THE GIRL IN THE NET

THE
GIRL
IN
THE
NET

GENE GROSS

BookPress®
publishing

Published in Des Moines, Iowa, by:

Bookpress Publishing
P.O. Box 71532
Des Moines, IA 50325
www.BookpressPublishing.com

Publisher's Cataloging-in-Publication Data

Names: Gross, Gene Francis, author.
Title: The girl in the net / Gene Francis Gross.
Description: Des Moines, IA: BookPress Publishing, 2024.
Identifiers: LCCN: 2023924284 | ISBN: 978-1-947305-92-2
Subjects: LCSH Attorneys--Fiction. | Murder--Fiction. | Iowa--Fiction. | Iowa Great Lakes Region (Iowa)--Fiction. | Mystery fiction. | Thrillers (Fiction) | BISAC FICTION / Mystery & Detective / General | FICTION / Crime | FICTION / Thrillers / Crime
Classification: LCC PS3607 .R67 G57 2024 | DDC 813.6--dc23

First Edition
Printed in the United States of America
10 9 8 7 6 5 4 3 2 1

For Vicki, my Frau Nägel.

He needed to stay sharp. No one would notice a snow machine at night, but this late in winter, ice could be treacherous. The recent hard freeze should have firmed things up but to be safe, he rode close to shore. The steady drone of the snow machine was reassuring and the sled, heavy with its load, trailed easily over the ice and recent snow.

But damn, it was cold! He'd rather be back in Arizona. He liked the heat but right now Arizona had become too hot and it had nothing to do with the climate. No, it was safer in Iowa. Besides, business was good—very good, better than they'd planned. Tonight's accident was inconvenient, but he was good at solving problems.

Earlier that day, at the Sports Shop, he'd witnessed the game warden chewing out Weird Willy for not removing his ice fishing shacks on time. Too bad for Willy but fortunate for him.

He didn't fish, but knew Lake Okoboji well enough to spot which shack Willy had placed over deep water. As he arrived, he turned off the machine and headlight, dismounted, switched on his headlamp, and stood looking at the ramshackle shelter. He thought aloud, "He must've raided every dumpster in the area to build this pile of junk." Ignoring the padlock, he slipped his fingers between the door and frame, and with a sharp tug, the hasp gave way.

He paused to listen for any unwanted attention, but the only response was a loud boom echoing through the ice and water. It was harmless, caused by the change in air pressure as a new front moved in, but unnerving, and motivated him to finish the job and get off the lake.

Retrieving the spud bar from the sled, he ducked his head and stepped into the shack. The state of the interior was no improvement over the exterior. He removed a plank covering a hole in the floor, exposing the portal to the dark water below. He chopped away the thin layer of ice that had formed since the last time Willy had dropped a line and expanded the size of the cut.

Returning to the sled he moved some rope and a large piece of broken masonry aside and lifted the small form from the sled. She was light but the throw wrapped about her, though part of his improvisation, made it awkward. He grunted as he bent over to reenter the shack and unceremoniously dumped her wrapped up body on the floor. Retrieving the rope and masonry he folded back the covering, secured the rope around her ankles and tied the other end to the masonry. It was too much rope but at this depth, it wouldn't be a concern.

Sliding her over to the newly enlarged opening in the ice, he paused to stare at the form made luminescent in the glare of his headlamp. Such a beautiful body. What a waste. Now just meat, fresh meat he noticed, still warm. The angry wound on the side of her head had swollen, looking even larger than when he'd wrapped her in the throw. She wore small gold earrings and a ring mounted with a large red gem on the index finger of her right hand. The throw and her clothes could be scattered among various dumpsters, no problem, but he knew from experience disposing of something as personal as jewelry was more difficult and in this case, it was better left with the dead.

With a shove he pushed the masonry into the icy gap and guided the body to follow. With her legs and torso submerged, he released her. To his horror, there was a sharp gasp and by the light of his headlamp he saw her eyes open wide in terror, mouth agape, fighting for breath against the frigid water. She reached out to him but the weight dragged her down until only her fingertips gripped the ragged edge of the shack floor. One at a time they failed; the last adorned by the blood-red gem. She was gone.

***

Federal Prosecutor Michael Cain awoke with a start—another bad dream. Gabriel had been messing with him. His twin had passed soon after their birth, but visited Michael often during childhood, in pleasant, vibrant dreams of them playing together as brothers. It was long ago but Michael still trusted in the memory. Yet since his return to the family's lakeside home to recover from what the media characterized as "A shootout worthy of the Old Wild West," he dreaded sleep. Gabriel had reappeared as an identical adult, but looked animated, struggling in the midst of an intense tempest filled with unintelligible violence.

Michael threw back the covers, shivered at the room's coolness, and stepped into his old Nike sandals. Pulling on his father's ratty robe, he slowly made his way along the dark hall and down the stairs. The bright reflection from moonlit snow lit his way through the family room. Pouring a small Glenfiddich, he stood before the large lakeside window and sipped the amber liquid and the view of a calm winter's night.

He was only mildly surprised to see a snow machine pass by

near the shore below. He considered, "Some knucklehead out for a late night ride ripping across thin ice."

Had Michael been truly prescient, as his family thought him to be, he would have discerned that this lone rider could tear mending wounds anew and place Michael and those he loved in mortal danger. He would have been forewarned and with Gabriel by his side, steeled for what he did best. Battle!

He reached down from on high and took hold of me;
He drew me out of deep waters.

2 Samuel 22:17

Willy DeWeerd, Weird Willy to some, was a big man past his prime, who knew the waters of Lake Okoboji well. When young, he had volunteered to assist the Iowa Department of Natural Resources with gillnetting game fish. This spring Willy was "volunteering" in the form of community service for his "failure to remove fishing shacks in a timely manner," as cited by Department of Natural Resources Officer "Picky" Piccard.

It was the same routine—lay the nets before dark, pull the nets in around midnight, throw back the immature and undesirables, and transport the selected mature fish to the hatchery in Spirit Lake. They eventually would be returned to the lake, but the eggs and milt stripped from the fish at the hatchery would become the fry and fingerlings needed to restock and maintain the high level of sport fishing in the Iowa Great Lakes. Since fishing was an integral part of the area's economy and he was a commercial and sport fisherman, fishing consumed much of Willy's time.

It had not been a typical winter for northwest Iowa, nor was this a normal spring. Except for a sharp cold snap that had extended the end of the season, the winter was mild. Now, as if Mother Nature believed in the law of compensation, the work of netting spawning fish was taking place during a late, bitter storm whose snow, freezing temperature, and strong northwest wind coated the workers and equipment in ghostly white.

As he worked, the icy crust on the arms of Willy's coveralls and insulated rubber gloves cracked and broke off only to be replaced by successive blasts of spray as waves hit the side of the boat. His face was raw and his beard hoary with frost. Even his exhaled breath seemed to hesitate in a momentary state of frigid disbelief.

Willy looked back at his two companions and in the dim light of the lanterns could see their deep fatigue. This was the third consecutive night placing and pulling nets, and all three nights they'd faced harsh conditions. Tonight was the worst. If their misery demanded justification it was coming in the form of nets heavily laden with mature walleyes.

Kneeling near the bow of the flat-bottom boat, Willy pulled and passed the net back to the original cause of his misery, Officer Piccard, who removed fish from the net and passed them to the third man, a DNR hatchery biologist, for sorting. Willy's back ached, but as tough as it was, he was determined to show "Picky" he could do his part.

Fish after fish came over the boat's gunnel. Willy marveled at the large iridescent eyes of the walleyes. The piercing light of his headlamp could pick up their pearl-like luster several feet below the water line. While eager to see the species and number of fish, what excited him was the possibility of handling a record-sized walleye, or maybe even a northern pike or musky.

The weight of the net suggested how many and the size of the fish ensnared, and it was now that Willy felt the hulking resistance of a possible trophy. On the next pull he was surprised, not by the heft, but by the lack of fight in the finny prize. Slow as his fatigue-numbed brain might have been, he became alarmed. The fish could be stressed, or so enmeshed, it was unable to move and pass a sufficient amount of water over its gills to survive. Willy hauled the net back with urgency until finally he could see the pallid form that began to materialize from deep in the water.

With a powerful heave, he pulled the catch near the surface. Expecting to see the massive head of a pike or musky, he was surprised by the appearance of the tail, a tail distinctly separated into limp, thick splayed spines. From one of the spines, something shiny, like a metallic lure, reflected the beam of his headlamp.

"What the hell?" Bending over the side of the boat, he drew the netted fish to him. Suddenly in a blood-red flash, a pale, grotesque hand broke from the water, grasping for his throat. Reflexively dropping the net, Willy's body snapped back violently in terror from the apparition. His hoarse primal scream was cut off by the sharp blast of icy air mixed with freezing spray that choked shut his nose and throat.

***

Night dispatcher Duane Fridlay hesitated. There had been something unusual brought up in a DNR netting operation off Pillsbury Point and the excited caller wanted the sheriff's office to respond immediately. In his experience "respond immediately" calls in the middle of the night this time of year were usually pranks or a drunk who needed a ride home. Duane waited until the caller caught his breath, then calmly suggested what he should do is contact the lake patrol for assistance with any netting problems.

There was a pause and then a verbal explosion. "We are the lake patrol. Who the hell do you think does gillnetting? Send the sheriff!" Duane, startled by the fierce outburst of anger, stammered and then tried to recover.

"I hear ya! I'll send one of the deputies. What is the nature of your situation and where exactly are you?"

He immediately was subjected to another verbal blast. "Don't send a friggin' deputy! We need the sheriff! We've got the body of a dead female, and it's not a fish! We're beached just east of Pillsbury Point, out of the wind, and we need the sheriff NOW!" Duane knew Sheriff Conrad wouldn't like this, but considering he was between a hook and sinker, he made the call.

***

The jangle of the phone on the nightstand was like barbed wire ripping through the sheriff's slumber. Grabbing the receiver, he spoke in a voice gravelly from sleep. "Duane, this had better be important."

"Sorry, sheriff, but we just got a call from the DNR that something unusual was brought up in their gillnet."

There was silence on the line and then, for the third time within minutes, Duane suffered more verbal abuse. "Gillnet! Is this some sort of joke? What the hell is so important about netting fish that you would call me at 2:00 in the morning? So help me Duane, if you fell asleep again and had one of your so-called night visions!"

"No, sheriff! No! Please, listen. It's a body! I didn't get it at first either but it was a DNR officer and he insisted they needed the sheriff. I told them I couldn't do that…well sort of, and that I'd send a deputy. The DNR guy had a goddamn meltdown and insisted I call you. They've got a dead body. It's a woman!"

Sheriff Conrad sharply sucked in his breath. The report of a body was cause enough, but the "goddamn" from Duane did it. A bit of a prude, Duane was not one to use profanity, and Sheriff Conrad had never before heard a blasphemous obscenity uttered by his longtime deputy and part-time dispatcher. "Okay, Duane. Calm down. Tell me what, where. You know the drill."

***

Sheriff Mark Conrad—Connie to family and friends—was a taut-line, by-the-book, no-nonsense officer of the law. His tall broad-shouldered frame served him well in his chosen career. More than once a violent situation was resolved by the appearance of a sheriff with the stature and look of a tough, seasoned lawman who could have stepped right out of the pages of a Western novel. The animal intensity and focus from his deep, dark, intelligent eyes clearly communicated there would be only one outcome and it would be what Sheriff Conrad expected.

Most of his duties during the off-season involved obvious, even mundane matters. Summer brought the types of problems found in larger communities and with young people in particular, issues more like those encountered on a college campus. Still, the motive and perpetrator tended to be obvious. Random acts often fueled by alcohol or drugs nearly by definition did not reflect great planning or require complicated solutions. If there had to be crime, Sheriff Conrad preferred it that way. What he didn't like were the muddled cases, the occasional serious crimes not readily explained through standard police procedure and straightforward investigation.

He had the skills, was diligent, and possessed a talented

imagination, but he and his well-trained staff knew that unintended consequences touched upon so many when investigating a complicated case. A possible drowning this soon after ice-out was unusual. His experience and the innate qualities that made him good at his job provoked in him the sense that this case would quickly become "complicated."

Sheriff Conrad had seen bodies pulled from the lake, victims of boating or swimming accidents. All were tragic, but most were impairment-related or the result of other variations on poor judgment. This was something else.

It was the body of a young woman, nude, stretched out on the bottom of the boat and still entangled in the gillnet. Framed by long hair dampened to fair brown, her face glowed alabaster by the light of the lanterns. For a moment Sheriff Conrad gazed upon what he'd only seen in museums and never in the form of a living soul. She was an angel rendered in marble. The grubby deck, dying fish still in the net, and the rude setting of the old boat were an obscenity to this perfection.

She couldn't have been in the water long. Even from where he stood beside the boat, Sheriff Conrad could see a darkened area just underneath the hairline on the side of her head. Raw red ligature marks circumvented each ankle, and her arms lay crossed upon her torso. On the index finger of her right hand was a ring with a single large red gem.

The ring! Something stirred in his memory. Connie carefully climbed into the boat and aimed the beam of his flashlight directly at the victim's face. Stooping over for a closer view, Connie confirmed what his recall of the ring had suggested.

"Oh, damn!"

Connie paused and took a deep breath to find his professional place, but there would be no easy separation of professional and personal about this. In a gruff voice, without looking up, he addressed the three men. "Other than pulling her into the boat, did you do anything that might have compromised the situation?"

The three looked at one another and each shook his head. It was Willy who spoke.

"No sir. We lifted her into the boat, recovered the net, and came ashore."

Connie gave them a hard look. "Stay here. We're going to treat this as a crime scene. Don't do anything that might compromise what we have. Give me your phones. I'll return them before you leave."

***

Sheriff Mark Conrad stood out of the wind at the top of a low bluff on the eastern side of Pillsbury Point overlooking Smith's Bay. The lake was shrouded in darkness. The storm had passed and the Moon had set. As the sky cleared, the few remaining stars were fading as if trying to flee the anguish below. He drew out his phone and hit the speed dial for dispatch. On the first ring he heard Duane's voice. "911—what is your emergency?"

"Duane, this is Connie. Contact the Arnolds Park Police Department and our night patrol deputies, and send them to this location. Then I need you to wake some people up. Tell them it's urgent. Tell them we have a body, and tell them where they're to meet me. Do not—and I mean this—do not give them any other information. Put a lid on this and keep it there. Any questions come into the office, direct them to me. And Duane, if you stop for breakfast on the way home, not a word. Do you read me? Not a word!"

"Yes sir. Not a word. Who do I call?"

In addition to the local police and night deputies, Connie requested the hospital EMTs, the county medical examiner and part-time pathologist, the Dickinson County Sheriff's Deputy most skilled in crime scene investigation and photography, and one of the department's two homicide detectives. "Duane, one more person. Call Father Barney over at St. Theresa's. Tell him to bring his Gates of Heaven kit. He'll know what I mean. Make sure it's Father Barney and not the new guy."

There remained one more call to be made, and the sheriff needed to do this personally. "Duane, I need you to look up a number for me."

Standing there in the dark listening to the signal ringing in his ear, it all seemed surreal. The wind was subsiding, but snow still swirled about in eerie contrast to the black below. Connie felt that one misstep at the edge of the bluff, and he'd fall forever into a bottomless ebony pit. A shiver shot down his back when on the fourth ring a small, thin voice answered.

"Hello?"

"Miss Lawery? This is Sheriff Conrad. I apologize for calling like this, but I know that you would expect to be contacted immediately." Drawing a deep chill breath, Connie paused then pressed on. "Miss Lawery, can you hear me?"

A few seconds passed with some indecipherable words filling the gap, then a stronger voice came on the line. "It's OK, Hoepe, I've got it. Hello, Connie. This is Faethe."

"Miss Lawery, I'm sorry to be calling you in the middle of the night."

Before he could say another word, Faethe interrupted, "Connie, we've known each other for over thirty years. Call me Faethe." That was Faethe Lawery, who insisted upon her version of decorum.

"Yes, Miss…yes, Hoepe…I mean Faethe. I'm sorry, but I have the worst kind of news. It's your niece."

***

It was daybreak, the sun's arrival announced by the glow on setting clouds and exalted by the brilliant sparkle on water. The recent snowfall and heavily frosted trees provided a pure white crown to the deep blue water of Okoboji. Such joyous beauty lifted the spirits of Father Barney. It was a dawn like this one that affirmed his faith in the promise of rebirth for the souls of those he shepherded.

Though he still preferred to be addressed as Father Barney, he was now Monsignor O'Brian, an honorific title granted by the Pope in respect for Barney's many years of valuable service to the church. During his fifty years as a priest and pastor, Father Barney was assigned to various Midwestern parishes. But for his final posting, the Monsignor requested and was reappointed to St. Theresa's, his former parish that served the Lakes area. It may have been unusual for a priest to return to a congregation served so many years before, but technically he was semi-retired and acting as mentor to Father Jim, a recently ordained priest. The parishioners were responding well to a combination of wisdom born of experience and the enthusiasm of the newly minted.

For any priest the performance of what was once known as Last Rites was common, but the call from the dispatch officer that specifically asked for Father Barney and his Gates of Heaven kit meant this case was different. He was directed to meet Sheriff Conrad on

Pillsbury Point, and as he turned off Highway 71 onto the narrow residential street leading to the point, he could see a police car with lights silently flashing and further on, an ambulance. An officer stood near the police car.

Ahead of Father Barney, an old sedan came to a stop and, after a brief check of the occupants, was allowed through. As he drove past, the Father waved at the young police officer who simply nodded. Parking his car, he was surprised to see two of his elderly parishioners, the Lawery sisters, getting out of the sedan. Beyond, he could make out the sheriff, another policeman, and the EMTs.

Collecting his kit, Father Barney stepped out and followed quietly behind the sisters. As he approached the bluff's rim he could see lights below that illuminated a boat and several figures. A large man was in the bow, and even at this distance Barney recognized him to be Dr. Matthew Hunter, county ME and a respected area physician.

Sheriff Conrad greeted the Lawerys and Father Barney, then took Barney by the arm to draw him aside. "Father, we need to talk first." Connie's face was drawn and the red of the morning's early light emphasized the deep lines in his face carved over time by his dedication to duty. "This is a bad one, Barney. It's Virginia Lawery."

Father Barney started, stepping back and nearly stumbling. "No, no, no, please! It can't be."

"I'm sorry Father, but there's no doubt."

Father Barney's aged body sagged. Bowing his head, he spoke softly, "God help us. Please, Lord be with us."

"We'll need all the help we can get, Father. That's why I had Duane call you and not the newbie."

"Ah, yes. I understand. It's because of her Aunties. But is it wise they should be here at this time?"

"Father, of all people, you know better."

"Yes. Yes, I suppose I do."

Sheriff Mark Conrad had known Father Barney since childhood. Some of his earliest recollections were of a younger Father Barney at the church altar and in the parochial elementary school.

Barely an adolescent, Connie was present when the Rites of the Sick were performed for his mother, Anne. The rite may have helped spiritually, but physically, the medical doctor's diagnosis prevailed, and his mother had passed on quietly from the cancer that had suddenly devastated her body and his life.

Personally skeptical about the veracity, he understood from experience the importance the ritual held for some, especially for family members. It provided them a semblance of order when thrust into a state over which they had no control. And while Last Rites were intended for the faithful's final stage of living, Connie knew there were Prayers After Death to accompany the souls of the deceased on their journey.

The small ensemble followed Sheriff Conrad down the steep path, and, as if finding comfort in proximity, clustered together on the shore. It was surprising how well the elderly sisters managed the rocky trail. There was a grim resolve to their efforts as they assisted each other.

The ice that coated the boat's gunnel and ribs reflected the light from the lanterns and gave the appearance of a frozen crib. The body remained on the floor of the boat but had been sheltered by a section of rough white canvas used to cover gear. Only her face, framed by hair now dried to its true golden color, was exposed.

The medical examiner finished the preliminary tasks, stepped out of the boat, and joined the assembly. With the sheriff's assistance, the priest took his place, and Connie handed him the kit.

Father Barney slowly knelt, placed the implements of the ritual on the seat, kissed then placed the stole over his shoulders, and quietly began to speak the words of passing for such a prematurely released soul.

Without any sign or word, the lanterns on the bow and stern were extinguished. The subdued glow of the boat's running lights reflected off the surface of the dark water like a halo surrounding Father Barney and the body of Virginia Lawery. The solemnity of the rite, the humility of the elderly priest, and the reverential tableau on the shore bore witness to the sanctity that consigned an incongruent dignity to a heartrending scene.

"Is that me?"

"Yes, or rather, it was you."

"I don't look so good."

"It is what you left behind."

"If that's what I left, shouldn't the rest of me be somewhere else?"

"Yes."

"Then why am I here?"

"What you were is finished. What you become is yet to be."

"I don't understand."

"Nor do they. That is why you remain."

"Can I help?"

"No."

"What should I do?"

"Wait."

"How will they understand?"

"I am with you."

Do not be overcome by evil, but overcome evil with good.

Romans 12:21

Sheriff Conrad was off duty when he pulled into the drive of the family home of his longtime friend, Michael Cain. He loved the old place. The warm memories of living with Michael and his family were strong and important to him. His younger life had been troubled, and his success as a man, husband, father, and even officer of the law, was due in no small part to Michael's family.

Old Judge Cain was not known for "coddling law-breaking delinquents," as he put it. But when his son, Michael's father, represented Connie and expressed a willingness to take him into his own home and to foster him, the elder Cain agreed to modify the severe sentence he had intended to hand Connie.

Michael had his sixteen-foot Lund Pro Angler in the driveway and was busy hosing out the inside of the boat. It was a cool day but with no breeze, and the afternoon sun in a cloudless sky gave a sense of warmth. It was one of those glorious spring days that blessed those who lived in the Lakes region.

Michael wore tattered cutoffs, water shoes, and a bright yellow T-shirt with a green parrot printed on the front and "My Therapist is Jimmy Buffet" on the back. ZZ Top's "Sharp Dressed Man" blasted from an ancient CD player, and a Finland Beer koozie massaged a bottle of Corona. Michael was deep into mellow, and Connie regretted that this visit was about business.

Reaching over he picked up the portfolio with the case file inside and stepped out of his Ford 150. Michael looked up from his efforts, flashed his brilliant white smile—part friend, part shark—and drew out the greeting, "Well, helloooo, Sheriff Conrad! Welcome to my version of Margaritaville. Grab a libation from the cooler. How are the wife and kids?"

"Kids are fine, but Madge is on a tear to get the school district and city council to agree to work together and do something about the soccer fields."

Michael shook his head. "Why don't they just play baseball and football, like we did?"

"According to Madge, we are not about to let a pack of bureaucrats limit the opportunities for young men and women to explore their talents."

"Explore like we did, Connie?" Both laughed. "Well, maybe Madge has a point."

Growing serious, he said, "Michael, I hate to take you away from preparations for next weekend's walleye opener, and on such a fine afternoon, but I'd like to pick your mind a bit."

Without taking eyes from his work, Michael replied, "Let me guess. The Lawery investigation? One of your deputies is teaching a class in photography and I spoke with him over at Iowa Lakes Community College. He didn't tell me any details but mentioned that unless there was luck involved, it was going to be a long, difficult slog."

"Yeah, that's what I want to talk to you about."

Michael stopped in his efforts to scrub several years of worm residue from the boat's floor, turned off the faucet, and wiped his hands on his cutoffs. "Well, come inside—we'll find some chips and salsa to go with the beer."

***

They sat at the old kitchen table, the same table where "delinquent Mark Conrad" had enjoyed after school snacks with the rest of the kids while Mrs. Cain went about preparing supper or other tasks. In her kindly way, she got every child, younger and older, to tell her about his or her day and what each had for school work.

"There were many good times spent at this table, Michael. I miss your folks." He felt a twinge of sadness at the thought of his foster parents.

"Yes, there were, Connie. And I'm glad, we all are glad, that you became a part of the family."

The face of the hardened lawman softened and his eyes glistened. "I've said it before and I'll keep saying it. After my mom died and dad ran off, I was angry at everyone. I would have been on the other side of this badge if it weren't for your parents. They saved my life."

"Maybe, but I think you may be selling yourself short. There was a lot of good and potential in you, and my folks saw it, even if you didn't."

Connie sighed. "I guess that's one of the reasons I'm so crazy about Madge. If she can, she's going to see to it that every youngster has a chance to succeed."

"Yeah, she's a lot like mom."

With that, Connie reached into the portfolio, took out a folder marked in long hand, "The Girl in the Net," and placed it on the table before Michael.

***

"'The Girl in the Net?' A little dramatic, isn't it? I'm surprised it's not 'Lady of the Lake'!"

"Well, I may not have the literary sense you have, but in this case it seems appropriate. Everything we've learned is in this file. To start with the high points, we know that Virginia Lawery was a student at Iowa State University and that she drove to Okoboji on the afternoon of Friday, March 4, the week prior to spring break. According to a credit card statement, she gassed up her car at 1:18 PM, at the Gilbert corner Casey's, two miles north of Ames on Highway 69. She arrived at The Lodge on Okoboji a little after 6:00 PM and spent the evening visiting with the owners of the Lodge, Anthony and Lucia Sandoval. Anthony Sandoval saw Ginny leave the Lodge, at or shortly after 11:00 PM.

"When she didn't return the following Monday, her roommate thought she had decided to stay an extra day or two. Her aunts thought she was at school but became concerned when they didn't hear from her and couldn't reach her to learn whether she planned to come home for spring break. They called the roommate midweek and that was the first anyone thought something may be wrong."

Michael was silent so Connie continued his recitation. "According to the Iowa State University Registrar's office, she was still enrolled and had not given any notice about dropping out. An investigator from the ISU Police Department interviewed her roommate, her university friends, and her ISU advisor. None of them were able to shed any light on what may have happened.

"As you know, especially in the case of a murder, we may request help from the Iowa Division of Criminal Investigation, and the DCI has agreed to assist us. However, the cause of her death isn't clear and has been listed as indeterminate, possibly suspicious. The Dickinson County Sheriff's Department remains the lead investigating agency, but it's a shared effort with the Iowa Division of Criminal Investigation, assisted by the Ames and ISU Police Departments. Between the DCI, ISU PD, Ames PD, and our office, we've interviewed and in some cases reinterviewed her family, friends, professors, employers, and the people she worked with at the Lodge. No one knows what happened to her or, for certain, when she disappeared. What we know is conjecture."

"Did she have a boyfriend?"

"No, not that we know of. She had one last school year but they broke up months ago. His name is Grant Laxton."

"Did anyone talk to him?"

"ISU tried but couldn't reach him, and when his parents were called, they insisted their son couldn't possibly be involved in anything like what we're investigating."

"Sounds like parental denial."

"Likely. When the investigator asked where he was they said he should be in school. They added that their son was of legal age and he could account for himself."

"And that would be parental delusion. Is he still enrolled at ISU?"

"Yes, but it's reported he skips more classes than attends. He lives alone in an apartment off-campus and attempts by Ames PD to contact him have been unsuccessful. Their investigator questioned the neighbors, but they hadn't noticed whether he was or wasn't around. He's not been sociable, and they're busy with their own lives.

However, according to the mail carrier, someone picks up the mail about once a week and he assumed it was the recipient."

"Sounds mysterious."

"Maybe, but it's all pretty flimsy. There wasn't any recent connection that could be found, and since the breakup was long past, it may not have been considered a high priority that early in the investigation. Remember, any attempt to interview him took place before her body was found."

"That's understandable but circumstances have changed. It's a loose end. He'll need to be run to ground and questioned."

"Agreed, if and when we can find him."

"What about physical evidence?"

"Not much. Her mother's ruby ring was still on her finger, and she had a single earring, a gold cross, in her right ear. The earring in her left ear was missing, and according to her aunts, she should have been wearing a gold cross and chain that went with the earrings. They too were missing. Everything we could find at her home or in the apartment—her clothing, books, correspondence—everything simply pointed to a normal twenty-something college student."

"What about the rest of her stuff?"

Connie inwardly smiled. It was for good reason he was seeking Michael's insight. "We haven't been able to locate her phone, laptop, or car."

"Whoa! That's more than a big red flag on a tip-up."

"I know. We have a national alert for her car and are monitoring pawn shops and the internet. No one, including her roommate and friends, has any idea where those things have gone. Her roommate assumed that Virginia took everything with her. That would be reasonable. Other than her body, there is no other significant physical evidence."

"Were you able to obtain a record of her phone calls and texts?"

"Yes, with the help of a warrant, the carrier cooperated, but what we learned only corroborated what we already knew, with one exception. There was a number we couldn't trace. We have no idea whose it is and we think the number must be for a burner phone. According to Ginny's log, she called it about once a month, including the Thursday before she drove to Okoboji. Her last call was to that number and made at 10:33 PM, Friday, March 4. It lasted less than a minute and originated from the Lodge, all of which was corroborated by the Sandovals and the ping from an area tower. When we tried calling, there was no response—it was dead. We've tried dozens of times with the same results. The burner's a nonstarter unless someone tries to use it again."

"Can you monitor the number?"

"We can but whether that's useful depends on the phone. Some numbers of burner phones disappear or are replaced with a new number after a set period of time, or the user can cancel or change the number. We're not hopeful. Besides, the burner is probably in a landfill by now."

"What about the computer? Were you able to download her email?"

"Yes, again with a warrant, the carrier was cooperative and Ginny's friends and aunts volunteered access to their computers. We also checked her social media. Nothing helpful was learned, and of course since it's missing, we have no documents or information that may have been saved on her computer."

"How about the cloud?"

"What about the cloud? Without a password, we're locked out and not likely to get help. The FBI may get access but it's a high standard and our chances are slim."

"And the autopsy?"

"The medical examiner's preliminary report indicated that death

was likely due to drowning, and bruising to the side of her head suggested she was unconscious when or shortly after she went into the
water. There was very little water in the lungs but what was found
was lake water. There were ligature marks around her ankles and
some cuts around her lower legs. Otherwise, her body was relatively
free of perimortem or postmortem marks or injuries."

Drawing and releasing a slow breath Michael asked the necessary question. "Was there evidence of sexual assault?"

Connie looked down at his broad hands and shook his head in
response. "The body was nude, but there was no evidence of sexual
intercourse. However, she was pregnant. County ME thought about
two months."

The sound of the old grandfather clock ticking in the hallway
measured the silence that fell between the two men. "Connie, do the
Aunties know she was pregnant?"

"No. It's public knowledge she was found nude, but besides
myself, only the county and state medical examiners, county attorney,
my lead homicide detective, the DCI agent assigned the case, and
now you, know that detail. We've kept it from the public, and we
need to keep it that way."

"Do we know who the father was?"

"No, we don't. There was viable DNA evidence recovered but
without a donor, no way to match it. We ran it against the Iowa database, FBI database, and even the military database. No hits."

"If my math adds up, two months prior would have been around
winter break. Was she home for Christmas?"

"She was. According to her aunts she spent some time at home, but
since she worked long hours at the Lodge, she slept over a lot of nights
at one of the employee apartments. We spoke with everyone concerned
and learned nothing about a possible father or any motive for her death.
The people at the resort adored her. She was an exceptional employee

and got along well with everyone, especially the guests."

"Not quite everyone. What is it you want me to do?"

"I'd like you to do what you do better than anyone else I know. I'd like you to review what we have. I can't leave the file with you, but I had it all copied onto a flash drive. Fresh eyes may find something we've missed. You are meticulous and have a weird, excuse me, different way of thinking that goes beyond the investigator cum lawyer thing. I'd really appreciate your insight."

Michael sat quietly looking at the open folder before him. "It looks complete. I don't know what else I could find."

Clearing his throat, Connie added, "I'm not one to get between a man and his fishing, but after reviewing the file, if you're willing, I'd like to officially have you assist with the investigation. I've already spoken to the DCI and they're willing to cooperate as long as our county attorney agrees to my request. Our county attorney suggested he temporarily hire you as a Dickinson County Assistant Attorney. It's a little unusual, but as such, you would have access to all information relative to the case."

"I would need to clear it with my boss for the Southern District."

"Is that a problem?"

Michael hesitated, then admitted, "No. Since I'm still on personal leave, I'm sure he'll approve. But what about the county supervisors? Will they agree to this?"

"They already have."

"Wow! They agreed to adding an attorney? That may be a first."

"Just don't expect a big salary."

"Still, I'm surprised everyone's on board."

"I know, but we've hit a wall. Even as good as my people are, with tourist season about to begin, my office won't have the time or manpower to do this justice. That, and the fact that the Lakes area business community would have a fit if it was on the front page of our newspapers every day."

"You mean tourists read our newspapers?"

"You bet. Most businesses advertise and run specials in the newspapers each week. Tourists generally check them out. Besides, news media from the outside would splash it all over."

As they talked Michael leafed through the papers in the file until he came to an 8"x10" photo of the victim. It likely was her senior picture and showed a lovely, smiling woman with the optimistic glow of someone excited to embark on the next stage of a promising life. But it was her eyes, clear and bright, that fixed on him, challenged him, and demanded answers. Anxiety bonded to a searing rage began to well up inside him.

Sharply turning over the picture Michael responded, "OK. I'll review the file, but I won't promise to investigate."

"I understand. Anything you suggest or may do to help is appreciated. Let me know not if, but when you have questions." With that, Connie handed Michael the flash drive, collected the file, thanked him for the libation and chips, and apologized for not staying longer.

He drove away with less of a burden than when he arrived; if only Michael had been left with a similar sense of solace.

5

Located in the northwestern corner of the state, the Iowa Great Lakes region includes Big Spirit Lake, the largest lake in the region, and five interconnected lakes: West Lake Okoboji, East Lake Okoboji, Upper and Lower Gar, and Minnewashta. Of these, West Okoboji is the crown jewel with an area of 3,825 acres, 19 miles of shoreline, and depths up to 136 feet. A glacial remnant, it's known for its spring fed waters; rock, gravel, and sand bottom; and clarity that replicates the deep blue of the sky.

From Memorial Day to Labor Day, families flock to the resorts and parks to enjoy the variety of activities on and off the water. Part-time residents return to open summer homes, permanent residents look forward to Labor Day, business owners obsess over financial success or failure, and fishermen revel in the prolific fish species that inhabit the lakes.

Of the variety of species available, many anglers consider the walleye as the most highly prized. Although a native species, the natural reproduction of walleyes from year-to-year is inconsistent and to maintain a fishable population, the lakes are stocked with fry and fingerlings from the Spirit Lake Fish Hatchery.

From mid-February until the first Saturday in May, no walleyes are permitted to be taken from West and East Okoboji and Big Spirit Lake. Gamefish spawning during this period become easy prey for fishermen. The closed season allows fish to spawn without risk and is an opportunity for the Iowa DNR to net game fish and harvest their eggs and milt.

The first Saturday in May, locally referred to as the walleye opener, is the unofficial start to the tourist season, and the Iowa Great Lakes Area Chamber of Commerce supports the opener with a walleye tournament. Fishermen from Iowa and beyond converge on the area to take part in the event and local motels, resorts, restaurants, and bait shops enjoy a boffo business and a kickoff to their summer season.

The walleye opener was a tradition Michael had missed in recent years. With the optimism and primal instincts of a fishing fanatic, he believed it represented a time of rebirth. As he thought about the file before him, Michael experienced that old conflict between what he wanted and the pull of what he felt compelled to do.

A string of crises had forced Michael to confront his underlying conflicts. The result was a detour in his being. He had stepped away from his all-consuming work, his colleagues, and the mess his life had become. He had a good deal of money and incentive to rethink his life, and with some help, he did.

Time and therapy had provoked a remarkable change. It was as if he was given permission to be happy. He regained interest in life but with a new normalcy that didn't require him to obsess over the exaggerated expectations of others at the expense of his own health, happiness, and relationships. It all seemed so obvious now but had been long-submerged.

There was the occasion when his therapist was briefly called away during a session, and Michael's chart was left unattended on the desk. Curious, Michael read his diagnosis and was shocked to learn: "The subject exhibits mild characteristics of obsessive-compulsive personality disorder with schizophrenic tendencies." By now he understood, accepted, and could deal with his personal OCD quirks. It was the schizophrenic part that concerned him.

But sometimes he did think he saw someone or heard his name spoken, although no one was there. And when solitary, he had a sense he was not alone, but rather that there was a presence with him. It was calming. It was reassuring. It wasn't paranoia but was simply how he felt and the way his mind existed. He considered it normal, and rationalized that the deviations were the result of an overactive imagination.

When it had come up in one of his sessions, Michael admitted to his therapist as a little kid he had an imaginary playmate for a constant companion. It was not until kindergarten that he traded his imaginary friend for reality.

Years later, a serious conversation with his older sister, Melanie, illuminated their parents' concern. "I just thought you were an odd little brother. The thing is, sometimes I could have sworn there was someone else with you."

"How's that?"

"Lots of things—like building blocks that fell over by themselves and you laughing, clapping your hands and saying, 'Do it again!' And a ball you would roll to your imaginary friend."

"So?"

"It rolled back to you."

"There must have been some explanation."

"That's what mom and dad said. But I think they knew."

"Knew what?"

"I don't know. They just knew. I overheard mom and dad talking about it. Mom said it was Gabriel."

Although Michael was born robust and healthy, his twin brother Gabriel had died at birth. The priest at the time had expressed a hopeful thought to his parents. "Perhaps the physical energy went to Michael, and their spirit is shared by Gabriel."

He rarely gave it thought, but since returning to the lakes, memories of his earliest life popped into his mind at the oddest times. It was an enigma with no logical solution.

He finished cleaning the boat, if for no other reason than on the principle you should complete what was begun, and now was seated at his desk in the study. He plugged the flash drive into the computer and saved the material onto the hard drive. Accompanied by a large Glenfiddich, he began the first step in his process—a quick read through the entire file followed by a second slower read with methodical consideration of each detail.

Other than the implication of a serious crime, there was little evidence to go on. The investigation was well documented and followed standard procedures. As Connie had indicated, investigators from the sheriff's office, ISU PD, Ames PD, and DCI had collectively interviewed everyone available who may have had any relationship with Virginia Lawery in the months leading up to her disappearance. Michael knew from experience that "interviewed everyone" seldom provided all possible information and often fell short of everyone. Besides the ex-boyfriend, who else had been unavailable, and should be included in the inquiries?

The interviews were written out and some video-recorded. All the proper paperwork was done. The county ME's report was in the file as well as dozens of pictures from the scene of discovery. Several photos were of Father Barney kneeling in a boat with everyone else huddled together as witnesses.

Michael knew everyone pictured except two, a deputy he hadn't met and, he assumed, the hatchery biologist. He recognized DNR Officer Picard and remembered him as a by-the-book agent—hard-nosed and intelligent—who reportedly was fearless when confronting lawbreakers.

He was surprised to see the tall, lanky, older man Willy DeWeerd, aka Weird Willy, a character well-known in the Lakes region as an eccentric. Michael also knew the Lawery sisters. Aware of their connection to the victim, he reread their interviews several times.

As he read through the entire file a second time, Michael wrote questions and listed the names and contact information of everyone interviewed. A series of lists provided one way he managed to make sense of his research. Legal pads devoted to different topics were displayed on clipboards hanging on the wall behind his desk. He was skilled in the use of computers, but had an affinity for paper and pen. It was tactile; it just felt right.

He also believed in redundancy. Writing on paper and then reorganizing it on the computer provided thoroughness. Sometimes the very act of repeating what was known would trigger a new direction in his thoughts. Most of the time it was merely repetition.

Michael added his notes and lists to the computer and printed a hard copy of the file, including pictures. The sound of the printer at work brought Michael back from a deep state of concentration. Taking out a fresh legal pad, he drew a vertical line through the first page, and on the right hand side began writing a random list of tasks to be done. On the left side he numbered the sequence of tasks. Both would change many times. In spite of scant hard evidence, what was provided did suggest avenues for investigation. In his own way, he vaguely discerned a beginning and means to a possible solution.

By now Michael felt a familiar excitement, a sizzle throughout his nervous system, the anticipation of what he thought of as conflict, of battle. The demand for aggressive mental and physical action was a strong stimulant. It was a distraction from, rather than cause for, anxiety.

Michael was not the only person thinking of Virginia Lawery. While he learned the details of the investigation into her demise, someone else was brooding over memories of the desirable young woman.

His nickname was "Dum Dum." When very young he had watched re-runs of *The Flintstones* on TV and latched on to the character Bam Bam. He was only three years old and when he said it, instead of Bam Bam, it came out Bum Bum. That became his nickname until about second grade when kids begin to notice these things, and observed that he not only wasn't the brightest bulb in the pack, he was likely missing a few filaments. After that his nickname depreciated from Bum Bum to Dum Dum, a liability that had little effect on Harold. The fact his last name was Krumm only exacerbated the taunting. But Harold Krumm went about his life in a happy state, greeting everyone as a best friend, and eventually "Dum Dum" became infused as an expression of endearment to most who knew him, much to the amazement of his taunters.

He liked to sit on a bench on the bluff above Pillsbury Point and watch the boats as they motored or sailed in or out of Smith's Bay. When he was young the boats appeared large. He was now older, but some of the boats still looked large. Indeed, the average size had increased along with the wealth of the region.

Today as he sat on his favorite bench he was not watching boats. He was lost in thought over the young woman he had adored and loved. Even Dum Dum knew they never would have been together that certain way, although he was not sure why. He only was aware of something from the crude comments and jokes of some of his friends and from his boss who picked him up each weekday to help make deliveries to businesses that sold live bait. He couldn't bring himself to think that such vulgarity would be a part of her life or their friendship.

They had met last summer. It was early morning, and as he was going into the Sports Shop near the Lodge resort, he dropped a flat of containers filled with night crawlers. Jolly, his boss and the driver of the delivery van, was screaming at him using a few descriptors that were new even to Dum Dum. Nearby, she was getting out of her little green car and seeing his sad, beaten-down appearance, ran over to help pick up the recently liberated invertebrates as they attempted to crawl across the hot parking lot.

Dum Dum was repelled at the memory of Jolly screaming at Ginny. "Leave them crawlers alone! It's Dum Dum's fault. He has to clean up the fuckin' mess."

Startled, she had stepped back and walked away. As Dum Dum watched, she turned and gave him a smile and small finger wave. She was made of sunshine! That was when Dum Dum first began to learn how happiness so great also could be painful.

Besides bait delivery, Dum Dum did odd jobs at the Lodge, and they saw each other several times after that but only exchanged smiles and waves. She was so wonderful! It was a month later, on a Saturday morning, when he saw her at the farmers market.

Her golden-colored hair was pulled back, and it cascaded down to the middle of her back. She wore a yellow sundress with matching yellow sandals and over her arm carried a blue canvas bag with little white whales printed on the outside. Cheap large-framed sunglasses covered half her face. She had not seen him, and he stood transfixed, his heart pounding. As much as it frightened him, he just had to talk to her.

She was discussing varieties of spring lettuce with an elderly Asian woman when she looked up and their eyes met. She removed her sunglasses and dropped them into her bag and the smile that lit up her face looked to Dum Dum like the sum of all the joy he had ever known.

His face grew hot and his mouth went dry. He tried to say, "Hi!" and wave, but all that came out of his voice was an inarticulate croak and his wave managed to knock over the sign announcing Green Beans Are Here! She laughed, a lovely, sparkling laugh, and quickly came over and asked, "Are you okay?" Dum Dum nodded his head and tried to think of something, anything, to say.

Suddenly she thrust out her hand and said, "Hi. My name's Ginny. What's yours?"

After first wiping his sweating hand on the side of his jeans, he reached out and gently took her hand and said the only thing that he seemed able to remember. "Harold Krumm, but…but call me Dum Dum."

Her eyes seemed to grow larger and she said, "Dum Dum? Would it be alright if I called you Harry, Harold?"

Confused by the Harry-Harold proximity, he coughed lightly and said, "No one ever called me Harry-Harold before."

Her eyebrows shot up, and she burst out laughing. "That's funny!

I like you! How about I just call you Harold?" He managed a quick smile and again nodded his head.

They walked about the market and Ginny kept up a stream of chatter directed at him and sometimes to the market vendors about the importance of treating our food and environment with respect. Dum Dum mostly nodded and said yes, no, and okay. Ginny did not ask personal things. She just seemed to enjoy his company.

Finally she had announced, "Well, I've got to get ready for work. My shift begins at noon." And then she did something Dum Dum would never have dreamed possible. Turning to face him she wrapped her arms around him and gave him a quick hug. "Thanks for the company. See ya!"

Dum Dum stood there dumbfounded, waving a limp hand and watching her disappear into the crowd. He felt like this was the most beautiful thing to ever happen to him. But it seemed so strange, and he experienced an anxiety that this was something fragile. He wanted to see her, talk to her, or at least listen to her again. He was afraid. Would this all disappear because of something he might do or say to her and never understand why?

He need not have worried. Each time she saw him, if place and time allowed, she would come over and say a few words. That's all he needed. And each time she left she would say, "See ya!" And although she didn't give him a hug, she would squeeze his arm or pat his shoulder in a friendly way. Sometimes he would get a ride over to the resort just to stand out-of-sight and watch for her.

It was during another morning delivery to the Sports Shop by the resort that it happened. He saw her through one of the resort's large windows and stopped to stare. Suddenly Jolly gave him a push from behind and said, "So, Dum Dum, you've got yourself a girlfriend. You're dumb as a box of rocks, but you have good taste in pussy. That's a good-looking bitch. Out of your league by a mile, but maybe I could take care of her for you. I'd bet she'd like my night crawler." With that he let out a loud crude laugh, part bark, part growl.

From some place he'd never known, Dum Dum felt fury explode inside him. With a screech he wheeled and leaped onto Jolly, driving him to the ground.

While Dum Dum was tall and gawky, Jolly was average height but with powerful arms and thick chest. They rolled about the driveway, Jolly profusely cursing and Dum Dum flailing at him as if in a raging fit. It ended as abruptly as it started when Jolly landed a blow to Dum Dum's nose.

Dum Dum stood up, staggered back and sat down on the pavement, nose bleeding and the flesh around his nose and eyes already beginning to swell.

"Jesus Christ! What the hell is wrong you, you dumb sonofabitch!" But Dum Dum just sat on the pavement bleeding and crying. Jolly walked to the van and returned with a roll of toilet paper. "Here! Clean up! It's just a pop to the nose for Chrissake. Quit crying. It's embarrassing for a grown man to cry, even a dumb one."

After that, Jolly said no more about Ginny. He was a crude, obscene beast but intelligent and understood something about the unattainable. Dum Dum didn't speak of Ginny and made a point of not looking for her in Jolly's presence.

What he feared had happened. It didn't seem possible such beauty could evoke ugliness from anyone. Dum Dum was more determined than ever to do anything and everything he could to protect his glorious friend. He would keep her safe and pure, and if he couldn't, no one would.

It was what he had meant to do, but now she was gone.

7

Sunday morning found Michael attending mass at St. Theresa's, followed by a visit over brunch with Father Barney in the rectory. At least that was how Michael used to know the living quarters for the priests. When he had called the night before, Father Barney had suggested they meet after the 10:30 service, a suggestion heavily laden with the implication that Michael should be there anyway. The fact that Michael seldom attended any service was not lost on Father Barney.

"I'm so glad you called, Michael. You're looking well. How have you been?" Father Barney was one of the first people Michael had called when his mental and emotional wheels became mired. He was a touchstone. It was Father Barney who helped Michael reignite a sense of purpose and the old determination to never give up. Life could still be good or at least better than it was.

Even when struggling, Michael was interested in what the next day would bring. He knew he would never harm himself, if for no other reason than he didn't want to miss out on something. He thought it curious that someone could be simultaneously depressed and optimistic. He had needed guidance, and he'd turned to the most optimistic person he'd ever known. He would not disappoint Father Barney.

"I'm fine, Barney. I'm glad you've come back to St. Theresa's. It's almost as if you never left."

"Well, in this business, you don't always know. That's why we call it faith. I hope you don't mind decaf."

"Father, decaf coffee? Must you make such a sacrifice?"

Barney smiled, then replied, "It may be God's will, but more timely, it's the will of Doctor Hunter. And, I admit, I was a bit too fond of the caffeine." After a lively visit about family and business, there was a pause in the conversation and Barney asked, "Why don't you tell me what's on your mind, Michael? I'm happy to see you, but I sense there's another purpose to our visit."

"I'm sorry, Barney. I should've been over to see you sooner. I guess it's one of those things a person takes for granted and intends to do until it's too late. But having said that, I do have something else on my mind."

Michael related his meeting with Sheriff Conrad and the subsequent requests. "Barney, I agreed to review the case and make suggestions, but after carefully studying the file, I'm hesitant. In spite of work by the sheriff's department and the other authorities, there's little to go on. Knowing the family as I do, it's difficult to be objective."

"I understand. What may I do to help?"

"Other than confession, did Ginny meet with you at any time between last Christmas and when she disappeared?"

"No, I can't say that she did. I saw her at Christmas mass and at mass a few times last summer, but she didn't try to arrange nor did we have a private meeting of any sort."

"Have her Aunties shared any worries they had concerning Ginny?"

"Like what, Michael? What are you driving at?"

"Ginny may have made a decision or decisions about her future that could have a bearing on the case. Did Hoepe and Faethe have anything to say about Ginny struggling with a big decision or an anxiety that Ginny shared with them?"

"I've visited with Hoepe and Faethe several times since Ginny was found, but it's a mystery to them. Ginny called each week, usually Sunday morning, and the last time they spoke, Ginny seemed excited about school and was her usual, upbeat self. They knew of nothing troubling her, nor did they know Ginny was even in the Lakes area when this horrible thing happened."

Michael took time to sip his coffee, then continued. "Barney, I am of the opinion that priests, as well as leaders of any faith, are very aware of what goes on in the community as well as within the lives of many in the congregation. I'm not asking for a breach of confidentiality, but from your perspective, have you noticed anything, even remotely, that might suggest a motive or reason for what happened to Ginny or something that could happen to any young person living in the area?"

Father Barney leaned back in his chair, looked up at the ceiling and then back to Michael. "I've given this some prayer and thought. I know bad things happen, but if Ginny's death was the result of an unfortunate accident, why would someone need to dispose of the body? This humble old priest suspects there was an effort to cover it up. And even if her body was found, there was an attempt to mislead authorities. I believe that takes cold, rational thinking under pressure." Michael nodded his head and remained silent.

"Also, I was told that she still had her mother's large ruby ring. I thought if this involved robbery, all the jewelry would have been missing, and if the motive were something else, isn't it true that many attackers take a souvenir? You're the expert in this sort of thing, but wouldn't the ring be the obvious choice?"

"Barney, you could've been a detective."

With a bit of twinkle in his eyes Barney responded, "That may be part of a pastor's unwritten job description. Besides, I read your book."

"Let me ask this, and again, I'm not trying to get inside the confessional, but is there anyone or anything you would suggest that might be worth investigating?"

"Well, nothing definite, but there are many changes going on in the Lakes region. It's not so much a fact as a feeling of uneasiness I get from some of the old-timers. Some comments go beyond the usual gripes concerning the amount of wealth and property held by fewer people leading to a Rich Man's Club and the average Joe getting pushed out."

"There always has been some of that in the region."

"Yes, but this seems different. I don't know how it relates to your interest, but it seems there's a notion that something unsavory is driving much of it. Greed and jealousy do not explain the comments. Something more is happening. I think some might call it 'a disturbance in the force.'"

"That's interesting. I'm not sure how this all fits, but it may mean we need to broaden our view of possible motives."

"Ah, I see. As usual, you are engaged in a grand quest for justice."

"What?"

"Oh come now, Michael. You must remember from elementary parochial school. After that little stunt with our guest priest, when you and your friends helped Janneke pass as an altar boy, the nuns began calling your little group of friends the four apostles—Matthew, Mark, Luke and Janni. To Sister Felicity you were Michael the Archangel, the fierce protector of your friends, always ready to battle against real or imagined inequities."

Now it was Michael's turn to stare at the ceiling. "Well, other than insisting there should be altar girls that sounds a bit overdone."

"Perhaps, but your willingness to challenge others intellectually and your determination to stand for what you thought was just were what earned the epithet."

"Ah, but Father, I have to point out, you're one to talk. Do you know what we considered the best time ever in high school religious ed class? It was the day you took a swing at Daugherty."

Father Barney appeared puzzled. "I'm not sure that I recall ever striking a student."

"Of course you do. Besides, you didn't strike a student, he was short and quick and you missed. We all respected you, but when you tried to slug Dickhead Daugherty, it was a Pentecostal moment."

A slight blush climbed up from Barney's collar. "Now Michael, I couldn't have. It would have been traumatic to such young, innocent children."

"Ha! We weren't that young or innocent. On the entertainment scale, you made the top ten in hits, even with a miss."

"But why would any priest do such a thing?"

"I remember it clearly. You were standing in front of the pews, Daugherty was in the first row, Mary Josephine was kneeling beside him, and I was on the other side of Mary Josephine. You gave the blessing to dismiss us, and as we stood up, Dickhead said to Mary Josephine in a loud whisper, 'Do you want to have sex?' Although that's not how he phrased it.

"He had this big grin on his face. Mary Josephine nearly fainted and Daugherty turned just in time to see what was coming. Darn, I wish you had landed one. But the look of terror on Daugherty's face after he realized what had happened was almost as good. It was the only time I've seen someone literally running out of church."

Father Barney's face flushed a deep red. "But to see someone you trusted and depended upon, to do such a thing, what must you have thought?"

"Barney, you are God's good servant on this earth. I just decided it was His will, the bolt of lightning tempered by forgiveness. You know—you swung, he ducked."

With that, Barney roared in his great Irish laugh until tears ran down his ruddy cheeks. Father Barney believed in and preached that the divine scales of judgment would balance, even if it took a little earthly assistance.

Before saying their goodbyes, Barney encouraged Michael to visit the Lawery sisters. "The Aunties were very important to Ginny, and they adored her. I know Sheriff Conrad spoke with them, but now that some of the shock has passed, they may remember more clearly. I'm sure it would be a comfort to them to know that the investigation is ongoing and not set aside as a cold case."

"Thank you, Barney. In fact, I've arranged a visit for this afternoon."

After a warm hug from the elderly cleric, Michael took his leave. As he drove off, Michael waved to Father Barney, who waved in return. Looking back in the rearview mirror, Michael saw Father Barney bless him with the sign of the cross.

As he stopped then turned to enter the traffic stream on Highway 71, he said to no one in particular, "I'll need that and more when I see the Aunties."

8

To visit with the Lawery sisters was to take a step into the living history of the Lakes region. Michael's grandmother had passed on to her grandchildren the tale of the courtship between Dr. Lawery and his intended wife-to-be. As she explained, it was not unusual for a family of stature to insist that a young suitor, in this case a veterinarian just getting established, demonstrate to be a man of means or potential means in order to be worthy of their daughter's hand in marriage.

It had taken two years, but in addition to long work days as a veterinarian, Dr. Lawery designed and built this resplendent home for his beloved Elise with the help of farmer clients who paid for his services with their labor. With that, as they say, the rest was just details.

Grandmother told about the wedding at St. Theresa's and the reception that followed, held on the expansive lakeside lawn of the home. Though the list of those invited was reserved in number, it was profound in the importance of family members and guests, including Michael's grandparents and the parish priest. When listening to this part of the story, Michael liked to imagine how his grandparents, especially his grandfather, would have appeared. The dignified sobriety of Judge Cain alongside the Catholic Church's consecrated celebrant would have combined to elevate the occasion to social and moral heights not often experienced in the relaxed resort atmosphere of the Iowa Lakes region. In Michael's young mind the occasion held status appropriate for royalty or at least the landed class, and in a way, it was.

The marriage was fruitful. First came Faethe and then Hoepe. Chaerley, the son Papa so wished for, came along a few years later, but tragically died at a young age of scarlet fever along with Papa's dreams for his son. When the fever was passed on to Faethe and Hoepe, three graves were dug, but only Chaerley succumbed. Then, much later, a surprise—there was Chaerity!

In spite of hard times, the veterinarian's business continued to be successful and eventually included a farm, dairy, creamery, and feed store. The family's prominence was still evident through the wealth and beneficence made manifest by the stately old home.

Faethe Lawery's response to Michael's call was cordial but to the point. Cordial because of the longtime relationship between their families, and to the point because—well, because it was Faethe. "Of course we'd love to see you Michael. Why don't you come by at 2:00? Hoepe will have a fresh batch of cookies. Be prepared to tell us all about what you've been up to these past months."

The last statement was less a request than a command and tinged with the implication that, since Michael was back in the area and their families were closely entwined, he was remiss in not stopping by to see them sooner. After all, maintaining such relationships was expected if your family had a long history in the region.

So that afternoon it was with a mixed sense of nostalgia and apprehension that he turned into the entrance, past the ornate but slightly rusting iron gate. Daffodils, a smattering of tulips, and an abundance of fern and hosta plants lined the short pine- and oak-sheltered drive to the remarkable home of an equally remarkable family.

The house stood as he remembered, an odd combination of Victorian, Queen Anne, and Farmhouse Revival architecture. In spite of its eclectic nature and dubious provenance, it exhibited a grandeur that reflected a personal interpretation by its designer that surpassed the character of each style.

Michael had to admire the ingenuity and evident skill of the farmer-craftsmen that formed this extraordinary structure. And there, on the extended wraparound porch, framed by the large entry door, stood the dignified grand dowager herself, Faethe Lawrey.

At the sight of Faethe, Michael's unease increased then assuaged with the appearance of her sister. With a childlike wave and an angelic smile radiating from her beaming face, Hoepe exuded a warmth of greeting that, even at some distance, seemed to surround and shield one with love and good cheer. Hoepe provided a needed counterbalance to the imposing figure of her older sister. Parking in the small set-aside, Michael took a deep breath, stepped out of the truck, and greeted the sisters.

With a firm handshake and a "Do come in, Michael," Faethe ushered him into the entry where suddenly he was swathed in a generous hug against Hoepe's ample bosom.

"It's wonderful to see you, Michael!"

With a slight smile, Faethe mildly remonstrated, "Now that's enough, Hoepe. Let's all go to the sitting room. Michael, do you prefer coffee or tea?"

Now Michael had to smile. There was no question whether he might but rather an expectation that he would have coffee or tea. "Coffee is fine, thank you." With a slight bob of her head, Hoepe dismissed herself to fetch the coffee.

"Hoepe, remember the cookies." And with that Faethe showed Michael into the parlor and to his seat on the horsehair couch.

Once intended for formal reception, the great room was now a repository of family history. Warm-toned paneling matched the beautifully carved mantle, and family pictures covered the wall on either side of the natural stone fireplace. The grandfather clock, antique couch, high wingback chairs, finely finished end tables, and richly woven throw rugs could have overwhelmed the space but for the bold outward view. Framed by French doors, the sight of the spacious lawn and stone stairway that fell away to the shore was a preamble to the panorama of the lake beyond. It was a commanding statement on the taste and status of those who dwelt within.

Following the obligatory exchange about himself and family and some compliments on the cookies—he ate three—Michael considered how to transition to the main reason for his visit. Leave it to Faethe to lead the charge.

"Michael, I had a call from Sheriff Conrad—he's been so conscientious about keeping us up to date on the investigation—and Hoepe and I are very encouraged that you've agreed to solve the mystery of this obscene act against our dear Virginia." A sharp cough, emitted by Michael, startled the sisters as much as Faethe's pronouncement had startled Michael.

He croaked, "Must be a cookie crumb." After taking a sip of coffee, Michael responded, "I should clarify that I only agreed to review the case, and I offer no illusions about solving any mystery."

"But Michael, you are here, and you said you spoke with Father Barney, so you are investigating, is that not so?"

"Ah, yes…but mostly to review and perhaps add to the facts as they are known." With the subject breached, Michael decided he may as well plunge in. "Although we met, I really didn't know your niece, and it may help if you were to tell me about her. For that matter, I know almost nothing about her mother. I apologize if this is intrusive, but perhaps there's something about Chaerity's past that might be relevant?"

"Well, yes. That is reasonable." Faethe paused, "Perhaps more coffee?" While Hoepe refilled Michael's paper-thin Lenox cup, Faethe turned her gaze to the lake, her eyes transfixed on another place and time. Sitting tall, she steeled herself for what was to come.

"To better understand Virginia, we should begin with Chaerity, and you may decide what is relevant. You must understand that there are gaps, parts of Chaerity's life that we know nothing about. Where to begin? How about with birth?

"Chaerity was the youngest, the baby of the family. She was doted on by us all. To Hoepe and me she was like a doll. We loved dressing her up and having tea parties. Mother smothered her with attention. Papa was still grieving over the loss of Chaerley and, at first, was deliberately remote. But as time passed Papa's attitude changed, and he came to adore her."

"She was beautiful. She had a glowing complexion, honey-colored hair, prominent cheek bones, and wide-set bright blue eyes. Her high forehead evinced intelligence. Chaerity was our golden child.

"Unfortunately, as a teenager her name seemed appropriate, because she freely gave it away, so to speak. But for Papa, Chaerity could do no wrong. He gave her everything... and now none of that matters."

Faethe paused. Michael remained silent, recognizing how difficult it was, even for this strong-willed woman, to be objective while speaking of those so dear to her who were now gone. Taking a deep breath, she glanced at Hoepe, then continued on. "She ran off at seventeen with some drifter ne'er do well. It wasn't her fault. We spoiled her, she was vulnerable, and we failed to protect her from that scoundrel. After that, she was in and out of our lives. She came home when she needed something, and the last time she returned, she was very ill and very pregnant."

"The delivery was difficult, but she gave birth to a healthy baby girl, our Virginia. There was no father in the picture, and as soon as she recovered, Chaerity ran off with the child. Ten years later, Chaerity died. By then Papa and Mama were in poor health and too old to care for Virginia, so Hoepe and her husband Ernest adopted her. Your grandfather facilitated the adoption.

"We had Virginia baptized. Our priest at that time, Father Andre, was very understanding and performed the baptism with little fuss even though Virginia was old enough that she could have been required to take instructions as an adult, before receiving baptism— a bit of nonsense, if you ask me. I was godmother and my long-time personal friend, the late Arlo Schnelling, was godfather. Soon after this, Ernest died of a heart attack, very unexpectedly.

"Hoepe was trying to care for Virginia, Papa, and Mama, and it was a struggle. I moved back in to help but not long after, Papa and Mama were gone."

"It was a very difficult time. Papa attended church with Mama, but he was not religious and wished to be cremated. He loved the lake. I think…rather we think, it helped to sustain him after losing Chaerley. When Mama passed, we put some of Papa's ashes in her coffin and sprinkled the rest out in the lake."

Suddenly Hoepe interjected, "Virginia saved us!"

Reaching out, Faethe took Hoepe's hand and looked to her sister with deep affection. "Yes, she did. She was our joy, and it was a chance to amend for some of the failings we may have had with her mother."

Then, as if to regain her more objective composure for the narrative, Faethe released Hoepe's hand and redirected her attention to

Michael. "Hoepe and I agreed that Virginia would keep her mother's name as Virginia Lawery. By the way, we know and don't mind if people refer to us as the Aunties or Lawery sisters, but legally my sister is still Hoepe Lawery-Johansson. I advised..."

"You mean insisted! It was scandalous!" Hoepe was clearly displeased.

"Yes, well my intentions were good, and it has become a common practice for a woman to use her maiden and husband's name. You were just ahead of the times. Now what was I saying? Hoepe, you've confused me!"

Hoepe bowed her head and softly reminded Faethe, "You were speaking of our lovely Virginia."

Faethe glanced at her sister, took a deep breath and, with a contrite tone to her voice, continued. "We never really knew what Virginia had experienced before coming home. There were few pictures and personal items. She always wore her mother's gold cross and ruby ring. Her mother told her as long as she wore the ring, she would be by her side, and the cross would keep her safe. Chaerity promised Virginia they would be together again in heaven. When Virginia's body was discovered, she still had the ring on her finger but the cross was missing. Ironic considering the cross was to keep her safe. The beauty of Chaerity's life was Virginia."

The little group sat quietly as the ambient afternoon sunlight passed through the windows of the French doors, holding them in a warm embrace. The start of a distant lawnmower intruded faintly, but Michael waited politely to be certain Faethe was finished speaking before he pressed the issue. "Do you think there's anything in Chaerity's past that could bear on what happened to Virginia?"

"Hoepe and I have considered that, but there is nothing we can recall that may be relevant. And of course, Chaerity has been gone for quite some time."

Michael continued, "May I see a picture of Chaerity? Sometimes my memory is better if associated with an image."

"Yes, her picture is to the left of the mantel. In fact there are several of her and other family there."

Rising from the couch, Michael stepped over to the collection of photos displayed about the wall and, finding the picture Faethe indicated, was startled to see an older version of Ginny staring at him.

"The resemblance is quite remarkable, isn't it, Michael? Such beauty. Yet there is a difference in the eyes. Virginia appears so innocent and bright. Chaerity looks at us through worldly eyes, as if having seen so much, she sees everything in us."

To escape the censorious scrutiny, Michael shifted his attention to the large original oil painting over the mantel. The effect of late afternoon light brilliantly played upon boisterous pheasants taking flight from a golden field of grain. Below the picture, resting on the mantel, was an old side-by-side shotgun.

Hoepe, so silent during the account of Chaerity, now piped up. "That was Papa's favorite painting. Papa loved pheasant hunting. He hunted our farm and went to South Dakota each fall to hunt with friends."

Michael nodded in approval, then remarked, "This is a beautiful shotgun. I believe I've never seen one quite like it."

"That was Papa's shotgun. It is a Sauer double-barreled 12 gauge, with external hammers and hand-carved scrolling on the receiver. He brought it back from Europe."

Michael was impressed by Hoepe's recital. "Was he in the war?"

Hoepe covered her mouth and giggled. "Heavens no! You can't go to war with a shotgun. He just went to Europe. He was so proud of the gun. He hunted with it until he got too old."

Faethe, not to be outdone, added, "We were never allowed to touch the Sauer except when Papa took us out shooting. Hoepe is a very good shot, much better than me. Papa had a gunsmith rework it for modern shells but stopped using it because it wasn't safe. He said sometimes the hammers slipped. We need to get rid of it. I don't like a gun in the house, but Hoepe insists we keep it."

Hoepe's response was quick and prickly. "It is Papa's! We'll get rid of it someday, but I'm not ready yet."

"It's alright, Hoepe. I promise I won't spirit it away when you're not looking."

Mildly chastised, Hoepe said, "I'm sorry. You're right. It's been so long, we probably should get rid of it, but not today."

As the visit came to an end, Michael thanked the sisters for their help and hospitality and promised to stay in touch. While Hoepe prepared a parting gift, Faethe followed Michael to the door. "Michael, I should explain. Losing Ernie was very hard on Hoepe, and when we lost our parents soon after, it was difficult for both of us, but especially painful for Hoepe. Hoepe has never truly recovered. Please consider this when we talk about family."

"I will. And Faethe, again I apologize for not seeing you both sooner and under better circumstances."

Reinforced with a half-dozen cookies in a plastic bag, Michael made his way to the truck and drove off. As much as he marveled at the relationship between the sisters, he was subdued in spirit, recalling the small, saddened smile that shadowed the face of Faethe while listening to her sister speak of their father.

9

Although Michael was on extended personal leave as an assistant attorney and prosecutor for the U.S. District Court of the Southern District of Iowa, he had agreed to be a temporary substitute instructor at Iowa Lakes Community College. He remained an officer of the court and, as the author of several highly regarded papers and a book on the relationship between the enforcement and practice of law, was in demand as a consultant and lecturer. Having served both in law enforcement and prosecution, the connection between them was clear to Michael—as one of the students succinctly put it, "How Sherlockian!"—but he understood that the two did not always blend seamlessly.

Monday found him at his 9:00 AM class feeling foggy. The semester's end was near, and following Sunday's visits with Father Barney and the Lawery sisters, Michael had been up late grading papers and preparing this morning's lesson. Even his third cup of coffee did little other than increase the need to pee.

Fortunately, the students were engaging, even eager for today's review on criminal investigative techniques. He respected the maturity and motivation displayed by his students, some of whom were recently honorably discharged from military service or still in the reserves. The keen satisfaction of working with committed young men and women, even on a temporary basis, was a surprise. The interaction with students was stimulating, and it was liberating to have more time to indulge, on his terms, in his passion for research and writing reviews and opinions for investigators and prosecutors. The intense focus Michael had applied in the courtroom was replaced by something reflective and meaningful in a different way.

Still, on occasion, Michael missed that recent period in his career when opportunities seemed limitless, only waiting for him to choose. He had been on the fast track for Attorney General or a judgeship, and there had been other possibilities, perhaps as a future professor at a major university or a lucrative partnership in a law firm. Hell, he could have started his own successful law firm. And then the world crashed down around him. He was left blindsided by the unanticipated dismissal of a high profile case which was followed by the subsequent murder of the primary witness and her young child.

It all spun out of control when the killer eluded capture and attempted to assassinate Michael and his wife—resulting in what the *Des Moines Register* called, "A shootout worthy of the Old Wild West." Michael used two full magazines in his Beretta 92FS to ward off the attack. Five rounds found their target and killed the assailant. Miraculously, Michael and his wife were unharmed—at least physically.

The collapse of his marriage due to his wife's serial infidelity was long in the making, but the attempt on their lives was a closer. Considering the professional debris at that point in his life, their divorce was of relatively little consequence. But the blow that pushed him to a place he never knew existed inside himself was his father's sudden death. He had been piloting his own airplane when it had crashed.

Engulfed by crisis, and on the advice of family and friends, Michael stepped away and took time to work with a private counselor.

Michael had felt lost, utterly destroyed. Life as he had known it had shifted. Little by little, with guidance and reflection, he grew to accept that he'd been dissatisfied for a long time. So much of his work as a prosecutor seemed inadequate. His personal life seemed devoid of the values for self and others that had been instilled in him as a child. He was forced to face his mortality, and the result was a tipping point in his life. At the suggestion of Father Barney, he decided to return to the family home and the Lakes region.

Rather than seeing his return as a step back in life, he was surprised by the joy and restored confidence it nurtured in him. The past few months had been a chance to redirect his life, and the blue water, on which so many of his memories sailed, was restorative—a source of healing and peace. By his choice, the future may not broil in that intense, laser-like focus of a high-powered prosecutor, but was the better for the brilliant sparkle on sunlit water, the warm glow of sunrise and sunset, and the quiet serenity late at night of the lake at rest. The waters helped to mend him and he was wise enough to be grateful.

His needs were modest; many wants had already been realized, his separation from his wife financially amiable—there were no children—and between his investments and inheritances, including the use of the family lake home, he was well off. Though a work in progress, he slowly was reconnecting with family and long-time friends. He better appreciated that time was precious, and what time there was only increased in importance as it diminished in duration. How you used the time you were given did in fact matter.

After class and several brief student consults concluded, Michael went to his office to clear the flotsam and jetsam that daily cluttered his voice message account and email inbox from various parts of the school and places unknown. He was eager to dispense with busy work and make time to call Dr. Matthew Hunter, better known by friends and patients as Dr. Matt, and discuss Ginny's autopsy.

Dr. Hunter had found irregularities during his examination, and owing to the circumstances of the death, an autopsy was done in Ankeny by the state medical examiner. Although it was being treated as a suspicious death, Dr. Matt and law enforcement were waiting for the state ME's final report to confirm the cause of death and whether it was considered a homicide. Michael understood the report would be forthcoming only after the lab work was concluded, but he was interested to learn more about the irregularities Dr. Matt found.

As he looked up the number for the clinic, the sharp demand of an incoming call on the landline interrupted his search. "Hello, Michael? This is Matt Hunter. I just received the autopsy report on Virginia Lawery from the state ME's office, and when I called to inform Sheriff Conrad, he asked me to call you. Connie thought it might be helpful if you and I were to meet and review it together. I checked with the county attorney, and as you're an acting assistant attorney for the case, he approved providing you with a copy of the report. The results are interesting and unusual. It won't take long to read, but it may seem more problematic than helpful. You'll have questions, some of which I may be able to answer."

"Reviewing it together is an excellent suggestion, but I've got to ask—bottom line, how did she die?"

"Technically, her death was by drowning, but it's not that simple."

Michael responded, "Sounds mysterious. Do we know when she died?"

"That may be more mysterious than how she died."

"Okay. When can we meet?"

"How about Lyle's Deli, today at 1:00? Monday is busy but my staff can manage the office long enough for us to meet and eat a quick lunch."

"Sounds good. See you at Lyle's, 1:00 o'clock—my treat."

10

The noon crowd was thinning by the time Michael arrived, and while there were dishes to be removed from most tables, he found a cleared booth near the back and ordered coffee. From its inception ten years prior, Lyle's Deli had looked tired and overused. The furniture could have been manufactured preowned and the splits in the vinyl booth seats looked repaired by a product that predated duct tape. The positive qualities of the grubby tiled floor included a nonspecific color that obscured many sins but not a multitude of cracks that offered some unfortunate customer or employee an opportunity for enrichment due to a fall. Dim lighting was advantageous at night, but on a sunny day like today, the walls seemed to pulse with a gloss unknown to any type of paint from the neighborhood Sherwin-Williams store.

In spite of the ambiance, the number of luncheon patrons, whether eating in or taking out, was nearly more than the small business could handle. The price was right, the food excellent, and it was fast. Lyle still managed the kitchen and could be heard exhorting those under his command to greater glory. Lyle's seemed less like a deli and more like the type of "mixed plate" eating establishments Michael had experienced on Maui. Though not on the Pacific Ocean, the impression was reinforced by a spectacular view of Smith's Bay.

When Dr. Matthew Hunter appeared at the doorway to the eatery, Michael waved him over. The doctor was a large, robust man, and the waiters, or in this case diners waiting for their orders, parted on his approach. He vigorously shook Michael's hand, asked about family and health and, to Michael's relief, didn't chide him for any social negligence. After resolving lunch orders to the satisfaction of the gum-smacking waitress, he handed Michael an official-looking folder with a facsimile of the seal of Iowa stamped on the front.

"As I said to Sheriff Conrad, I'm sorry this took so long, but I wasn't satisfied with the results of my preliminary autopsy. I thought it warranted a closer look by some of our folks in Ankeny. I know it takes time, but the state medical examiner's lab has the expertise and resources to perform tests unavailable to those of us out here in the hinterland, and the state folks are very thorough."

Michael nodded, opened the folder, and began to read. It was difficult. The jargon was familiar but trying because Michael knew the family of this promising young woman. Though required by Iowa State Code whenever cause of death was indeterminate, something within him rebelled at what he considered a violation imposed by an autopsy.

After some minutes, Michael stopped reading and closed his eyes, nearly volcanic with a mix of rage and sorrow. He swallowed hard to suppress the demons, as if he could dissipate the blackness piercing his mind and soul. When he opened his eyes, he realized the food had been served, the coffee gone cold, and Dr. Matt was midway through this noon's special gastronomical delight. Glancing over, he got the waitress's attention. He apologized and asked for a fresh cup of coffee, and then resumed reading. He was determined to absorb as much information from the report as possible before Dr. Matt's impending departure.

Finishing, Michael remained deep in thought, continuing to ignore his Ham and Swiss piled high on rye. Finally, after taking a sip of coffee, he said, "I don't understand."

"Which part?"

"Matt, I'm familiar with autopsy reports. I reviewed my share as a prosecutor, but some of the conclusions in this report are confusing."

"That's the interesting part."

"It may be interesting to a medical examiner but not to an investigator. I'll reread this more thoroughly, but according to the autopsy, and I quote: 'A blow to the head contributed to a likely unconscious state before or shortly after the victim entered the water.' It goes on to say that the cause of death was drowning, yet the evidence seems to indicate she did not drown."

"Quite the contrary, Michael. There is evidence of death by drowning. In order to understand, one must consider the pathology of drowning. Most people think, perhaps from an abundance of popular crime shows, that the victim will have any number of easily detectable indicators related to drowning, the most common of which is water in the lungs. The reality is that, although rare, evidence of drowning can be subtle and more problematic."

"But Doc, there was next to no water in the lungs and, if I take this at face value, it sounds like she had a heart attack."

"No, if that were the case there would be several definite markers for a heart attack. This is what one might call an atypical drowning. As a reflex caused by the sudden immersion in very cold water, the pharynx and larynx may close up causing the loss of consciousness and within a few minutes, cardiac arrest. The conclusion is still death by drowning. If you require a more detailed explanation, I'd suggest you call the state medical examiner's office and ask for Dr. Phill Goulet. Dr. Goulet is the pathologist who performed the autopsy and is the proverbial expert on unusual causes of death, especially in the case of a suspected drowning. In fact, and you didn't hear it from me, some colleagues call Dr. Goulet 'Dr. Le Ghoul' because of an obsession with circumstances of death described as unusual or even macabre. Whatever that suggests, in my opinion Dr. Goulet is exceptional even within that small dedicated group of honorable doctors who choose to work as pathologists. The phone numbers and email address are listed on the inside of the folder." After a quick glance to his wristwatch he said, "I'm sorry Michael, but I must get back to the office. You may keep that copy of the report."

"Wait, Doc. What about the time of death? According to the autopsy report it appears that she could have been found within hours of death, and yet we know she was missing for several weeks."

"I know, but it is possible for a body immersed in cold water to have little deterioration. Although I agree, for our region, several weeks sounds excessive. Michael, I'm sorry but I have to go. Call Phill. You'll get more information than I can provide and a better conclusion concerning the time period involved. Then, if you still have questions, call or email me. In fact, call me anyway. I'll be curious to hear what you learn. Oh, and Michael, don't be put off by, shall we say...the unorthodox. Sometimes an acquired taste is rewarding, including that of someone absolutely nutty over death. I'm certain you'll find any insights shared are of great value."

"Thanks, Doc. I'll get the check." Although it was not intended to sound like a dismissal, Dr. Matt took that as his cue and without further conversation stood up and rushed out, waving to several patients and acquaintances as he departed, successfully avoiding the floor's latent horizontal pitfalls.

For several minutes Michael remained lost in thought, staring at his uneaten entree. Abruptly he rose from the booth and, with no thought of an expense receipt, threw down cash for the lunches. On his way to the restaurant door, he exhibited such a foul-appearing countenance, no fellow denizen of the deli felt anything over his departure other than relief.

Following his 2:00 PM class, Michael had planned to review the state autopsy report in detail and list additional questions and tasks. He also needed to touch base with Connie and the county attorney. But in spite of his best intentions, the switch from teacher to investigator had him feeling unsettled and out of sync. He needed a break. After checking his watch for the third time within the same minute, Michael pushed back from his desk, shoved his class notes and the autopsy report into his book bag, and headed for the gym.

A long jog followed by a round of resistance training at the ILCC weight room left him pleasantly fatigued. The demands on his body had diminished the mental aggravation and after a light supper, Michael decided to use the upcoming walleye opener as an excuse to see if his boat and motor were ready for a late night of fishing. It also was an opportunity to check out the new version of the Lodge. Officially now renamed The Lodge on Okoboji, most area inhabitants continued to informally refer to it as the Lodge.

***

The fire that had damaged the old Lodge three years prior had been less noticeable from the lakeside than the damage visited upon neighboring homes. Michael was not living in the area at the time, but he followed the news and saw the aftermath during a brief vacation at the family home. Soon after the fire, the Lodge and the damaged homes nearby were sold, the homes torn down, and the Lodge rebuilt and expanded to the new owner's specifications.

Before heading for his boat, Michael checked out the resort's website. There was a long list of summer and winter outdoor activities, two restaurants, indoor and outdoor swimming pools, a variety of rooms to fit different needs and budgets, meeting rooms, a ballroom, and a lengthy list of services. The site included a comment section by guests and even a cursory check favored a preponderance of four and five star reviews.

There were pictures that featured examples of the renovated facilities with before and after comparisons meant to demonstrate improvements over the older structure. Found within the digital promenade was an exquisite photo of the owner-managers in their combination business and personal living suite. Anthony Sandoval was posed standing behind his wife who was seated before him on a large leather couch. He was wearing a well-fitted dinner jacket, a classic white shirt with French cuffs, and bowtie. To Michael, the formal attire suited Anthony's image as the conventional tall, dark and ruggedly handsome type, all desirable assets for representing the public face of the Lodge. In contrast, Lucia exhibited a sensual but refined elegance that softened their image. Her long dark hair framed a face of striking beauty with bright eyes, sensual full red lips, and a small but slightly equine nose that suggested a hint of Spanish heritage. She wore a brightly-colored chiffon dress that seemed to flow over her body and revealed just enough to be suggestive yet not enough to satisfy the prurient interest of someone with an imaginative nature. A finely embroidered throw draped over the couch's back added a stately touch. Together the Sandovals appeared professional and self-assured. Impressed, Michael mused whether if taken separately, each would project the same degree of competence as displayed in their duality.

All in all, the refashioned Lodge seemed to be a remarkable effort to cater to the needs and wants of a varied clientele on a year-round basis. The possibilities were intriguing, but Michael was curious as to the financial viability of such an enterprise. Area resorts went full bore during the summer months, but shortly after the end of tourist season, most resorts adjusted to the limited amount of business by reducing the number of activities and requisite employees, or by simply closing their doors for the winter.

Slipping a life vest on over his favorite Outdoor Research fleece, Michael descended the nineteen wooden steps from his porch to the dock and cranked the Pro Angler from lift to water. Climbing into the craft, he disconnected the bow and stern ropes from the lift and pushed off. With a sharp pop the motor responded to the electric starter, and Michael slowly backed the boat away from the dock. Sometimes Michael imagined that he might have been a sailor in a previous life. The simple act of leaving terra firma for water, even on such a limited nautical sojourn as this, provided a welcome sense of freedom from land-locked obligations.

It was cooler on the water, but the breeze was mild. The view of the greening shoreline engaged in the life-affirming rite of spring appealed to his higher spirits in spite of the many oak trees that displayed bare angular limbs anguished in repentant supplication for the redemption of new growth.

Maneuvering further out onto the deep blue lake, the Lodge

came into view. It dominated the far shore and the scene from the bayside was impressive. A third level had been added to a portion of the original structure, and the grounds encompassed a wider area, likely as a result of acquisitions of fire-damaged houses next to the resort. His first impression was "Wow!" But then he felt a sudden quiver, whether from the light breeze over the water or an uneasy pre-science. Increasing to full throttle, Michael directed the bow straight toward the Lodge. The 40-horsepower Mercury motor responded smoothly as demanded and pushed the Lund swiftly across the bay.

Nearing his destination, Michael slowed the motor to a trolling speed, or what might pass for a trolling speed from a 40-horse motor. He maneuvered the boat parallel to the shore to better take in the scope of the old and new. It really was changed. Again, Michael wondered how such a facility could be financially feasible beyond the normal tourist season and made a mental note to ask that question of his long-time personal friends, business leaders, and, according to Father Barney, biblically-referenced apostles Luke and Janneke.

Having secured his boat at the marina dock, he walked the concrete path that separated the lawn from the sandy beach. Gone were the small cabins that once stood between the shore and the main facility. In their place was an expansive grassy area where guests could lounge and children enjoy a variety of playground equipment.

As he strolled past, Michael marveled at the appeal of the spacious glassed front of the restaurant and bar and its ingenious design. The outdoor seating on a great stone patio appeared to be a continuous extension of the interior. Nearby, chaise lounge chairs and umbrella-festooned tables surrounded the outdoor pool and flaunted a South Seas motif, probably an expected feature, but in Michael's opinion a bit tacky. A row of cabanas lined a portion of the beach.

Further along the path, visible through windows framed to appear like the stern of a sailing ship, was an interior pool and recreational area elaborate enough to compare to a small water park. Adjacent to the interior pool was an exercise room with aerobic devices and multi-stationed Nautilus equipment, all situated to take advantage of the view of the lake.

An enclosed walkway connected the principal building to the variety of rental options that ranged from "affordable," whatever that implied, to "luxurious." The rooms and suites stretched at least a city block and ended in a faux lighthouse.

He knew from the floor plan on the website that the main business suite was rebuilt and located on the first floor of the main building. It had a private employee entrance that provided ready access to and from the staff parking lot and the resort's maintenance yard.

Walking about the grounds, it appeared that every square foot of the property was used to good effect. Duly impressed, Michael retraced his steps and found his way to the front entrance.

***

The original modest lobby, with a short registration counter and nearby concierge's desk, imparted a bit of nostalgia for those who remembered the old Lodge. As soon as he stepped inside, Michael knew he'd made a good decision. Emanating from the second floor ballroom, or what he assumed was still the ballroom, were the great sounds of the Big Okoboji Band, playing an arrangement of Herbie Hancock's jazz classic, "Watermelon Man."

The big band was a Monday night standard for the old Lodge. Michael had heard that following the fire and during the rebuild the band had broken up with members going their separate ways largely due to disagreements over venue and who owned the "book," the collection of arrangements performed by the band. Michael considered that this may be a recording, but the sudden halt to the sound followed by muffled shouts and the words, "Sound check!" confirmed that the band was setting up to play their first set. It was a joyful surprise to hear the sounds of what he hoped was now a resurgent feature of the Lodge.

Michael was a jazz fanatic and on occasion had sat in with the band. His father did not object when Grandmother insisted upon giving young Michael piano lessons. But when introduced to the genre by his middle school-high school band director, Michael went absolutely gaga over the jazz piano greats.

Regardless of any personal disposition, it was thought Michael would follow in his father's footsteps. When his son chose to be a piano major at the University of Iowa, Michael's father correctly assumed that it was done mostly to piss him off. Michael found an additional rebellious cause to again assert his independence when his university piano professor made it clear he considered jazz piano degenerate noise and the progeny of demons. The result was a freshman year largely devoted to playing piano in any type of jazz or pop group that would hire him, and once they heard him play, they all did.

Michael followed the inviting sounds, brushing past the posters and autographed pictures of Marilyn Mae, BB King, and of so many other luminaries that graced the walls of the staircase. Most were originals from the old Lodge, and Michael wondered how they managed to survive the flames. Reaching the top of the stairs, he arrived at the dais manned by the same diminutive maitre d' he had known for years.

"Jeez Louise, look who's here! Michael Cain, as I live and breathe!"

"Sammy, I thought you went down in flames with the old Lodge."

The wiry little man with large lively eyes and tobacco-stained teeth nearly leaped over the stand to hug him and attempted, with an ineffectual effort, to lift Michael off his feet. Stepping back Sammy exclaimed, "You are a sight for sore ears! Ha!"

"And you, Sammy, are as annoying as ever, but…lookin' good!"

"Yup! Beauty has never been my problem. I heard you were back. Really, how have you been?"

"Better now. I needed to come home to work some things out."

"Work out, hell. I heard it was so bad, someone could have tied an anchor to your leg, thrown you in the lake, and you wouldn't have noticed."

A sharp sensory spark flashed across Michael's cortex. Something tugged at his consciousness but was gone as quickly as it struck. Michael stood unseeing, a frown on his face.

In less than a 4/4 bar in swing time, Sammy broke the awkward silence, "Come with me. Ya gotta say 'Hi' to the band."

12

After enthusiastic greetings from longtime band friends and introductions to new members, Michael agreed to sit in on a tune if the tune could be of his choice. He had a Tanqueray and tonic (with two olives rather than a lime slice), listened to the first set, and during the break visited with the rhythm section. The music requirements clarified, Michael was asked how his work at ILCC was going and if it was true he was assisting the sheriff's office with the Lawery investigation.

"How do you know about that?"

The group laughed and guitarist Danny Barley, "Digger Dan" to his friends, spoke up, "Are you kidding? Everyone knows about it. It's practically buzzing electric here at the Lodge." It was understood to the area's populace that information, rumors, gossip, and outright lies were like currency and thus freely exchanged. Having broached the subject, Digger and the rest of the group expressed condolences over the sad circumstance of someone they had come to know while playing at the Lodge. The potential onset of melancholy was diverted by the bright call of a trumpet that insisted on their immediate return to the portable stage.

Michael played in the opening number of the second set—his choice: "I Don't Get Around Much Anymore." It was hard to beat Duke Ellington. Though out of practice, by the final chorus Michael found his groove. The richness of friends and fine music was regenerating.

***

The moon was rising late and stars were abundant in the clear sky as he guided his boat slowly along the shoreline back to his home. The stillness of the night accompanied by the soft slap of waves against the side of the boat and the occasional splash of water-fowl nurtured his mellow mood. The aroma of an aquatic environment stirred up by the motion of boat and motor was like a perfume. In his experience, each body of water had a slightly distinct fragrance, and to Michael, Okoboji was like Chanel No. 5.

Many homes remained in winter slumber and exuded little illumination. There were a few whose bare bulbs glowed harshly over recently placed docks and expectant boat lifts. Evidently the folks at Marv's Marina and Lake Service had been busy. Michael knew the way well, and a scarcity of light was no hindrance to his progress.

Suddenly a voice yelled, "Boater, stop!" Michael's anxiety level immediately peaked. Abruptly the flash of a piercing white light blinded him. "Turn off your motor! Turn on your running lights!"

Thank God. Or in this case, the DNR.

"I'm coming alongside."

Lost in the afterglow of the reunion at the Lodge, Michael was guilty of a significant mistake. He had failed to turn on the boat's running lights. It was a cardinal sin of boating that put himself and others at risk.

The bright spotlight was redirected downward onto Michael's boat, and now he could make out the form behind the blinding light. Michael flipped the switch that engaged his boat lights, turned off the motor, and prepared for a deserved lecture on water safety.

And the lecture came, enumerated by the book from no less than "the world's greatest DNR officer," Richard Piccard, or "Picky Dicky" as he was known to the less enthusiastic of his admirers. Having cited the offense and performed the requisite rites of inspection of the accused reprobate's boat and accruements, Piccard went on, "I recognized you as you pulled out from the Lodge. Nothing personal, but what're you doing out here without running lights on? Have you been drinking?"

With his lawyer sense beginning to kick in, he carefully responded, "I thought I'd do a little cruise as a night trial for my boat before the walleye opener and was curious to see the changes at the Lodge. I stopped to hear the Big Okoboji Band, had one drink, and without intending to, invited this reminder to use running lights after dusk. I have no excuse. It was a case of inattentiveness and I do apologize. It won't happen again." Then, after a pause, he added, "I'm sure, had I seen the running lights on your boat, I would have remembered to turn on mine."

The implication bobbed on the water between them for several seconds. Following a rather theatrical clearing of his throat, Piccard responded with a less than amenable tone. "Well, it's early in the season so I'll give you a pass, but remember, if there is a next time, it means a summons and hopefully not something more serious."

"Thank you, Officer. It won't happen again."

"Good. See to it and remember, on opening night, I'll be out here looking for you and all the other goofballs that consider themselves sportsmen."

The exchange seemed to have developed into a pissing match over who would own the final word until Michael recalled that Piccard was listed in the sheriff's report as one of the three members of the gillnet team who discovered Ginny's body.

"Yes, sir. Officer Piccard, is it?"

The response was drawn out, sounding like a challenge. "Yes?"

"This may not be the best time, yet here we are. Sheriff Conrad asked me to review the case of Virginia Lawery. I know the reported facts, but as an experienced law officer and one of the men who found her body, hearing your impression of that night would be helpful. It may save both of us some time, and I'd appreciate knowing what your thoughts may be on the case."

Piccard snarled from the darkness, "You want to know my impression? Here's my impression: Young women shouldn't skinny dip in ice water. You want to know what I think? Scofflaw, self-entitled lawyers shouldn't be asking questions when out alone at night in the middle of a lake. That's what I think." With that, Piccard hit the starter and, with no regard for the wake, gunned the motor, going from hole to trim in a matter of seconds.

Michael's boat was rocked by the hasty departure but not his mind. He spoke to no one in particular, "The nickname fits. What a dick! He must have a theory or at least an opinion. Telling me now would have saved time for both of us, but we'll see how he reacts to an interview in a more formal setting with Sheriff Conrad present. He won't like it, but it doesn't matter. He's a witness, and even a hostile lawman makes a better witness than most civilians."

With the help of his deck light, Michael steered the boat in an easy glide to the lift. Attaching the lines, he stepped onto the dock, engaged the lift, and secured the boat a good two feet above the water line. Vaguely, Michael processed that the winter season had been drier than usual which left the lake's water level down slightly from average. There was enough of a difference to suggest the need for extra caution when fishing over his favorite points and reefs in the dark early on Saturday.

Michael tucked that knowledge into his mental tackle box and headed for the steps. In one of those odd tangents his mind sometimes took, it occurred to him that rather than a twelve-step program, his program for recovery involved the nineteen steps between his home and the lake.

When Michael stepped into the broad front room, he could hear the quiet beep of the answering machine. A bit old school, he maintained a landline to the combination portable phone and answering machine that his mother had left behind. It was ironic in a way. Now retired in Arizona along with many Iowa ex-patriots, she had acquired a taste and skill for modern technology. A telephone landline was "so retro," she told him. It sounded pretty funny coming from his mother. Still, whether due to sentimentality or inertia, he had kept it there when he moved back.

After punching the button, the resonant baritone of Sheriff Conrad greeted him with a question, *"Wie geht's? Como estas, mi amigo?"* This was a game of salutation Michael and the Four Apostles had devised in junior high. It might have been playful, but in this case served to remind Michael that he had not touched base with Connie today, as promised.

"Damn. It was on my Must Do list, and I still forgot." Dialing the Dickinson County Sheriff's Office from memory, dispatcher Duane Fridlay answered him on the second ring. "Hey, Duane. This is Michael Cain. I'd like to leave a message for Connie."

"Well, Connie's still here if you want to speak with him." Then in his best verbal imitation he confided, "It's been one of those nights here at the ranch, if you know what I mean, pilgrim."

To the irritation of the sheriff, Fridlay's fascination with all things John Wayne was prone to exhibition anytime and anywhere and according to the sheriff demonstrated a distinct lack of professionalism. But he was a skilled, experienced communicator and, to the relief of the other dispatchers, he liked to work the night shift. Sheriff Conrad had shared with Michael that he wondered if Duane was part bat or just batty.

"Hello, Michael. Thanks for the call back. It's been busy, so if you tried to reach me, I'm sorry I missed you."

"No, my apologies, Connie. I simply forgot to call. I don't have a lot to report. Yesterday I caught up with Father Barney and the Lawery sisters and today met with Dr. Matt for lunch to go over the autopsy report on Virginia Lawery."

"Right. I have it here somewhere." Michael could hear the shuffle of papers and then through the muffle of a poorly covered phone receiver, "Duane, have you seen that autopsy report from the state?" Duane's response was undecipherable, but after a pause, Connie was back. "Got it. Found it in the fax machine tray. Haven't had time to read it."

"Well, it was informative but confusing. Read it over when you get the chance. I'll be interested in your reaction. Are we still on for the walleye opener midnight Friday?"

"I'm planning on it, but if business heats up, I may have to bail on you."

"Got it, I understand. Maybe if you can't go I can ask a DNR officer."

"What? What're you talking about?"

"Oh, I had a little run-in with the DNR's least admired diplomat."

"Let me guess, Richard Piccard."

"It was my fault. I was on a trial run and forgot to turn on the boat lights."

"*Uff da*, that's a biggie. Did he give you a summons?"

"No. He saw me leave the Lodge marina and ambushed me without his running lights on. I think he may have decided he didn't want to argue the point with a lawyer."

"Ha! You're lucky—or maybe he's getting soft."

"I told him that I was assisting in the Lawery case and asked him for his thoughts on that night. His response was informative but not useful."

"Yeah, I can imagine."

"But at some point, I will need to interview him. I thought you and I might do that together at the office."

"That's the best approach. He's a smart, hard character, but he and I have history. We've assisted each other in several cases. When would you like to meet?"

"Let's wait on that. The end of the semester at Iowa State University is a week from this Friday, and I'm concerned that if I don't get to it soon, I'll miss an opportunity to interview Ginny's roommate before she leaves school. Her recall may be better while she's still on campus. While I'm at it, I thought I'd visit with the ISU Police Chief and the state ME who did Virginia's autopsy."

"Sounds good. When are you going and what can I do to help?"

"Well, as of Thursday, ILCC classes won't meet. It's an abbreviated week so our students can prepare for finals. I thought I'd make arrangements tomorrow or Wednesday at the latest, and if it works out, do the interviews on Thursday."

"Maybe we should cancel our plans for the opener. The interviews are more important."

"No, I'll be back in time. I thought I'd fly the family Cessna 172. I need the flight hours to maintain my license anyway, and if your department will pick up the hotel and car rental, I'll pay for gas."

After a few additional words over fishing arrangements and a promise from Michael to call by Friday afternoon, the two seekers of justice hung up, ending what had been a very active day.

With the end of the spring term so near, Michael realized a follow-up interview with people who knew Ginny at ISU would become considerably more difficult and time-consuming if he didn't act soon. Enough time had already passed that reliable information would be less forthcoming. With that in mind, Michael's first call of the day was to his longtime friend Barry Seward, Chief of the Iowa State University Police Department.

Michael had worked with or advised Barry on cases involving students in more serious situations and understood any university had unique student and public issues to address. On more than one occasion, Barry had reminded Michael that though university-level students were capable of remarkably sensitive and unselfish behavior, they were not yet fully mature which at times led to utterly idiotic, self-destructive choices.

Barry answered on the third ring and after exchanging greetings Michael asked, "How are things at the University? Busy, I bet."

"Yeah, this time of year is borderline insane. Everyone is stressed and trying to reach the end of the school year in their own way. Most students are fine, but we deal daily with those who are struggling. Some students try to make up for lost time and act out the stress, and some have given up and are spending their last couple of weeks making even poorer decisions. It's interesting to say the least. I understand you've taken on a professorial role at Iowa Lakes Community College. How's that going?"

"Well, you know, I think it's going okay. I'm subbing for one of the instructors, Pam Schneider, who's on maternity leave. Pam is incredibly well organized. I follow her lesson plans, spice it up with my own experiences, and I think students are getting the better benefits of two instructors with differing backgrounds."

"And you're feeling better? Life is good again?"

"Life is much better. Coming back to the family home, slowing down to the point where I can manage my life rather than life managing me, and reconnecting with old friends and family have all been a big help. Not to be overdramatic, but living by the lake seems to promote a better perspective on life. Funny that I didn't appreciate that before."

"That's good to hear. Many of us were worried about you."

"I know, and thank you. Speaking of the lake, I've agreed to help local law enforcement with the case of Ginny Lawery, an ISU student whose body was found in Okoboji. I know your department, Ames Police, and the DCI investigated her disappearance and I have copies of all the reports sent to Sheriff Conrad. But I wondered if anything additional has come to light since her body was found."

"The case is still open," Barry responded, "but nothing more's been learned specific to her disappearance or subsequent to the discovery of her body. However, I recently pulled the file and did a general search for anything that may be related, even remotely, to Virginia Lawery or people connected to her here at the university. I didn't find anything further about her, but I did find some interesting things that were not part of the original report. They were separate events that happened after the investigation into Lawery's disappearance began, but may be relevant."

"Such as?"

"I learned the apartment Ginny shared with her roommate was burglarized on the Tuesday after spring break."

"Shouldn't that have been included in the report on Ginny's case?"

"Not necessarily. You'd be surprised how often things like this happen thanks to relationships gone bad, jealous roommates or friends, outright thievery, and sometimes, just stupid or drunken behavior. Besides, it was not considered part of the Lawery investigation because Virginia Lawery had already been reported as missing two weeks before and her body not found until much later. What should have set off alarms was that Lawery's roommate, Sally Grosfeldt, was mugged the same night the apartment was burglarized. She was crossing campus from Parks Library after dark, and someone she described as 'a big ugly biker type' knocked her to the ground and stole her backpack and keys."

"What? With the burglary, that can't be coincidental."

"I agree, but again, events like this one are often considered on a case-by-case basis. Also, the attack was on campus and handled by the ISU Police Department, but the burglary was off-campus and handled by Ames PD. With multiple agencies involved, associations are not always recognized, at least not initially. When we did make the connection, we thought that both crimes had to do with someone who was targeting the roommate. And there's more.

"Following the mugging and apartment break-in, the roommate dropped out of school, or rather, her parents pulled her out, and she took incompletes for the semester."

"What? Where is she now?"

"Believe it or not, she's living near you, in Spencer with her parents. Federal law protects student confidentiality and prevents me from sending you her personal information that the university has on file. But you can find her name and contact information in the Ames Police Department's report. Besides, if you want to talk to her, I doubt there are many Grosfeldts in Spencer."

"I'll do that. Do you know of any other reported incidents involving her since she returned to Spencer?"

"No. I only learned of her change in status when I did my search earlier today."

"How about a boyfriend? I understand Ginny had an on-again, off-again relationship with some guy, but they broke up months ago. Any information on him?"

"He's a head case. He was questioned more than a year ago on a different complaint, but since we didn't know exactly when and where Lawery went missing or whether she even really was missing, we didn't have much to go on that would connect him to her disappearance. Funny thing, when I checked on the roommate I also checked on the ex-boyfriend and learned he's no longer at ISU. Officially, he dropped out a week ago. He was enrolled until then, but according to his professors, he hasn't attended class since the week before spring break."

"Where is he now?"

"I don't know. I have his contact information and reached out to the family. There was no answer. I left a message this morning but haven't heard back. Do you want me to keep trying?"

There was a thoughtful pause occupied only by the soft crackle of unshaved stubble on the phone. "No, if they call back, fine, but otherwise let it rest for the time being. He seems to be an obvious suspect, but I can understand why, at first, he may not have been considered relevant. Let me do what I can to see how he fits into the frame before we proceed any further in that direction. It could be important, or it could be a waste of time."

"That's fine but the university's also invested in this. I may try calling the family again, anyway. Do you still want to speak to her advisor?"

"Yes, please. I should meet with all her instructors from this semester, but considering commencement is a week from Saturday, it might be more critical to interview her advisor and the four students who, according to your investigator's report, were close to her. I'm emailing you the students' names as we speak. If I need to, I can check on other staff members or students later. Do you have a suggestion how I might arrange to meet with the advisor and the four students I requested?"

"I'll reach out to them and see what I can do. How much time would you need?"

"Not much, no more than an hour with each."

"I'll let you know what I can arrange. When do you think you'll be here?"

"I can get away tomorrow. If you and I meet first thing Thursday, then maybe I could speak with the rest sometime later that day? I also hope to see the state forensic pathologist who did the autopsy and then fly home by Friday afternoon. I got a call back from the DCI investigator and there's been nothing new. I'm waiting for a call from the Ames PD."

"I can help with that. Last Saturday I had coffee with Ames PD Captain Romo and the detective he assigned to the case. It was our unofficial monthly breakfast for interagency cooperation. Detective Hawkins reviewed his notes about the burglary and did so again last week but had nothing additional to report."

"I didn't really think there would be. I'm hoping the pathologist can help determine a useable timeline. Almost every way to go in this investigation is hung up on knowing when she died. Right now the window is at least six weeks wide."

"We'll do what we can on this end. Why don't we plan to meet here at my office around 9:00 AM Thursday? Park in the visitor's area and I'll have a permit for you so you won't have any hassles parking on campus."

"Good, 9:00 AM is fine. Unless something comes up in the meantime, I'll see you Thursday."

After signing off, Michael considered whether he should try to reach out to the roommate; instead he dialed Sheriff Conrad's office for another update.

***

Barry Seward sat quietly thinking about his conversation with Michael Cain. "Interesting guy, my friend Michael. I wouldn't want to be the person of interest in any of his investigations, or worse yet, prosecutions." With all that was on Barry's plate, taking time to arrange meetings with students and staff was definitely a buzzkill. Yet, there was that small irk in the back of his mind that had been with him since the discovery of Virginia Lawery's body.

Barry enjoyed working around young people and was deeply dedicated to serve and protect all the citizens of the university. Before law enforcement, he had been a classroom teacher and still had a sense that each student, not just the group, was important. He counted members of his department as family, and he insisted his officers consider students and faculty the same. Baldly stated, Virginia Lawery was ISU family, and to Barry, what happened to her was personal.

He vaguely considered a fresh cup of coffee, sharpening his pencils, getting a supply of staples from the storeroom—anything that might help him avoid the maelstrom of demands on his attention for a few more minutes. As he did so, a slight smile formed, and a notion evolved into an idea. "Why not?" he thought then shouted, "Mavis! Would you come in here, please?"

Mavis was the central control and go-to colleague, or as Barry called her, The Maven of Marvel, when it came to unraveling a Gordian knot. She was agreeable up to a point but with a slightly intimidating edge in manner and voice that mildly implied that while she was willing to cooperate with others, the work required of her immediate boss was a priority. Indefinite of age in appearance, Mavis was a member of the legion whose presence was to be found in an office in nearly every department at the university. They were individuals of stature acquired by a history of proven excellence, who knew of everything that crossed their orbits, and were absolutely committed to maintaining decorum, privacy, and loyalty to their sponsors. Yet each was accessible, in a quid pro quo way, when called upon by a peer of their legion.

"Mavis, I need a favor—a big favor. I know we're swamped but this may help in the case of one of our lost kids."

"Is this about Virginia Lawery?"

Barry's jaw dropped slightly and he thought to himself, "Remarkable. How does she do it? Maybe Mavis is our university family's Mama."

"It is. I'm forwarding you an email with some names, and I'd like you to see if you may be able to arrange a meeting with each person on the list. The details are outlined in the email. I added a couple of names and some questions that may be relevant to the investigation.

"But here's the favor. Would you reach out to others in your magical web and learn if anyone has information about this case that might be of use? I know that's vague, but before I meet with this special investigator, I'd like to be as up-to-date as possible. Opinions are also acceptable."

"I'll get on it right away."

"Thank you—and Mavis?"

"Yes?"

"Be sure you include your opinion about her case and the stuff that doesn't always appear in an incident report."

"Of course, Barry. I'll have an update by lunchtime tomorrow and the results to you by the end of the day."

***

As Mavis prepared to rally the troops, Dr. Phill Goulet, the aggressively recruited graduate from one of the nation's top forensic schools and recent addition to Iowa's medical examiner staff was rereading the email sent the day before by Michael Cain. The potential response felt vicarious, in part due to the unusual results of the autopsy, but also because of the opportunity to meet Mr. Cain. Goulet had heard of Michael's work before moving to Iowa and had made a point to read his book on the relationships and correlations between investigation and prosecution. Although some of the procedures referenced were common practice, there was something imaginative and thought-provoking about Cain's insights. His suggestions proposed intuitive avenues of perception to decipher what could be learned beyond using only dogged procedure and deduction. Time was definitely worth carving out of a busy day for a meeting with Mr. Cain.

The preflight check went as expected, as it should have, since the annual inspection on the Cessna 172 Skyhawk had been completed the week before. Atmospheric conditions were good: barometer rising, high wispy clouds, visibility ten miles, temperature in the upper 50s, and a light wind from the northwest—a welcome push for the small plane. It occurred to Michael that the cold front that moved in overnight was bad news for walleye fishing. The wave action over some of his favorite fishing points would be good, but the high pressure associated with the front would give the walleyes lockjaw. Fishing success this Saturday would be a challenge.

He had not piloted a plane in several months, and although a little apprehensive, the takeoff was smooth and the rate of climb easily within the range of the Cessna. Tactile memory imprinted through time and experience took over, and soon Michael began to regain confidence.

Briefly deviating from his flight plan, Michael took a few minutes to circle over the lakes noting, as he always did, the distinct difference between the azure of West Lake and the decidedly sludge-green hue of East Lake. With a smile Michael recalled his first flight over the lakes, courtesy of an elderly pilot who was a family friend intent on demonstrating to Michael's father the ease of flight. As they passed over the lakes the pilot pointed out the difference in water color between West and East Okoboji.

"See how blue West Okoboji is? It's a natural blue-water lake, one of only three in the world. And see how green East Okoboji is? That's because of all the allergies in the water." Allergies! The pilot's intention was commendable but even a very young Michael had doubts about the effect of allergies on the coloration of water.

The lakes sparkled like gems set in the dark browns and blacks of the fertile soils of Northwest Iowa and highlighted by the green of emerging vegetation. Adjusting the throttle to cruise, he banked south, and in minutes flew over Spencer.

Spread before him was the expanse of land known as the Des Moines Lobe, an area flattened over 12,000 years earlier by the last glacial incursion into Iowa. As it receded, the glacier left the land so level that the flow of water was restrained and great wetlands were formed. Now most wetlands were drained by extensive ditch and tile systems. The current quilt-like patches of farmland outlined by square miles of country roads, broken up only by farm homes and small towns, were the result of the greatest environmental transformation of a landscape in North America.

Though at altitude it appeared idyllic, Michael knew that as contemporary agricultural practices and ownerships evolved, rural Iowa would continue to lose its population and services. Already, small towns were no longer the centers of farm business and social life they once were. Michael understood the impact that shrinking resources and increasing needs had on the remaining citizenry and law enforcement.

Though respectful of gravity's dictates, Michael enjoyed the temporary separation from the demands below. From this elevated view the world seemed embraced by a grandeur of scale that set daily life in perspective.

Opening the window on his left a couple of inches, Michael felt the cool breeze and was thankful for the fresh air that dissipated the odor of a few drops of fuel his jacket's sleeve had absorbed as he had topped off the wing tanks. He waved at the red-tailed hawk circling far below, enjoying the same thermals gently lifting them both.

His father had been the flying enthusiast, and the Cessna 172 had been part payment, part gift for representing a well-known Iowa business. The case was lost but not for lack of skills. Still, he had secured a significantly diminished financial cost for the company whose grateful owners felt their representative did exceptionally well for them.

Neither of Michael's sisters had taken any interest in learning to fly, but Michael dutifully had taken lessons, gotten his pilot's license, and used the plane for business and recreation. Perhaps owing in part to recent changes in his life, today he felt greater appreciation for his father's passion for what birds and angels did so well.

As the landscape passed by below, Michael began to ruminate over recent events. Knowing matters at ILCC were managed was a relief. The day before, he had helped the class review information needed to prepare for finals. The tests were written, and Pam planned to monitor and grade the results. Pam also was available during the rest of the week in the event a student needed help.

And then there was the walleye opener. Boat and tackle were prepped, and his anticipation grew. Thinking about it was enough to get the juices flowing. It was exciting for sports fishermen to stalk and catch quarry, but to Michael and many who grew up in the Lakes region, it was more about being a part of the annual ritual.

As he considered it, Michael was even optimistic about Ginny's case. With a review of what was known and a bit more research, the when and where of her disappearance would help point to a solution. He was less sure of an ultimate resolution. The challenge at this point in the process was establishing a definite timeline. He remained hopeful that the pathologist would provide a direction for inquiry that would, at least, help to narrow the window.

Before leaving this morning, Connie's office assistant had facilitated Michael's contact with Alice Grosfeldt, the mother of Ginny's roommate. Michael had assured her that the interview would be done with consideration for her daughter's emotional state and agreed to her parents being present during the interview. Still, it would be a challenge, and he began to consider whether he should have a partner with him for the task, someone like Pam Schneider. As a parent of three, including her newly born daughter, Pam would provide a counterbalance to Michael's aggressive tendency and help to avoid creating an emotional quagmire. Besides, Saturday afternoon he might be less mentally alert than usual after a night of fishing.

Lost in thought, time and distance passed quickly and on his left, the city of Ames and the ISU campus came into view. The northwest wind had pushed him slightly further east than he intended and checking the GPS, he recalibrated his bearing to take him over the city of Ankeny. A final turn of 180 degrees, give or take, should put him on the correct approach to the runway of the Ankeny Regional Airport.

With only 20 miles to touch down, Michael tweaked the throttle to slow the Cessna's air speed and begin a gradual descent. The soothing purr of the Skyhawk's dependable Lycoming engine was reassuring, until suddenly, it stopped. The abrupt silence stunned him, then Michael became acutely aware of the sound of air rushing over the cowl of the plane as it tilted downward.

Momentarily stunned, experience and training took over as Michael quickly ticked through his mental checklist. There was no indication the gravity-feed system had failed. The fuel selector valve was set for both tanks, and gauges read left and right tanks partially full. Everything that followed on the list checked-off positive. The engine should still be running.

Hitting the starter, the engine coughed, sputtered, and died a second time. The 172 was easy to fly but not intended to act as a glider. Any experienced pilot had to be attuned to considering emergency landing sites, and Michael, with panic setting in and his heart pounding in his ears, was desperately looking for possible places to put down.

In a flash of insight, Michael understood the desperation his father must have experienced when his plane went down. He thought aloud, "If I had the guts to outshoot an assassin, I sure as hell can land this plane. I'm not going down without a fight."

"Turn east." Startled, Michael was not sure if he had spoken aloud or if someone was speaking to him over the head set. It sounded like his voice. Whatever the source, he agreed.

"It just might work." Sacrificing some altitude, Michael banked sharply back toward Ames and began calling the airport.

"Mayday, Mayday, Mayday! This is Skyhawk 56632. Engine Failure. Two miles southwest of Ames. Pilot only. 56632. Mayday! Ames Municipal Airport, do you read me?"

There was a sharp crackle and someone answered. "This is Ames Municipal Airport. What is your status Skyhawk 56632? Over."

"Skyhawk 56632 has experienced engine failure and is approximately two miles southwest of your airport at five thousand foot altitude. Need clearance for emergency dead-stick landing. Over."

"Roger that, Skyhawk 56632. Be advised, the runway is occupied and not clear for landing. Over."

"Ames, will land on grass west of and adjacent to runway. Over."

"Skyhawk 56632, be advised of aircraft parked on grass adjacent to runway near hanger area. Probability of colliding with aircraft may be high."

"Ames, Skyhawk 56632 is on final approach from the south. Touchdown in approximately forty-five seconds."

Desperately Michael looked about one more time, but there was no alternative. There were only trees, buildings, and too much traffic on State Highway 69 to the east of the airport for an emergency landing. Airspeed was sufficient for control, but a quick check of his altimeter told a different story. Frantically he tapped the glass of the gauge, but the vertical speed indicator held steady. The Cessna was losing altitude too rapidly—he wasn't going to reach the strip.

Less than a half-mile out and hoping for the impossible, Michael gently lined the 172 up with the bright green new-growth grass to the west of the runway. He could see a tow plane and sailplane poised to take off from the runway. From midfield to the hangers, Michael could see the line of aircraft parked as if in salute to passing siblings.

If he set down just past the bordering chain-link fence, he might make it. If he miscalculated, trees, buildings, fences—none of it would matter, all would become irrelevant.

He adjusted the flaps and tried to remain calm. The reliable little plane shuddered, and Michael realized too late that he was dangerously close to stalling. With the stall alarm assaulting his ears, Michael made the decision—better to maintain control than simply drop—and tipped the yoke forward.

Time and space dissolved when suddenly the 172 began to rise. It was as if a giant hand lifted the Cessna, creating precious distance between ground and plane. Glancing from the side window Michael saw freshly worked black soil below him.

"Thank you, God. And thank you, Farmer Jones, or whoever you are." The black surface, warmed by the sun, had sent a rising thermal to lift the small aircraft. Enough altitude was gained that there was a chance to make the grass strip.

Increasing the pitch to recover his glide path for touchdown, Michael punched the electric contact to full flaps and saw the chain-link fence pass below with a few feet to spare. Turning the fuel selector, mixture, and magnetos to Off to avoid fire, he adjusted the rudder to allow for the northwest breeze. But, as airspeed decreased, the Cessna again began to stall. Unable to add power and with only a few feet remaining between plane and touchdown, Michael eased the yoke forward to fly the airplane onto the ground and applied as much pressure as he could to the aft elevators to keep the attitude of the craft nose-high. There was a single hard bounce, but the main gear held, the nose wheel touched, and he was down.

With the first parked airplane before him quickly filling his windscreen, Michael left the flaps down and applied max braking. The 172 moaned in protest and the rear of the plane began to rise and cant to the right. As he eased pressure on the right pedal, the plane straightened out, the trusty front landing gear held strong and true and, with only feet to spare, the Cessna settled to a dead stop as Michael released the brakes.

"Skyhawk 56632, welcome to sunny Ames, Iowa, home of the Iowa State University Cyclones. Way to stick it, dude." Drenched in sweat, heart still pounding, Michael burst out in relieved, uncontrollable laughter.

Exhaling, he expressed a brief, "Thank you, God!"

The radio crackled again, "You're welcome!"

Regaining a semblance of poise, Michael responded. "Thank you, Ames! Do you happen to have an airplane mechanic on hand?"

This time the voice countered with laughter. "That's a big affirmative. Would you like a tow and change of underwear?"

"That's a yes on the tow, and I'll keep my lucky underwear, thank you."

"Roger on the tow and underwear."

***

Nearly experiencing death was concerning but now that he was safely on the ground, the immediate issue to face was a cure for the ailing Cessna. Ames Municipal Airport maintained their own mechanic licensed to repair and perform annual checks on single- and twin-engine aircraft. Michael helped to roll the 172 into the work hanger. The inspection began with the fuel tanks and went no further.

"Tell me, Mr. Cain, do you really think water is a good substitute for aviation fuel?"

"What're you talking about?"

"Get that other ladder, the one by the door, and come up here."

Michael moved the ladder next to Patrick Hannah, the crew-cut former army motor pool sergeant and fixer of any piston motor whether on the ground or in the air. Climbing up two steps Michael watched as fuel was drawn from the sump of the right-wing tank. Hannah handed Michael the glass container.

"What the hell?"

"Water. A lot of it. You can see the separation and it's mostly water with a little fuel on top. This is my fourth extraction from the sump. The other three were all water. The other fuel tank checked out the same way."

"I cleared water from the sump when I did my preflight check but there was nothing like this."

"Notice anything else? Besides the water?"

"It's cold?"

"No, it's ice cold." Hannah retrieved a shop rag lying on the wing next to the fuel cap. On the rag was a small elongated piece of ice. "I found this floating in your tank. It's crude but effective. Someone gave you fuel on the rocks—probably water that was flash frozen in chunks that would fit through the port of your fuel tank."

"I don't see how. After I topped off the tanks and did my pre-flight check, I went inside to record the fuel. I was only gone a few minutes."

"Well, someone, somehow slipped your plane a Mickey. They probably did it just before you got to the airport. I'm surprised you made it this far. Did you see anyone else around your plane?"

"No. It's a small regional airport, sorta run on an honor system."

"No people, other planes, cars?"

Both men stood balancing on step ladders staring at the contaminated tube of fuel, when Michael exclaimed, "Ha!"

"What's that mean?"

"It means there was someone else, someone on a motorcycle. It sounded like a Harley. But I didn't see him or her. I didn't pay any attention. I heard it start up and leave from somewhere behind the airport repair shop."

"Well, you pissed somebody off. It doesn't take much know-how to understand what will happen if you mix water and fuel, or in this case, ice and fuel."

"I can't think of anyone who might try something like this. The kind of people who want to hurt me would be more direct, face-to-face, personal. I'll deal with a threat, if that's what it is, later. What do we need to do to get this plane flight-worthy?"

"When did you have your annual?"

"It was just finished last week. My guy has been doing annuals for over twenty-five years. He did both planes for my dad, and there's never been any problem with his work, not in the slightest."

"Well, since the annual is only a week old, I doubt if we need to tear-down the engine, but we need to drain and check the fuel tanks, lines, filter, and carburetor to be sure there are no additional surprises. Who's your mechanic?"

"Bobby Randall. He's self-employed but certified and does a lot of annuals and small-plane repairs. He lives in Spirit Lake but works all over the region, sometimes as far away as Sioux Falls."

"I know Bobby. I've been to workshops with him. Good man and an exceptional mechanic when it comes to small aircraft. I think I even have his cell number. I'll give him a call. How long are you in town?"

"I hoped to be back to the lakes by Friday evening."

"You sound like a fisherman."

With a smile and affirmative nod of his head, Michael confessed to the accusation. "So what's the verdict? Can you make time to check out my Cessna and get me back to Okoboji by late Friday?"

"I'll see what I can do. It may not take long if there are no further complications, but it depends upon what I find. Where are you staying?"

***

Several calls later, Michael was seated in a rented Ford Taurus sedan and headed for the Marriott in Ankeny. He had missed his meeting time with Dr. Goulet and called to possibly reschedule. The receptionist said Dr. Goulet had proposed it may be more convenient to meet over supper, perhaps at the Green Oak in Johnston?

The suggestion was a win as far as Michael was concerned. He was a regular at the Green Oak up until he had left the area some months prior. The food and wine were excellent, the service was professional, and the ambiance a comfortable combination of reserve and local pride. The receptionist said he would make the reservation for 7:00 PM. That left time for Michael to check in at the hotel and to call—for the third time this week—the DCI agent assigned to the Lawery case for any updates.

Traffic in the southbound lane from Ames on Interstate 35 this time of day was light, and Michael made good time in spite of the multiple orange signs announcing Road Work and their relatives urging caution and slower speed. As he turned off from I-35 onto Oralabor Road, he smiled, recalling the reference to local traffic made by his favorite *Des Moines Register* columnist as "the Des Moines fifteen-minute traffic jam."

***

Ex-army motor pool-cum-airplane mechanic Pat Hannah had drained both of the Cessna's fuel tanks, found no additional issues, and was enjoying a chat by phone with his longtime acquaintance, Bobby Randall.

***

Meanwhile another call was being placed. "Have you heard anything?"

"No, not yet. But believe me, by now whatever is left of Mr. Cain is in a junk pile of airplane hell. Like father, like son."

"I hope so. If not, we'll deal with Mr. Cain as needed. Are you sure no one saw you at the airfield?"

"I'm sure. Besides, I'm there every now and then anyway. Airplane mechanics have the best tools. If anyone noticed, I was working on my bike. And it's a good thing I spend time there, otherwise I wouldn't have heard about him flying to Ankeny."

"And if someone starts asking questions?"

"When the authorities investigate, they'll learn the crash was due to pilot error for not clearing water from the fuel tanks."

"Wouldn't he check for that before taking off?"

"Doesn't matter. It's a little technique I learned in prison. Investigators will find water in the fuel tanks. It just wasn't there when Mr. Cain went through his preflight checklist."

16

The Green Oak shared parking space with a strip mall. As he parked, Michael noticed that all the business spaces of the mall were filled, an improvement over last year, but that the asphalt lot remained in need of repair. The abundance of vehicles parked around the restaurant corroborated the popularity of the place, even on a Wednesday evening. Michael, along with a contingent of greater- and lesser-known figures, had made the Green Oak a popular choice for mixing fine food and business.

He walked under the green awning, pulled open the brass-handled wooden door, and entered the small foyer. Welcomed by a smiling young woman, he was ushered to a booth on the far side of the dining area and introduced to his waiter, or as his father with his preference for ribeye steak used to say, "Greeted, seated, and meated!"

Deferring to the arrival of Dr. Goulet, Michael thanked the waiter and used a private moment to consider the person he was about to meet for the first time. He knew quite a few pathologists and had learned not to reduce all to a stereotype. Yet, with all due respect, the service they provided did tend to bend one's opinion.

In that frame of mind he noticed a newcomer, a striking woman who stepped up to the hostess, nodded, and entered the dining area unescorted. Michael was mesmerized and not the only patron, male or female, to be so affected.

Then, like an ethereal vision, she stood before him holding out her slender right hand. On the third finger she wore a golden ring noticeably crowned with a green emerald rendered modest by the luminous green of her eyes. "Michael Cain? So pleased to meet you. I'm Dr. Phillipa Goulet."

Extending his hand and attempting to rise, Michael nearly pushed the table off its pedestal. Catching his balance if not his composure, he said, "Excuse me. I'm not usually this clumsy. Hello, I'm pleased to meet you, too. Phillipa?"

"Yes, but please, call me Phill." Releasing Michael's hand, she sat down and slid far enough into the booth to qualify for meeting Michael halfway. Turning slightly to better face him, Phillipa broke into a brilliant smile. "Okay. Let's get this out of the way."

With a sharp pang of disappointment, Michael nodded, "If you wish. I thought we might have dinner together as well."

With a playful laugh and touch of her hand on his shoulder, she replied, "No, you misunderstand me. I'm looking forward to a lovely meal while we visit. I'm speaking about the proverbial elephant in the room. My name is Phill, I'm a pathologist for the state of Iowa, and yes, I'm a woman."

Michael hoped his jaw had not hit the table. Then it was his turn to laugh. "You got me, but I'm sure I'm not the first to be sidetracked when first meeting you. And by that I mean, yes, you are a woman, a very lovely woman. And now I'm babbling."

With a tilt of her head, she gave him a sly sideways look. "I hope that's not a problem, Michael?"

"Funny thing about that, Dr. Goulet. I don't think I would mind if it was."

A soft cough interrupted them and was followed by, "May I tell you tonight's special?" It was the waiter standing at a discreet distance, venturing a tentative yet dutiful salutation with the hope that the mood of their meeting wasn't irreparably disrupted by his question.

"What? Oh yes, please."

For the entree, they both ordered the duck breast lightly sautéed in white wine, thinly sliced and drizzled in plum sauce, accompanied by wild rice, locally-sourced steamed asparagus, and a modest but appropriate Sauvignon Blanc. The repast was finished with decaf coffee, snifters of B & B, and Dr. Goulet's detailed primer to clarify some of the rather esoteric conclusions regarding the autopsy.

It was a lovely meal, a lovely time, and yes, incongruently instructive in the ways that water, temperature, and the lack of oxygen could so thoroughly challenge a pathologist in determining an accurate reason and time that a victim's spirit departed their body. It had been a long time since Michael had enjoyed an evening such as this, even though it was shared with a ghost.

17

Michael was exhausted yet slept fitfully. He dreamed of sound-less airplanes with propellers that would not move and strange women who smiled and drank wine. There was a barren land viewed from high above that transformed into a mirage of shimmering blue water and two identical young boys on the shore, laughing and skip-ping rocks as far out onto the water as possible. He awoke with a start as the door of a nearby room banged shut, his room faintly lit by early light.

After a hot shower followed by a breakfast which included three cups of coffee, Michael's hazy dream-induced state began to dissi-pate. He returned to his room, made a call to Pam Schneider for Sat-urday help—she agreed and seemed much too cheerful for early morning—then checked out of the Marriott.

He had immensely enjoyed the previous evening's company, but any wishful thought on his part of extending the social portion of the night with the divine Phillipa Goulet had been diminished with considerable prejudice after Dr. Goulet's account of the autopsy. He had recorded the details on his phone, and as he turned onto I-35, he played the recording. The sound of her voice renewed the delight he'd experienced the evening before, though it gradually lessened with the description that followed.

She described a body submerged in very cold water, below a thermocline, thus with little oxygen present to degrade the body. As Michael understood it, under such conditions, an undisturbed body might remain in a reasonably preserved state for quite a long time— that is until there was a change in one of the factors required to preserve the body.

As for drowning, Dr. Goulet considered it an atypical case. "Due to the constriction of the wind pipe caused by the shock of cold water, there was a catastrophic failure of the organs, specifically the heart and lungs, which quickly resulted in death."

Dr. Goulet agreed with Dr. Hunter that because of a blow to the head, Ginny was certainly unconscious when or soon after she entered the water. Goulet went on to opine that the cuts found on the lower legs were postmortem and likely the result of something needle-like that stabbed, then tore the flesh. She further explained that there was evidence of both premortem and postmortem injury— wounds around Ginny's ankles that were likely due to the restraints.

Michael had asked about the fibers the pathologist had found on the body.

"There were only three strands found in her hair. They were animal, not plant fiber, likely llama, and brightly colored with a natural dye used by weavers in South America."

"I understand how you might determine the llama part but how do you know it was a natural dye from South America?"

Michael recalled the brilliant smile Phillipa had flashed at him. "Have you heard the expression, 'Better living through chemistry?'"

"Yes, but how does that help?"

"I have an overdeveloped interest in poisons derived from plants. I've studied a great deal of plant pathology from sources around the world. Much of it has nothing to do with poisons, but if I apply what I know about plant chemistry, I can provide a pretty good guess of the dye's provenance."

With the account of fibers and natural dyes that followed, Michael had reconsidered and ultimately judged Dr. Matt's description of her as "absolutely nutty over death" a disservice to Dr. Goulet. She ended by restating the logical conclusion to be drawn from her insight.

Michael responded, "That's amazing!" He had enjoyed the blush that briefly colored Phillipa's high-boned cheeks. He would have enjoyed exploring what else might make her blush but given the conversation's topic had saved that inquiry for another time.

"You wrote that her stomach's contents included red wine and blackened fish. We know she spent time with the managers of the Lodge the evening she returned to Okoboji. I checked the menu at the Lodge, and on Fridays, one of the specials from their kitchen is blackened swordfish."

"That sounds about right. I assume the wine was a light red, possibly a Pinot Noir."

That was another little surprise, but he let it pass. "Based upon the food remaining in her system, can you make an educated guess when she may have died?"

"I referenced that in the autopsy report."

"I know, but I'm having trouble establishing a timeline. I just wondered if you could narrow the possibilities a bit."

"Allowing for ambient water temperature and variations in individual body processes, it is likely she died within five to six hours of eating her last meal. If you can confirm that what she ate at the Lodge matches what was found in her stomach, you may have a basis for the start of a timeline." A brief frown passed across her face. "Although I didn't include it in the report, there was something I thought peculiar. Her teeth were clean, as if she had flossed and brushed them shortly before she died."

***

From the moment he accessed I-35 until his exit onto Highway 30 headed toward University Drive, Michael turned the information gleaned during last night's dinner over and over in his mind. It was exquisitely detailed—yet he was still confused.

Perhaps it was too complex? There had to be a simpler, more common-sense reason for the condition of the body. He could not shake the conviction the victim had been in the water for only a short time before she was found. Then, recalling the previous evening again, it occurred to him he may be fixating on the wrong body, something that would need to be remedied in the future.

His spirits rose as he passed by the Reiman Gardens and saw the soaring Jack Trice Stadium beyond. Driving around the gentle curve east of the football stadium, the rest of the Iowa State Center complex—Hilton Coliseum, the Scheman Building, Stephens Auditorium, and Fisher Theater—came grandly into view.

Michael was a graduate of the University of Iowa and a Hawkeye through and through. But his time in law enforcement and law practice nurtured a respect for the quality of education throughout the state and appreciation for the devotion of fans to their favored teams. Thanks to the differing school loyalties of people in his life and the ebb and flow of success by their teams, Michael employed an ambivalent acceptance that it was all good. (Unless, that is, it conflicted with the Hawkeyes.) Perhaps it was a family trait. His father said on many occasions, "A good football Saturday is when Notre

Dame, University of Iowa, Iowa State, and Nebraska all win!" (a challenging task in the best of years.)

By the time he arrived at the visitor parking lot by the Armory building, he was upbeat. The energy and optimism of a university campus was special in his experience, and it felt good to step out of the car and pause a moment to take it in.

Entering the Armory building, he made his way to the Department of Safety, where the receptionist greeted him by name and directed him to Barry's office. Mavis met him at the door of the anteroom with a big smile and extended her hand. A coffee cup with "Cy" imprinted on the side graced her other hand. "Welcome back to ISU, Michael. It's wonderful to see you."

Ignoring the proffered hand and nearly tipping the cup's contents, Michael hugged her. "Mavis, you're as charming as always. How are you and how are things among the members of your legion?"

"I'm fine, thank you. The so-called legion continues to soldier on in support of the university. In fact, I believe there's something about that on Chief Seward's agenda. I'll let him know you're here." After knocking lightly on the open door, Mavis said, "Chief Seward, Michael Cain is here."

Seated behind his desk, Barry interrupted a conversation and covered the telephone mouthpiece. "Thank you, Mavis. Please have him come in."

Stepping inside the small office was like walking into some sort of bizarre blizzard of paper. Stacks of memos, reports, and binders were everywhere in various stages of use or abuse, of which Michael could not discern. A computer occupied a portion of the desk's surface but seemed superfluous compared to all the paper clutter.

With a few noncommittal words to the party with whom he was speaking, Barry hung up the receiver, jumped up from his chair and came around his desk to lift Michael in a bear hug. At a burly, well-conditioned 5 feet, 9 inches and 180 pounds, Barry could be as tough as any lawman. Releasing Michael, he stepped back.

"You look great! Whatever you're doing is agreeing with you."

Michael smiled, and his face actually reddened. "Thanks, Barry. As I said when we spoke on the phone, I'm enjoying my time back at the lakes, and at least for now, plan to make the most of it. It feels good to be home. If you and your family ever get time off, come up and see me. I have lots of room, and you're always welcome."

"Thank you—maybe someday. Please, have a seat." Barry went back to his leather executive chair and Michael sat across from him in the only chair not covered with work-related detritus.

Visiting about personal matters could have taken the entire morning, but Mavis, ever-cognizant of demands on her boss, politely tapped again on the open door to ask if either would like a cup of coffee. Barry recognized the gentle reminder to get down to business, no coffee needed.

"Mavis, would you join us, please? Here, let me re-file this pile." Barry transferred a chair's worth of paper to a corner of the room. Mavis got a folder and steno pad from her desk and returned to assume the recently liberated space.

Barry handed Michael a three-ring binder. "This is for you. I had my administrative deputy review, copy, and put all the information we have on the case into a binder. We've scheduled interviews with the four students and advisor as you requested. They want to cooperate, and the meetings will take place here in the center's conference room. The schedule is in the front sleeve of the binder. There should be enough time allotted, but if you need more, we'll do what we can."

"Officially, there's not much to add to what's been reported. However, Mavis put together a memo summarizing information, including gossip as gleaned from her personal network. Mavis, would you like to go over that with us?"

Mavis handed Michael a folder similar to one on Barry's desk. "Yes, I'd be happy to share what I learned. You, of course, will draw your own conclusions, but the consensus of colleagues is to take a hard look at the boyfriend or rather the ex-boyfriend. The university is very protective of its students, but that comes with a built-in conflict when it involves serious matters between students or among a group of students. There is procedure to follow, but the administration is constrained to deal with students in a manner which is different from that of the public. In many cases this better serves students, and, frankly, the university."

Mavis exuded a presence which implied interruptions, other than a nonverbal signal of interest or understanding from her listeners, were unnecessary and questions would wait until she was finished. "While none of this is official, what my colleagues suggest is that her ex-boyfriend was persistent in his desire to regain a relationship with Miss Lawery. Although it is not clear what level of intimacy they shared before, it seems he highly anticipated and expected a renewed liaison. We agree that he was obsessed with and ultimately stalking her.

"And this was not his first fixation with an attractive young woman. There was another instance that we know of here at the university. Reportedly, he struck that girlfriend and, in a drunken state, threatened to do her serious bodily harm. The young lady agreed to not press the issue after the authorities made it clear to him that any further attempt to engage the lady in question would result in his expulsion and arrest.

"It is our opinion that the young man should have been arrested and expelled, but no one pushed the issue and no official complaint nor medical report was kept on file. By the way, that drunken state was not unusual. It was generally understood he abused alcohol and likely other drugs.

"Now Michael, keep in mind that some of this is hearsay, or as Chief Seward says, gossip, but it comes from enough different sources to imply a valid duck test. Beyond that, I'm sorry to say, I have no solid facts that I may add to the case."

Before Michael could respond, Barry spoke up. "And Mavis, what is your opinion?"

"Well, you should take a good look at the one-time boyfriend. Frankly, I think he's a nutcase. However, if this is ever solved, the person or persons responsible for this horrible crime will be from outside the university and will have no association with ISU."

Michael stared at Mavis. "Wow! I understand that's your opinion, but how did you come to such a conclusion?"

"The ex-boyfriend was a stalker, but what happened to Virginia Lawery seems beyond anything in his known history. Furthermore, I don't think the ex was up to dealing with the aftermath of such a level of violence. It seems that whoever did this was not an immature, obsessive, addle-brained schmuck, but rather someone calculating, someone who's cool, thoughtful, and experienced. Again, this is my opinion, but Michael, be careful. I think you're dealing with someone far more sophisticated and dangerous than an immature, overly smitten young man."

Michael frowned but had to ask, "You don't think anyone at ISU is capable of such a crime?"

"Capable, yes, likely, no. Faculty members are more subtle, students leave too many clues, and there would be an electronic social footprint. Don't quote me, but digital communication flowing through the university's system can be accessed by authorities. And since the body was retrieved from Okoboji, it seems more likely the crime, motive, and solution lie in that region."

As Mavis spoke, Michael jotted down a few reminders to himself. "I have some questions, but I think Barry can answer them. Will

I see you before the interviews?"

Mavis nodded her assent. "Let me know if there's anything more you require."

Mavis returned to her desk, leaving the door open. Michael turned to Barry, "Who was the other girl that the ex attacked?"

Clearing his throat, Barry took the official line. "According to the administration, that information is unavailable."

"I could get a warrant."

"Good luck."

"Do we have any idea where this guy is now?"

"No. As I told you before, he dropped out of school. I can add he took incompletes for his current courses. After you and I spoke, I decided to try reaching his parents again. Let's just say they weren't cooperative. They threatened to call their lawyer and take action against the university and anyone who came after their son."

"Not helpful."

Barry agreed. "Not helpful and it implies they're trying to hide something serious. It might not even have anything to do with our investigation. Maybe the kid finally got in so much trouble they shipped him out of the country. I've heard of more bizarre cases, and so have you."

Nodding in assent Michael went on, "Was he capable of breaking into Ginny's apartment?"

"Not sure. He could have. But the break-in was the same night the roommate was mugged. Her key to the apartment was taken and Ames PD believe it was used to gain access to the apartment. As to the ex-boyfriend, we've been unable to verify if he was in Ames at that time. In fact, thanks in part to his parents, we've been unable to learn where he was the night of the mugging and break-in. If you'd like, I can arrange for you to see the apartment."

"Yes, please—that would be good." Pausing briefly, Michael

went on. "Do you think he attacked the roommate?"

"No, not likely. He didn't fit her description of the attacker. Not even close. The attacker was shorter, heavier, a very rough-looking character. He didn't say much other than to threaten her and tell her to shut up and keep her head down. But as he ran away, she took a quick look and he appeared to have a slight limp and wore leather, like a biker.

"Try as we could, we were unable to fit the former boyfriend into the description. That's not to say he couldn't have hired someone to do his dirty work, but we've found no evidence of that. And before you ask, there were no witnesses to the attack and no security cameras in the area. We can't afford to have cameras everywhere, and there are serious privacy issues to be considered."

***

At the workday's end, after dutifully delivering each student and the advisor to be interviewed, Mavis sat quietly at her desk considering what she had shared with Michael and Barry. Eyes closed, she mentally ticked off each point. Finally, with a nod of her head, Mavis opened her eyes, took a deep breath, and spoke aloud as if for her own assurance. "Yes. Not the boyfriend. Not the university. Somewhere, someone else."

18

Michael ate supper at the Memorial Union's food court then departed the university and scored a room at the Southgate Holiday Inn. Patrick Hannah had called, and Michael could fly home the next day. Smiling at the thought of calling Dr. Goulet—she'd given him her cell number—he instead called Sheriff Conrad and was pelleted by a storm of questions.

"Michael! Good to hear from you. Are you okay? I understand you had an eventful flight yesterday. Water in a gas tank? Are you kidding? That was the cause of your dad's accident in the Cessna 152. That's an awfully big coincidence. Aren't you supposed to do a preflight check for that? Will you be back by tomorrow night? I'm still planning on the midnight opener."

Michael was amazed at how quickly information traveled through the law community. "I'm fine, and yes, I plan to be back by late afternoon. The plane's cleared for flight, and the boat's on the lift and rigged to go." It was nice to contemplate something other than the case. "The water in the gas tanks was no accident. I'm not universally loved, but I have no idea why someone would do that. I'll worry about it later. I called to give you an update, courtesy of our fine folks in central Iowa, and to see if you heard back from our favorite game warden."

"Conservation officer."

"What?"

"Conservation officer, not game warden. You're a bit behind times on job titles, Michael. Officer Piccard agreed to meet with us in my office anytime on Tuesday. Does that work for you?"

"Yes, that's fine. I'll have a chance to speak with a few more people before then, which may be useful."

"Good. I'll check back with him and set a time. Other than that, I've got nothing new on this end. So, did you break the case yet?"

"Not quite. I have some additional information but not enough to satisfy your optimism. What's all that noise?"

"I'm at home. Madge and the kids just got back from soccer. Give me a moment to go to my den of solitude…There, is this better?"

"Much better."

"So, what did you learn?"

"I interviewed Ginny's advisor, four friends who knew her well, and one of the profs for her major. Everyone thought she was doing well, in fact thought she was happy and upbeat about school and life in general. Two of the students were of the opinion she had started a relationship with someone, but they had no idea with whom. The advisor said Ginny told her that she enjoyed her experience working at the Lodge the past two summers, and that she had advised her that adding the minor in hotel and restaurant management to her major in finance would mean more possibilities for employment after graduation. The prof shared that Ginny was an excellent student and in her opinion, likely to be successful in whatever she chose to do."

"That would seem to match up with what we know about her.

What did Barry have to say?"

"I spoke at some length with Barry and with Mavis, his executive assistant. Barry checked with his people and the local police but had nothing new. Mavis also checked with her colleagues and the consensus is the former boyfriend was involved. On the other hand, Mavis was unequivocal in her opinion that whoever did this was not the ex-boyfriend nor anyone at the university. She made some good points. Anyway, it remains critical that we find and speak with the boyfriend, or whoever he is."

Connie wasn't encouraged. "That may be easier said than done. Has anyone gotten through to him or his parents?"

"Not effectively, and they have a wall of lawyers that we'll need to scale."

"I know the university and Ames police tried to contact him at one time or another and were unsuccessful. The parents were not forthcoming and insisted he would not hurt anyone."

Michael waited until he was sure Connie had finished before responding, "It seems common knowledge that he has a temper and abuses alcohol and other drugs. I asked all four of the friends several times if there was anything else they could remember, and one of them added that the last day Ginny was seen on campus, she saw Ginny and Laxton in a brief argument, some yelling, name-calling. She said she didn't remember it before because she hadn't made the connection.

"The funny thing is, soon after Ginny may have disappeared, the guy stopped going to classes. He had an apartment off-campus and remained enrolled until about a week ago when he officially dropped out of school. As far as the university is concerned, Laxton is no longer their problem. Barry tried calling the parents again yesterday and was told to speak with the family lawyer who told him to get a warrant. In other words, go piss up a rope."

"Are you going to seek a warrant?"

"I'll try, but it's circumstantial. Other than hearsay, there's no witness or physical evidence that ties him to the Lakes region between the time she left campus and when she was found. Add to that the lack of an original crime scene and a firm timeline, and I doubt a judge will grant the warrant."

"Was there any help with the timeline?"

"Her professors and the ISU police know Ginny was in class that Friday, but it was the last anyone at ISU saw of her. Laxton went to class that morning, and although there's some disagreement, it may have been the last anyone here saw of him. It's fairly certain the timeline begins with the Friday Ginny left school but what happened between then and when her body was found is a blank. No one is able, or in the case of the ex-boyfriend's family, willing to account for her or the ex-boyfriend during that time."

"What did you learn from the state medical examiner?"

"I learned that Dr. Phillipa Goulet is an engaging, lovely woman who is every bit the skilled pathologist as advertised. Unfortunately, her conclusions only complicated matters. It seems that cause of death really was an atypical drowning, but owing to possible environmental conditions, the time frame could be even more ambiguous. However, the good doctor was willing to hypothesize that if we can confirm what Ginny ate at the Lodge the night she visited the owners and if it matches what was found in her stomach, it would be reasonable to accept the evening of Friday, March 4 as the beginning of our timeline. I'll include the details when I write it up."

"Well, that's something. Anything else?"

"I did see Ginny's apartment. I was told entry was not forced. The lock, doorknob, frame, and door itself were all intact and substantial. Unless someone forgot to lock up, it would be difficult to break in. Kids do share keys with friends, but none of them claimed to have one, and the landlord is at a loss as to how anyone could have gotten in without a key or without damaging the entrance. Ames PD concluded and I agree—whoever attacked Sally, took her key and used it to gain access to the apartment."

"Were there security cameras?"

"No. It's an older apartment building off campus."

"Sounds like someone with experience."

"I agree."

"Well, Michael, what's next?"

"Let's carry on reinterviewing everyone to see if new details or names come up. Let's also continue to focus on the former boyfriend. You know as well as I that often the solution lies with the obvious suspect."

"Okay. I'll have my detectives and the county attorney continue to review what we know and ask the DCI agent assigned the case to try his luck again with the parents."

"And I'll speak with the family's lawyer, and attempt to get a warrant. If the kid is innocent, it would be to his benefit to cooperate. Also, I have a meeting arranged with Ginny's roommate for Saturday afternoon. Perhaps her memory has improved."

"Or perhaps you can help her remember. You do seem to have a way of doing that."

"Perhaps, but she may still be upset. I've arranged for Pam Schneider to sit in on the interview to help me avoid pitfalls with her or her parents. Besides, it helps to have a second set of eyes and ears."

"Excellent! If Pam can keep the peace with her husband Darell and the in-laws, she should be able to manage you. Besides, I've seen her with her kids at ball games and school programs. She really has the magic touch with youngsters."

"I haven't spoken to the owners or staff at the Lodge but will try to do that Monday. If you can arrange it, why don't we take some time Tuesday, after we speak with Piccard, to review where we're at in the investigation."

"I'll have my homicide detective, Jack Donahue, join us. But don't be surprised if I get called away. The tourist season seems to begin earlier every year."

"Understood. It shouldn't take much time. There's not a lot to discuss, but we can plan on how to proceed. We need to do everything we can as soon as possible before this gets any colder."

"Yes. Now, about the opener."

"Right! Why don't we meet at my place early evening, go over our fishing stratagem, and be on the walleyes at midnight? I've got snacks. You bring live bait and, short of dynamite, whatever you want to get the job done."

"Michael, do you realize this is the first time in years that we've been able to do the opener together? Tomorrow night we fish, we snack, and we talk family and friends. Business is verboten!"

On that hopeful note they disconnected. The past two days had been intense and Michael wished he was already dockside. Time on the water would be a welcome relief.

19

Although their plans were well-laid, the opener was a bust. A cold front gave the walleyes lockjaw, and at 4:00 AM, with two modest walleyes in the live well, Michael and Connie called it a night and headed back to the dock.

"Well, Michael, at least we weren't skunked."

"True, and the misery we endured was fine and pleasant."

"Why, yes it was. All part of our annual offering in tribute to the art of fishing. I need to check in at the office and go home to catch a few hours of sleep. Why don't you keep the fish?"

"Are you sure? Catch a couple more, and you'll have a meal for the family."

"Nah. They'll make two meals for you, and Jeremy alone would eat both of them."

"I have a suggestion. Why don't we fry them up quick along with some eggs and hash browns and call it a fisherman's breakfast? It won't take long, and you can call the office while I pretend to be a cook."

"Well, if you don't mind, I think that's a great idea! And by the time we finish we should be thawed out."

***

Fresh walleye and a few hours of sleep made some difference, but a still-groggy Michael awoke feeling anxious and wishing for more z's rather than an afternoon meeting with Ginny's roommate and parents. After a shower, Michael made coffee, called Pam to confirm when he would pick her up, and sat down to list what needed to be covered in the interview. As he considered possible questions, Michael could see the need for a more nuanced approach from his typical manner of interrogating. He was thankful Pam would be at his side.

As they drove to Spencer, Michael rehearsed with Pam his intended line of questioning, and omitting the drama of his flight, briefly related what he had learned on his recent trip to central Iowa. Pam was quiet, trying to process as much of the rushed flow of information interspersed with opinion as she could. Finally, when Michael seemed to have summed everything up, she asked her questions.

"You said you visited their apartment."

"Yes."

"If I may play devil's advocate—in your opinion, if they didn't have a key, could anyone but a professional break in without damaging anything?"

"Hard to say. It would be difficult but not impossible. My first reaction would be more likely a pro or at least someone experienced at breaking and entering."

"Okay. Is there anything that would clearly implicate the boyfriend in the break-in or the mugging?"

"No. It seems incongruent, but both appear to be unrelated to the ex-boyfriend. It would help if I could talk to him."

As she considered the boyfriend issue, Pam continued her questioning. "So, if the ex-boyfriend had nothing to do with those events, it seems to me that either there is an unlikely coincidence or the scope of the investigation may be greater than you thought. I'm not saying the boyfriend couldn't have arranged matters, but considering his history, is there anything to indicate he had help?"

"No, just the opposite. What we know suggests he would act personally, impulsively, and directly, one-on-one."

"Michael, your plan to interview Ginny's roommate is logical, but my impression is that most of the questions seem to invite answers that imply it was the boyfriend."

"That's because I think he did it."

There was silence. They passed the city limit sign, entered the southbound fork of Highway 71, and drove by the KICD radio station. With a deep sigh, Pam went on. "All I'm saying is, whether the boyfriend is the prime suspect or not, she may be more forthcoming if we are sympathetic in our approach."

"Like how?"

"Ask fewer questions, let her tell the story. Encourage details with questions about her day and her circumstances. This is still a kid, and she's been traumatized. Put the focus on her, less on the boyfriend or Ginny. We're looking for a narrative, not a semester final."

Michael nodded his head. "OK, how about this: After we meet, greet, and commiserate, why don't you take the lead? At some point, if needed, I'll ask questions, but you set the tone and direction as you described, and we'll see where it goes. Agreed?"

"Are you sure?"

"Yes."

"Agreed. Then, if you think we should, we'll bore in harder with your questions."

"OK. Now, let's see if we can find the place. Siri, where is Nicholas Drive?"

Nicholas Drive turned out to be the newest housing subdivision in Spencer. Recently annexed, the development appeared to cater to a certain homeowner, someone more interested in privacy than community. Michael had not heard of the newly transformed area and was surprised by the aloof attitude. Considering the modest nature of the populace and the unabashed boosterism by its business owners, he thought it odd.

Still, Michael knew that due to the 80's farm crisis and changing fortunes in the economy, it was not the same burg once featured by Forbes Magazine as a vibrant, progressive small town for business. Though changed, Spencer remained the regional center for business, education, and medical care. An echo of the Iowa Great Lakes could be found in some of the local businesses, and although the Milford Chamber of Commerce would argue the point, Spencer was still the southern gateway to the greater Lakes region.

Elaborate stone and iron work announced the entrance to the latest development while wide streets and a modest green space proposed that the residents therein considered themselves a step up from average. But in spite of a proliferation of three-car garages, metal fences around expansive lots, and towering peaks and dormers, the houses did not appear as opulent as one might reasonably expect. The emphasis appeared to be on shallow and audacious rather than substance.

Siri confirmed that 1002 Nicholas Drive was indeed the residence of the Grosfeldt family. In contrast to others in the area, this home was older and of modest size with a garage for two vehicles and trees and shrubs more mature than those on surrounding lots. There was no fence.

If Nicholas Drive was a surprise to Michael, it was nothing compared to what followed.

20

Having parked in the street just past the mailbox, Michael and Pam approached the house then stood before its single large door with an unusual double clapper. "Nice knockers," said Michael. A stern look from Pam was enough to say, "No more of that, buster!"

"Sorry, I couldn't resist."

Ignoring the clappers, Pam used the doorbell and on the second ring a tall, slender, cadaverous-looking man with trim greying hair and languid Peter Lorre eyes slowly drew back the door. "Well, well, Michael Cain. I see they sent the A minus team."

Taken aback, Pam looked from the greeter to Michael and was startled to see the transformation in her associate. With his face scoured red, jaw muscles flexing, and an angry intensity in his eyes, Michael's appearance displayed the taut posture of a violent creature on the edge of attack. "Hello, Dennisss. "

The silence that followed was broken when Pam spoke up. "Mr. Grosfeldt? Hello, sir. My name is Pam Schneider. I gather you know my associate. Thank you for the opportunity to speak with your daughter."

Without breaking his stare-down with Michael, he retorted, "That's Erickson, E-R-I-C-K-S-O-N, Dennis Erickson. Alice and I were recently married and society has yet to catch up."

"Oh! I apologize—Mr. Erickson. May we come in?"

Without a word, Erickson stepped aside allowing his guests to enter the foyer. Closing the door, he commanded, "Follow me."

Pam shivered, a reaction intensified by the cold tile floor and stark white of the unadorned walls. Her first impression was of entering a mausoleum with an emaciated ghoul as their guide. Leaning close to Michael, she whispered, "What was that about?"

Michael's countenance hadn't changed. "History. I'll explain later."

Following Erickson down the hallway and past the staircase, they turned into the dining room. Like the foyer and hall, the walls were unadorned, but a magnificent dining room table with six matching chairs and highboy stood in contrast. They featured a unique combination of flawless carving and simple, warm wood tones enhanced by a beautifully hand-rubbed finish. Though she was no authority on the subject, to Pam the design appeared custom-made and the workmanship done with remarkable expertise.

"This is my wife Alice and her daughter Sally." Then, pointing to Michael and Pam as if they were the accused in the witness box of a courtroom, he introduced them. "This is the renowned Michael Cain and Pam…I'm sorry, what was your last name?"

Michael thought, "Cheap trick—put her in her place in the scheme."

Pam, without pausing, stepped around the table, and reached out to take Mrs. Erickson's hand, saying, "Schneider, Pam Schneider. Thank you, Mrs. Erickson, and Sally, thank you so very much for agreeing to visit with us. We know this may be difficult, but it is important."

Michael said sotto voce, "Touché! Well done, Pam." He wasn't certain if he had spoken too loudly or if he was the only one to hear. No one else reacted, so Michael just smiled. Pam had made it clear her interest was in mother and child. And as for Mr. Erickson? Well, Mr. Erickson was relegated to observer, sans participation.

With a loud, theatrical throat-clearing, Erickson attempted to reassert himself. "Be seated."

By choosing the chair across the table from mother and daughter, Pam had an opportunity to make a quick study of both. Their similarity was striking. Each was blond, attractive, tall, and of strong build. In fact, Sally's broad shoulders and muscled upper arms looked like an athlete's. Neither appeared nervous, but Pam assumed both had been prepped as if testifying in court. They were casually but neatly dressed. On the table before mother and stepfather were legal pads and pens at the ready.

Without direction from Michael, Pam began by addressing the daughter. "Sally, you probably have been questioned repeatedly about your roommate, but Mr. Cain and I would be interested in hearing what happened to you and your memory of the assault and burglary. As unpleasant as it is, could we have you just talk your way through from beginning to end, and tell us what you recall? It really is important for us to hear, firsthand, what happened to you."

Sally paused, flicked a cursory glance at her stepfather, and then looked directly at her mother who simply smiled. Turning to her husband, Alice communicated with a tilt of her head an incisive, wordless warning as if to say, "You're not in charge of this show." Indeed, except for his initial rudeness, Mr. Erickson sat quietly and made no attempt to interrupt his stepdaughter's account.

For nearly an hour, Sally related her experiences and answered questions about her assault, the apartment break-in, and her subsequent early departure from her second semester. Known facts were repeated and no new facts were given, but both Pam and Michael began to reconsider that there was a connection between what had happened to Ginny and to Sally.

The quick, violent assault had likely targeted Sally's computer and phone. But Sally's phone was locked down and none of her stolen credit cards had been used. The burglary and assault together made better sense if considered within the context of what happened to Ginny rather than a random attack to steal electronic devices and credit cards.

Sally was composed throughout the interview and her recall of details excellent, though her voice trembled as she first began to describe the attack. As the account progressed, she found her courage. Her initial timidity was subsumed by a resolve that barely concealed anger. It became clear to Michael and Pam that this was no physically weak nor emotionally dependent child.

The mugger had knocked her down and as she tried to look back at him, he struck her twice on the side of the head with a gloved fist. In a deep, rough-sounding voice he told her, "Keep your head down, you dumb bitch." He was like an animal, she said, his voice a growl. He had ripped off her backpack, groped her jacket pockets, took her computer, phone, ID card, keys, and small wallet, then stomped on her back with his boot. Bending over her he had snarled, "Stay down, bitch, or I'll be back."

She had stayed in place for what seemed like forever, but risked a quick glance and saw he wore a leather jacket, gloves, and military style boots, and walked with a limp on his right side. There also was something odd about the gloves, but she couldn't say exactly what it was. Two students passing by on their way to a late study session at the Parks Library found her sitting in the middle of the sidewalk, dazed and unsure whether to remain or to run.

She was admitted to Mary Greeley Medical Center for an overnight stay as a precaution and, with the approval of the attending physician, was released the next day into her mother's care. An interview with the ISU police left Sally exhausted and eager for a shower and rest. Her mother accompanied Sally back to the apartment. The assault was bad enough, but finding her apartment ransacked really freaked her out.

Michael knew from the Ames PD investigator's report that the bookshelves were swept clear, drawers pulled and emptied, containers dumped, and furniture, mattresses, and even a lamp shade thrown onto the floor. In the maelstrom of rubble some things stood out by their absence. Anything having to do with digital data—flash drives, even a camera and memory cards—were gone.

As she described the condition of the apartment, Sally lowered her head and wrapped her arms around her body as if to protect herself from further harm. Sally's mother reached over and while she gave her daughter a hug looked directly at Michael and added, "Nothing that was taken has been found—no pawn shop, no charges to credit cards, no use of her phone or other devices, nothing. We don't have or any longer expect answers to our questions. We're moving on."

Nodding her head in acquiescence, Pam quietly added, "May I ask one more question? Sally, it's been some time now, but do you remember anything else, perhaps something unusual, something you could smell, taste, or even feel in that moment beyond the pain and shock of the attack?"

With head slightly bowed in recall she suddenly looked up directly at her mother. "I do remember something. I didn't think of this before, but he smelled. He smelled funny. I don't know exactly how. Kinda like dirt. Moist dirt, mulchy, like in a garden. It must have been on his hands or gloves. I smelled it when he grabbed the back of my neck and held my head down."

Closing her eyes, Sally took a deep breath, relaxed her shoulders and began a mental sequential review of the attack from the initial slam down to the release of her neck. Then, as if in a seance-induced state, she said, "He had gloves that didn't cover the tips of his fingers. That's what bugged me about his gloves. His fingers were rough and strong but not real long. When he squeezed my neck his fingers only went about half-way around. I think he was right-handed because he switched from his right to his left hand on my neck so he could yank off my backpack and check my pockets." She paused, then continued, "His fingernails were dirty. I saw his right hand when he reached around to take off my backpack."

Everyone sat stone still until Sally finally opened her eyes and leaned back in the chair. "That's not much, but maybe it will help. I've only been asked to remember what I saw or heard. No one asked me how he smelled."

Michael assured her, "Sally, in every investigation, many details are collected. We sift through, look at them in different ways, and apply them to theories. Often small details may seem unimportant but produce a lead or fill in a missing piece. What you just told us is all new information. It could turn out to be very helpful. If you recall anything else, no matter how insignificant it may seem, please let us know.

"This is my business card and Mrs. Schneider will give you her card. Call, text, or email us, anytime day or night. We want you to know we're concerned about what happened to you and want to help you."

And with that, Michael handed Sally his card, as did Pam. With the requisite thank you for their time, they rose to leave, escorted to the door by the dour Erickson who offered them nothing but silence. Michael's attempt to briefly emphasize to Erickson the interview's importance as a way to amend their departure was cut short when he abruptly shut the door in Michael's face.

21

Erickson returned to the dining room and found his wife and stepdaughter with heads tilted near one another, engaged in whispered confidence. He paused to appreciate the similarity in appearance and mannerisms between mother and daughter, a likeness which stirred in him a disturbing attraction. Softly clearing his throat he interrupted what he considered their shared intrigue. "That went well. Nicely done, Sally."

Alice responded, "Yes, it did. However, while Sally and I understand their concern for her may be sincere, it's still a means to an end. They're more interested in solving Ginny's case. They will be back."

"Yes, that's likely, and the questions will be about Ginny."

Jutting her jaw in defiance, Sally took up the challenge. "I don't care. I've nothing to hide, and I told them everything I can recall about the attack. That was a good idea the woman had. I really did just remember something about the way he smelled and that stuff about his hands."

"Dennis, Sally and I wondered if she should say anything about Ginny's behavior last fall."

"What behavior?"

Sally gave her stepfather a quizzical look. "You know. I told you both about how much more social Ginny was this year. Last year she wasn't interested in going out or dating. She was friendly, studied hard, and we respected each other's space, but she just was not interested in the rest of college activities. Then this fall, it was like she couldn't get enough of the social life—lots of new friends, out several nights a week, she was just more fun to be around. It was such a change. She didn't do drugs or really drink very much. She just wanted to go out with a lot of different people. We became closer, more than temporary roommates. She became a friend, my best friend. I don't want to say anything that could make people think she was doing something wrong."

"Sally asked me if there may be legal problems if she doesn't say anything about this. What do you think, Dennis?"

He hesitated, took a deep breath, and released it. "If you deliberately withhold evidence in an investigation, that's a problem. If you don't recall or, in all sincerity, don't think the information relevant, it may be less a legal question than one of judgment. Frankly, I would consider her behavior this fall fairly typical for a lot of students when they first go off to college. In her case, it took more time for the college life to kick in. I don't think it's relevant, but if you are specifically asked about it, answer truthfully. If your answer is challenged simply say you didn't remember or didn't think it was important. But I wouldn't volunteer the information. It would only spread a wider but thinner net over more people who had nothing to do with this. Tell me, Sally, did you know any of these new friends?"

"Not all, but most of them. Some of them were more like acquaintances. We texted, shared pictures, and gossiped, but everyone does stuff like that."

"That's my point. Her behavior this fall was more typical of college students. It just took her longer to arrive at that phase. Everyone matures at their own rate."

"I know. It just seemed so different from last year."

"Did you see any warning signs? Did you feel she was putting herself at risk?"

"No, not really. Everything seemed fine to me. It was more like someone had given her permission to come out of her shell and enjoy people."

"Then I don't think volunteering any of this is an issue. Put your mind at ease, Sally. Let the investigators investigate or do whatever they do. You've done all you need to do."

"But wouldn't it help me if they solve Ginny's murder?"

"It's hard to tell at this point. Right now it's more important for you to take care of yourself. You need to take time to work past this whole mess."

"What about last summer?"

"In my opinion, it's irrelevant. You have enough to deal with. Better to let sleeping dogs lie."

"Sally, I agree with Dennis," her mother interjected. "I've spoken with your advisor at ISU, and she told me your professors are willing to give you incompletes and allow you to take your finals this summer or even in the fall. She said your scores are good and that even if your final tests are not as high as you'd like, your grades will still be solid." With that she gave her daughter another hug. "Now, enough of this talk. Take a break. Later today we can discuss those final exams."

***

As Pam and Michael walked to the truck, neither spoke but

instead exchanged looks of understanding. They knew the interview had been valuable. The focus had remained on Sally and nothing was said directly about Ginny. But the violence of the attack, as recounted by Sally, had impressed Michael and Pam. Rather than a random mugging, it sounded more as if Sally was targeted, and if so, then there was a greater likelihood the crimes against Ginny and Sally were connected.

Turning the truck around the cul-de-sac at the street's end, Michael drove past the Erickson home observing nothing further of interest in the property but instead was keenly interested in discussing with his partner what they had heard from Sally.

Michael, in semi-lawyer mode, waited to see if Pam would speak first. Pam, familiar with the ways of lawyers, looked at Michael, smiled but said nothing, knowing Michael was nearly bursting with eagerness to discuss what had taken place.

Grimacing, Michael gave in, saying, "Okay, tell me what you think about what we just heard."

Pam had no intention to let Michael off the hook. With a sharp sidelong glance Pam went right after him. "First, about that history, what is it between you and Erickson?"

"What history?"

"The history you referred to. The history that was obviously at play and nearly provoked an attack when we were greeted by the less than agreeable Mr. Erickson. What's it all about?"

"It's not important."

"Talk!"

Michael glanced over at his co-interrogator, judged how much to say, and realized he would need to be at least somewhat forthcoming. He took a big breath and dove in. "It's an old professional feud he had with my father that has been extended to include our family."

"I need more detail."

"My father was involved in a case over patent rights. He lost the battle but won the war."

"Come again?"

"He represented a large company whose use of a minor bit of technology in their product was in question. He lost the case but his argument and the supporting evidence he presented was thorough, detailed, exquisitely sequenced, and a textbook example of how to deal with a specious charge. That, along with a superior closing argument, exposed the claim against the company as minimal, more a nuisance, and although ruling in favor of the claimant, the damages assigned by the court resulted in a minuscule cost to the company and allowed them to continue with no further liability."

"Let me guess. The opposing counsel was Erickson."

"Correctamundo! Erickson likes to brag that he beat a Cain in court, but he and everyone evenly remotely involved knew what the real outcome was, and it's a burr under his saddle that the win was meaningless. Basically, my father handed him his head. The company was very generous in its gratitude to my father. So much for history—now you tell me what you heard in the interview and your impressions, and I'll share mine."

They agreed that the attack had been and remained a great shock to Sally. They didn't know how but accepted that her recent recall was helpful and that it was possible that Sally knew more than she was willing to tell. The description of the attacker reinforced the possibility that someone outside the university family was involved. The boyfriend could have had help, but it was hard to see to what end. If he was worried someone would learn he posed a threat to Ginny, that boat had long sailed. There were multiple witnesses to his behavior and little need to add digital corroboration.

All the drive back, Michael continued to churn over what was learned with Pam. "Violent attacks in two different places but connected by the close relationship of the victims is too much for a coincidence. One person may have carried out both attacks, but I think we're dealing with more than a single perpetrator."

"I wouldn't discount anything at this stage." Pam's brief response was followed by a big sigh and silence except for the hum of tires on the pavement.

Michael knew there was more. "What?"

"Tell me, Michael, isn't it odd that nothing known to be stolen has shown up in some way?"

"Definitely. But I don't think this was robbery. I think it was an effort to eliminate information or learn what Ginny or Sally might have known.

"OK, Sherlock. But what did Ginny or Sally know that was so important?"

"Ah, Watson. That's the question."

"Well?"

"Well, what?"

"Well, what's the answer?"

"I've no idea. We need to continue to investigate and do exactly as I described to Sally, review what we learn and see where it takes us. It's not about coincidence, it's about the facts. Follow the facts, sort, compare, contrast, and synthesize."

"So, do you still say it was the ex-boyfriend?"

"Why Pam, you know I would never speculate before considering all the evidence."

"Right. And porcine flight is a common occurrence."

"Ah, you saw right through me."

"Easy enough in this case. I'll email you my notes and any additional thoughts. Oh, and before I forget, don't worry about the tests and year-end reports. I'll finish things up, and that should give you some time for the case—or cases if it's more than one."

"Thank you, I appreciate it. Frankly, it's probably better for the students as well, but I would like to thank the students and to pass along what I hope is a bit of wisdom. I'll have a brief written summation with suggestions for each student."

"Great! I know the students have enjoyed working with you and would appreciate your advice."

"When's the best time to come in?"

"How about 9:00 AM, Friday? It's the last day of classes and it won't take long to review test results. You had the same students in your afternoon group, so feel free to double-up. There should be plenty of time for you to do your thing."

"Friday it is. I'll be sure to touch base with you during the week. If anything comes up or you need help, just let me know."

Pulling into Pam's driveway, Michael had a sudden rush of recognition how important Pam had been in today's efforts. "I want you to know how much I value your expertise. Frankly, without your help, it would've been a disaster. You turned a potentially bad situation around, and made it possible for Sally to recall new details. And you gave Sally and her mother needed assurance. Great work, Pam! Thank you."

Crimson colored her cheeks as Pam smiled with a nod of her head. "I'm glad I could help. Let me know if there's more I can do."

As he exited the driveway Michael considered something he often observed, namely that in the right situation most people demonstrated greater skills and intelligence than normally expected. And experience had taught him that if the right people were brought together to solve a problem, the results could be amazing. He might need to expand membership in his investigative posse for this case, but not right now. The rest of the day called for organizing his thoughts and an early bedtime, maybe with dreams of a walleye bite on calm blue waters.

22

He had decided to go on an impulse, but whether due to his conscience or simply the need for something normal from his past, Michael found himself looking forward to Sunday mass. He awoke early, refreshed and motivated by abundant sunlight streaming through his bedroom window. Lying there, he watched dust motes lazily drifting through the rays and felt a silly affinity with them, floating free. He couldn't remember when he'd last sensed such contentment.

So many experiences, so much love, so many people important to him were associated with this place. All had contributed to make him into who he was, and the memory would continue to help him become who he would be. Rather than burdened, he was relieved.

If there was any revelation, it was accepting that his long descent into discontent lay in repudiating what was most important to him. Why did he run away from this? Had he been fearful he would disappoint his family? Did he really intend to separate himself from his father? He certainly tried to do so in early adulthood. But why? His father had been the most loved and respected person in his life. Was it so important that he be an entity singularly distinct from everyone else? As if anyone entirely escaped the source of their existence.

He decided this mental self-flagellation needed to be locked away, the key discarded, and his mental home renovated as a place of revival rather than recrimination. And if he was to entrust his future happiness to lakes, family, friends, and remain here in the family home, he'd better call the house and grounds keepers and set up a schedule. The place was a mess.

On his way to church, everything about him felt bright and airy, which may have accounted for his late arrival. Slowly opening the great door he made his way across the small narthex as if on cat's paws. Fortunately, there was just enough room for him in the pew chosen by the humble or relegated to the remorseful Saturday night miscreants. Keeping his head down, he quickly genuflected and squeezed into the back row, hoping Father Barney did not notice his overdue entry. A sign of the cross, a quick Hail Mary, and Michael rose with his adjacent pretenders for the mass Introit.

But Father Barney wasn't the leader of the pack. Having failed to check the church bulletin—truth be told, he didn't have one—he was disappointed to find the tenderfoot, Father Jim, in charge.

Father Jim was a nice enough fellow and was commended in ecclesiastic circles as an "up-and-comer." Father Jim liked his job, especially the sermon, which tended to drone on at a pace seemingly commensurate to Gibbon's *The History of the Decline and Fall of the Roman Empire*. Yet, the place and ritual pleased Michael, and lost in past memories of church, he strayed from Father Jim's earnest contribution on the scripture "Many are called but few are chosen."

Vaguely looking over the congregation for familiar faces, his reverie (and perhaps his sanctity) was disrupted by the vision of someone he once held dear. There she was, up front before God and all—the song leader. It was Janneke. How extraordinary! Could it be related to Father Jim's message of the chosen few?

***

Janneke had noticed Michael entering and taking a place in the last row. She knew he was back but hadn't seen him since before her divorce. What was it now, nearly two years? She had heard of his personal troubles, a separation from his wife and some sort of breakdown, but due to mixed emotions and the demands of her career, she hadn't given in to daydreams, much less acted upon the local favored son's return.

They had been in the same elementary class in parochial school and graduated together from Okoboji High. They had a searing carnal relationship their senior year, tamped down post-diploma by allegiances to different universities and threats from their parents. The affair was reignited during the following "summer of whoopee," as her mother characterized it in her lecture on the subject.

After all these years, Janneke could still hear her mother's voice. "A roll in the hay or even a summer of whoopee may be understandable, but it's time to start using the instrument above rather than below your neck!" It was to be understood that, though it may be acceptable for a normal hormonal young woman to "make whoopee," there was a point at which said young woman should get it out of her system and get on with reality. Janneke always had to smile when she pictured her prim and virtuous mother as a salacious young woman boinking her way through her own "whoopee summer."

Marriage was not out of the question but was discouraged for a couple so young by both families' proffered argument that a university degree was the priority as well as its result: a secure financial future. To drive home the point, in the event of rebellion the insurgents would be on their own to pay for college and the likely tenuous life to follow. Perhaps more significant than generous financial support were family expectations. Both families boasted numerous professional and business leaders, and the children, even for that time, were expected to follow the dictate laid down by their elders.

The smoldering bond between Janneke and Michael had gradually abated, and though never entirely extinguished, time and circumstances resulted in a case akin to Frost's "The Road Not Taken." Of her four years in college choir, Randall Thompson's musical setting of Frost's poem remained her favorite. She still could recite the words. How did that part go?

> *"Oh, I kept the first for another day!*
> *Yet knowing how way leads on to way,*
> *I doubted if I should ever come back."*

Now, after all this time and in all places, there he was. Contrary to Frost's melancholy reflection, could they come back to the path kept for another day?

For the celebration of communion, song leader Janneke began to direct communion-takers and pew-kneelers through a hymn whose intended virtue was to inspire devotion, but in Janneke's esteemed opinion, was musically betrayed by the less than poetic use of common language and an unimaginative melody.

Janneke's clear soprano voice pierced the din, like a beacon on the path to redemption. However, distracted by Michael's approach to the rail, she failed to observe the dal segno. To the confusion of the organist and less so the congregation, since few actually sang, the final chorus became the penultimate chorus, a redundancy that eventually and mercifully found its way to the proscribed coda. Truth be told, except for Gladys Simpson, parish scold and music teacher for the local school district, few noticed nor cared about the unintended deviation—or rather, repetition.

The final blessing and response was lengthened slightly and leavened by Father Jim's entreaty that as they departed the church, their sense of Christian brotherhood might extend to the parking lot. Good-natured laughter acknowledged that the availability of parking space immediately around the church was limited and competition keen. Indeed, the parish joke was a multiple choice question concerning whether the earliest arrivals for service were those: (a) of greatest faith, (b) of greatest sin, or (c) who coveted the best parking spots. Some thought (b) and (c) should be combined. The humor was less appreciated by neighbors who were indisposed to surrender street parking to churchgoers each Sunday. As one scalawag put it, "If it came down to lions and Christians, I might pull for the lions. They don't drive."

Finally liberated to the promise of the day, Michael made his way to the church entrance used by the priests when walking from rectory to sacristy. As he came around the corner buttress, he delighted in the fragrance of the blooming lilac bushes. The long untrimmed limbs reached out to caress everyone, sinner or saint, who passed by on the narrow path.

Waiting outside the doorway she would use to retrieve her car from the small parish lot, Michael felt as he had his junior year in high school, trying to screw up his courage to ask Janneke to be his prom date. At that point, they had been out together in groups, but never dated each other. At the time, Michael had no answer for his anxiety. He certainly was interested in her, which sounded pedantic. But he was insecure around girls and unsure of his own motives. He felt his interest was too strong to be relegated in rank to a mere crush.

Both were socially awkward at that age, but the summer of their senior year, Michael was surprised by Janni's increased confidence in their relationship, as was happily made clear when late one night they went skinny dipping off the family dock. Their nervous anticipation was interrupted when his mother turned on the deck lights. It was Janni who called out to reassure his mother, "It's just us going for a swim."

After a short pause, the lights were turned off and Michael's mother responded, "Well, have fun, but be careful." And a little later, on the swimmer's float, they did—and were.

"What are you smiling about?"

Gazing at the traffic in the lot and momentarily taken up in memory, he had not heard the door open nor her footsteps down the stone stairs. He turned and stood there unmoving, marveling that the pleasantness he felt earlier that day could be exceeded by the joy of seeing his first and perhaps most enduring romantic love.

"Well, Michael, don't just stand there—give me a hug."

Parted for so many years, now they were within arm's length. Reaching out they enfolded each other in a long, warm embrace. Disengaging, Michael blurted, "You look great!" and continued to hold her shoulders, elated by her smile and the affection radiating from her face.

"You look great, too." Then with a slight turn of her head and an exaggerated frown, "Now tell me, Michael Cain, why haven't you called?"

Dropping his arms, embarrassed to explain what he knew was a failure on his part, he attempted a lame meandering defense, suddenly interrupted by her bursting into a bright robust laugh. "Michael, you're still so easy."

Feeling self-conscious but recovering some composure, Michael persevered. "I know. I should've called. I'm sorry, but seeing you now is such a wonderful surprise. If you'll allow me, I promise to amend my behavior."

"Well, against or maybe because of my better judgement, I will give you the chance to make up for your negligence."

"Anything."

"How about meeting me for an early lunch, say tomorrow at the Lodge? I have some business with the owners and should be finished by 11:30."

"Excellent, 11:30 lunch it is. In fact, I planned to call the manager for an appointment."

"Oh, are you thinking of investing?"

Surprise and curiosity passed quickly across Michael's face. "No, but should I be?"

"Quite a few area investors have committed to the Lodge. There's a lot of interest in residential and business realty, and the Lodge is currently the leader as a destination for a variety of visitors. Just last week I gave Faethe and Hoepe Lawery the grand tour of the Lodge and after the tour they met with the owners, Anthony and Lucia Sandoval, in the their private suite. The Aunties were impressed with the changes to the resort and by the Sandovals. Faethe called me the following day to say that she and Hoepe were interested in making a modest investment in the Lodge. I was thrilled with their decision. Faethe, especially, has been supportive of my career. I owe her so much."

"The lakes always draw vacationers. I've been to the Lodge. It's undergone quite a transformation, but I'm not sure I'd invest in any tourist spot."

"Yes, but this is much more. It's not only intended for families on summer vacation, but for winter recreation, too. And it provides a venue for special events and for professional conferences that cater to business and political leaders. Have you met the Sandovals?"

"No, not yet."

"Why don't you meet me at Anthony's office at 11:00, and I'll introduce you? You'll like him and his wife. They share a great vision for the area and have a business plan that respects and maintains the integrity and quality of the Lakes region. Just ask at the desk, and they'll direct you. It's a bit out of the way by design. Their inner sanctum is a combination business and personal living space."

"I think that's a good idea, but I'll warn you, my interest has to do with the investigation into the death of Virginia Lawery. She worked at the Lodge the past two summers and during breaks from school, and I want to question her employers and the people Ginny worked with. They've been interviewed, but I still want to meet with them."

"I'm sure they'll cooperate and see to it you have access to staff members. I've heard both Anthony and Lucia say how much they respected and liked Ginny. But wasn't her death an unfortunate accident?"

"Perhaps, but the investigation into her death has come up short on answers, and with the advent of tourist season, the sheriff's department doesn't have the resources to continue to investigate in a timely manner. Sheriff Conrad asked me to review the case, and I'm interviewing everyone listed in the file."

Dropping her eyes and leaning forward to speak in an intimate voice, Janni said, "I'm sorry, but I have to go. Promise me something, Michael. When we have lunch, no talk of business or investigations. Okay? We have so many other things to talk about."

Surprising even himself, Michael reached forward to raise her chin, looked into those gold-flecked violet eyes, and spoke from the heart, "I would like that very much."

She took his hand and pressed it to her cheek, smiling. As she walked away she turned to say, "Tomorrow, at the Lodge."

He watched her drive off, took a deep breath, and the spell was broken—at least until tomorrow.

To Michael's parents, especially his mother, the argument over whether a child's development depended upon nature or nurture was specious. The dictate was faith in God, family, and citizenship. Competing philosophical ambiguities only muddled matters. What they preached they tempered in practice with unrelenting love and care for their children. But when the Cains agreed to foster a proven juvenile delinquent, community skeptics gleefully anticipated that the effort would expose the fallacy of such facile faith in the family's philosophy.

To the disappointment of skeptics and their kinsmen, the cynics, the transformation in Mark Conrad was stunning. It wasn't all peaches and cream, but it was unnecessary to argue whether nature or the Cain family had imbued Connie with the character that defined him. The reality was it was doable and it had been done.

Michael and Connie were not related by blood nor name, but through a similar disposition and a deeply shared sense of moral integrity fueled by passion for justice and fair play. The path for each had been circuitous amid rebellion. For Michael it began with an interest in music suborned by a desire to break from his father's influence and for Connie it was a need for respect, impaired by impatience while also enhanced by a proclivity for action. But given time and guided by desires to practice values both inherent and burnished by experience, they traveled trajectories that culminated in the business of law, Connie by enforcement and Michael by statute.

Similarities aside, their present contrasts were striking. One was self-confident, fulfilled by family and profession, and firm in faith that his life had purpose. The other, once outwardly favored by the same attributes, had seen it quickly fall away and now struggled to understand why and what to do about it. Whether due to fickle fate or his own deeds, it was Michael who faced an existential dilemma, either to regain what was or choose a new path to revival.

An invitation was waiting for him on the answering machine. He smiled as he listened to his sister tell him to join them tonight for a good home-cooked meal which, as she pointed out, was certain to be better than anything his limited culinary efforts could concoct. On the way home from mass Michael had stopped at the Dairy Queen and indulged in two chili dogs, french fries, and a large milkshake. He knew the invitation was an order rather than a request, but considered it dispensation for any guilt associated with his indulgence from Dairy Queen.

***

His sister was too modest. It was not just good, it was a great home-cooked meal. "This chicken and gravy tastes just like the way mom used to make it."

"They're her recipes. It took lots of practice, but I'm getting close."

"How did you get the potatoes and veggies to taste this good?"

Madge looked at Michael like he was dense. "They're real."

"What?"

"They're real, not canned or boxed, and with extra butter and not overcooked."

"Oh yeah. Just like I do them."

Connie paused, a forkful of spuds and gravy before his mouth, and both of them laughed out loud. Only little Ginger looked puzzled, but Uncle Michael had not been around enough in recent years for her to experience Michael's version of cuisine aptly described by Connie as "fodder food."

As expected, everyone remained at the table until the meal was finished. Dessert was ice cream and home-baked cookies (Grandma's recipe—chocolate chip with walnuts). Michael didn't say much, but enjoyed listening to the family's conversation about school, Jeremy's girlfriend, schedules for the upcoming week, and the typical familial hubbub. The post-meal ritual involved everyone rinsing and placing dishes and silverware in the dishwasher and helping to tidy up the remains.

After accepting Connie's offer for a Bud Light longneck, Michael and Connie made their way onto the deck. Madge indicated she would soon join them. Before she arrived, Connie hurriedly warned Michael, "Heads up, Michael. The buzz on the gossip train is that you were in church this morning and sitting in the last row. Madge is going to drill you on it."

"What, for being there or for sitting in the last row?"

"Does it matter? Inquiring people want to know and here comes the inquisitor. Oh, and you'll be encouraged to visit more often. Just thought you'd want to know."

Flopping down on the only padded deck chair with "Mom" imprinted on the cushion, Madge took a big swallow of Bud Light, sighed, and looked over at Michael.

It was Michael who spoke up first. "Madge, thank you. I'll admit it—I enjoyed a real home-cooked meal. You have Mom's touch."

"Thanks. Now brother of mine, down to business."

"What business?"

Being a bit myopic, Madge tipped her head back out of habit and stared at Michael through the bottom of her lenses. "Gladys Simpson called to tell me you were in church this morning. Were you thinking of re-upping or was it the end of the night and the last place you staggered into?"

"Hey, it's not like that."

"Well, what should I think, Michael? You've been back to the lakes since early January, and in spite of numerous invitations, this is the first time you've come over. Phone calls and emails are helpful, but what should I make of it when I never see you? And then you show up at mass, without letting us know so we might sit as a family and you don't even sit in the family pew. Do you even remember which pew it is?"

"How could I forget? Grandma Cain was the one who started the rhubarb about putting family names on brass plates on the end of each pew."

"Yeah, that was great! Grandma Cain really didn't like it when the Reinhardts sat in 'our pew.' Remember all the jokes we made about 'someone else sitting in our P U'?"

Connie had emphasized the P U with air quotes and both Michael and Connie began to laugh and yuck it up until Madge cut them off.

"That's not helping, Connie. You stay out of this. This is about Michael."

Quickly humbled by his petite wife, the big lawman began an intense effort to peel the label off the beer bottle, glanced over at Michael, and shrugged his shoulders as if to say, "I tried."

"Madge, this isn't the first time I've been over to St. Theresa's."

The look on Madge's face only intensified. "And I'm just learning this?"

"Before you say anything else, let me explain. I went to see Father Barney. I hadn't seen him since I returned, and I wanted to express my appreciation for his help. I also had some questions about the Lawery girl's case. Barney was there that night shortly after she was found, and he usually knows what's happening in our parish and in the Lakes area. I thought he could be of assistance and he was. We arranged to meet after mass."

Michael was not sure how determined Madge was to continue this family-motivated grilling, but at the mention of Father Barney there was a slight change in her posture and he decided to press on. "As for this morning, it was a last-minute decision. I arrived late and the church was nearly full, so I sat in back with the slackers."

"Seems appropriate."

"Don't encourage him, Connie!"

"Yes, ma'am." Connie smiled and sipped his beer. He really was beginning to enjoy this. Madge was not one to nag or be unkind, but had the same well-honed technique for engendering guilt as her mother. As long as you weren't the one being grilled, it was entertaining.

Madge huffed, "Well, I don't mean to imply that I hold you to Mom's expectations. After all, you are a grown man."

Connie thought, "Here it comes, just like in a comic book. 'Pow! Biff! Bang!'"

"I just thought it would be nice if we went to church as a family."

"I understand." Holding up his right hand, Michael performed a mock oath. "I promise that by all that is good and Mom's recipe for chicken and gravy, sometime in the near future to go to church with the Conrad family and sit in the…what is it now, the Conrad pew or still the Cain pew?"

Mid-swallow, Connie began to laugh and choked on his beer. Madge threw him a withering look then went on, "Now you're just being a smart ass. Speaking of which, how was your conversation with Janneke?"

Connie was still stopped in mid-swig, but Michael, knowing well his sister's artful modus operandi to obtain information—she should be a detective, he thought—only smiled and asked, "What do you mean?"

"Oh, come on. Gladys Simpson saw the two of you talking after mass. Was this also an appointment or did the grace found within the tabernacle give us a miracle?"

"Ha! Okay, Madge. In fact, it was totally serendipitous. After mass we talked and decided to meet for lunch tomorrow at the Lodge. I guess she knows the owners, and she's going to introduce me to them. We'll mix business with pleasure. Janni assures me they'll cooperate and be willing to help in any way with the Lawery investigation."

"Hmmm…"

"Now what?"

Connie considered to himself, "Should I bestow a conversational intervention?" But before he could, Madge pressed on.

"Janneke knows the Sandovals very well. She and Luke helped them negotiate the purchase of the Lodge and some additional property. I'm sure they hold the insurance on all of it."

"So?"

"Nothing. I agree—she knows a lot about them."

Connie finally stepped in. "Madge, just tell Michael what's on your mind, besides the stink over the pew." There was another sophomoric guffaw, this time from Michael, and another dirty look from Madge.

"Michael, let's begin with Janneke. We all know there's history between you two, so what are your intentions?"

For the first time this evening and perhaps since his return to the lakes, Michael felt testiness over a familial intrusion—one possible drawback of proximity to relatives, or at least it was in his family. "How do I know? I just saw her today."

"You've been back this long and you haven't spoken to Janneke or Luke?"

"Madge, we've already established my negligence to family and friends, but wouldn't you agree that this is an opportunity to make amends?"

"Do you know about the break-up of her marriage, about Luke, about anything they've been through?"

"I know they're divorced, but not why or anything else for that matter. It's been a long time."

"Yes, well obviously you're both adults, but I'm concerned for you. You seem to be doing so well and I—we don't want anything to disrupt your progress."

Feeling a little guilty over his irritation, he responded, "I understand, but don't worry. I'm still working through a few decisions, but things are so much better, renewing a past friendship should be a good thing."

With a serious tone to his voice Connie interceded. "I don't think it's the friendship she's concerned about."

"So what? It's still a chance to reconnect and maybe atone for some of my past behavior. And what about Janni? What is it about her that should raise a concern?"

Glancing first at Connie, Madge went on. "We aren't worried about Janni, but keep in mind that after all this time, you've changed and so has she."

"So tell me. What's so different that it causes you to worry? Has she had problems since the divorce? Is Luke causing trouble? Is business bad?"

"No, no. Rather the opposite."

"Then you'd better explain."

First collecting her thoughts, Madge resumed. "It wasn't just a divorce, it was an annulment. Father Garnier was the priest at St. Theresa's and he assisted with the annulment. Since there were no children, it was relatively simple. Go figure. Anyway, in spite of the opinions of both families, Janneke and Luke were not a match made in heaven—maybe they were business-wise, but not personally. Janneke wanted…wants a career, that's her priority. Luke wants a family, that's his priority. You'd think they could have worked it out, but it became apparent their feelings for each other weren't strong enough to overcome their differences, a realization they arrived at late in the game. So, the annulment was more a meeting of the minds, a mutual acceptance with respect for each other. They still work together, they each have their strengths, and the business is flourishing. Luke minds the office and staff and Janneke is in promotion and development, although they both keep an eye on the finances. That seems reasonable considering they still answer to the board of directors or, in other words, family members who hold shares in the business."

"So what does this have to do with lunch with an old friend?"

"It's just a heads-up. Janneke has her own goals and notions about what her life should be."

"What about Luke?"

"Well, Luke has gone on to remarry, since the bride was conveniently on staff and their first offspring was born six months after the annulment."

Connie had to say it. "A serendipitous event, the miracle of the firstborn."

"Firstborn?"

Madge stared at Connie, shook her head and continued. "Yes,

Michael, and they're expecting a second miracle, but I'm pretty sure in the normally allotted interval of time."

"Wait. How did Janni take all this business of pre-divorce... excuse me, pre-annulment replacement and miracle babies?"

"She was okay. She was genuinely happy for Luke, but the annulment probably hurt the most. She doubled down on work, and thanks mostly to her, the Lodge has become an important part of their business. She's also made a serious personal commitment."

"How's that?"

"It's commonly known she invested some of her own money. She also was appointed to the board of directors and has been actively promoting the Lodge to potential investors. Not everyone in the area's business community is happy about the new competitor. There's that 'old family, old money' expectation to conserve the Lakes region as it was. Hypocritical if you consider how much of the old money was gained by families taking advantage of what the Lakes region had to offer. I guess I'm just suggesting you keep all this about Janneke in mind. Mea culpa, I'm sorry to sound like an old gossip. I thought it would be better if you knew. I don't want you hurt."

Michael got up, walked over and hugged his sister. "Thanks, Madge. It's okay. I know where your heart is." Stepping back he saw the glisten forming in her eyes, smiled at her and said, "Thank you."

Madge returned the smile, wiped her eyes and began a different tack. "By the way, you need to call Mom. She thinks you're avoiding her."

"Why would I avoid her? Madge, I've called and left messages, I even wrote a letter, but I can't reach her. Every time I call, she's out or Aunt Louise answers and says Mom's not available. What does 'not available' mean?"

"Well, they're both busy. They play bridge and golf and Mom joined a dance club."

Connie interrupted, "Tell him about Fred."

"Who's Fred?"

"It's nothing—it's all innocent, I'm sure. I mean, good grief, the lady is seventy-five years old."

"Hey, that's no lady, that's my mother."

Connie interjected, "Bad joke, bro."

Ignoring the digression, Madge explained. "Fred is a retired stock broker and widower. Mom met him at a dance club, and they seem to have hit it off. Louise says they enjoy each other and it's all perfectly fine. But when, not if, you talk to her, let her bring him up. She may not respond well if you sound nosy."

"I'm nosy? Alright. I'll keep calling and won't ask about Fred."

"She'll appreciate that. It's important to respect each other's personal lives."

With that Connie and Michael erupted into laughter followed by poorly imitated mockery of the recent interrogation and unsolicited advice. Madge, with bright red face, got up and stalked into the house, throwing back the words, "You two are awful!"

After the final hoots of derision died away, a gratified Connie added, "God, I love her. I love her more every day."

They were quiet, each with their own thoughts, serenely enveloped by the evening's twilight. Almost as a postscript Michael agreed. "You are blessed...we both are blessed by that woman."

On the drive home Michael savored the afterglow of a well-spent day. There came a voice of affirmation, whether aloud or in his mind, "Life *is* better."

24

While Michael enjoyed a restful night, Janneke's attempts at sleep were fitful at best. The remainder of her Sunday had been spent at the office preparing for the Monday morning meeting with the Sandovals. The fledgling season at the Lodge was promising, but success this summer was critical to the enterprise, and Janneke knew better than most that they were sailing close to the wind. It was a make or break summer, and this meeting, intended to be an objective review of the financial numbers required for success, was consequential.

Janneke was accustomed to the stress of business; in fact she thrived on the challenge. She was ready, and the numbers were encouraging. The board of directors was in lockstep with the strategy and she was confident in the abilities of the owner-managers to achieve the required objectives. In spite of all this, something was niggling at her confidence. She didn't have time to ruminate on the cause and demoted it as her inclination to overthink, a tendency she considered an indulgence which wasted time rather than improving results.

As she was about to step into the shower, she caught the sight of her image in the mirror. Pulling back her long auburn hair, she turned her head first to the left, then the right. Her complexion was clear and naturally healthy. She had a tendency to burn in the sun, but work had kept her indoors, minimizing time she could devote to her alter ego, outdoors woman.

Releasing her hair, then curling a few strands around a finger, she admired the highlights and the lack of any greying or invading white threads. Turning to view her profile, she lifted, then released her modest breasts, admiring their firmness. She may be "annulled," but it hadn't been for a lack of Luke's interest in her body. She still looked good.

Michael should be so lucky. Sure, he had those gorgeous eyes and all that wavy hair. He looked to be in good shape although the slight softness around his middle could use some work. And that great smile and cute little ass. Whoa! What was she thinking?

But God, he looked so good! She had even daydreamed about him when jogging this morning. Enough! Time for a shower (maybe cold, she thought), breakfast, and then to work—she had a big day ahead. The time to think about Michael was secondary, maybe tertiary. He would have to wait.

***

Michael's day began with an early phone call. The machine picked it up, but Michael could just make out Stan Dorian's voice. As its nominal personnel manager, Stan had to be sure the Big Okoboji Band was fully staffed for every performance.

"Hey, Michael! This is Stan. How would you like to play with the band? Ronnie got a fishhook in his finger courtesy of the walleye opener. He'll be fine but suggested you might like to take his place tonight. Give me a call sooner than later. It should be fun. We're breaking in some new material for the summer season. I think you'll enjoy it. Hope you can join us."

Stan was a published composer, mostly for jazz bands, and his arrangements and originals were popular. He was in demand as a player and clinician, but truth be told, he enjoyed and preferred teaching, especially middle school students. He espoused, "Their energy is contagious. You get them moving in the right direction and they can achieve anything!"

Michael had to admire Stan's optimism. His own experience at that age was less memorable, and he had long ago resolved that whatever happened in middle school stayed in middle school.

Sitting on the side of his bed, Michael picked up his cell, called Stan and, with a mix of eagerness and annoyance, accepted the offer.

"Warm-up's at 7:00 and we play at 8:00. It's an early night; we'll be done by 11:00. Will that work for you?"

"Yes, it's all good. I'll be there. Tie or casual?"

"Casual, don't overdo. We're all poor working stiffs."

"Yessir! Got it. 7:00 and no tux."

Considering whether or not to flop back into bed, Michael was startled by the Jimmy Buffet inspired ring of the phone still in his hand. It was Connie. "Michael! Sorry to call so early but I'm glad I caught you. My lead homicide detective, Jack Donahue, checked with all our deputies to see if there was anything they could add to the Lawery investigation and specifically asked about the ex-boyfriend, Grant Laxton. He just informed me that one of our deputies, Deputy Don Warren, responded to an early morning call last summer from the Lodge regarding a disturbance. The folks at the Lodge refused to file a complaint but asked Deputy Warren to escort someone they had just fired off the premises. He remembered the 'someone'—it was Grant Laxton."

"What?"

"You heard me correctly. Don filed a report but it just stated that he'd been called to the Lodge for a possible assault that was resolved without incident. Now we have another reason why we need to find the missing ex-boyfriend." There was silence on the other end until Connie asked, "Michael?"

"Oh, sorry. I was thinking it's interesting that none of this came up in any of the reported interviews with the Sandovals. I'll be sure to ask why when I meet with them today."

"Good! I'll be interested in what they have to say."

By now Michael was fully awake with time enough for a good run, breakfast, and a review of his notes and questions for the anticipated interviews at the Lodge. "Need to remember to check in with Pam later today," he told himself. Then he smiled as he thought of lunch with Janni. "If all goes well at the Lodge and with Janni, it should be another great day."

***

"Are we ready for this?"

"Yes, of course."

Anthony Sandoval nervously opened his binder a third time. A deep frown formed on his forehead and his jaw flexed, relaxing only to tighten again. For a moment he felt the conference room contracting around him. He took a deep breath, forcibly exhaled, and regained a semblance of control. He was eager for this planning session to begin, but not looking forward to meeting Michael Cain.

His wife sat at ease on his right. The cascade of thick dark curls framed her distinctive face and her bright eyes gleamed with anticipation. The soft fabric of her light summer dress caressed her body and whispered over her thighs as she crossed her lovely legs. The allure revealed by the low cut of her dress required no embellishment, but the modest gold chain and cross limited the potential delight of a voyeur. She was in full combat mode while her husband was too distracted to admire the beauty beside him.

***

Arriving a few minutes early, Michael checked in at the registration desk and was immediately escorted by an overly perky young woman to the office suite adjacent to the Sandovals' private quarters. It was only a three minute walk down the hall and up the stairs, but in that time Michael gleaned her name and that she was a student at ILCC working at the Lodge part-time during the school year and full-time this summer. She had heard about Virginia Lawery, but wasn't here last summer, so never met her.

After a light knock, the door was answered by a smiling Anthony. "How do you do, Michael? I'm so glad to finally meet you. I'm Anthony Sandoval." Reaching out to shake hands he glanced at the young woman and dismissed her with a nod. Stepping back he drew Michael into a spacious room that, except for the large desk, appeared to be designed more for entertainment than business. The fireplace, oil paintings, matching leather chairs and couch confirmed Michael's recent visit to their website. It was impressive, professionally appointed, and offered a magnificent view of the lake through the large glass doors leading onto the deck. If the intent was to impress a newcomer, it was successful. Before he had a chance to take it all in, Mr. Sandoval ushered him into the adjacent conference room, more modest in size, whose function was clearly intended for business.

Janneke rose from her side of the conference table to greet him. "There he is. Good morning, Michael." Hugging him a bit longer than was casual, she turned and said, "You just met Anthony. I'd like to introduce his wife and business partner, Lucia."

Rising from her place at the table, Lucia took his extended hand in both of her hands. "It's so good to meet you, Michael. We've just finished the boring stuff. Please, join us and have a seat. Can I get you anything—coffee, tea, water?"

"No, but thank you," he replied as he sat down next to Janni.

"Very impressive," thought Michael, his mind suddenly abuzz. "I need to focus. I'm in dangerous territory. The lady is stunning, her husband impressive, and Janni fits right in. I feel like I've been set up. This should be interesting."

Janneke began, "I was just explaining that you were brought in by the sheriff's department to review the investigation into the death of Virginia Lawery, and as part of the process, you were planning to reinterview anyone mentioned in the report."

Opening up his butter-soft leather satchel, Michael removed his notebook and a separate sheet with names listed in alphabetical order. Sliding the sheet across the table, Michael added, "That's true. I also would be interested in talking to anyone you may suggest whose name isn't on the list." As Anthony picked up the list, Michael went on. "I have to admit, the interviews appear thorough, and I'm not sure if there's much else to be gained. But, you never know."

Mr. Sandoval looked thoughtful, then passed the list to his wife. "I assume we definitely aren't talking about an accidental death?"

"Anything is possible, but at this point her death is still considered suspicious. I'm trying to learn as much as possible about the circumstances leading up to the time of her death."

"So you know when she died?"

Michael thought, "Interesting that he should ask."

"No, that's something we have yet to establish. I can't get into details, but I can say that the time or even exact date of death has not been determined."

The slight hint of a delicate floral fragrance wafted across the table as Lucia Sandoval leaned forward. "Michael, Anthony and I want you to know we are committed to helping you and the authorities in any way we can. What do you need from us?"

The conversation that followed was earnest, but other than his first impressions, the facts were known. Ginny was well-liked, an excellent employee, and a friend to all she met.

"I read in the interview that you saw Virginia the evening of Friday, March 4, the same day she left ISU. As far as we know, she may have disappeared shortly thereafter. Would you review for me what you told the detective from the sheriff's office about that night?"

Looking at each other for what seemed a nonverbal sign, it was Mrs. Sandoval who replied. "Why don't I start and Anthony can add anything as needed?" With a nod of agreement from her husband, she went on. "Ginny arrived here shortly after 6:00 that evening. She had called the night before so we were expecting her. She was excited and wanted to talk about her future. She told us about adding hospitality to her degree program and how much she was looking forward to interning here this summer.

"When she arrived, it was after office hours, so we met here in our suite, ordered a late supper for her, and visited for quite a long time."

Apologizing, Michael interrupted Lucia's account. "Do you recall what she had for supper?"

"Yes. It was the Friday dinner special, blackened swordfish. While she ate, we shared a bottle of Pinot Noir. Is that important?"

"Not necessarily. I was just curious. Please, continue."

"Ginny left about 11:00, give or take a bit. She said she was staying with a friend, and I offered to give her a ride, but she said she'd arranged for her friend to pick her up. She used her phone but didn't specify who she was calling. She used the restroom, and we visited a few minutes longer. I could feel a migraine coming on and needed to be up early for a staff meeting, so I excused myself and went to bed. Anthony walked with her to the employee entrance."

Anthony had remained silent but now took up the account. "We waited together no more than a few minutes until her ride arrived. I thought at the time whoever it was must have come from somewhere nearby. The glare from the headlights made it impossible to clearly see the driver. It may have been a man, but I can't even be sure of that. The sheriff's detective asked if I recognized the car, and I have to say, I didn't. It was late and cold standing there in the hallway, so once she was in the car, I waved and went back to the apartment. Sadly, that was the last time we saw her."

"What did you talk about?"

Lucia took up the question. "Other than what I already mentioned, we spoke of school, friends, plans for the summer, nothing of great consequence. It was a nice, comfortable chat, if people still call it that."

Thinking he'd received something, Michael decided to give a little in return. Redirecting the questions to Anthony, he shared, "Her car hasn't been found. Could it be her car you saw?"

"I didn't know that." Looking over to his wife, he shook his head. "I recall she drove a small bright green car last summer, but I'm sorry, I couldn't say for certain if it was the same vehicle I saw that night."

"Were there any other cars in the employee lot?"

"There were a few. The big band was playing and some of them park in the employee lot. I think the detectives questioned everyone, even the band members, but they didn't share with us whether anyone else saw her leave."

"Do you have security cameras in the parking lot?"

"Not then—we do now. I'm sure you noticed, we've been under-going a lot of construction. At the time, the cameras were yet to be installed."

Michael waited but nothing else was forthcoming. He decided to try some questions inspired by Deputy Warren's disclosure. "I didn't know that Grant Laxton was employed at the Lodge last summer and that midsummer, he was let go." Though not entirely truthful, Michael persevered. "He assaulted someone and according to the deputy, was given a choice: leave or be arrested. That seems serious. Why was he not charged?"

Anthony's face suddenly paled but he responded. "I'm not sure what's in your report, but we were uncertain of the circumstances and preferred to avoid any publicity."

"As personnel manager, I was responsible," Lucia interjected. "Frankly, as an employee, he didn't work out. He had a good refer-ence from one high school teacher but nothing more. We needed the help so I took a chance. He was fine at first, a good worker and bright, but also proved to be self-absorbed and manipulative. After a few weeks his attitude worsened, and he became ill-mannered, even rude to customers and staff."

Lucia hesitated, then continued, "We learned of at least one occa-sion when he was drinking on the job and his supervisor thought he helped himself to a bottle of liquor from the storeroom. So when we were told by the night maintenance workers that Laxton may have attacked one of our employees, we let him go with the clear warning that if there was any difficulty resulting from our action, we would turn the whole matter over to the police. He was sullen but didn't argue. The sheriff's department was helpful. We called and explained the situation and they had a deputy escort him to his car and off the grounds early in the morning, before the first shift reported to work."

Lucia's explanation may have been sufficient but to Michael it sounded rehearsed. His intuition suggested there was more. He took a shot. "Did you get a restraining order?"

She didn't hesitate, "Yes. The night after he was let go, our security caught him sneaking around outside the women's dormitory. He was escorted off the grounds a second time, and the next morning we applied for and quickly were granted a restraining order. The police located him at a motel in Spencer and served him the order. Other than mailing his final check to his home address, we haven't seen or heard from him since."

Still writing in his notebook, Michael asked, "Who did Laxton attack?"

Nervously clearing his throat, Anthony replied, "Well I'm a bit chagrinned, but please believe me, Lucia and I only learned of this recently."

At this Michael looked up at them sharply. The sudden change in his demeanor produced an awkward moment which, thanks to Janneke, was quickly smoothed over.

"Michael, Anthony and Lucia were just informed of this, and it may be totally unrelated."

Realizing his reaction had communicated something unintended, Michael apologized. "You're right…Sorry. Please, go ahead. Tell me what you learned."

As Anthony began, he folded his hands on the table, like a student about to recite a lesson. "We assumed the assault was against Ginny. We knew there was history between her and Laxton. That was why we kept it low-key. We wanted to protect Ginny."

Michael was not writing but listening intently. "How does this differ from what we know?"

Anthony looked at Janneke, who nodded at him, and he continued. "The assault wasn't on Ginny."

"What?"

"No. It was on Sally, Ginny's roommate."

Stunned, Michael stared at them both then blurted, "Sally! Sally Grosfeldt was assaulted? I thought Ginny was his girlfriend."

"We thought so, too. After we fired Laxton, everyone got very tight-lipped. No one talked about it, and we didn't encourage it. We didn't hear about Sally's relationship with him until her lawyer came by. He had some questions, and we tried to answer as best we could, but we were surprised to learn that Sally was the girlfriend in question, not Ginny. We think he thought we knew, and when he realized we didn't, he abruptly ended the interview."

"When did you speak with him?"

"Last Friday, late in the afternoon, downstairs in the conference room next to the business office."

"What did he want to know?"

"He wanted to know if we were in contact with Laxton and whether we had reported the assault to the police. He said Sally's family had a right to know what action we may still take in the matter and that's when he must have realized we didn't know it was Sally who was attacked."

Anthony added, "He stopped, closed his briefcase, told us this was a privileged conversation, and threatened us with a lawsuit if we told anyone."

Michael was writing again but looked up to say, "Did he inform you at the beginning that it was privileged?"

"No. He said he needed our help and acted like we were just having a conversation."

"Then it's not privileged."

"We know. We checked with our lawyer."

"What's his name? Not your lawyer, but the guy who interviewed you."

"Erickson. Dennis Erickson. I have his card right here. He may not like it, but you probably will want to interview Sally."

"Yes, I probably will want to interview Sally. Did you have any other surprises?"

"Thankfully, no. There's enough drama when preparing for the start of the summer season."

Michael sat quietly, then closed his notebook. Janneke accepted that as a sign the interview was concluded. "Well, if you will excuse us, Michael and I have a lunch date."

Smiling and visibly relieved, Anthony responded, "Of course. Michael, if you would meet Lucia in the business office downstairs, say around 1:00, she will have a private room for your use and will see to it that people are available. If there's anything else you require, just ask."

Michael sincerely expressed his appreciation to Anthony and Lucia Sandoval for their time and cooperation and added, "I do have one request. I wondered if I might have a tour of the Lodge. My family visited and dined here many times when I was young, but it obviously has changed a great deal."

Leaning forward in all her splendor Lucia said, "Of course. I'd be happy to be your guide. When you finish the interviews, I'll be available."

"Again, thank you. I look forward to it."

With that, Janni pushed back her chair and declared, "Michael, I am famished. Time to eat and…what was it? Oh yes—chat!"

25

Having placed their order, Janni, with her elbows on the table, chin resting on her hands, gave Michael a bemused look.

"What?"

"Tell me, Michael, what did you think of Anthony and Lucia?"

"I thought we were avoiding talk about business."

"This is less business than personal. How much are you looking forward to your personal tour of the Lodge with Lucia Sandoval?"

Michael had to laugh, "If I didn't know you so well, I'd say you were jealous."

Dropping her hands to her lap, she said, "Sorry. They both can be a bit overwhelming at times, especially when it comes to first impressions. So tell me, looks aside, what did you think of them?"

The food was excellent and after a short exchange of impressions and opinions regarding the owners, the conversation followed the natural course of two longtime friends who hadn't spoken to one another for years. It always surprised Michael that close friends, even though separated by time and distance, could so easily pick up where they left off. At the lobby they hugged and agreed to see each other again soon. As they were about to part, almost as an afterthought, Janni turned to say, "I'll send you the promotional materials I use for investors—it includes personal information about the Sandovals. You may find their story interesting."

***

While time at lunch with Janni passed quickly, the interviews had the opposite effect. Finished by 4:00, Michael was eager to start the tour if for no other reason than to finally be done with the small conference room and even smaller results from those he interviewed. Nothing new was gained and what he already knew repeated, though the recent revelation from the Sandovals was confirmed by the supervisor in charge of summer help. At this point Michael could not see a compelling reason to follow up with the few on the list who were no longer employed by the Lodge and reportedly had no other connection, remotely or otherwise, to Ginny.

If the interviews were tedious, the tour made up for it. Although some construction remained, the new version of the Lodge was fantastic. The planning and execution were first class and it was difficult to not be taken up with the results. He was even more impressed than when he had explored the grounds alone the other evening. Arriving back at the business office still in the company of his charming guide, Michael thanked Lucia for her time and consideration. "You're welcome, Michael. If there's anything else I can do for you, please call."

As he was walking to his truck, curiosity redirected him to the nearby Sports Shop. While not part of the tour, it was pointed out as one of the independently managed enterprises in a symbiotic relationship with the Lodge. As Lucia portrayed it, "We partner with private operators who manage the day-to-day business, and we provide promotion, data services, billing, bookkeeping, etc." She had further explained that, besides sales, the Sports Shop offered boats and a variety of gear for rent as well as instruction in water sports with deep discounts for anyone staying at the Lodge.

Pulling open the heavy glass door he was nearly bowled over by a scowling, smelly, rough-looking character who made no attempt to apologize for his ill-mannered exit. Following him was a tall gangly younger man whose unruly dark hair sprang out from under an oversized Berkley freebie cap. Unlike the older man, he stopped, tipped his cap in what appeared to be a sincere but somehow comic manner and simply said, "Thank you, sir." Then he hurried to catch up to the older man who was already climbing into a van.

"Sorry about that. Please come in." Stepping inside, Michael was confronted by a gnome-like man with a goatee beard who peered at him over the top of little round granny glasses.

"Who was that?"

"Oh, the rude fellow with the nice young man? He's Baitman with his sidekick Robin." The diminutive greeter smiled and tilted his head to the side as if waiting for the newly arrived customer to get his play on words. Unexpectedly mesmerized, Michael stared at the twinkling blue eyes made large through lenses perched precariously near the end of the owner's small, round nose.

"Come again?"

"Sorry, my sense of humor is an acquired taste. The older man distributes live fishing bait— crawlers, minnows, crawdads, leeches, grubs, that sort of thing—and the younger man works for him. If you think my little jest silly you may think the real thing isn't much better. His name is Jolly, Jolly Holiday, which is a misnomer if I've ever known one. His assistant is Dum Dum. I can't believe that's his real name, but I've only heard him called Dum Dum. He doesn't seem to mind. He's a bit slow, but friendly. Jolly is the opposite, a bit too smart and quite unpleasant. However, the bait and service are good and that's important. Now, how may I help you?"

The shop owner was affable and knew his business. The wide variety of quality sporting equipment for sale and rent were complemented by signs advertising lessons available through a stable of skilled area instructors. Michael was impressed and would have lingered over the variety of fly rods if there had been time. He definitely would return, but for now, he needed to hurry home to grab a snack, get dressed, and hurry back to the Lodge for his gig with the Big Okoboji Band.

***

"Get the hell out of that dumpster! And put a leash on your dog!"

Michael rushed across the parking lot, jumped into his truck, and headed for home. Had he not been in such a rush, Michael would have overheard the loud opening exchange between the foreman for the general contractor to the Lodge and a grizzled older man. Lonnie Davidson ("Stud Boss" according to the scrawl on his hard hat) was trying to impress upon Willy DeWeerd that the construction dumpsters were not within Willy's province.

"Kiss my ass, Davidson, and my dog's hairy ass, too!"

Davidson's shoulders slumped and he let out a deep sigh. "Willy, I told you before you can't dumpster dive at the Lodge."

"Can too! I helped Ms. Sandoval with her car, and she told me it was okay for me to help myself."

"I know. You told me before, but I have to answer to her husband, and he is the king of assholes around this place."

Willy set his jaw and flipped off Davidson. "Screw you and screw King Sandoval! I take my orders from the Missus."

"Yeah, well you tell that to her husband. I've never seen such an arrogant jerk. He gets his kicks bragging about how much smarter he is than everyone else."

"Tough! That's your problem. She's the boss. Besides, they're not married anyhow."

Davidson wasn't sure if Willy meant what he said or if he was high. "Are you nuts? Of course they're married."

"Not for real—they're married but it's 'n arrangement. They don't even sleep together. They have separate bedrooms."

Davidson was stunned. "How do you know that?"

"Those kids that work here in the summer? They like to go slumming. One of their favorites is that biker bar, Spokes and Suds. They drink, they talk, they drink more and they talk louder. I overheard some of them blabbing about cleaning the Sandovals' rooms—separate bedrooms and bathrooms."

"That doesn't prove anything. They work hard—they probably have different schedules."

"Is that why there's a lock on the door between the bedrooms?" Willy paused, then slowly grinned. "And the little pissants talked about seein' other women sneak up there when the Missus weren't around."

"There must be an explanation."

"There is—I just told you."

Willy was warming up to his audience. "Something else…I just happened to be walkin' by here late one night on a recon mission when two of the night security guys was out havin' a smoke. We talked and the big one, the one with the big beer gut, complained he felt like they were pimps. Before I could ask him what that meant, his partner told him to shut the hell up and get back to work."

"I can't believe it."

"I can't either. What a waste of a beautiful woman. Well, enough gossip. There's some primo stuff at the bottom of this dumpster and

I mean to get it!"

Davidson was unconvinced by Willy's sordid account, but his immediate problem was to get Willy out of the dumpster before one of Anthony Sandoval's peon ass kissers created a problem. "Willy, wait! Tell you what. I'll help you if you promise to leave and don't come back unless you check with me first."

Willy stood staring at Davidson and scratching his scraggly whiskers. "You mean I have to make an appointment?"

"Let me see your phone."

"Don't got one."

"Come on, Willy. I know the Lodge gave you a phone. I'm just trying to help."

Reluctantly Willy handed over his phone but Davidson handed it back. "Unlock it."

"Thought you knew everything."

With it unlocked, Davidson typed something into the phone. "That's my cell number. If you just have to go through our dumpsters, call or text me first, and I'll let you know the best time to come by. I don't wanna go all law and order on you but I will if you make me. Whaddaya say? Is it a deal?"

Willy took his time deciding. Finally he nodded his head in approval. "Is it true?"

"What?"

"What it says on your helmet."

"Yeah, I'm the stud, but right now I'm not sure who the boss is."

26

Anthony Sandoval stood staring through the large glass sliding door to the wraparound deck and outside stairs of his private second story business suite. If he'd bothered to notice, the evening sky, colored coral by the setting sun, and the water, transformed a deep indigo by the day's late shadow, were sights that would improve even the most dour of moods.

Behind him, a luxurious leather couch with two matching chairs faced an Italian marble fireplace. Over the fireplace hung an original oil painting, a triptych expressed in vibrant colors. The left panel was of a picador on his horse attacking an enraged bull, the center panel showed a matador and bull engaged in mortal combat, while the panel on the right depicted a beautiful dark-haired señorita with a rose pressed between hands as in prayer and reverence for her matador. Draped over the backs of the chairs were finely embroidered throws depicting scenes that corresponded to the left and right members of the triptych.

His large desk was across the room. Much of the wall behind it was covered with plaques and pictures of himself with politicians and entertainers. None of it consoled him.

Turning abruptly, he walked across the lush burgundy carpet and into the adjoining conference room. It was the inner sanctum where, with a few unfortunate but necessary exceptions, only those most important to the Sandovals' success were allowed to enter. The room was intimate in size but spartan, holding only the conference table and chairs and a modest sideboard. There were no pictures, but there was a large drawing that nearly covered the end wall. Here was the present and future of the Sandoval Lakes area empire, the source of both pride and anxiety.

In a brief time they had already achieved success beyond expectations. The first stage of development had gone well. The variety of accommodations, the wide appeal of activities available to all guests, the possibilities for dining that addressed sophisticated palettes or the more economical needs of families, had all proven promising. The revitalized resort was one reason the storied, slightly stuffy Lakes region was experiencing an entrepreneurial renaissance. And while the renewed energy was welcomed by area business communities, he knew the Sandoval enterprise was looked upon with suspicion by many of the longtime residents.

Their visit with Mr. Cain had gone well, but Anthony was left with the impression that to the wrong person, Cain could be dangerous. He was surprised to learn that investigators did not know the summer unpleasantness was over Sally, not Ginny. But then, they also hadn't determined when Ginny disappeared and whether her death was accidental. And they hadn't found her car. That really was unexpected news. Many missing pieces that probably would remain that way—an unsolvable mystery. That was better for him and for the Lodge.

Lucia had done well. She was in charge of human resources and personnel development and the one to answer questions having to do with staff. She also was the one to ask about whether there may be additional people to interview. He had to smile over Mr. Cain's obvious attraction to her or rather distraction by her, musing, "Sometimes I don't show enough appreciation for her talents."

Ginny's supervisor was still employed by the resort, and Anthony knew he would answer truthfully but not embellish nor volunteer beyond what was asked. Finally, they had expressed the appropriate concern about such a sad event and pledged to help in any way they could. They had anticipated everything, even the tour. This matter of Virginia Lawery was a diversion, but it shouldn't affect their plans.

He did miss her. Ginny truly was unique. He had not obsessed over her but had taken an interest. She had the most innocent way of flattering him whenever he was near. Their intimate dalliance last summer was briefly reprised during winter break but abruptly ended, seemingly on good terms. It was confusing, but Ginny hadn't explained why she suddenly pulled away. She was lacking in guile but exuded so much passion. Maybe it had to do with her mother.

He thought aloud, "That night we shared a joint, those were some strange things she talked about. Little girls should have dolls and frilly dresses, not the crap she had to live with. Mothers are supposed to protect their daughters, not bring home the scum."

The whole business was unfortunate, but frankly, it wasn't a problem. Lucia would get over it. There were more important issues to face, and having processed the interview, he confined it to a distant part of his mind. If needed, he would return to it at a more convenient time and then dismiss it. At least that's what he told himself.

27

It was nearly 6:00 when Michael arrived home. He had an hour to eat, change, and make it to rehearsal; his anxious inner monologue played but he dissuaded it with the words: "No problem."

There were four messages on his answering machine, the first was the old message from Stan and a second from Stan saying there would probably be a small crowd so 7:30 would be early enough to start. Micheal sighed in relief. The third was from Pam (whom he'd forgotten to call) telling him that she had emailed him her notes from the interview with Sally and suggesting they should interview her again—soon. "And the tests are ready to go. Don't worry, I have things covered. I'll see you Friday." The fourth message was from Connie: "Call me."

Connie answered on the second ring. "Has the budget been cut to the point that the sheriff answers his own phone?"

Connie scoffed, "I'm moonlighting. What do you need?"

"Good food, wine, and music. I'm returning your call."

"Oh, right. I forgot. It's been a zoo around here."

"Yes, I called your house, and Madge said you were still at the office."

"My poor wife, she's a saint. I assisted with a situation this morning and I'm trying to wrap up the paperwork."

"Something serious?"

"Not really, but it took time. Weird Willy took umbrage with some bicyclist in brightly colored plumage hogging the road, and decided to nudge him over to the road's shoulder. The biker wasn't hurt, and I talked him into not pressing charges on the condition I would take Willy in and I quote: 'Give him a stern talking to.' The biker was some kid I didn't know. They both gave my deputy attitude. Anyway, I'm glad you called. I learned a little more about Grant Laxton, Virginia Lawery's so-called ex-boyfriend."

"So did I, but you first."

"The DCI did a follow-up on Mr. Laxton after you spoke to the agent in charge last week. There was nothing new about the case but the kid has an attorney. Laxton's attorney states that the kid is unavailable for questioning, but if in the future Laxton should agree to be interviewed it only would be with his attorney present. Right now, we don't even know where the kid is."

Michael heard a rustling of paper, then Connie continued. "According to my notes the DCI agent's name is William Hitchcock. He spoke with my homicide detective, and they think it is suspicious, but agree we don't have enough to take to the Dickinson County Attorney for a subpoena. For that matter, there's nothing definitive to corroborate that Laxton has anything to do with the Lawery investigation. Hitchcock is contacting fellow agents for anything they may know. I'm going to do the same with county sheriffs and municipal police departments in the area. We want to find out if Laxton pops up on any of their reports at, or around, the time that Virginia Lawery left ISU."

Michael finished jotting down details and had a suggestion. "What about hospitals?"

"I hadn't thought of that."

"It's a long shot, but might be a possibility. I don't know if they would be willing to cooperate, but maybe Dr. Matt could get in through an emergency door, so to speak."

Connie agreed. "I'll call Matt and the administrator at the Spirit Lake Hospital to see what they can do. The clock is ticking, and once we pass Memorial Day, this investigation will get pushed aside and turn frigid fast."

Michael cautioned, "I know, but better to do this right in the first place rather than have it come back on us later."

"You're right, of course. There's something else you need to know. Our local newspaper is running an editorial the Sunday of Memorial Day weekend about the Lawerys and the investigation. They have a new hotshot intern who persuaded Milo Leadbetter to let her write a feature on the family. Her name is Stevie Carson, and she called me this morning to arrange an interview. The kid did some research in the paper's archives and now thinks she's an expert. I think she's flying by the seat of her pants and doesn't know it."

"She wants to interview you about the Lawery case? The area's business barons are not going to be happy. What is Milo thinking?"

"I don't know. He'd better be careful. A lot of advertisers may be uncomfortable having this raked over at the start of the season." There was silence, which Connie interrupted, "Michael, are you still there?"

"Yeah, I was just thinking. Local newspapers usually run a weekly report of police and fire calls and hospital admissions and dismissals. My mom used to check them religiously. Sometimes I'd tease her about keeping up with the neighborhood gossip. Maybe instead of calling the hospitals, why not ask Milo's hotshot intern for a quid pro quo: you'll do the interview if she'll do a check of area newspapers and see if there's anything that may help us."

"That might take a lot of time. I'm not sure they'll be willing to do that, and if it involves a hospital, by law the publication of admissions and dismissals are no longer permitted."

"Yes, but people like to gossip and a snoopy, excuse me, curious reporter might be able to suss out something helpful to our investigation."

Getting into the spirit of the exchange Connie added, "I'll call Leadbetter. If he wants our cooperation then there needs to be some give and take."

"Good. What about insurance companies?"

"What do you mean?"

"If there was an insurance claim during that time, it may be informative."

"We already did a check, no claims, and before you ask, no traffic violations issued recently, only a speeding ticket from a year ago. Now tell me your news. How'd the interviews go?"

"There was nothing we didn't know except for one important fact I learned from the Sandovals. It seems we've been operating under a false assumption. Last summer's assault by the boyfriend was not on Ginny. It was on her roommate, Sally."

After hearing in detail what had been divulged, including the short meeting between Dennis Erickson and the Sandovals, Connie stated the obvious, "We need to reinterview Sally, but this time at the courthouse with our detective."

"I agree but I have one suggestion."

"Which is?"

"Call Pam and have her sit in on the interview. She had a calming effect during our talk with Sally, and I respect her insight. By the way, it won't do any good to talk to Erickson. He'll just say he was representing his client and anything else is privileged."

"I get it. The lawyer will lawyer himself up. I'll have Jack arrange the interview with Sally. Stay in touch and have fun playing tonight."

"How did you know I was playing tonight?"

"Stan was interviewed on the local radio station. If I can, I tune in to listen to the early morning Local Yokel news to hear what's happening in the area, and they do interviews with some of our homegrown personalities. Oh, hey—I just thought of something else."

"Yes?"

"Is Jerry Foyle still the drummer for the Boji Badass Band?"

"You mean the Big Okoboji Band? Yes, last I knew of it."

"Would you please remind him to get his old Hafner boat off the public beach next to Fordham's resort? He left it there last fall, and county sanitation is about to haul it to the landfill."

"Is it that junky old boat with more wood than paint?"

"Yep. Last time I checked it was upside down, and the snowmobilers were using it for a ramp."

"Okay, I'll tell him. He'll probably donate it to the county."

"Well, the county ain't interested. It's Jerry or the landfill."

"I'll pass the word along. Good luck with Willy. Don't be too hard on the old guy."

"I let him go with a warning not to drive if he's self-medicating for PTSD."

"PTSD?"

"Long story, short version. Think Vietnam. Willy is one of our vets with more locked up inside than should be allowed. I know something of combat, but some of these guys deal with stuff we cannot imagine. Enough of that! Take a break. Enjoy tonight."

28

Michael made it just in time for the downbeat. It took a few minutes to work the kinks out of his fingers, but by the end of the rehearsal his hands and mind were in sync.

The crowd was small, not a surprise for this time of year. Once they were into the high season there would be standing room only, but tonight even the hard-core fans were gone by 10:00 PM, and the band shut down early.

As he was replacing the piano book in the folder case Michael remembered he had a message for the drummer, who was just packing his equipment. "Hey, Jerry. I thought you would leave your equipment up. Isn't the band playing this weekend?"

"Yeah, but I have a little gig at the Spirit Lake nursing home Wednesday with our blues combo. It's a good time and the residents really enjoy it. Who knows, someday we may be sitting there listening while trying to remember how to tap our toes."

"Maybe, but let's not be in a hurry to find out. By the way, I have a message from Sheriff Conrad."

On his way home, Michael puzzled over the conversation he'd just had with Foyle. Connie's message had evoked a quick response from him, "I know. I'll take care of it, thanks." But the conversation hadn't ended there; a couple of bandmates had gathered around and wanted to know how the investigation was going. Michael said nothing that wasn't generally known except they were pretty certain someone had picked Ginny up around 11:00 the Friday night she disappeared.

"We don't know who it was, and we don't know where they went."

Stan Dorian was standing by and joined the conversation. "We figured as much. The band played the night they think she disappeared, and we were questioned by the detective."

"I know. I read the reports. We also can't find her car."

"What kind of car?"

"It was a lime green Ford Fiesta."

Foyle was still packing his equipment but stopped and stood there with a deer in the headlights expression on his face. Finally he spoke up. "What kind of car did you say it was?"

"It's a lime green Ford Fiesta. Why?"

"I just remembered. That night, while I was taking in my drum set, I saw a greenish car. I'm not sure of the year, but it was a little green Ford. The passenger was a young woman. She got out of the car and took some bags out of the back. She and the driver, a guy, gave each other a big hug and then she walked right by me and went into the Lodge. I was late arriving and busy with my stuff and didn't give it a thought. I didn't remember until now. When you said green Fiesta, it came back."

"Was it Ginny?"

"I think so. I remember she worked at the Lodge last summer. She was carrying a computer bag and wearing a big back pack. She had enough stuff to be moving in."

Michael took out his phone and pulled up her picture. "Is this the same woman?"

Looking intently Foyle confirmed, "Yes, that's her. I remember her hair, and she was talking on her phone and she smiled at me as she went by. She had a great smile."

"How about the guy? What did he look like?"

"There were quite a few vehicles in the lot, and he stopped back by the fence. The light wasn't very good, but I could tell he was about her age, fairly tall, slender, dark hair."

Michael pulled up another picture. "Is this him?"

Foyle took the phone from Michael and stared at the picture of the driver's photo and license.

"Well?"

"I think that's him."

"Are you sure?"

"Pretty sure. I'd have to see him in person, but from the picture, I'd say 80 percent. Who is he?"

"An on-again, off-again boyfriend." Almost as an afterthought Michael asked, "Jerry, did you tear down your equipment and take it with you when you were done?"

"Yes, I had a club job the next night."

"Do you remember what time it was when you loaded your drum set into your van?"

"Well, we played until 11:00, I packed up, used the restroom, and then carried stuff to the van. It was probably 11:15 or so by the time I went outside."

"When you loaded your equipment, did you see the green Fiesta again?"

"No. There were a few vehicles still in the lot, but I didn't see the Fiesta."

Michael looked to his fellow musicians who had gathered. "Folks, you must not share this with anyone. It may be nothing or it may be something. But until we know more, don't say a word about this. Got it?"

As a chorus, they replied, "Got it." It was Foyle who gave him a poke. "Listen to you, Michael. The cool cat lawyer who plays piano."

***

It was a mild evening and as he pulled into his drive Michael decided to leave the venerable truck outside. Stepping up to the back door, he was surprised to find it unlocked. "Huh, I must be getting senile."

Stepping inside, he paused. It was a feeling, a nameless unease that something was about to happen. He heard nothing other than the family grandfather clock ticking through the darkness. Flicking on the kitchen light, everything appeared in place. He stood still, waiting. There was no sound, no movement, nothing to validate his sense that there was a threat. "I must be getting senile and paranoid."

Throwing his keys into the whatever bowl by the back door he headed for the stairs. He froze when he heard a whisper, "Michael!"

He turned, but not soon enough. The blow staggered him; he tasted blood and his vision blurred. Defenseless, the second blow drove him to his knees. Barely conscious, he tried to raise an arm for protection, but the effort was too great, and he fell to the floor.

He didn't know how long he was out. As he came to, his head was spinning and he felt nauseated. The first thing that came into his head was "Mack the Knife." They had played Stan's new arrangement and the introductory bars sounded repeatedly in his brain. He was on his back, staring at the ceiling. His head felt like a gong that someone was pounding with a giant beater. Still in shock, the next thing he thought was, "It really smells bad in here. I've got to call my house cleaner."

Struggling to his feet, he staggered to the first floor bathroom. It was a nasty reflection that looked back at him in the mirror. "No wonder it hurts."

Carefully washing the blood from his face, he could see the swelling and purple discoloration already at play. Taking a hand towel from the linen closet, he stumbled his way back to the kitchen. Placing a hand on the refrigerator to steady himself, he opened the freezer door and took out a handful of ice cubes. Wrapping them up in the towel, he gingerly placed the make-do cold pack against the side of his head. The pain was sharp, but he held it in place.

He needed help but stubbornly deferred. "First, let's see if anything's missing, then I'll go to the ER. I can call the sheriff's office from there." Michael lost track of time as he lurched about the place. It was illogical, but in his muddled state he thought it necessary. The effort was fruitless.

Finally conceding the greater need for medical aid, he retrieved his keys, then stopped. He was certain he was alone in the house, but if someone was bold enough to attack him in his home, they may be bold enough to hang around outside. He dialed the sheriff's office.

"Dickinson County Sheriff's Office, Dispatcher Fridlay speaking. How may I help you?"

***

By the time Michael had come to and began to bumble about the house, the intruder was far away and dialing a number on a burner phone. The recipient answered on the first ring and immediately asked, "How did it go?"

"Not the best."

"What happened?"

"Cain came home early. I had to get out before I was done."

"Did you learn anything?"

"Yeah. Mr. Cain is fussy. He picks up his clothes, washes the dishes, and doesn't leave reports out for anyone to read. He also has good security on his computer. Even with more time, there was no way I'd get past the encryption."

"You didn't leave any trace that you'd been there, did you?"

"Well, not exactly."

"What do you mean?"

"Let's just say I gave Mr. Cain a welcome home greeting."

"What?"

"I slugged him twice. It felt good."

There was silence, then, "Did he see you?"

"Not a chance. All he saw were stars."

There was irritation in his response. "We don't need the extra attention this will bring. Stay away from Mr. Cain."

"Whatever you say. I've had enough entertainment, for now. You know how to reach me."

After the disconnection and in spite of his bravura, the caller felt slightly less confident than he had expressed. "I wonder why he turned just before I hit him? I don't think he saw me. Besides, he probably has a concussion. He's not going to remember much. Still— maybe, just maybe, I should do a little investigating of my own."

We are hard pressed on every side, but not crushed; perplexed, but not in despair... struck down, but not destroyed.

2 Corinthians 4:8

Michael lay there, opened his left eye, and then tried to open the right, as he attempted to focus on a box with blinking bright numbers.

"Wake up, sleepy head." It was Janni, and as he turned his head toward her, pain and vertigo reminded him of the previous night's event.

"What day is this?"

"Tuesday."

"What time is it?"

"7:30. I got the call from Connie and needed to see for myself how you're doing. If you're trying to impress a gal by looking tough, mission accomplished."

"Thanks. Do you know what the doctor had to say?"

"She's right here. Ask her yourself."

Michael slowly turned his head to see a smiling Dr. Harding.

"I'll leave you to the good doctor. I'll be back in a bit," Janni said, stepping out of the room.

"Michael, you may have a mild concussion, nothing serious, and in a day or two you should be up and about. The bruising around your eye looks worse than it is. We do want to keep you another day for observation. If you're a good patient, you may be out by some-time tomorrow."

"I need to get home to see if anything is missing."

"No, I'm keeping you here for another day at least. Dr. Hunter stopped in earlier and agreed—the only way we can be sure you'll follow the doctor's orders is to keep you here."

Dr. Harding checked Michael's vitals, typed something into his chart, smiled, and placed a hand on his shoulder, "You'll have some discomfort for a few days, but you'll be fine."

When Janneke returned, Michael was sitting up with an ice pack against his face, looking pale, bruised, and annoyed. "I was careless. I should have taken the sabotage to the gas tanks seriously."

"What sabotage to gas tanks?"

"Never mind. I need to go home. I want to check what was taken and I need to talk to Connie. Get the doctor back here, please."

"No can do, hotshot. For now you stay in limbo. You can't go in your house anyway. The police have it taped off and the crime lab is at work."

"The crime lab? For a mugging and breaking and entering?"

"Connie said that until they determine what happened, they're treating it as part of the Lawery investigation. Let them do their job, Michael. Your job is to rest. Connie said he'd come by later to fill you in. Someone will want to question you again anyway. I under-stand you were less than coherent when they brought you in to the ER last night. Something about someone whispering your name and that you saw him. They asked you if you got a good look at the attacker and you said, 'No, I saw *him*.' Pretty Twilight Zone if you ask me."

"I don't remember. It's all fuzzy."

"Dr. Harding said that should be expected but that it would clear up in a day or two. Do you remember our lunch yesterday?"

Michael smiled. "That I remember."

"Good! Now, I have to go to work, but I'll be back to see you later. Be a good boy. The folks are here to help. They're not the bad guys. Oh! And Luke says, 'Hi' and 'It's a good thing you're so hard-headed.'"

"He's one to talk."

"Yes, well…later. Behave, Michael."

Lightly kissing the unbruised side of his forehead, she squeezed his arm and as she walked toward the door, turned back just long enough to flash a smile at him.

***

It had been a very long day for Connie and Detective Donahue. They received the call around midnight. Both went first to Michael's home, then the hospital for an interview in the ER (brief due to Michael's confusion), and returned to Michael's home to meet with the crime scene people. In the morning, Donahue reinterviewed Michael. About the same time, a call came in to the sheriff's office from Alice Erickson, Sally Grosfeldt's mother. She said simply, "Sally wishes to volunteer additional information which may be helpful to the Lawery investigation."

***

That afternoon, Sheriff Conrad watched from the other side of the one-way window as the interview unfolded.

"The time is 3:45 PM, Tuesday, May 10. Those present include Sally Grosfeldt, her mother Alice Erickson, their attorney Ron Stafford, my assistant Pam Schneider, and I am Detective Jack Donahue of the Dickinson County Sheriff's Office. Mrs. Erickson called the courthouse at 10:00 AM today to say her daughter wanted to make a statement. Sally, I understand you have information that is an addition to what you've told us in prior interviews. Would you like to start?"

But it was Sally's mother who spoke first. "Before we begin, I want it clearly understood that no information was knowingly withheld to impede any investigation. With the exception of when Virginia Lawery first went missing, all interviews have been about the attack on my daughter and the burglary of her apartment. After several conversations between Sally and me, Sally decided her attack and Ginny's disappearance must be connected in some way. With that in mind, she has agreed to volunteer additional information that you may or may not already know but, if not, might still find useful. Also, please remember that her reluctance to come forth with this information was influenced by a desire not to say anything that someone might distort or use to damage Ginny's reputation. Understood?"

"Yes."

"In that case, go ahead, Sally."

With that, Sally took a big breath and began, "I didn't think it was important before, but when we got back to school this fall, Ginny was different."

"Different? Different in what way?"

"I don't know, just different. She was still Ginny—a good student, happy—but social, very social."

"How so?"

"Well, she always enjoyed her friends but usually as a group. She still had lots of friends, and we still went out together, but this fall she seemed to have more relationships—a lot more. It wasn't like her."

"What kind of relationships?"

"I'm not sure."

"Was she sleeping with anyone?"

"Well, maybe. Not everyone, but I thought maybe some of them. I don't think she was serious about any of them."

"Why?"

"She would only go out with them a few times then drop them. Some were really interested in her, but she made it clear she wasn't interested in anything permanent."

"What about her ex-boyfriend, Grant Laxton? What can you tell us about him?"

"Well, I'm sure you must know, there was a big blow-up with him last summer."

"What was it over?"

"Jealousy. He was overly possessive. Anytime anyone else showed interest in Ginny, he had a meltdown. Finally, she had had enough. She told him it was over, that it had been for some time, and to stay out of her life. After that, he was devastated. I felt sorry for him and we started talking. I saw a side of him I hadn't seen before."

"Like what?"

"I don't know. I guess I thought he was sweet. He's good looking and can be charming if he wants to. And I hear his family's loaded."

"How would you describe your relationship with Mr. Laxton?"

"We're not in a relationship."

"Did you sleep with him?"

"Well, yes...I slept with him, but Ginny didn't care."

"She didn't?"

"No. I think she felt sorry for him."

"What did Ginny say about you sleeping with her ex?"

"I told her I liked him, and reminded her she didn't want him. And she said, 'It's ok with me, but be careful. He may be trying to get back at me, and he may want to hurt both of us.'"

"Why would he want to hurt you?"

"She said he knew that she and I were close friends, that we told each other everything, and that made him jealous. He didn't want anyone to be closer to her than he could be. Ginny said he might use me to get to her and hurt us both. I told her she didn't have to worry. I wouldn't let that happen, and I could take care of myself, but…she was right."

"Why? What happened?"

"Grant and I were in bed in his room at the Lodge. I told him I thought I might be falling in love with him. He seemed pleased, he even blushed a little and said he wanted me to know I was important to him. And then I told him something I shouldn't have. I told him I didn't agree with Ginny. He asked me what that meant, and I told him Ginny thought he was bad for me and wanted to hurt us both.

"He went ballistic. He was furious. I thought he was going to hit me. He wouldn't calm down. He jumped out of bed and paced the floor yelling, waving his arms. I got up, pulled on some clothes, and then the phone rang, and he grabbed it and threw it across the room."

"What was he yelling about?"

"He said I took advantage of him and used him. It was all Ginny's fault. There was something wrong with her and with me, too. He was the only man for Ginny. She just didn't get it, but she would and so would I. He'd get us both. He said, 'You're both dead meat!'"

"Did he physically attack you?"

"No, but I was afraid he would and not let me go. Then someone began banging on the door telling us to stop making so much noise. I ran for the door and got out before he could come around the bed to stop me. I ran down the hall as fast as I could. He didn't chase me but kept yelling about us, over and over. If someone hadn't knocked on the door and if I hadn't been able to run out, anything could've happened. I might not be here!"

"Do you remember who knocked on the door?"

"Yes, but I didn't know them. They were from the night cleaning crew. I ran by so fast I didn't even look at their faces. There were two of them, both men, and I think that's why Grant didn't chase me."

"What did you do next?"

"I went back to my room. I was awake all night, crying and talking to Ginny. I was sick with worry. The next morning we got ready for work as usual and went to breakfast. Ginny insisted that I had to face him and take back control. I didn't want to. I couldn't have done it without her. She's so strong." Lowering her head, she corrected herself. "Was so strong. But when we got to breakfast everyone was talking excitedly. Grant had been fired and already escorted off the grounds by a sheriff's deputy. That was the last we saw of him until we returned to ISU in the fall."

"Is that everything from last summer?"

"Pretty much. We had six weeks left and everything was normal. We finished up, said goodbye, and then met back at school a week later."

"How did Ginny act after Laxton was fired?"

"I think she was relieved. She regained her usual enthusiasm and really got into the business at the Lodge."

"What business?"

"I know she had an interview with the manager, Mr. Sandoval, and he sent her to his wife for another interview. I think they recognized her talents and wanted to mentor her. She talked about possibly interning in the business office. Mrs. Sandoval spent quite a bit of time helping her understand the financial and personnel parts of the business. Ginny was really excited. She even talked about adding to her business major to include a minor in hospitality."

"That matches up with what we've learned. What happened with Laxton in the fall?"

With a big sigh of resignation, she admitted, "He ignored me. When I saw him he wouldn't talk or even look at me. Frankly, I was glad. But he kept harassing Ginny and calling, sometimes late at night, but Ginny wouldn't pick up. He'd leave a voicemail but she'd just delete it. Other times he'd be standing outside our window, and once he sent flowers, roses and lilies. You'd think he'd just send roses. They came with a card, and he wrote the roses were for when they first met and the lilies for when their love died. It was creepy."

"How did Ginny react?"

"She insisted he was harmless and said he had enough problems without her making it worse. Typical Ginny, being more concerned about someone else than herself."

"Ginny said he had problems. Do you know what kind of problems?"

"You mean besides being a head case? He was a boozer and sometimes a druggie. I heard he was into a little cocaine. It's pretty easy to score drugs on campus. When he was using, he was calm, but when he got on the booze or if he hadn't had anything for a while, he became mean, bad-mouthed people, including his profs, and got into fights. He almost got kicked out of school last fall, but except for harassing Ginny, he must have cleaned up his act or at least stayed out of trouble until about the time Ginny went missing."

"Why, what happened then?"

"I think he lost it and got into more trouble, because I heard he's not at school anymore."

"When was the last time you saw or heard from him?"

"The day Ginny left for Okoboji."

"The same day she went home to take care of something she said was important?"

"Yes, I saw him that afternoon."

"What did he say?"

"It was early afternoon; I was reviewing notes for my 2:00 class. I opened the door, and there he was. He insisted he had to see Ginny. I told him right away she wasn't there, and he called me a liar and demanded to see her. He was a mess. I could smell the booze, he was swaying back and forth, his eyes were all bloodshot, and his nose was runny—he kept wiping it on his sleeve. I told him she didn't want to see him, and I was going to call the police if he didn't leave. I started to shut the door, but he jammed it with his foot. So I told him she had gone to Okoboji to see her aunts. He stepped back from the door, and I slammed it shut and locked it. I could hear him breathing on the other side—I think he was crying. Then he hit the door hard once and said, 'You're a lying bitch! You'll be sorry. You're both dead meat.' And he left."

"And you haven't seen or heard from or of him since?"

"Not a word, nothing. He just vanished."

"Is there anything else you want to add?"

"No, I don't think so. I'm sorry I didn't talk about this before. I really didn't think it was important, and I didn't want to get anyone in trouble. Laxton's a jerk, but I just couldn't believe he would do something this terrible. I guess I was wrong."

"So you think he harmed Ginny?"

"Who else had a reason to hurt her? Everyone liked or even loved her. I tried to warn her. He terrified me, but she wouldn't listen. She kept saying it would be alright. So like Ginny!"

"Okay. I think that's enough for now. I have to say it would've saved us time and effort if you'd mentioned this before."

"I'm sorry. After I was attacked, the attack was all I could think about."

Detective Donahue asked, "Anyone else have a question or anything to add?"

Only Pam spoke up. "Sally, this is so very helpful. It took a lot of courage for you to voluntarily come forward. We know you were trying to protect your friend. Before we stop, can you tell us if Ginny had any other relationships during the summer?"

"No, not really. There was a guy who hung around. She called him Harold, though everyone else called him Dum Dum. But she was just being nice to him, I wouldn't call it a real friendship."

"What would you call it?"

"A lost kitten."

30

"How's he doing?" Connie asked as he walked into Michael's room a few minutes before visiting hours ended. Janneke was seated on the edge of the bed, reading something from the local newspaper aloud to Michael.

She stopped to say, "Oh! Hi, Connie. He's better."

Michael peered around Janneke. "Hey, Connie."

When questioned the night before, Michael had been irrational. Detective Donahue had returned the next morning for what he hoped to be a more cogent interview. Michael's head had cleared somewhat, and he had remembered that Foyle had identified Ginny and her ex-boyfriend. "Foyle said he was unloading his drum set and saw them arrive together in a little green Ford. He didn't know if they left together but the car wasn't there when he reloaded his drum set around 11:15."

Unfortunately, Michael recalled nothing more of the mugging. In turn, Detective Donahue reported that nothing from Michael's home seemed to be missing or damaged.

Donahue went on to explain, "You'll have to determine whether anything was taken. I'd like to meet you at your home when you leave the hospital and have you walk me through events beginning when you first pulled into the driveway. Right now your house is taped off as a crime scene, but once we go through it and the grounds together, assuming we find nothing relevant, we can take the tape down."

Between naps and short visits from Father Barney, Madge, and Janni, Michael had reviewed the previous night repeatedly in his mind. Now that Connie had returned, he was eager to learn of any new developments.

"You know, Michael, if you got an eye patch to go with that bandage around your head, you could pass as a pirate. That may be the biggest black eye I've ever seen."

"Thanks for the observation. I've always liked pirate movies. I'm a lot better than last night and Dr. Harding said I should be dismissed tomorrow."

Connie went on. "That's good news. In the meantime, take the opportunity to get a good night's sleep."

"In a hospital?"

"Grumpy much? You must be feeling better."

Brushing off Connie's jab, Michael asked, "How's the investigation going?"

"Which one? Nothing more on your assault, but it's been a big day for the Virginia Lawery investigation. I thought I'd stop by and fill you in personally. I think we're closing in on the little bastard—pardon my French, Janni."

"I may, but if Madge was here she might not."

"You're right." It was well known by family and friends that the standard in the Conrad family was the mantra: "What would Madge say?"

Janni stood and placed the folded newspaper on the nightstand by Michael's bed. "I'd better get going and let you guys visit. Michael, call me in the morning, and let me know what time you'll be dismissed. I'll pick you up."

"No, I can drive myself home."

"That might be difficult without a vehicle."

Recalling his transport from the night before, Michael replied rather sheepishly, "Oh, yeah. I forgot."

"Good! It's settled. Call me."

"Thanks, Janni."

With a peck on the unblemished side of his face, Janni smiled and turned to go. "Bye, Connie."

"Bye, Janni."

They both watched as she walked out the door. Connie cocked his head and gave Michael a curious look.

"What?"

"I was just thinking, that's quite a woman. I don't mean to sound critical, Michael, but you may have let your best gal get away."

"That's a discussion for another day. Tell me what you learned."

"My, you *are* grumpy. Well, your suggestion to check with area newspapers paid off. The Storm Lake newspaper listed under the Patrol and Courts Report that police responded to a call for assistance from the hospital due to a man who was out of control. They identified the man as Grant Laxton. Laxton was subdued then admitted to the hospital for observation. We don't know the time he was admitted. It could've been any time past midnight Friday—the same Friday Ginny left ISU. There was no dismissal reported. Milo's intern may be on the ball after all. She called the newspaper and asked why the admittance was listed but not the dismissal. She was told it was part of a police patrol report and not a hospital admittance or dismissal report.

Michael was listening intently. "So the admittance was published as part of the police report and there was nothing about the dismissal."

"That seems to be the case."

"That would fit the time frame, assuming it began earlier that Friday."

"I've asked the good folks at the Storm Lake Police Department to check to see if they can learn any more about what happened. If it warrants, I'll have one of my detectives go to Storm Lake."

"Remind your detective to tell whoever he speaks to that this is an investigation into a possible homicide. Since the police report is public anyway, they should be willing to cooperate."

"I'll do that. Now as promising as that may be, here's the big news. Alice Erickson called and Sally voluntarily came in today for a second interview. Sally was holding out on us, but claimed she was trying to protect Ginny. She had a lot to say about what happened between her and Laxton and between Laxton and Ginny. The guy must have serious problems. Anyway, rather than explain it all, I come bearing a gift."

With that, Connie pulled a laptop out of the bag he had with him. "The interview is loaded onto the computer. Everything we learned seems to incriminate this guy. We'll wait until after we hear from the police and hospital in Storm Lake, but I think we have enough for the county attorney to get a subpoena to interview the kid."

"He's not a kid—he's of legal age and he does have rights. It's the county attorney we need to convince."

Connie's face clouded. "As you said, this is a murder case. That should mean something."

"Not necessarily. It may work against us. We need to clearly show probable cause or our request may be considered a fishing expedition and refused. Did you bring the DCI up to speed with this latest information?"

"Yes, and after you told Detective Donahue this morning what Jerry Foyle had to say after you showed him Laxton's picture, Donahue talked to Foyle. He confirmed what he told you, that he was 80 percent sure it was Laxton he saw driving Ginny's car the night she went missing."

"Yeah, I was still a little confused this morning but I definitely remembered talking to Foyle." Michael tipped his head back, looked up at the ceiling, and uttered, "Ha!"

"Ha, what?" asked Connie.

Michael returned his gaze to Connie. "Under certain circumstances, if there is probable cause and a person is a necessary material witness, the Iowa code does allow us to arrest that person as a material witness with or without an arrest warrant. We may have a better chance of getting to Laxton using that approach. Talk to the county attorney and see if he agrees."

The PA system's computerized voice declared it was time for visitors to leave. Walking to the door, Connie spoke over his shoulder, "Don't stay awake all night with that laptop. Get some rest. We'll talk again tomorrow."

Pausing at the door he turned to add, "Before I forget, I spoke with Officer Piccard and he agreed we'd reschedule our meeting when you've recovered."

"I forgot all about that. Thank you, Connie."

"You're welcome. See you tomorrow."

As Michael was opening the interview file on the laptop, his evening nurse came in for a brief check. "Is there anything I can get you? Do you need more water?"

"No, I'm fine as long as I don't have to take another one of those horse pills."

Nurse Natalie smiled, "Two more before bed time and then you should be done with the supersized Tylenol until morning. Let me do a quick check of your pulse and blood pressure."

After she was done, she hung the blood pressure cuff back in place and reported, "122 over 78. That's very good."

"Thank you."

With a tilt of her head she went on, "You must be a popular fellow."

Rather surprised Michael asked, "What do you mean?"

"Well, you've been here one day and received a plant, an arrangement of flowers, several calls, and visits from two lovely women, a priest, a detective, the sheriff, and one biker-type character."

With a frown Michael asked, "What biker-type character?"

"The one with the leather jacket. He stopped at the nurse station around 3:00, during shift change. I was coming on the floor and saw him talking to the charge nurse."

"Who was he and what did he want?"

"I asked about him but the charge nurse said she didn't know who he was and he didn't give his name. When I asked what he wanted, she said he wanted to know how you were. He said he was a friend and had called, but was told that information couldn't be shared over the phone. He told her he didn't have time to visit but just wanted to stop by to check on you. It was odd."

"Why?"

"If he had called, they would have transferred the call to your room."

"Did you get a good look at him?"

"Yes and no. Besides his jacket, he wore a sweatshirt with the hood up. He had on an old cap pulled down over his forehead, and wore gloves and dark glasses. I noticed he smelled musty, too."

"If you saw him again, would you recognize him?"

"I'm not sure. Is it important?"

Michael said, "Probably not but I would like to find out who he is and speak to him. I know that the hospital has security cameras. Could I arrange to see the video for this floor and the entrances?"

Natalie smiled and said, "OK. I'll be right back with the Tylenol and then I'll check on the videos for you. In the meantime, if you need anything else, just push the call button."

31

It was shortly after 10:00 AM when Janneke dropped Michael off at home. "Good grief! Do you think they used enough police tape?" The house, garage, grounds and drive were all bordered by tape. "I'm sorry I can't stay to help unwrap your house, but I have a meeting in fifteen minutes. But Detective Donahue is here—he can help."

Getting the hint and eager to inspect his home, Michael gave her a quick hug. "Thanks, Janni. I'll call this evening to let you know what we do or don't find."

The inspection of the house and grounds revealed nothing missing nor was anything out of place other than what the crime scene investigators moved. There remained traces of fingerprint powder and a residue of something on the floor that Michael didn't recognize. For all that, the team had done a good job of picking up after themselves.

Michael didn't expect anything to be stolen. There could be several reasons why someone would want to attack him, but it was more likely he interrupted someone who meant to gain information. That information was likely related to the Lawery investigation.

The detective thanked him, gave him his card with the request that Michael call if he discovered something was missing, and drove off with a trunk full of used police tape. Finally, Michael was home and had the place to himself.

He ground some coffee beans, filled the water reservoir, and pushed start. While the coffee brewed he took another slow walk around the inside of the house but found nothing different from the inspection with Detective Donahue. All his notes were safely locked away where he'd left them, and the computer keyboard was coated with a light remnant of powder.

He intended to check the computer but instead filled a cup with coffee and made his way to his father's old leather recliner. Michael's early morning call for a warrant had resulted in a copy of the requested security video. Placing the flash drive into Connie's laptop computer, he opened the drive and hit play.

After repeatedly watching the visitor at the nurses' station, he used the time stamp to focus on videos of the entrance and parking lot. His "friend" was shown talking to the charge nurse and arriving then departing the hospital, but he found no more details than those described by Nurse Natalie. Michael's brief conversation with the charge nurse only confirmed what Natalie had observed.

The video of the parking lot did capture the visitor walking across the lot, but if he was parked nearby, it was outside the parameters of the security cameras. There was something about the figure's appearance that tugged at a corner of Michael's memory, but despite further repetitions, it remained elusive.

***

In Michael's dream he was with his grandfather. It was nighttime, and they were out on the lawn with a flashlight and coffee can hunting night crawlers. It seemed so real. He could feel the squishy reluctant crawlers as he plucked them from the ground. He heard his grandfather's hushed voice cautioning him, "Don't pull too hard or you'll tear them apart." He could see the muted light from the flashlight, its lens covered with his grandfather's linen handkerchief. They stepped softly across the lawn, but no matter how hard he tried, there was noise. "Shhh. Be quiet."

And then he awoke with a start. "Shhh. Be quiet." But this time it was his voice and the noise was the mobile phone resting on the end table by the recliner. As he groped for the phone, he could still smell the hint of something like mulch or freshly turned earth.

It was Connie. "Are you OK? I tried calling your landline earlier. I thought you were home."

"I am. I fell asleep and was having the craziest dream."

"I'm sorry to wake you, but I have some news you'll want to hear."

"Hang on, Connie. Let me go to my desk." There was a pause and then he said, "I'm ready. What's up?"

***

Connie had decided that it was worth the time for Detective Donahue to interview witnesses at the hospital and police department in Storm Lake. "It paid off big-time, Michael." Connie's appraisal was an understatement. Using the detective's notes and his own, Connie related in detail what they'd learned.

"We now know that on Friday night, Laxton was traveling on Highway 71. His car was low on gas so he attempted to drive into Storm Lake. He ran out of gas about a mile outside of town. It was cold, the wind was blowing hard, and all he had on was a sweatshirt

—no gloves, no coat, no cap, no boots. He made it as far as the ceme-tery on the edge of town when some guy driving by spotted him stag-gering down the street and picked him up. This was sometime between 1:00 and 2:00 AM.

"Laxton insisted all he needed was gas, but the driver could see he was confused and might have frostbite. He promised to get him gas if he would go to the hospital and be checked out.

"The hospital ER folks told Laxton he needed care and should be admitted. The kid tried to leave, but the guy who brought him in was gone. They found out later the good Samaritan had been drinking and didn't want to stick around to answer questions.

"Laxton had a meltdown. He became violent, and they had to call the police for assistance. After he calmed down, he started to cry uncontrollably. They finally got out of him that he had a sister and brother-in-law in Storm Lake. He didn't want them called because of his brother-in-law. I quote: 'Don't call them. I don't want that ass-hole coming over here.' Unquote."

Connie continued. "The sister and brother-in-law were notified and while the brother-in-law remained at home and attempted to reach Laxton's parents, the sister came to the hospital. She talked at some length with Laxton and finally convinced him that it was too late to retrieve his car and that he should remain in the hospital for observation. He was admitted and remained in the hospital for two days, ostensibly for frostbite, and then released to his parents. We understand they took him directly to rehab, but we don't know where.

"When it came out that Ginny was missing, his parents did what they could to prevent anyone from questioning him without their per-mission or the lawyer present. The folks at the hospital said he was a big mess, very upset, and he did have a minor procedure for frost-bite on his ears and his fingertips.

"There's more. The family had a towing company put gas in the car and drive it to the brother-in-law's warehouse. We understand he owns a music store and the warehouse is part of his business."

There was a pause and Michael took that as an opportunity to ask questions.

"Do we have access to the car?"

"We do now. When I told the Palo Alto County Attorney and the judge this was a murder investigation and explained why the boyfriend was the prime suspect, they were helpful. We were granted a warrant to seize and search the car. We already have crime scene tape up, an officer on site and, get this: a DCI Crime Scene Team is on its way to Storm Lake. They want to process the car where it sits and then transport it to Ankeny for impoundment in their lot. I might add, the kid's brother-in-law wants to cooperate but I don't think he's as concerned about the car as he is someone unauthorized having access to the warehouse."

"Wait until he and the rest of the family are charged for conspiracy to withhold evidence and impeding a felony investigation. Then he'll really have something to be concerned about. This could break the case wide open."

"I hope so. Everyone I've spoken to in Storm Lake has heard of the bizarre way Lawery was found and, except for Laxton's family, everyone's been willing to help."

"How soon will you hear from the crime scene team?"

"We may have a preliminary report as early as tomorrow."

"Connie, if they find something incriminating that can be added to everything else that we've learned, we may be that much closer to a subpoena. Just the threat of a subpoena might be enough to persuade the family it could be of benefit to their son to voluntarily answer our questions."

"Okay, we'll talk to the parents and their lawyer. But if that doesn't work, and even if nothing additional is found in his car, I'm all for trying to force the issue."

"I want to be present when he's interviewed."

"This is still a joint investigation, so that may be up to the DCI. I'll let you know after we hear from the crime scene team. By the way, how're you doing?"

"Much better, thanks. My headache is gone and the good Dr. Harding gave me a clean bill of health. If I had a concussion, it was fairly mild. Tell Madge thank you for the visit and flowers. I'm sorry I was sleeping when she came by."

"That reminds me, Madge is bringing you supper. That will give you a chance to thank her yourself." There was a muffled voice in the background. "I'd better let you go. I've got an issue that just popped up that needs my attention."

By the time Michael visited with his sister and called Janni, he was exhausted. That night sleep came quickly, without any need of persuasion.

32

The next morning, Michael desperately wanted to call the sheriff's office, but stopped himself. This was the most trying part of an investigation—knowing something important was going down but that he could do nothing but wait. He did feel better physically—no headache, his black eye was turning a lovely green and yellow, and his bloodshot eye was less red.

He busied himself with a walk rather than a run, a light breakfast, and a short call from Madge. Afterwards he made a longer call to Pam to thank her for her help and confirm that he would speak to the class the next day.

Considering what he might do with the remainder of his morning, he recalled that during his visit with the Lawery sisters, they'd touched on the subject of old wooden boats. The Lawerys had a Garwood Commodore, a magnificent classic and a reminder for Michael that he had yet to retrieve his mother's Chris Craft Riviera from winter storage. The Riviera had been a gift from his late father to Michael's mother in celebration of their twenty-fifth wedding anniversary. Christened *Frau Nägel*, his father's pet name for Michael's mother, it was expected Michael would maintain the classic wooden runabout in pristine condition as a prerequisite for his taking over the family lakeside home.

Grabbing his phone and a fleece, he walked down to the dock and lowered his fishing boat from its lift. There was a light chop on the clear blue water, compliments of a westerly breeze. The old line "Wind from the west, fishing's the best" popped into his head, and he vaguely considered that this evening would be a good time to make up for the slow walleye opener.

He stepped into the boat, started the engine, and slowly backed away from the lift. Following the shore line, Michael crossed Fort Dodge Point, entered Smith's Bay and headed for East Okoboji. Passing below the Highway 71 bridge, he waved at some of the regulars fishing from the public dock and directed his boat toward Marv's Marina.

As he had expected, the inboard engine had been tuned and the boat prepared for the summer season. After a brief visit with the folks at Marv's, arrangements were made to have the boat delivered to his dock where it would repose in its own lift, opposite the fishing boat.

Slowly putt-putting his way back, he decided to stop for lunch at the funky old diner known as Five B's nestled on the hillside near the bridge. Tying up at the dock and climbing the stairs, he marveled at the lack of change in the place. It was an anachronism, stubbornly resisting the so-called progress that surrounded it. An old long out-of-use gas pump stood at the dock, its handle seized at 12:00 and its opaque globe dimmed by time, a stubborn icon of a simpler time and place.

The original Five B's had been named Billy's, but he had drunk all the profits. Billy was smart enough to know he couldn't run the business and drink, so he sold half-interest in the place to Betty, his most-of-the-time girlfriend. To Billy's chagrin, Betty changed the name to Bill and Betty's Beer, Bait, and Bagels, and converted the smelly old place into a nice breakfast and luncheon diner. It turned into a smashing success. It had a great location and was the only place on the lakes that served bagels, along with incredible cream cheese, the finest pork tenderloins in Northwest Iowa, and hash browns made from fresh potatoes with homemade gravy to die for, as well as still selling beer and bait to go. For Billy it was cause for another separation, except for booty calls.

Both Billy and Betty were retired, so their daughter Veronica was now the manager and ran a tight ship. Walking up to the counter, Michael was reminded of the cheap steak place where he used to eat in downtown Iowa City, a type of Greek eatery that had been mimicked in a comedic sketch on Saturday Night Live. There were, however, no Greeks in sight. Instead a young, blond, bearded man greeted him and took his order for a bagel, cream cheese and coffee.

Going to the opposite end of the counter, Michael paid for his order, poured a cup of coffee from the urn, and then selected a small table by one of the many south side windows. For the time being, he set aside the anticipation of Connie's update and simply enjoyed watching the variety of boats as they passed by.

"Hello, Michael. Here's your bagel and cream cheese."

Looking up he recognized his server. "Hey, Veronica. How are you?"

"I'm fine. Busier than a beaver in a lumberyard, but it's all good. Donnie got a new job that pays well, Katie's growing like a weed, business is booming, and mom and dad stay away."

"Speaking of, how are your folks?"

"Good. Billy stopped drinking about two years ago."

"AA?"

"No, he just stopped. I think he got tired of the hangovers, and mom told him to quit or die, meaning she was done with him for real. Kind of shook him up. Otherwise life is the same for them, unusual that is." It was a humorous statement considering Veronica and her companion of several years weren't married, shared a young daughter, and were known for their own prickly relationship.

"Are they married yet?"

"Ha! Good one. Last time I asked if they would ever get married mom said, 'Hell no, I'm not marrying that old fool!' Good to see ya, Michael. Gotta get back to work and set a good example for the employees, you know. Don't be a stranger."

Watching the manager's lovely beam sailing back to the kitchen, Michael took a sip of coffee, and on an impulse unrelated to the receding distraction, took out his phone and called the Aunties. The call went to voicemail and with it came a little disappointment. "Hello, Faethe? Hello, Hoepe? This is Michael Cain. I thought if you would be around this afternoon, I might stop over and give you an update on the case. Sorry to miss you. I'll try again later."

Within a breath, his ringtone sounded.

"Hello, Michael. This is Faethe. I'm sorry we didn't answer when you called, but we get so many computerized molestations that we've descended into the purgatory of screening our calls. We'd love to have you stop by anytime this afternoon. We'll have the coffee and cookies ready."

"Great! I'm coming by boat. See you in a bit."

Michael cruised his way back home. As he pulled into the slip he heard the deep rumble from the inboard of the *Frau Nägel*. Stepping onto the dock he admired the sleek eighteen-foot classic as it was slowly driven into its designated slip. Speaking aloud he announced to himself, "There's my ride to see the Aunties."

33

The visit with the Aunties proved to be more social than informative but obviously was appreciated by the sisters. It was a pleasant
distraction while waiting for Connie's call which, mercifully, came
later that same afternoon.

"The DCI Crime Scene Team found hair samples of at least two
different donors on the passenger's head rest. Preliminary says one
is a match to Virginia Lawery. They also found a blood sample and
semen. The car's less than a year old, but the interior is a mess. Food
containers, unpaid parking tickets, even a couple of condom wrappers. Kid didn't clean up anything."

"How did they determine it was Ginny's hair so quickly?"

"They came prepared. They brought hair and blood samples
from Ginny's autopsy and were able to offer, under duress I might
add, a preliminary statement to the effect that the hair sample was a
match to Ginny and the blood sample the correct type but would have
to be tested for DNA to be certain. The DCI lab will make this a priority and should have more definitive answers quickly. The car is

already on a flatbed truck on its way to Ankeny."

"That's encouraging. But you know as well as I do, that especially in a homicide, the evidence or possibility of evidence should be compelling before charges are made. It's a pretty high standard we need to meet."

"The evidence may be considered circumstantial at this time, but it is strong. Less than an hour ago, the DCI was granted a warrant to interview the boyfriend. His parents and lawyer could be notified as early as this evening. Since we don't really know where he is, we'll have to wait for their response. If it works out, a meeting may be set for as early as tomorrow."

"I want to sit in on the interview."

"I know. Michael, I'm sorry, but the DCI said no. They don't want any of what they referred to as 'further complications.' Detective Donahue will represent the county, and the DCI will share a copy of the unedited video of the interview. I made an argument on your behalf, but I don't always get to make the rules."

"That's disappointing, but understandable. I'll want to see the video as soon as I can."

"Of course and maybe you, Jack, and I can view it together. It will be helpful to hear Jack's opinion as to how it all went down."

"Connie, we're here on the ground in this investigation. I'd feel better if we could take a more active role."

"I know, but the DCI has been read into and kept up-to-date on all aspects of our investigation, and they'll do the same for us. I'm confident the interview will be done well. They may just be throwing us a bone, but they did promise if there was a need to do a follow-up interview, they would reconsider allowing you to observe."

"Well, that's something. You'll let me know ASAP what they learn?"

"Of course. The DCI wants this cleared up as much as we do.

The Lawery family is still remembered and respected, especially in northwest Iowa. There are important people who are pressing for a solution. That's something we can all appreciate."

"And we do. In the meantime, is there anything else we should be doing?"

"No, let's wait until after the interview. The looney factor of tourist season is already in full swing. My deputies have plenty to keep them busy. This may be a good time to update Hoepe and Faethe."

"Already done—they were encouraged by what progress we've made but felt bad that Sally was harmed."

"That sounds like them. They want justice but understand the implications." There was a drawn-out silence. "Michael! Are you there? Is it me or did you doze off?"

"Sorry. It's not you, it's me. I was thinking of what you said."

"What's that?"

"About the Lawerys. It's just an impression I had after speaking with them this afternoon. Given the chance, I think the Aunties would prefer to execute justice on their own terms."

***

After an early supper of Madge's leftovers, Michael sat himself before his computer with a dose of Glennfidich at hand—his first taste since the attack—and began a meticulous review of his notes and the case file. He was hopeful the investigation would conclude with the interview of Grant Laxton. He had no reason to doubt the subject's guilt. The guy was unstable, used drugs, had a history of violence against women, and threatened Ginny and Sally at least twice. Those interviewed who had more than a passing knowledge agreed: if angry, he was capable of seriously harming another and, a few thought, even of murder. Michael did wonder, however, why

Ginny hadn't shared their opinion.

Laxton had motive, means, and opportunity, and fit the possible time frame. Somehow, it almost seemed too easy. The theory was sound on the face of it, but were they putting it all on the boyfriend and ignoring other possibilities? If so, what other possibilities? Even if they were, Michael understood that if you mixed anger, drugs, and booze with Laxton's proclivity for violence anything could happen, even murder.

34

The final day of class was a necessary deflection for Michael from the recent intensity of the Lawery investigation. Most students did well on the semester exams and everyone completed their assigned projects. Michael found it strangely fulfilling to know he had a part in their success. He spent as much time as needed answering questions, passed out what he characterized as his personal evaluation with suggestions for each student, and they in turn filled out course and instructor evaluations. Finally, he thanked them, and Pam announced that she and Michael would be available in their offices from 1:00 to 3:00 for any further questions or considerations.

The first text from Connie came early: "The warrant was executed late yesterday and the interview is arranged to take place this morning. The kid's in a locked-down, ultra private rehab facility in Iowa City. Jack drove down last night. Now you know what I know."

As he sat in his office, Michael was in high spirits. His first excursion into teaching had been rewarding. His help on the Lawery case had led to the long-sought interrogation of the ex-boyfriend.

The doubts of the previous evening dissipated like the early morning's mist over the lake. Justice would be served.

Connie's second text pinged on Michael's phone at 2:50 PM. The cryptic message said: "Call me!"

It took a great deal of self-control but Michael waited. At 3:01 he closed his office door and called Connie.

"The kid didn't do it."

There was stunned silence until Michael asked, "What happened?"

"Laxton never made it to Okoboji. He only got as far as Storm Lake. Jack is on his way back with the video, and I have the updated report from the DCI lab. Let's meet here at the sheriff's office in the courthouse this evening, say at 7:00?"

***

The long-sought interview with Grant Laxton was informative but a big disappointment to the investigation. Laxton insisted he was forthcoming about everything concerning Ginny. He could afford to be. She was dead and couldn't contradict him. But the answers he gave were easy to check and quickly confirmed. Laxton's alibi also was supported by the latest results from the crime lab. The DCI investigators concluded that while Laxton remained a person of interest, he was no longer the prime suspect in the investigation.

Detective Donahue just made it to the courthouse by 7:00. Connie and Michael were waiting for him, eager to view the video. Prior to that, they reviewed the latest report from the DCI crime lab, and Detective Donahue shared his opinion that there was nothing to suggest Laxton had hired someone to hurt Ginny. "In fact, Laxton's state of mind at the time appears to have rendered him incapable of conceiving anything that complex."

Donahue explained that from his threat to Sally until his hospital admittance, there was sufficient time for Laxton to drive to Okoboji and back to Storm Lake. But, he went on to say, Laxton's car had been serviced a few days before his intended trip to find Ginny. The mileage on the receipt found in the car was compared to the odometer and the information confirmed with the dealer. The DCI lab had meticulously inspected the car's computer and components finding no manipulation of the car's data.

Donahue summarized, "There weren't enough miles recorded for him to have driven from Ames to Okoboji and back to Storm Lake. There were only enough miles to have gone from Ames to Storm Lake."

"If that isn't enough, it turns out Laxton and Lawery had the same blood type and the lab determined that the blood likely was his, although it'll be awhile before they have the DNA results. The sample was found on the driver's side, likely the result of a nose bleed, courtesy of Laxton's indulgence in nose candy. The sample contained traces of cocaine which matched blood drawn at the hospital at the time of his admission. By the way, the blood sample taken at the hospital also showed he was over the limit for alcohol."

"The semen was his, though the traces of a female donor weren't from Ginny—wrong blood type. The strand of Ginny's hair could've been there for months. There are still some loose ends to process, but DCI investigators have concluded that Laxton did not attack Ginny that night."

Looking to his associates, he asked, "Any questions?"

Connie shook his head no, and Michael answered, "Let's see the video before we ask questions."

"Okay. It's movie time."

In the video the kid was calm and articulate. He admitted he had been a mess and out of control. He claimed his trouble with Ginny was a symptom, not the cause.

He went on to say he was frustrated and delusional. He believed if he and Ginny had talked it all would be better. "I couldn't accept she really rejected me. I was out of my head. I thought at the time she even cared more about that goofy worm guy than me."

DCI agent Hitchcock looked intently at Laxton. "What worm guy?"

Laxton seemed mildly surprised. "You know, that goofy guy who helped deliver bait to the Sports Shop by the Lodge."

At this, Agent Hitchcock had deferred to Detective Donahue who continued the questioning. "You mean Jolly? Jolly Holiday?"

"No, not that bastard. I mean that Dum Dum kid."

"I know who he is. What did he have to do with Ginny's disappearance?"

"Nothing that I know of. I was out of my head. I was jealous of everyone who even talked to her."

Michael took notes throughout and at the end sat there shaking his head. "Why didn't the parents just tell us all this before? Why put up the barrier?"

It was Jack who responded. "We asked them that. They explained that at first they were trying to help him get clean. When they learned Ginny was missing, they weren't sure if he had hurt her or if there was anything to incriminate him. When they picked him up, the kid was practically incoherent and his recall was vague. At the time, even in his own mind, he wasn't sure what he'd done. So they got their lawyer involved. Ironic, but it was the DCI lab that cleared him. By the way, the kid's father is a piece of work."

Connie allowed a bit of parenthood to slip in, suggesting, "He was trying to protect his son."

"Maybe, but he was angry, and determined to get his way. It was like a sick competition. Another case of the fruit doesn't fall far from the tree."

It was quiet for a moment, then Connie went on to another point, "What about our eye witness?"

Exhibiting some discomfort, Michael replied, "That was my responsibility. It was a little questionable to begin with. I'll check with Foyle, but I think he made a good faith guess. Whomever he saw, it was not under the best of circumstances."

There was another pause, then Connie asked what was on all their minds. "Now what?"

Michael spoke for them all. "Now we review what we know and start over."

***

It was a subdued trio that departed from the courthouse. Connie had asked Jack and Michael to meet with him Monday to consider their next move and any tentative theories. "I'll get back to you about a time."

As Michael walked to his truck, Connie called out, "Wait up, Michael! I have a personal favor to ask."

35

The high school track field was not where Michael had envisioned himself spending his Saturday afternoon. After their meeting the evening before, Connie had explained that Detective Donahue and two of the deputies were given the weekend off and that Connie was helping to fill in on Saturday and Sunday.

"You can imagine, Madge isn't pleased. We can go to early mass on Sunday, but Saturday is the conference track meet. It's the last meet this year on the home field, and Jeremy is competing. This is a big thing to ask, but would you consider standing in for me? I know it would mean a lot to Madge and Jeremy."

"Of course I will. Anything to keep peace in the family."

"Great! If I can get away, I'll be there as soon as I can."

In spite of the cool, drizzly weather and the change in his weekend plans (though truth be told, he had none), he was enjoying the afternoon. Madge was happy he could be there, the competition was good, and he was impressed by his nephew's performance.

Jeremy placed third in the half-mile, second in the quarter-mile, and had taken his final turn in the broad jump. Between events Madge kept up a barrage of family and community gossip. It was of some relief to Michael when Madge shared, "I need another restroom break. Watch the kids, please."

Michael felt a little out of his element sitting there with his nephew and little niece, an unease compounded by the presence of Jeremy's girlfriend. When introduced he was gracious to her, but thought to himself, "Girlfriend? Jeremy's old enough for a steady girlfriend? Good Lord, I'm becoming more and more like my father."

He sat there looking over the crowd while trying to think of something vague to say when he was surprised to see Officer Richard Piccard, "Picky Dicky" himself, at the end of the row.

"Hello, everyone." Turning back to the group, Michael was pleased to see Connie approaching. "Business is slow so I was able to break away. I think the cooler weather helped. Dispatch will call if I'm needed. How're we doing?"

After Connie was caught up on the meet and how well Jeremy was doing, Michael pointed out to Connie, "I'm surprised to see Officer Piccard here at the meet."

Connie leaned forward to look past Michael. "I'm not. His son Jordan is on the same relay team as Jeremy. The kid's been in some scrapes since the divorce and Piccard has been trying to do the right thing, but it hasn't been easy. They're too much alike—hardheaded and apparently never make mistakes. Difficult to tell either of them what to do, although I have a good relationship with Piccard. We share problems in law enforcement, and we've had a couple of talks about families."

"I'm surprised to hear that…I mean the family part."

"I'm not saying Piccard doesn't deserve his reputation, but there's more to the man than most people know."

Michael looked over just in time to see Piccard glance his way and thought, "Well, he knows I'm here."

The final call for the 4x400 relay was announced and Jeremy took his place on the sidelines with the other members of the relay team. All seemed to be taking turns jumping up and down or pumping their legs in an effort to manage their nervous energy.

Michael saw Madge coming up the stairs as Connie turned to his little daughter who was telling him how well her big brother had done. Michael tapped Connie on the shoulder to get his attention. "Here comes Madge. I'll be back shortly."

As Michael approached him, without even looking up at him, Piccard spoke first. "What brings you here, Counselor?" Using the spirit towel provided by Madge, Michael wiped dry a place on the empty bench next to Piccard and sat down.

"Same as you, Officer—to cheer on the local team." Looking at the groups of relay participants waiting to take their places he asked, "Which one's your son?"

"The one who needs a haircut. He's standing by Coach Tingle."

Michael didn't know the coaches, but he spotted the burly young man standing next to a large man wearing a jacket with the home team's name emblazoned on the front. "The 4x400 isn't easy. He must be good if he's in this relay."

"He could be better. This is our compromise. Jordan agreed to go out for track if he only ran a relay. It was his way of being in control and getting me off his back. I spoke with the coach and Tingle was happy to put him on the 4x400." As the participants took their places, Michael found it interesting that rather than Jeremy being the anchor, he would run the first leg and Jordan would run the last, suggesting he was the strongest runner on the relay team.

The race began and the competition was keen and the pace fast. Jeremy had a perfect start and finished his leg of the race a good two meters ahead of the closest competitor. But by the time the baton was exchanged for the final leg, they were in third place—several yards behind the leader.

The handoff was clean and with the baton secure, Jordan blasted down the lane as if shot from a cannon. The crowd responded as one, suddenly jumping up and beginning to shout encouragement. The competition fell away as the young man's electrifying performance became the focus of the entire stadium. The transformation in Piccard was striking. He jumped up, yelling as Jordan hit a higher gear and blazed down the final one-hundred meters. The crowd's shouts rose to a roar as he came down the home stretch and thrust his upper torso across the finish line. The time on the clock was frozen at a full two seconds better than the conference record.

At the finish Piccard stood there pumping his fist, shouting "YES! YES! HELL…YES!" Michael was shocked when Piccard turned, pounded him with a double high five, then wrapped his powerful arms around him lifting him clear of the aisle. "That's my son! What a race! What a great team! If they can run like that, they'll win state!"

At that moment, Jordan looked up to the stands, saw his father, smiled and gave him a thumbs-up. Piccard responded with two big thumbs-up of his own and another fist pump. "Yeah!"

Michael would not have believed what followed if he hadn't seen it for himself. The lantern-jawed, hard-nosed conservation officer suddenly had tears running down his face. "Damn, I knew he was good. I didn't know he was that good." Finally regaining his composure and looking a little sheepish, a more subdued Piccard apologized, "Sorry, I got carried away."

"It's OK. It was a great race. You have a reason to be excited and proud."

With the excitement around them dying down, they took their seats and Michael decided to take a chance. "I want to apologize for not meeting with you Tuesday. I hope Connie explained why."

"He did, and it's fine."

"Would you mind if I asked you a few questions now?"

First pausing to release a tension-filled breath, Piccard replied, "Sure. Why not? What would you like to know?"

What started as Michael asking questions soon became a conversation.

***

According to Piccard, the biologist that called in the discovery was a recent hire named Nick Brauser. Brauser knew his business but had never heard of the Lawerys or Ginny. All three of the gill-netters had been shaken by the discovery, but Piccard could add nothing new to his observations of the night.

"How about the boat?"

"What about it?"

"Where is it now?"

"It was trailered back to the hatchery for storage. It's an older rig and doesn't get used much."

"Was it inspected by the crime scene folks?"

"I don't know if it was or not. I do know the boat with all the gear and the net is still sitting where we parked it the morning after. The quota for milt and eggs was filled by the next day, and there's been no reason to put the boat back into service, although that could change at any time."

Piccard also recounted that, at Connie's urging, he had put out the word to all bait and tackle shops as well as the Iowa Great Lakes Fishing Club to contact Sheriff Conrad if anyone had information that might help. Nothing came of it, but even that was meaningful.

After Michael's initial questions the discussion went beyond the events of the night Ginny was found. If the body was dumped before ice-out, how and where? If after ice-out, was there any suspicious activity reported? There wouldn't be a lot of boats out that early in the spring. Docks? No. Marina and homeowners had not begun the activity in earnest until after the walleye opener. It wasn't likely any-one would dispose of a body in daylight. Any boat launched in the daytime that early would draw attention. Lots of retirees who were fishermen rode their boats around the lake to check for remaining ice in the bays and canals. They would be interested in any signs related to fishing that seemed encouraging.

Michael asked why Weird Willy was in the picture, and Piccard explained that Willy was helping because he failed to remove his fishing shacks by the deadline set by the DNR. Piccard gave a short laugh and shook his head. "Willy thought since the season was extended, he was justified to extend it a little more. He provides guide service for the Lodge through the Sports Shop on an as-needed basis. It's a nice supplemental income, probably non-taxed, and he didn't want to screw up the deal.

"I threatened to ticket him for each of his six shacks and tell the Lodge, but Willy's a good worker and experienced waterman. I let him off with a warning provided he removed the shacks and volun-teered to help the hatchery with gillnetting."

"When did you warn him?"

"It was a Friday and, before you ask, it was the same Friday the Lawery girl was last seen."

"Did Willy remove his shacks right away?"

"I checked the following week, and there was one left. I went out to see if there was a problem—sometimes the shacks get buried in ice—and I caught Willy using it. You know what I thought was odd? I mean, I wasn't surprised that Willy would stretch things, but the shack I caught him using was over deep water. It was maybe okay for a passing school of perch earlier in the season, but not good late in the winter. I asked him what kind of fisherman would be out this deep, and you know what he said? He said I should keep an open mind. He said he hadn't used that shack since he last moved it and decided to try it himself before he took it in. He said that he had hooked a monster fish, and it broke his line. He lost one of his own handmade lures. I've seen his lures. They look like they'd really work at the right time and place. Anyway, he says that he tied on a second lure, dropped it in, and slowly jigged it up and down. He told me the damn fish took it and broke off again. He said the fish was heavy and had to be huge. It stayed on the bottom and he could hardly budge it. He thought maybe it was a catfish or record musky.

"I told him he was full of shit. He was fishing below the thermocline and nothing like that would be down there. It's a dead zone, no oxygen. I don't know if there was really a fish or if he was pulling my leg. He looked pretty relaxed, maybe under the influence. Anyway, we talked, confirmed we had a deal, I helped him free his shack from the ice, and that was the end of it."

"I read about the extended season and new deadline in the paper. Willy wouldn't have removed his shacks until nearly two weeks after the published deadline. As flagrant as it was, that was pretty generous of you."

"Yeah, well we were short-handed and this was an unusual winter. The week the shacks were originally supposed to be removed a huge Arctic cold front moved in and drove the ice down another good four inches. Because of that, the DNR decided to extend the time for fishing shacks. Willy just took advantage of the situation."

Both men were silent for a moment until a very interested Michael asked, "Where was the shack Willy was using?"

"Roughly two hundred yards west of Pillsbury Point. It's eighty feet deep there. Why? Is that important?"

"I don't know. Maybe. I'll let you know. I'd better have a talk with Willy."

"Well, I'll warn you—he won't like talking about that night, he was really spooked. But I'd recommend you talk to him anyway."

"Why's that?"

"Willy's good at three things—fishing, dumpster-diving, and gossip. We may disagree on the law, but we both enjoy fishing, and we like to talk about it. Don't quote me, but I've used him as a source of information. Lots of it's hearsay, but people tend to ignore him and say things around him they probably should keep to themselves."

"That's interesting, good to know."

With the track meet about to end, Michael stood up and retrieved the spirit towel. "I'd better get back to the family. Thank you for your time, Officer Piccard." Michael extended a hand, and Piccard stood and accepted the handshake.

"You're welcome. Let me know if you have more questions."

As Michael returned and took a seat beside him, Connie commented, "You and Picky looked pretty serious. What were you talking about?"

"I'll let you know. I need to check on something first."

Connie added, "I have an update about our Monday meeting. The DCI agent assigned to the Lawery case and I have a little online confab scheduled for Monday at 9:00 AM. Jack will be there and you're welcome to join us. You, Jack, and I will have our session after we speak with the DCI."

"Great! I'll be there."

"Thanks again for subbing this afternoon."

"My pleasure. I really enjoyed watching Jeremy and that 4x400 was outstanding."

As he made his way out of the stadium, Michael needed no notebook to remember: "Check boat and talk to Weird Willy."

36

It was a cautious Michael who unlocked the back door. With a hand on his Beretta he stepped inside and stood there listening. He hated that someone could, even temporarily, take over his sense of security. After a quick walk-through, the only disclosure was a blinking light on the answering machine. It was Janni. "Hellooo, Michael. I just had a fantastic day. The board approved all our recommendations to go forward with a charter and formally reorganize as an investment group focused on business in the Lakes region and...they appointed me board treasurer. I want to celebrate! I have a reservation at the Lodge for 8:00 tonight. Call me, ASAP. Oh, and Michael, you really need to turn on your phone. Good things happen when you do! Bye." Reaching into his jacket pocket he checked his phone—dead.

Michael was a social animal. Whether professionally or personally, he greatly enjoyed the company of others and they enjoyed him. It was out of character for him to avoid people, but since his return, with the exception of ILCC, Michael had acted more like an ascetic. He hadn't avoided dating, it simply didn't occur to him. Yet, gradually he was lowering his self-imposed barrier and re-entering the lives of some important people from his past and in turn, inviting them back into his life.

Teaching students at ILCC was acceptable; he could do it part-time, control the amount of interaction, and then retreat to his imagined invulnerability. Now he found himself thrust into a case that demanded justice, requiring him to use his knowledge, experience, and skills in a way that stirred his emotions and re-immersed him in this place and its people. It had awakened and reinstated something in him that had been suppressed for a long time.

***

As the host directed him to the booth in the far corner of the dining room, Michael had a strange sensation of déjà vu. He wondered if Janni noticed his arrival in the way he had when watching the approach of the divine Dr. Phillipa Goulet.

As good as the drinks and meal were, they weren't as pleasing as the time spent with Janni. There was much talk about family and business, and after coffee Michael found he didn't want the evening with this captivating woman to end so soon. "Why don't we go for a short walk along the shore?"

"That sounds lovely, Michael. Let me use the restroom and I'll be right back."

It was early spring, but to anyone watching, the chatty couple appeared to take no notice of the nighttime chill off the lake, absorbed as they were in each other. They walked, talked, and midway back stopped to admire the reflection of lights and listen to the gentle sound of waves on the beach below. Janni said, "So beautiful."

Looking at Janni rather than the water, Michael replied, "Yes, she is."

Turning, she smiled, leaning in to kiss him gently. As they separated, she looked into his eyes. He smiled and bent toward her again and they exchanged a lingering kiss that grew in ardor. As they resumed their walk, with Michael's arm around her, Janni looked down at the path and said, "You know Michael, there is something more that would make this night perfect."

***

"I feel like we're back in high school."

Janni smiled, "I feel like we never left." She had reserved the room when she had excused herself earlier. After a few fumbling efforts, what barrier remained between them was obliterated by their long-denied desire and the passionate joy of first love reignited. Later, with her head on his shoulder, the heat and perfume of their love about them, Janni noted, "You're quiet. What're you thinking?"

"I'm thinking I should've never let you go."

"Well, you have me now."

"I mean I should've married you."

Laughing gently, she responded, "Oh Michael, don't you know? I love you far too much to marry you."

Turning toward him, she pressed her naked body against his, kissed him lightly, and leaned back, smiling. Her eyes bright, she exclaimed, "Oh!"

Their second time was even better.

***

Something woke him. Sunlight was streaming through the crack between the curtains. He lay there as the memory of their shared intimacy came back to him. Reaching beside him, he found the pillow vacant but warm. Sitting up, he heard the sound of running water in the bathroom. Seconds later the door slowly opened and by the early light he saw the fully dressed version of his recent bedmate.

"Janni? What're you doing?"

"I'm sorry, Michael. I was trying not to wake you."

"It's okay. Where are you going?"

"Well…I'm the song leader at the early service this morning."

Michael had to laugh. "Do you want me to come with you?"

A mischievous Janni replied, "No, I think you did enough of that last night."

"And I wasn't the only one."

"Yes, and lovely orgasms they were." Bending over to give him a kiss full of longing, she backed away, "As tempting as it is—and it is—I've got to go. Call me later."

He lay there basking in the previous night's delights and thinking, "That was unexpected…or maybe not." When he finally threw back the covers, he smiled and said aloud, "Yes, I will." But sitting on the side of the bed he couldn't help but think, "Now what?"

***

After mass, Gladys Simpson could hardly wait to tell Madge about seeing Janneke and Michael together at the Lodge's restaurant the previous night. "They looked very cozy, if you know what I mean. And guess what? This morning, Janneke had on the same dress she was wearing last night. You know what that means! And she's up there leading us like nothing happened AND she went to communion! How disgraceful!"

Madge looked squarely into her eyes, "And who just went to communion, but then couldn't wait to start a rumor?"

Ms. Simpson's mouth dropped. Then she snapped it shut and

with the words, "Humph! I know what I saw," she stalked off.

Madge watched her leave then smiled to herself. "Good for you, Janni! Good for both of you!"

37

Michael's arrival outside Willy's ramshackle cabin was greeted by loud barking and a blurry-eyed Willy at the door whose first words were, "Who are you, some sorta religious nut?"

Willy wore an ancient, faded Henley shirt under overalls of the same generation. The overall cuffs were rolled up and exposed stick-like shins and bare feet, all white as bleached bones. Long arms terminated in meaty hands, the fingers like sausages. In spite of his age, he stood tall and menacing.

Michael approached the narrow porch, introduced himself, and explained he was helping Sheriff Conrad with the Lawery case. Willy stood there silently formulating his decision, then grabbed the dog by its greasy collar, stepped back and gestured for Michael to follow them inside.

The cabin's interior was as esoteric as the exterior. Willy certainly lived up to his reputation. Inside and out, the place appeared not so much landfill modern as construction discarded. The main room was illuminated by a keroscne lantern resting on a solid but well-worn wooden table, though an unlit lightbulb dangled by its cord from the ceiling. Michael had noticed the long line of sagging electrical wire emanating from the woods nearby, its provenance hidden from view.

There was a closed door, presumably to a bedroom, and a second doorway, minus the door, open to a combination mud and utility room in which a leaky hot water heater stood, likely serviced by the rusted propane tank only a few yards from the cabin. In spite of the mild day, a wood fire crackled in an ancient iron stove. The stuffiness of the room enhanced a sweet, musty herbal essence, an olfactory assault which suggested a likely illegal indulgence.

"Have a chair. Would ya like coffee?"

"If it's not too much trouble, yes, please."

There was a speckled blue and white coffee pot, the kind used for camping, sitting on the side of the stove. As Michael sat down on a wobbly captain's chair, Willy carried the pot over to a badly-chipped 70's style green enamel sink and turned on a faucet already dripping sufficiently to provide at least a cup of water without much encouragement. "I hope you like Kenya AA, it's all I got."

"That's fine." Fascinated, Michael watched as the beans were poured into a small white grinder, transformed to a finer state, then dumped into the coffee basket. Michael thought it interesting that he and Willy shared a taste in coffee beans.

With the pot on the stove and a pair of gimme cups printed with 4K Construction placed expectantly before them on the table, Michael asked about the night in question.

Willy grunted through a grin that revealed bright white teeth suggesting oral care was an exception to the general hygiene practiced by the owner. Wrinkles spread like cracks in thin ice from the corners of his eyes. Variations were sculpted about his face and incised deeply around his mouth, sending his grey whiskers strangely askew.

Now within his citadel, Willy proved to be gregarious to a fault, and with someone interested in what he had to say, he held forth, enthralled by his own words, like a Father Jim moved by a Holy, if lesser, Spirit.

In rambling fashion, he expressed his opinion of Picky Piccard, the lack of sportsmanship in today's fishermen, the ignorance of the public when it came to preserving the lakes, the degradation of civilization in general, and was at the point of predicting the apocalypse when he caught himself, backtracked, and briefly related details matching what Piccard had said.

Michael discerned this may not be only about imposing opinions and philosophy on a newcomer. If Piccard was correct, the prolonged nervous jabber was Willy's way to avoid reliving the moment he pulled in Ginny's body.

Willy admitted that guiding and taking care of the fishing shacks for the resort was an easy winter job. "That hard-ass Picky snuck up and threatened to fine me and tell the resort. He knew I had a good thing going and said the lake patrol was short-handed, what with so-called budget cuts, and told me that if I'd help, he'd drop the charges."

Willy got back up, retrieved the perking pot of coffee and filled the cups with aromatic steaming brew. The first sip was excellent.

"Catch any fish?"

"What?"

"The shack you were using when Piccard stopped by."

"Nah, it was too deep, but thought I'd try. Sometimes I've caught perch in deep water, an occasional school moving through. Something broke my line…didn't matter, it was past time to take the shacks off anyway. Technically I own 'em, that's why Picky threatened to ticket me and not the resort."

Michael hesitated then decided to revisit the subject of the broken line later. Instead, he asked if Willy had noticed anything in general that might relate to the case.

"Like what?"

"You're out on the lake a lot. See anything unusual that might raise the flag on your set line? You know, something suspicious, someone causing trouble or who may have looked out of place?"

With a snort, Willy said, "Out of place? I'll tell you who's out of place. That dim-witted kid that works with Jolly, the bait douche. The kid helps deliver bait so he thinks he knows how to fish. I almost stopped putting locks on my shacks because he and some of his friends thought it was okay to use them whenever they liked. They tore off the locks and, from all the beer bottles, they weren't just fishing."

"Are you sure it was him? Couldn't anyone break in?"

"I'm sure. I caught him and a couple of his friends trying to use a shack. Unfortunately for them, I was in the shack at the time. I know those characters seem harmless, but they aren't and believe me, they're not that dumb. They know what's going on."

"Like what?"

The more he talked, the more animated he became, rocking from side to side, arms and hands in motion. "Like when you talk to them, they look at you with their mouths hangin' open and pretend they don't understand. And that Dum Dum kid, he had a thing for your victim."

"What do you mean he had a thing for the victim? You mean Virginia Lawery?"

Willy leaned toward Michael and in a conspiratorial tone, "More'n once, I'd be over at the resort takin' care of business and I'd see him just standin' there, staring at her through those big windows." Willy excitedly stabbed the air with a crooked finger to make his point. "And I know for a fact, he and Jolly got into it once cuz of his stalking her."

"Stalking is a pretty strong word, and it's not against the law to stare."

"The way he did it, it should be. It was spooky. He'd stand under those trees on the other side of the parking lot, just waitin' for her. And I saw him following her other places."

"Like where?"

"Everywhere! He'd hang out at the farmers market and sometimes walk behind her. And I saw her car parked outside his place."

"What?"

"Yeah! It blew my socks off! One time it was there overnight."

"When was this?"

"I don't remember. I'm not a human calendar!" Willy was getting tetchy.

"Are you sure it was her car?"

"Sure, I'm sure. It was that little pukey green thing she drove last summer. Hey, if this is so important, shouldn't it be worth something—like a reward?"

Ignoring the solicitation, Michael pressed on. "How do you know all this?"

"I get around. I see things, ya know? People ignore me because they think I'm nothin', but I notice. I'm pretty handy and you'd be surprised what people throw away."

Michael paused. The mood was intense, and this was important. He was certain Willy knew more, much more. But Willy was wired and probably in need of something to calm his irritation. Michael decided to slow things down, maybe approach Willy from a different direction.

"Willy, you like an occasional drink, yes?"

"Is that an invitation?" Willy responded with a ragged smirk.

Michael smiled and said, "Maybe. And you enjoy the occasional mood-altering substance? Not that I care."

Abruptly the smirk disappeared. Willy's eyes grew hard and

closed to mere slits. His jaw clenched shut, but his lips drew back in a sinister grimace. Leaning back in his chair Willy defiantly tilted his head. "Look, pretty boy. Let's cut the crap. I'm nobody's fool. I've said more'n I should. It's not my business. I don't bother others and they don't bother me. Lord help the soul of that poor girl, but there's nothin' I can do to help her now. Get your coffee somewhere else. I'm a busy man and your time is up. There's the door. Boxer will help you if you need an escort."

With that, Boxer's head jerked up, teeth exposed, and from deep in his broad chest came a rumble. Michael let out a sigh. Obviously that had been the wrong approach.

Rising, Michael took out a business card and laid it on the table. "I appreciate your time. I'll leave you my card if it's alright with you. If you think of anything else, please give me a call—anytime."

"Can't. Phone's not connected—don't like interruptions."

"Okay. Then let someone in the sheriff's department know, and I'll contact you."

Closing the door behind him, Michael was exasperated with himself. He shook his head. "I should've had Connie or Pam with me." He heard a whinny and looked over to see a large, grey-muzzled draft horse standing at the rail of a small corral, its ears expectantly perked up. Even the corral and its lean-to shelter looked to be the product of an incomplete scavenger hunt.

Willy's first years back had been bad. The flashbacks died away with time, but not the nightmares. Sleep was the enemy. If he closed his eyes, he drowned in a flood of anxiety and despair. Eventually they became less frequent, but that night the nightmares attacked, raging with an intensity he hadn't experienced since his first year back from Vietnam.

In his dream, he was smothered in heat, the air thick with a humid, smoky haze. He sucked in the taste of napalm and burned flesh with each breath. His jungle boots were laden with glutinous mud from the rice paddy. Staying low, he struggled through the clinging muck, finally diving against a protective berm.

Hootches exploded in flames as his squad advanced. A burst of gunfire ripped into their right flank and in the next instant his squad leader was down, torn in two. Setting his M-16 on "Rock and Roll," he blindly charged into the chaos and obliterated the enemy. The enemy—a girl and small child. "No…God, no! It's just babies—killing us!"

"Incoming!" The searing blast ripped his body, the shock wave driving him to the ground. Disinterred, a pale amorphous figure rose from the blast pit just in front of him, long tangled hair framing a face with empty eyes, mouth opened wide, gasping. It spoke, but deafened by the blast, he heard nothing.

All around blurred ghostly forms writhed in anguish; hot frozen tracers rushed by. The cold bitter wind fried his skin. The specter with the empty eyes faded, stealing away accompanied by the anguished spirits.

Willy crawled over to the edge to peer into the crater, now filled with dead fish, nets, and bottomless black water. In a flash of crimson, a stone-cold claw seized his throat. He tried to break free, but the net entangled him, pulling him down. He struggled, but the net dragged him deeper and deeper into the abyss, drowning him in the horror below.

A shriek cut through the darkness, a horrendous scream to eviscerate the belly. His body convulsed as his eyes stared into the blackness. Drenched in sweat but freezing cold, he tried to move—another scream. It was unclear if he was alive but he could hear the screams—his own screams.

Willy lay still, lost, feeling the roar of silence enveloping him. His heart hammered as he began to suffocate, unable to inhale or exhale. Fire and terror seared his brain until the intensity woke him and with it came relief.

Gradually, ever so gradually, breathing became easier. His heart continued to pound but remained beating. His head cleared but for a faint, high-pitched whine. Something was close by—something alive!

With all his might, he listened. The sound was near him but everything was dark. Gripped by dread, he needed to find out what it was. He had to reach out. Holding his breath, he closed his fingers and extended his shaky fist. The whine stopped. He felt a puff of hot air then suddenly a touch of something wet and raspy.

Willy pulled back his hand and released his breath in a sudden burst of laughter, loud and maniacal. He yelled, "THANK YOU, JESUS! Hoowhee!" He took a few deep breaths. "Hello, Boxer! It's you, dog." With a sharp bark, Boxer leaped onto the bed and planted a big wet lick on the awakened warrior's face. Willy hugged his canine champion. "It's okay, Boxer. You're okay! *We're* okay."

Swinging his legs over the side of the bed, Willy squinted at the luminous dial on his battered military issue wristwatch: 12:05 AM. "Shit! Gillnet time."

Rising, Willy stumbled to the door of his shack, stepped outside, and walked to the end of the ramshackle porch to relieve himself on the weeds below. Boxer relieved himself at some distance from the shack. Willy waited at the open door until Boxer returned, then drew a fresh cup of water from the faucet for the dog's bowl and another for his own long, cool drink.

By the moon's light dimmed by scattered clouds, Willy found a half-burnt roach in the tray on the kitchen table and fired it up. It would not kill nightmares. It would not amend history. But the toke-induced haze would ease him mercifully into a temporary truce.

***

"Oh! I know him! He's that old guy who was around when I was growing up. Some people called him a hobo because he lived in a shack he built himself. But he couldn't be a hobo because he had a shack and a dog. I only spoke with him once. It was a sunny day and I was riding my bicycle, and he was digging up Mrs. Mallory's vegetable garden. The plow was pulled by two big horses. I told him his horses were beautiful. He looked at me. I thought he was angry, but

his eyes got wet and he smiled all ragged through his whiskers. All he said was, 'Thank you.' Then he turned back to his horses and I remember he had these huge hands and used one to wipe his eyes. He was a nice man. I hope he's OK. Is he OK?"

"Yes."

"How do you know?"

"Because you remember him."

There were donuts on the conference table and fresh coffee in the carafe. Connie had DCI Agent Hitchcock up on his computer for their online meeting and Donahue nodded to Michael as he came into the room. "We're just starting."

The final results from the DCI lab didn't change anything. "I'm sorry, but that's all we have." Agent Hitchcock was as disappointed as anyone in the conference room. "The evidence only shows she was in the car sometime in the past. There is drug residue, and we know he was a user, but there's nothing to physically tie him to Ginny's death. On the contrary, the evidence and the testimony given by everyone on this end confirms he didn't do it. To be frank, without more to go on, we still can't even prove beyond any doubt that it was a murder."

After a few questions, a promise to keep the case active, and another expression of disappointment from Agent Hitchcock, the videoconference ended.

It was Michael who spoke first. "Any thoughts on how you want to proceed?"

Connie and Donahue looked at each other. Connie took a deep breath and sighed. "As committed as we've been to this investigation, there's work we've set aside that needs our attention. Jack has two new cases in addition to the stack on his desk. The new fiscal year isn't that far off and I'm up to my eyebrows in formulating a preliminary budget for next year. That's the reality for sheriffs in this day and age."

They sat glumly with their own thoughts for a moment until Michael began to share his conversation with Willy DeWeerd. After an account of the visit, Michael asked, "What can you tell me about Willy and about a couple of characters called"— Michael turned back to his notebook to confirm—"Jolly Holiday and Dum Dum?"

Jack pointed to Connie. "You know Willy better than me."

"Right. Well, Willy is a character, but there are things about him that are not widely known. He enlisted in the army right out of high school and did two tours in Vietnam. That was around 1970. Shortly before the truce in 1973, his company was caught in a fierce firefight that went on for two days. Willy was wounded, decorated for his actions during the battle, and spent months in the hospital. He was honorably discharged, but in my opinion, never totally got over it. He was one of those people that society used up, then threw away. Sorry to sound cynical but I've seen too much of that over the years. Anyway, he likes to live on the edge of the community, he scavenges, loves his dog and old horse, and will either talk your ear off or spit in your eye. He's pretty calm except when he rages about what he considers social ignorance and fascist politicians who send other peoples' children to war."

"Is he violent?"

"Not usually, but it's interesting you ask and want to know about Jolly. Jack, you've handled them both with the deputies. You fill us in."

"Right. Willy and Jolly don't get along. Willy thinks Jolly's bait is crap and is generous in expressing his opinion. It was all harmless until they got into it early last June at that biker bar, the Spokes and Suds."

"What happened?"

"One evening some of the seasonal workers from the Lodge went out drinking and wound up at Spokes and Suds. Willy and Jolly were both there that night. As I understand it, everyone was minding their own business when Jolly went up to the kids from the Lodge and hit on Virginia Lawery. He was drunk and he wouldn't take 'no' for an answer. He got rough and abusive…said something like 'If you like to fuck Dum Dum, you'll love a real man.' Anyway, Willy walked up to Jolly and clobbered him with a beer bottle. Shirley had the bouncer throw them both out. Someone called it in, but when the deputy got there it was over. I went back the next day and got the story, but no one wanted to press charges."

At that point Connie chimed in. "Willy's never been a real problem. We've had a few complaints over the years of someone fitting his description going through dumpsters, urinating on private property, and having his dog unleashed, but nothing serious. Now Jolly, that's a different matter."

Jack picked it back up. "Oh yeah, we know Jolly. Tough guy with a bad habit of assault when someone disagrees with him. We've arrested him twice and both times the charges were dropped. We've got a pretty extensive file on him. He's still a person of interest in several open cases back in Arizona."

Jack turned to his laptop. "His name really is Jolly—Jolly Holiday. He was born on Christmas Day. When we first interviewed him, he told us that when he was born his father thought he looked like a chubby little elf, sort of a miniature Santa, and celebrated by getting drunk and naming his son Jolly.

"Jolly came to the attention of law authorities his freshman year at ISU—nothing major, mostly suspected harassment and underage drinking. His sophomore year though he was accused of rape and assault to commit great bodily harm, but the charges were dropped when the woman suddenly left school and her boyfriend, who was badly beaten, refused to testify. This was all around the time he began to hang out with some gang types.

"I'll skip some of this stuff." Scrolling down the screen, Donahue picked up the narrative. "He began his junior year by assaulting one of his wrestling coaches in a bar and that ended his scholarship. He was booted second semester due to charges of assault and dealing drugs. He was suspected of manufacturing meth, but no one could prove it. He worked out a deal with the university and county attorney. He agreed to plead guilty and leave the university in exchange for lowering the charges to misdemeanors and a suspended sentence.

"After that he returned to Arizona and dropped out of the scene until three years later when he was arrested and charged along with four gang members for assault, extortion, dealing drugs, and racketeering—a federal beef. The victims changed their minds and did not press charges, and the racketeering charge was dropped in a deal for him to plead to aggravated assault and possessing drug paraphernalia. He did some prison time and was released on probation. According to his probation officer, he checked in sporadically but did check in. When his probation was up, he left Arizona and returned to Iowa."

Connie added, "Lucky us."

Michael was amazed. "Wow. That's quite a file for a local trouble-maker."

Jack agreed. "He earned it. Shortly after he popped up in our area, we received a complaint that he assaulted a woman because she wouldn't pay for drugs. She wouldn't testify and there were no other witnesses, so we dropped the charges."

Connie emphasized, "That's when we became very interested in Mr. Holiday. He's become Jack's personal project."

Jack closed his laptop. "It turns out that Jolly is on the Drug Enforcement Administration's watch list. Most of our file is courtesy of the DEA and Arizona authorities. Unfortunately, we've had even less luck nailing him than they had."

Michael waited, then asked, "What does he do?"

"He owns and runs a distribution business, mostly bait, some fishing tackle and sundry supplies for resorts and area businesses. He gets minnows and leeches from local trappers, but some of his worms and grubs and all of his other supplies come from out-of-state. At least that's what I've been told."

"What sort of supplies?"

"Bait containers, bedding, paper products, some janitorial supplies. Strictly small time. He has a barn he uses as a warehouse outside of Spirit Lake north of Highway 9. He lives in a trailer next to it. He's a case of wait and watch. We know he's going to screw up. It's a matter of when, not if."

Michael was curious to learn more about the other person of interest. "Who's this guy that works with him, Dum Dum, and what kind of name is that?"

Jack deferred to Connie. "Dum Dum's real name is Harold Krumm. A sad case, but in an odd way, inspiring. He's another area character. His parents left him long ago and no one knows where they went. He was passed from foster home to foster home. He's not trouble, but slow—he has special needs. He lives on his own, so must function pretty well. We don't know how he started working for Jolly, but they seem to get along in a weird sort of way."

"How's that?"

"As far as we can tell, Jolly looks out for Krumm, and in turn, Krumm works hard and is willing to put up with Jolly's crap. We've never had any complaints about Dum Dum."

"Didn't Willy complain about him breaking into his fishing shacks?"

Connie had to smile. "Willy complains about a lot of things. We listen, write it up, and before we take time to investigate, Willy comes back and tells us to forget it. It's like choreography, and whether intentional or not, that's how it plays out. Frankly, I think Willy gets lonely, and it's his way to get a little attention."

"He said people don't take him seriously."

"Well, maybe they should. Anyway, that's what we know about Harold Krumm."

"What about the relationship between Krumm and Ginny Lawery?"

"What relationship?"

"Relationship may be the wrong word but his name keeps popping up. Both Sally and Willy said Krumm and Ginny knew each other. Sally implied Ginny befriended Krumm because she felt sorry for him. Willy told me Krumm was fixated on and stalking Ginny. He said he saw Ginny's car parked overnight outside Krumm's apartment."

"When was this?"

"Willy wasn't sure, and after that I must have said something he didn't like because he told me to leave or he'd sic Boxer on me."

"Boxer?"

"His dog. I think it's mostly a Labrador."

Connie looked over to his chief homicide detective. "Jack, I believe we'd better have a little talk with Mr. Krumm."

"Sheriff?" They hadn't heard Delores enter the room. "You have a message from Richard Piccard. He said he has some information for Michael, but couldn't reach him." Delores handed Connie a Post-it with the return number.

"Thanks, Delores."

Connie looked at Michael. "Do you have your phone?"

"Yes."

"Is it on?"

"Let me check. Ah, no."

"Call him and put him on speaker."

Piccard answered on the second ring. Michael put him on speaker.

"You had a good idea, Counselor. I checked the boat and net we talked about during the track meet and found something. It's a fishing lure. It was snagged in the net with a thread from a rope. I know the lure—Willy DeWeerd makes them."

Connie broke in. "You're sure it's one of Willy's?"

"Hello, sheriff. Yes, definitely! It's a spoon with a deer hair tail. He makes them in different colors, sizes, and shapes and sells them through the Sports Shop. In the right situation, they work. I've even used them, but don't tell Willy."

Michael's mind began to buzz. "Officer Piccard, I know we talked about this, but do you remember exactly where Willy's shack was when you asked him to volunteer?"

"Approximately, but why don't you ask Willy? I'm sure he marked the location with the GPS on his phone."

"His phone? He told me he didn't have a phone. Oh, wait—he said it wasn't connected. There was an old landline phone on the counter."

"He has a cell phone. The Lodge gave it to him so they could let him know when they needed him to guide someone. Willy down-loaded a GPS app. I know because he showed me. He marks where he sets shacks, where and when he finds fish, and the most productive dumpsters around the Lakes area. What're you thinking?"

"It's just a hunch, but what if Willy broke his line on something other than a big fish? You said it was a dead zone, but what if he really hooked something? Like a body? And what if there's still evidence on the lake bottom?" The silence lasted long enough that Michael asked, "Officer Piccard, are you there?"

"Yes, I'm here. Let's go talk to Willy."

40

Donahue had the task of bringing in Harold Krumm, and Michael rode to the fish hatchery with Dickinson County's Junior Homicide Detective, Wayne Terrill, and Deputy Brian Graves, the department's most skilled crime scene investigator. While Wayne and Brian secured the evidence and documented the chain of custody, Piccard and Michael left to find Willy.

"Let's see. This is Monday, late morning. He's probably still at one of the landfills."

"How do you know that?"

"He has a routine. It's Monday, so he'll start at the county land-fill. A lot of people dump their stuff on the weekend, and he starts his week by checking out the recent additions. He also checks restaurants on Fridays and Sundays, Goodwill on Wednesdays, and construction sites on Saturdays."

"What about Tuesdays and Thursdays?"

"He makes up for days hc guides. He's organized and flexible. He allows plenty of time on any day to fish."

"Are we talking about the same guy?"

"Yes. People underestimate him. He likes it that way."

"Why?"

"I don't know. I guess he considers it an advantage."

"Let me ask again—how do you know all this?"

"Common knowledge among law enforcement—we notice things. We have to, that's part of our job—I'm sure you know that. We talk to all kinds of people. It's more than PR, it's an important way to keep up with what's going on, often right out in the open. It's the kind of stuff not in the news but useful for the public's welfare. There he is. He's a little ahead of schedule."

Michael recognized the ancient pickup truck. Willy's canine companion had his head outside the passenger window. With his lolling tongue, blinking eyes, and laid-back ears, Boxer looked to be in ecstasy, a stark contrast to the dark look on the countenance of the driver.

Stopping alongside the DNR truck, Willy went on the attack. "Now what the hell do you want? I paid my debt to fascism. Is the DNR so hard up they raid a poor old man's pickin's from the dump?"

Leaning forward Michael extended his greeting. "Hello, Willy."

"I should've known. You're in bad company."

"Willy, we need your help with something. Could we buy you and Boxer lunch and talk it over?"

Willy looked skeptical, but a free lunch was not to be passed over. "Mac's off 71."

"We'll follow you."

***

Willy said nothing until he was eagerly eating his second Big Mac (and Boxer's was in the takeout sack). "I only eat stuff like this when someone else is buying. It's not as healthy as home-cooked, but it sure tastes good. Whaddaya wanna know that's worth a free lunch?"

Piccard took the lead. "Do you remember the exact location of the shack you were in when I asked you to volunteer?"

Willy snorted. "Volunteer, my ass."

"Okay, but do you know the exact location?"

"NO! How would I know that?"

Michael was about to speak, but Piccard touched his arm.

Willy looked first at Piccard, then Michael, and back again. "Why?"

Piccard took out his phone and opened his photos. Turning it so Willy could see the picture, Piccard asked, "Is this one of your lures?"

"Could be. I'd have to see it to be sure. Is that why you bought me lunch—you're shopping for lures?"

"No, we think you broke your line on something besides a big fish. We found what we think is one of your lures and trace pieces of some kind of rope in the gillnet we were using the night we recovered Virginia Lawery's body. It's just a hunch, but if you could show us the spot you had your shack, we'd like to have our divers check the lake bottom."

Willy took the final third of the sandwich into his mouth followed by fingers full of french fries, a large swallow of root beer, and a larger belch. Reaching into the pocket of his well-worn barn coat he drew out a nearly new smartphone. "What? An old smelly guy can't use technology?" Both Michael and Piccard smiled, but remained silent.

Willy fiddled with the phone, took a pen from his shirt pocket and wrote numbers onto a paper napkin. "I don't remember, but my phone does. Here's Winnie's coordinates."

Piccard took the napkin, looked at Michael and then back to

Willy. "Winnie?"

"You know, like Winnie the Pooh! I like to name my shacks. Each one's a little different. I name them for things they remind me of. I have carpet inside Winnie that's the color of honey." Willy considered that explanation enough. He crammed the rest of the french fries in his mouth, downed the remaining root beer, and announced, "Gentlemen, some of us work for a living."

As Willy rose to leave, Michael thanked him then added, "Someone will need to come by to have you confirm that what we found is one of your lures. And, if it's all right by you, the sheriff's department would like to send over their crime scene people to take a look at Winnie. Is there a good time to see you?"

"Nope, but I'm 'round home most evenings unless I'm fishing."

***

Michael and Piccard returned to the courthouse, and arrangements were begun to have the Dickinson County Dive Team check the location provided by Willy. Piccard agreed to be on hand to help represent the DNR. He had a suggestion. "I'm not sure, but it might be good if Willy was on hand."

Connie agreed. "That's fine, but let's get the dive team organized first. It takes them at least an hour to get on-scene in an emergency and since this isn't an emergency, it'll likely take longer. Jack and Brian will be there to document evidence. Let me know if there's anything else you need from me."

"I'd like to be there, if I may."

"It's all right with me if it's all right with Officer Piccard."

"Yes, as long as he stays out of the way."

"Thanks. I'll stay clear of business."

Michael spent the rest of the day at ILCC. There were messages to answer and student evaluations to finish writing. Connie's call came late in the afternoon and was brief. "10:00 AM tomorrow, west side of Pillsbury Point."

***

The water was dead calm and the sky unclouded and bright. This early in the season the water was still ice cold, but visibility was relatively clear. Michael, together with Donahue and Willy, stood on the shore watching two boats hovering over the site provided by Willy's GPS. The larger carried four divers in dry suits and two handlers. Piccard and Graves accompanied them in a smaller lake patrol boat.

While two of the brightly shrouded divers took the plunge, the other two remained on the surface as back-up in the event of an emergency. The importance of this extra precaution was not lost on Michael. He had great respect for the expertise and professionalism of the small group of volunteers—mostly deputies and area firefighters—who provided this service for the Lakes region.

As Michael watched through binoculars, one of the handlers slipped a rope over the side of the boat. It took no more than fifteen minutes before the rope was drawn up, tied to something the divers had found below.

While the tender waited for the divers, the DNR boat came to the shore. The excitement over their discovery quickly subsided as they considered what had happened to the young woman in the final moments of her life.

A somber Willy quietly said, "I recognize the stonework. It's from the pile of broken masonry at the construction site behind the Lodge. That's the rope they used to hold the masonry bundles together." Pointing to the small metal object still attached to a strand of rope, "And that's the other lure I lost."

Jolly was clearly irritated. Standing outside the interview room, Detective Donahue explained to Connie, "We couldn't find Harold Krumm, so we brought in Jolly. He came voluntarily to answer questions about Krumm, but only after it was suggested that his cooperation might help him to avoid future trouble with the police concerning his bait business.

"He said he had to make out-of-town deliveries and gave Dum Dum the day off. We sent a deputy to Krumm's apartment, but no one was there. Our deputy said Jolly told him Dum Dum was 'probably off dickin' his new girlfriend…the dummy's a horny bastard.'" Watching Jolly from outside the interrogation room's one-way mirror Connie grunted and replied, "How sweet. Let him stew for a few more minutes."

The long, unpleasant interview did little to improve the mood of either the guest or detective. Jolly was a thug and experienced in dealing with law enforcement. He did confirm Krumm was fixated on Virginia Lawery. "Dum Dum was capable enough to try anything with her and too dumb to know why. I can't believe he even thought they were friends—disgusting."

There was nothing to connect Jolly to a known crime, but he did say that during the week Dum Dum ate breakfast at the McDonald's on Stake Out Road off Highway 71. "That's where I pick him up for work around 7:30 each morning."

Jolly was released with the admonition to not say anything to anyone about their interest in Harold Krumm and to call Detective Donahue if he should see Krumm before the next morning. As Jack watched Jolly pull out of the law center parking lot, he thought, "Ironic, expecting a career thug to agree to help us out."

Michael's efforts were even less fruitful. He spent most of the afternoon reinterviewing the employees at the Lodge for anything they might know about Willy DeWeerd, a bait supplier named Jolly, and his helper Harold Krumm, aka Dum Dum. Thanks to the Department of Transportation, pictures of all three were available to law enforcement, and Michael had their photos on his phone. Nearly everyone he talked to recognized the subjects, and though some knew who they were, no one had anything more to add. Late in the afternoon he met individually with Anthony and Lucia.

Previously, Michael had been impressed by Anthony Sandoval's poise and confidence, an effect enhanced by Anthony's bearing. Tall and athletic, with a chiseled chin, strong nose line, a high prominent forehead, and black hair that tumbled to the shirt collar in designed disarray, Anthony seemed to exude a masculinity that could appeal to others, women or men, with little effort.

But today, something was off. Anthony's manner was cool and aloof and his answers were curt. Rather than accommodating, his arrogance and impatience were palpable. As the interview progressed, or rather degraded, Michael's attitude became more assertive, and his earlier impression of Sandoval faded. Michael began to consider that his opinion of Anthony had been based upon a facade, expertly perpetuated, but which was now crumbling away under the onslaught of Michael's pointed questions and increasingly aggressive attitude. Sandoval was clearly annoyed by the continued questions concerning Virginia Lawery and her relationship to the Lodge and to its owners. The interview didn't end on good terms.

As Michael waited for Lucia, he thought about how much people were willing to ignore if they liked what they saw. Anthony Sandoval was handsome, personable if called upon, and did present the correct image for the Lodge. That likely was his value in this enterprise. Still, if someone bothered to look beyond the veneer, there was something unsettling about the man. Good looking, yes, but slick, even oily. When agitated, his eyes shifted nervously, as if seeking a way out.

In contrast, each response Mrs. Sandoval gave tended to be rambling and disingenuous—whether by design or unintentionally, Michael was unsure. Without her husband at hand, she was anxious, vulnerable, and to Michael the lawyer, susceptible to questioning. She also appeared even more stunning, if possible, than when they first met. To Michael the man, vulnerability enhanced her deeply sensual beauty. Still, he was disappointed. Other than his new impressions of the two, he'd learned nothing significant.

As he went to his truck he saw Jerry Foyle's van pulling into the rear lot. On a hunch, he changed direction and intercepted the drummer at the employee entrance. "Hey, Michael! Are you playing with the band tonight?"

"No. I'm here on behalf of the sheriff's office, following up on some questions we had for the staff concerning the Lawery investigation. Do you have a minute? I have something I'd like you to look at."

A few minutes later it was clear an interview with Harold Krumm was critical. When comparing the photo of Grant Laxton and Harold Krumm, Jerry's response was surprising. "Ha! If you hadn't shown me this second photo, I still would have said I thought I saw the boyfriend that night, but no more. This is definitely the guy I saw. I recognize the hair and the size and shape of his head. He just isn't wearing a cap in this picture."

"What cap?"

"I've seen him before. He wears a cap that's too big for him. He wears it low and his hair sticks out all around like a scarecrow. The guy I saw that night had on a cap. I'm sure this is the guy."

"You didn't say anything before about a cap."

"Sorry, but I really thought the picture you showed me the first time was of the person I saw. Anyone could wear a cap. I didn't even consider it until you showed me this picture. This is the guy."

"You were sure about the boyfriend, too."

"I said boyfriend 80 percent. This guy is 99 percent."

On his way home Michael stopped at the sheriff's office and spoke with a frustrated Detective Donahue. The workload on his desk was evident, and he was eager to get on with his other—now three—new cases, thanks to a file just added to the pile that afternoon. "If Jolly's information is good, we'll find Harold Krumm at McDonald's at 7:30 tomorrow morning. I'll give you a call when we have him. We're not the DCI, so you can sit in on the interview."

"Can you trust Jolly to keep his mouth shut?"

"No, but I think in this case, his self-interest will trump alerting Mr. Krumm."

After recounting what he'd learned from Foyle, Jack's frustration lightened a bit. "We shouldn't assume, but it's beginning to look like this could be our guy. Maybe we'll catch a break tomorrow and bring an end to this sorry mess."

The dimly lit side street was deserted except for a pair of raccoons making their way out of the storm sewer and waddling across a small side yard overrun by weeds and wind-blown trash. A dumpster in the center of the yard overflowed with construction debris and discarded remains of workers' lunches. It represented Valhalla for the raccoons but less so for the residents of this backwater neighborhood. Here, those fortunate to still possess the slightest incomes and skills for survival, precariously clung to dilapidated shacks and shabby apartments. The nearby presence of large construction equipment and signs posted by the developer promised that soon the drab scene would be regenerated with shiny new businesses and town homes.

Jolly knew his way though he normally came by van rather than motorcycle when his otherwise dependable employee failed to show at the usual place. His little story about McDonald's was true enough, but he had omitted the detail that Dum Dum had a tendency to oversleep. He understood what he had to do but couldn't help considering, "Krumm, you poor dumb bastard, what have you gotten yourself into?"

Dum Dum's apartment took up the front half of the storage warehouse's upper floor. A long, enclosed stairway led up the side of the building to the apartment. Pausing in the deep shadow provided by the sagging overhang of the stairwell, Jolly heard little sound that could be manmade. The odor of gasoline, putrefying fish parts, and moldy dust settled by years of passive indifference assaulted his nose. Remnants of old boats, motors, and a variety of parts were stored in this mausoleum of castoffs.

Snapping on his headlamp, Jolly adjusted the lens to red, and began a slow, silent climb. Dum Dum shouldn't be home, but it was best to be cautious. Although a passerby was unlikely, after today's interview it was important to avoid attention.

Staying close to the wall to minimize the inevitable complaints from the old stairs, Jolly did his best to step over the more decrepit boards and to avoid food wrappers, beer cans, liquor bottles, and even an old blanket, discarded by those seeking temporary shelter or concealment.

Arriving at the small landing atop the stairs, he gently tried the doorknob. It was locked, but it was the simple push button variety. It was old and very loose. Jolly applied the same technique he used when he needed to enter and wake the slumberous resident. Pushing on the knob while moving it back and forth, he was rewarded by a soft ping as the latch released. Applying steady pressure, the warped hollow wood door swung inward with a soft scraping sound but no squeak. Stepping inside, he pushed to close but not latch the door.

Jolly was experienced at B&E. He was calm, patiently listening for any sound of alarm and waiting for his eyes to adjust in the dim red light. He needn't hurry. This was the single night of the week that Harold, without fail, bowled and went for late snacks and beers with his friends, if that's what they were. "Such an odd bunch," Jolly thought. Certainly in that group, Dum Dum was normal by comparison.

Growing confident that his work would be undisturbed, Jolly switched his headlamp to white light and, with the addition of a small LED flashlight drawn from the inside pocket of his leather jacket, began to rummage through the meager spaces where anything obvious might lie.

He was surprised to find a phone but recognized it as a burner, useless to investigators. He'd used this particular brand and model himself on several occasions and knew it was untraceable. An attempt to turn it on failed—the battery was dead. But there was no charger that Jolly could find.

He took his time and was thorough in his search. Though not totally careless, he wasn't concerned whether everything remained exactly as he found it. He was good at this, but as it turned out, didn't need to be.

The dozen or so DVDs were all generic save for two that were obviously crudely pornographic. The latter he thought to take but deferred to his primary purpose. The CDs suggested musical interest limited to pop ballads.

Turning on the devices and playing what remained from their last use wasn't an afterthought, it was part of a meticulous search. He found what he was looking for in the combination VCR/DVD player housed below an old television, both resting on shelving made up of boards and broken masonry from the Lodge.

He had no great brotherly love for Harold but did feel a shared if vague affinity that was difficult to ignore. It would've been easier if there was nothing to be found, but instead here was evidence that Dum Dum, whether he recognized it or not, possessed information that in the wrong hands would put a crushing end to Jolly's freedom and very lucrative business interests. Whatever the case, it would now get personal. Jolly also was good at risk containment.

He put the damning DVD in his pocket. As he was leaving, he

saw but paid no attention to the car keys hanging from a nail driven into the door frame.

***

It had been a great day for Dum Dum, spent with his girlfriend Sylvia and followed by a fun evening out with their friends. They told the stories they enjoyed that had been told often before. They played little jokes on each other. Dum Dum's bowling scores were bad which meant much teasing and then encouragement. He'd do better next time, and someone else would get teased.

They drank three pitchers of beer, one more than usual, and it was late when Sylvia, the only one in their group who owned a car, dropped him off in front of the warehouse building. With waves and a few cheers his friends drove off. Harold stood watching the tail-lights disappear around the corner, then turned to stumble his way toward the stairs. Hearing his name called, he was surprised to see Jolly standing on the other side of the road beneath the dim glow of the streetlight. As Jolly approached, Dum Dum rubbed his eyes, tried to focus his fuzzy mind, and asked, "Is it already time for work?"

Jolly smiled and slapped Dum Dum on the shoulder and said, "No work tonight, Harold. We're together all the time but don't really talk much. I just thought we should get to know each other better. Whaddaya say? Let's you and me have a drink together. I brought my best vodka."

43

The call came early. Michael had just returned from his run. "We found Harold Krumm."

"Good."

"Not so good."

"Why?"

"He's dead."

Stunned, Michael asked, "What happened?"

"We're not sure, but it looks like suicide. You'd better see for yourself."

***

"Krumm didn't show at McDonald's. When Jolly arrived there he told us sometimes Krumm overslept, and he would have to go to his apartment to wake him up. We then came here, forced the door, and found him hanging from a beam. The medical examiner is almost finished and he just gave us the go-ahead. We called in our two best deputies for investigating a crime scene. Don't touch, but there's a note in situ. Follow the tape. Here, you'll need these."

Standing beside Detective Donahue on the small landing outside the door, Michael donned the proffered blue booties. "And you may want this." Michael looked at Donahue who nodded. "It's not a respirator, but it may help."

Stepping through the doorway, an amalgamation of odors scoured his eyes and throat; the thin, gauze-like mask did little to diminish the attack. Absorbed within the sour, uncirculated air was a fusion of dust, spoiled food, sweat, and urine overlaid by the recent addition of alcohol and vomit.

Brian Graves and Terry Mullen, occupied as they were in their macabre dance, ignored him as he picked his way to the table indicated by Donahue. The rambling scrawl on the stained note paper was nearly illegible, but the first line was clear enough: "Ginny, I am sorry I hurt you." Next to it was a pen, a half-empty bottle of cheap vodka, and a cracked juice glass. Propped against the vodka bottle was an unframed 5x7 picture of Ginny and Krumm, a selfie, with a smiling Ginny hugging a self-conscious Harold, his face fixed in a vacant expression.

Using his phone Michael snapped a close-up of the vodka bottle and photo. Except where Krumm presumably sat, the table was clean, in contrast to the grimy kitchen counter laden with unwashed dishes and the waste basket overflowing with takeout containers.

The room was large, fronted by windows facing the street, and truncated at the far end by a kitchenette. The windows were veiled by what may once have been attractive curtains, but now were faded, threadbare, and torn, allowing ample sunlight to filter through as if by osmosis. An open doorway to the bedroom showed an unmade bed and discarded clothing. A small, equally ill-kept bathroom was next to the kitchenette.

The entire quarters appeared more industrial than residential, likely a reassignment of space previously allocated to the same service as the warehouse below. Sheetrock was nailed up but untaped and unpainted. Rafters spanning the flat roof remained exposed. An open beam separated the primary living space from kitchenette, and now served as a gallows.

The body hung from the beam by a rope identical to that retrieved from the recent site off Pillsbury Point. Vomit stained Krumm's shirt front and congealed in small separate blobs on the floor below the suspended corpse. A nearby overturned chair suggested a means to the young man's intent.

"We should have some preliminary results later today. I'll let you know what we find, but the autopsy will be done by the state medical examiner's office." Michael had retraced his entrance and stood next to Jack as the detective spoke of the need for the state's expertise. Focused intently on the slowly evolving scene, they were startled by a call from below.

"Hello?"

Both turned to see Father Barney standing at the bottom of the stairs. As Barney took a tentative first step, Jack called out, "Stop! Please, wait where you are, Father."

In minor protest Father Barney responded, "I believe I'm needed here, Detective Donahue."

Holding out his hand as if he could stem the flow of any holy sacrament, Jack pleaded, "Please wait, Father. The body was just taken down. The coroner will be finished in a few minutes, and then you can send Harold on his way."

"All right, if you insist. At this point, a few minutes won't matter."

"Bad news travels fast." Michael gave Donahue a quizzical look.

"Father Barney is one of the volunteer chaplains for county law enforcement. I called him after I called you."

"I didn't know Krumm was Catholic."

"Neither did I. It's just the luck of the draw."

Both men stood silently watching the ongoing drama. Recognizing there was no further reason for him to remain, Michael thanked Jack for the call and with his reassurance of an update later in the day, descended into the bright light of morning and was greeted by Father Barney.

Though incongruous to the circumstances, they chatted as if they'd just met on the street. When pleasantries ran their course, Michael asked Barney if he knew the victim well enough to answer some questions.

"Certainly, Michael. I'll answer what I can."

"How did you know Mr. Krumm?"

"Harold and I met shortly after I returned to St. Theresa's. We spoke a few times, and he helped with some tasks around the church yard. Most of what I know about him I learned from Father Jim who learned from his predecessor. I understand that Harold was abandoned by his parents at a young age and was in and out of foster homes and facilities. He was uncooperative and kept running away. The last time he was gone a month. A local farmer found him hiding in an abandoned country school west of Milford. He was nearly starving and diagnosed with pneumonia. The farmer and his wife were deeply moved by his situation, and though elderly, insisted upon taking him in."

Father Barney went on to explain it had been difficult at first. The Department of Human Services and the local school district had diagnosed Harold and provided assistance, but it was the unrelenting love showered upon Harold by the farmer and his wife that ultimately made the difference.

Harold had graduated from high school, received some training through the state and ILCC, and moved into a shared home. His foster parents were now deceased, but had provided for him with a portion of their estate. Father Jim had heard, due to interest from the endowment plus a small income from working odd jobs, that Harold was financially independent.

"I believe Father Jim told me someone from your late father's firm manages Harold's finances. I never knew the foster parents, but they were members of St. Theresa's and had Harold baptized into the Catholic faith. He occasionally attended mass, I suspect mostly out of a filial-like respect for them.

"I was impressed by how happy the young man was and by his upbeat attitude toward a life that could have left him bitter. Michael, there was a joy about the young man, a natural joy nurtured by his loving foster parents. I may not have known him well, but I can't accept that he would harm himself or another. It contradicts everything I know or have been told about him."

"What are you suggesting, Father?"

"I'm not suggesting. I'm saying this is not the act of the man I knew. As for speculation? I'll leave that to the investigators."

Still standing at the top of the stairs, Jack called out, "Father Barney? You can come up now. The medical examiner's ready for you."

Turning at the first step Father Barney looked to Michael with a sardonic smile. "I sincerely hope he meant Harold was ready."

Watching Barney climb the decrepit stairs, Michael felt a profound admiration for the resilience of the elderly priest. Repulsed by violence, Michael remained sensitive to the broader destructive consequences it caused. There never was a single victim. Everyone who dealt with the aftermath, in effect, became a victim. Violent death spawned an insidious evil, touching all who came near.

***

From his office, Michael made calls and sent numerous emails, catching up with what he thought needed to be done to wrap up the school year. His time as an instructor for ILCC was nearly finished but when asked by the department chair, he had agreed to work with summer students doing internships related to studies in criminal justice. His ILCC colleagues had generously shared information on their work with past interns, and the transition to Michael's oversight looked to be smooth. He would confer with each cooperating supervisor and schedule meetings with the summer interns, but there was time. By late afternoon, Michael's patience was nearly exhausted. He was on the verge of driving back to the scene when Jack appeared at his office door.

"The keys to Ginny's car were hanging on a nail by the entrance. It's in the warehouse below Krumm's apartment. Even from the doorway, you can see it's covered in dust and bird droppings. It's likely been there for quite some time."

"Didn't the marina folks notice it?"

"No, this warehouse is like the last stop before the junkyard. They drive by or walk around it occasionally, but they insist no one from the marina has been inside since last December."

"Did they even know Harold was living there?"

"Oh, yeah. They wanted to have someone staying there. They said it tended to discourage vandals or squatters. The apartment, if you want to call it that, was intended originally for some of their itinerant workers. This spring the marina sold the warehouse and the land around it to a developer who agreed Harold could continue to live there until they were ready to raze the building. As you saw, the developer has already begun work."

"What did Dr. Matt say?"

"The body's already on its way to the state ME. Consequently Dr. Matt wrote up the usual 'Official cause of death to be determined.'"

"What was his unofficial conclusion?"

"He saw nothing to suggest Harold died any other way than what you saw. Determining whether or not it was self-inflicted was the task of the investigators. He set time of death between midnight and 2:00 AM."

Michael nodded, digesting this information, then went on. "Was there any evidence that Ginny had been in the apartment?"

"No, not yet. There aren't a lot of fingerprints. What there are will be checked at the county's lab. There's also a cheap mobile phone, a burner. The battery was depleted but our tech guy, Deputy Mullens, had a charger and was able to turn it on. It's our mystery number, the one we've been trying to reach. Ginny's number is in the contacts along with a pizza place and a few numbers we assume are for friends. We're in the process of contacting the friends to bring them in for questioning. We want to talk to them as soon as we can."

"Any chance there's a record of calls made and received?"

"No. Not with a burner phone, or at least with this burner."

"If Harold had a phone, why did Jolly have to go into the apartment to wake him?"

"He said he didn't know Harold had a phone. Jolly's cooperating but isn't much help. He admitted his prints were probably in the apartment since he'd gone there at times to wake up Harold. He insisted he hadn't seen Dum Dum after leaving the sheriff's office. He said he spent the rest of the afternoon and evening finishing out-of-town deliveries and didn't get home until after 1:00 AM. We'll check his alibi, but if he's telling the truth, I don't see how he would've been involved."

"Unless he had help."

"We'll try to check for corroboration but that may be difficult since we don't know his route and he was less than forthcoming."

"The rope looked the same as the one found off Pillsbury Point."

"Yeah, both it and the masonry he used for the shelving are a match. The rope was looped over the beam and tied off with a series of knots. It terminated in a crude slip knot at his neck."

"It seems the dump site for the construction at the Lodge got picked over pretty thoroughly. Anyone could've walked away with this stuff."

"I agree."

"Other than the obvious, did our deputies find anything useful?"

"Possibly—there were some anomalies."

"Such as?"

"Harold's fingerprints were on the neck of the bottle, but only the neck. The rest of the bottle was clean."

"I'd think there would at least be smudges from the person who stocked the shelves or sold the bottle."

"That's what Deputy Graves thought. He's our expert on finger-prints and trace. He'll do a more detailed check back at the sheriff's office."

"What about the glass?"

"It had clear prints, Krumm's thumb and first two fingers."

"Any smudges on the glass?"

"No."

Both men understood it was unlikely anyone, but especially an inebriate, could leave pristine prints without smudges on a glass. Michael hesitated then continued what was beginning to sound more like an interrogation. "What else?"

"He wasn't into house cleaning, yet half of the table was wiped. It appears as if another person could've been seated at the table. Unfortunately, there's no definite way of knowing when. There are scuff marks in the dust under the table, and Mullen, our expert on all things digital, took a lot of pictures and lifted what he could from partial footprints. Graves also collected a little mud and some dirt from the footprints for analysis."

"What about the note?"

"Penmanship was weak, but the message was clear enough. He was sorry for hurting Ginny. It was hard to make out, but he went on to say that he didn't want it to end that way."

"Didn't want what to end what way?"

"We don't know."

"Did he say he killed her?"

"No, but as a prosecutor you would know the significance. Until someone can prove otherwise, the note he wrote and the car hidden below speak volumes."

Jack looked away and then back to Michael. "There was something about the note that bothered me."

"Yes?"

"In spite of the poor penmanship, it was grammatically correct, and there were no misspelled words."

"Not bad for someone inebriated and intellectually limited."

"That's what I thought."

"How do you know he wrote it?"

"I found a short list of people with addresses and phone numbers written in a three ring binder. And get this, he wrote a poem about his girlfriend. The poem's pretty bad, but it's a good sample of his handwriting. The experts will decide, but I think it looks like a match."

"A poem. I don't know if that's touching or pathetic."

"The DCI Crime Scene Team arrived right before I left. They'll pick over the car, and if warranted, transport it to the secure lot in Ankeny."

"If we keep sending them vehicles, they may have to expand their impoundment lot."

Jack reacted with a cold smile and shake of his head. "Michael, I admit I don't know whether he murdered her. But whether intentional or not, it appears he may have harmed Ginny in some way, and in remorse, took his own life. We'll know more when all the physical evidence is in and after I interview his friends, but this looks like the sad ending we knew was coming."

44

If Wednesday had seemed long, the days that followed were interminable. Michael occupied time by meeting with interns and took a road trip to speak with sponsors. On his return he caught a limit in walleyes—the bite was on—and reread everything he had on the Lawery case.

"You do obsess over these things." It was late Sunday evening, and Janni lay snuggled next to him, her head on his shoulder.

It had been a winsome day, the afternoon spent on the lake cruising in the *Frau Nägel*, then drinks on the wide front porch. Michael prepared his specialty, a tossed salad distinguished only by the addition of anchovies (which Janni picked out). A pizza delivery completed the culinary requirements, and they spent a romantic evening with wine, time in the bedroom, and pillow talk.

"What do you mean?"

Lifting her head to look directly into his eyes, she spelled it out. "The case is never closed until Michael Cain says it is."

"Well, that seems a bit harsh."

Janni said nothing but continued to stare into his eyes. So he said, "Okay. Everything fits, but there are loose ends, and you know how I feel about loose ends."

"And how do you feel about my loose end?" she asked with a salacious smile.

Now Michael lifted his head and with an exaggerated grin, "I definitely need to continue my investigation."

"Oh? And how do you intend to proceed, Counselor?"

"By examining all the physical evidence I can." She squealed then laughed as he pulled her atop him.

***

It was morning and rain was softly falling. She had left a brief note on her pillow. "It was lovely. Got to run. Call me."

"Not again!" Michael tossed the note. The light in the room was dim as were his plans for the day. He showered, ate breakfast, and picked up around the house. His housekeeper was coming today, and as perverse as it seemed, he felt he needed to tidy up before allowing someone, even someone he knew and trusted, to give his home a thorough cleaning.

Finally satisfied that at least the worst was now presentable, he decided it was better to get out of Anna's path. She wouldn't mind if he remained while she cleaned, but she cleaned like a human tornado. Seeking shelter from the storm, Michael preferred to be out of the house.

Pulling into the ILCC lot on the southern side of the main building, Michael parked in a place designated for faculty members. As he entered the lobby, Michael was surprised to see so many people moving about with a purpose that seemed a combination of good spirits, excitement, and stress. Summer classes were to begin the day after Memorial Day. Distracted as he'd been, it hadn't occurred to Michael that registration and the myriad of other details students and staff needed to complete would be underway. Besides, he'd assumed everything could be done online.

Well-versed in the use of technology, he had a love-hate relationship with devices. He muttered under his breath, "Computers—good for some things, but education and law? It's still about people, not machines."

"Excuse me?"

Michael realized that his mumbling must've been overheard by the receptionist as he walked by her desk. "Oh, nothing…sorry. I was just ruminating about computers, and I must've spoken out loud."

The receptionist smiled. "Welcome to the club. I think everyone has wanted to ruminate a computer right into a dumpster at one time or another. By the way, I have a message for you. It's in your school email too, but President Benton asked me to tell you, he'd like you to call or stop by to see him today."

"Do you know why?"

"I can't help you with that, but I do have a little advice, if you'd like."

"OK."

"If it's normal business, his PA will email or leave a message on the phone system. If it's more urgent, he'll email or message you himself and have someone follow-up in person."

"What if it's really important, like critical?"

"He'll meet you at the door."

"What happens then?"

"It depends—if he's smiling, it's very good, and if he's not smiling, it's very bad."

"Good to know. Maybe I'll start using the service entrance."

Picking up his mail, he went directly to his office and skipped his usual serving of lounge coffee. It was no sacrifice since he thought the Styrofoam cup possessed better flavor than the oily sludge found in the stained carafe. "I really need to bring my own coffee," he thought.

After reviewing his email, Michael called President Benton who answered on the second ring. Michael responded in a slight state of confusion. "President Benton? Sorry if I sound muddled, I was expecting your personal assistant."

"Mildred is off this week. For now I'm president and PA, and I'm beginning to think Milly deserves a raise. Thanks for calling. I just wanted a quick update on the intern program and to remind you that the weekly reports are due on Mondays, beginning the Monday after Memorial Day. The state monitors our progress, and financial support depends upon the paperwork. It doesn't have to be detailed, but enough to feed the beast."

While it seemed trivial for the president to send a reminder, Michael understood paperwork was a part of administering any school. After the update on interns, they signed off, and Michael pulled up the required form on his computer. He was relieved to see its brevity, a welcome change from the layers of documents required in a criminal prosecution.

"Time to call Janni!" He hit speed dial only to be directed to voicemail. "Hi. Calling as requested. I miss you already. Do you want to do lunch? Bye."

Within seconds, Margaritaville rang. It was Janni. "I miss you already, but I can't do lunch. I'm swamped. It really was a lovely time. It's been longer than I care to admit since I've had a day like yesterday."

"Not to sound sappy, but to paraphrase you, I feel like we've never been apart."

"Michael, we've always been together. Now I sound sappy. Not to break the mood, but I had a question about the picture you showed me on your phone of Ginny and Harold, the one beside the vodka bottle."

"What about it?"

"I wondered, who's in the background?"

Pulling the picture up on his laptop, he replied, "That's Jolly, the guy that Harold worked for."

"What's he doing?"

"What do you mean?"

"I was curious. I couldn't make it out, but I had the impression he was handing something to someone and I wondered what it was."

"Let me enlarge that part of the picture." Michael made the adjustment on his computer. "It's a little fuzzy, but it looks like he's giving or receiving quite a wad of paper, maybe money?"

"Can you tell who he's talking to?"

"No, I can see a hand and forearm. It looks like a man wearing a suit coat, but the rest is outside the picture. I'll check with Detective Donahue. They have a copy and their equipment is better. I'll let you know what I find. Sure you don't want to get together at least for dessert?"

"Sorry, not today. I promise to make it up to you. This is a stressful week. The official opening of the remodeled Lodge is Saturday. All the big shots will be there for the ribbon cutting. There's a reception and banquet, Foyle's combo is playing for the dinner hour, and the Big Band will play until the huge fireworks display. We're going all out."

"We?"

"Well, so to speak."

After they disconnected, Michael smiled. "A question about the picture. Sounds like a good excuse to bug the law enforcement folks."

45

Donning his rain jacket, Michael exited the school, hurried up the street, and passed through the rain-scrubbed Veterans Memorial Plaza to enter the Dickinson County Courthouse. He went directly to the sheriff's office where he was informed that Sheriff Conrad was attending a meeting out of town. When he asked if Detective Donahue was available Michael was directed to Interview Room #1.

"I'm just about to interview Krumm's girlfriend, Sylvia Norris. Denise, one of our office employees, is with her in the interview room. I'm using a suggestion from your playbook. Sylvia was upset and crying when she arrived. Denise was willing to go in first to reassure Sylvia and see if she needs anything."

Standing outside the window to the interview room, Michael wondered how they had managed to soften the normally harsh glare of the overhead lights. What else was different? "You have different chairs."

"That was Denise's idea. So was the laptop."

"Why the laptop?"

"It's hard to see from here but the top is covered with brightly-colored flower stickers."

"Your personal laptop?"

He snorted. "Hardly. It belongs to Denise."

Sylvia was red-eyed, had the hiccups, and was rapidly adding to a pile of used tissues next to a small blue tissue box. An unopened bottle of water was before her on the table.

"Well, that's as calm as she's been since arriving. I'd better go to work. Denise is going to sit in on the interview. You can observe from here."

Michael was captivated less by Sylvia than by Denise, who appeared transformed from the bubbly office worker he knew, into a confident, reassuring advocate for someone who was in serious need of empathy.

The interview was circuitous and tear-infused, but meaningful. When not blowing her nose or wiping her eyes dry, Sylvia's fingers would grip and fidget with a whale-shaped pendant suspended on a gold chain from around her neck.

Jack took his time. His quiet, reassuring "I'm on your side" manner nurtured a rapport that gradually tamped down the emotional bursts of muddled libretto and evoked coherent answers. Though silent throughout, Denise's presence was calming. When asked a question, Sylvia would look first at Denise who would nod her head, sometimes with a slight smile, and thus encouraged, Sylvia would respond.

In response to his questions about the vodka and Harold's drinking habits, Sylvia frowned and insisted, "Harold didn't like strong stuff. He only drank beer."

When asked about Ginny's car, she replied, "We rode in it once. He said she let him borrow it for our date. I didn't see it again after that." Sylvia didn't know the car was missing and couldn't remember for sure when they used the car for their date. She added, "Harold really liked Ginny but they were just friends."

She knew Harold worked for Jolly, and Harold said Jolly was a good boss. But when shown his picture for confirmation, Sylvia's voice quivered, declaring she thought Jolly was scary because of the way he looked at her.

When the interview concluded, Michael met Jack in the hall and followed him to his office, while Denise escorted an emotionally drained Sylvia to the restroom. Michael spoke first, saying, "That was impressive."

"What do you mean?"

"The way you conducted the interview."

"Denise made a big difference."

"Yes, she did, but I've observed and done enough interviews and interrogations to know the difference, and what you did was exceptional. I'm impressed. You're one skilled interrogator."

With his face faintly reddened, Jack cleared his throat, "Well, thank you. Coming from you, that means a lot."

Michael went on, "So, what do you think?"

After a deep breath, Jack answered, "It fills in some of the blanks, but doesn't significantly change the narrative. The DCI is waiting for the autopsy report, but considers there to be enough evidence to close both cases."

"Do you agree?"

"Because of some of the circumstantial stuff, I'm not totally convinced. Deputy Graves did find human blood traces on Winnie the fishing shack, some on the latch and two contributors on the carpet. One of those on the carpet matches Lawery's blood type. We're waiting on any further results from the DCI lab, but it seems to support what we already know. Unless something unexpected turns up, I have nothing to challenge the facts. Sylvia added insight, but it won't change any minds. What do you think?"

"I agree with you. With only conjecture and no solid evidence to the contrary, I may question their conclusions but would have trouble refuting them." Both were quiet. Then Michael added, "She got a little testy when you said you admired her pendant."

"Well…I was too blunt. I think she got defensive because Harold gave it to her and she was afraid we would confiscate it. She admitted they had what she called a 'physic relationship.' I believe she meant physical, but I think it hurt her to know that when Harold committed suicide, if that's what it was, the last person he was thinking about was Ginny."

"Did you learn anything more from the other friends?"

"No, not really. It's a unique bunch, but what they said lines up with Sylvia. They knew he was infatuated with Ginny, but insisted other than a hug there was nothing physical between them. They all said he would never hurt her or anyone. He wasn't violent."

"We know that he attacked Jolly."

"Jolly is such a boor he even managed to provoke Krumm. It clearly was a one-time thing and out of character. What bothers me is all his friends said hard booze and suicide were not like him. If he was troubled he would've talked about it. He talked about everything. He was happy. He had a girlfriend. He liked his work. There was nothing they could see that would explain what happened."

Drawing his phone from his hip pocket, Michael opened it to the photo of Ginny and Harold. "Janneke had an interesting question. She asked what Jolly was doing in this picture. It appears he's exchanging with someone what may be a large wad of cash."

Jack went over to his computer to open the case file on Harold Krumm and brought up the same photo. "It's hard to tell what it is or what he's doing, but it's an interesting question. Deputy Mullen is our computer tech. I'll have him play with it and see if he can enhance it."

With a backlog of work made conspicuous by the heap of paper on his desk, Jack turned down an invitation to lunch, and Michael opted for something from the ILCC vending machines. Munching an energy bar at his desk, he considered the conclusions in both investigations and the reservations he held in accord with Jack. Few cases closed with all questions answered, but there should be enough evidence and facts known to dispel serious doubts. Despite the scribbled confession and physical evidence, there were flaws in the conclusion that Krumm was their culprit—flaws significant enough in Michael's experience to warrant reservations.

Although he and Detective Donahue remained skeptical, he understood that if the DCI's conclusions held, Donahue's job was done. Jack would move on to the next investigation. Michael was less restricted and wanted more answers. He took from his desk a new legal pad and began scribbling out his thoughts with no filter nor any particular order.

Why did Ginny come home?

What was so important that she came home a week before spring break?

There was some sort of big news.

What was the news? Was it only about adding to her business major?

Why didn't she call her Aunties?

Why did she spend the evening at the Lodge?

Did she leave the Lodge?

Did she stay with Harold?

Why would Ginny stay with Harold and not with her Aunties?

If Ginny was in Harold's apartment, why was there no evidence?

Why would Harold harm Ginny?

Was he capable of harming her?

He knew about the fishing shacks.

Was he capable of what seemed to be a calculated disposal of the body and cover-up?

If he did do it, did someone help him and who would that be? Who would gain from Ginny's death?

Love, hate, anger, fear, money, revenge?

Ginny was pregnant. Who was the father of Ginny's child?

Did the father need to eliminate the child and Ginny?

Is the father the prime suspect?

Father = Suspect

Michael hesitated. It was obvious the father would be a suspect. Had they made wrong assumptions about the father? Had Michael and the other investigators been so convinced of their first theories, or manipulated, that there were miscalculations? They were so certain and yet so wrong about the ex-boyfriend and the relationships between Laxton, Sally, and Ginny, couldn't they be wrong about other matters, including the relationship between Ginny and Harold Krumm? Was there really a connection between the attack on Sally and what happened to Ginny or was it only random?

And what of the change in Ginny's behavior and attitude? Sally Grosfeldt suggested Ginny may have been promiscuous, possibly with several partners. Was it possible that the father was someone not yet drawn into their investigation? And if so, was he desperate to cover it up, desperate enough to harm Ginny? What could be that critical? Did the father even know of the pregnancy?

Was Krumm, for some unknown reason, a threat to Ginny or was he a threat to someone else? Did he possess some sort of evidence? Was it all coincidental? Were the deaths of Virginia Lawery and Harold Krumm related? Was Krumm's suicide staged?

The flood of disorganized thoughts were tumbling out only to be caught up into an undecipherable web. Michael returned to his legal pad.

Motive

 Harold Krumm: None that we know of unless an accident.

 Baby's Father: To cover up relationship (pregnancy) in order to protect marriage, money, social or professional status, or conceal criminal activity.

Means

 Known outcomes, both possible.

Opportunity

 Too many unknowns, both possible.

Michael set down his pen and quietly sat staring at the yellow pad on the desk. He slowly sifted through and filtered everything he remembered about the cases, weighing details, comparing, contrasting, and rearranging evidence to fit differing scenarios.

Gradually from the cacophony there began to emerge an order suggesting several alternative paths, one of which, with work, could prove more traveled than others. Picking up his phone, he began calling.

46

With the exception of the removal of the body, the apartment was unimproved since his last visit. The sour odor lingered. Faint footprints, residual fingerprint powder, and items misplaced onto prior dust patterns attested to the documentation and attempt to ferret out any clues to understand the violence that had occurred. What remained were the big pieces and some smaller artifacts as he remembered from the photos of the site. Still, something about it didn't ring true.

He had prevailed upon Detective Donahue, and now that he was back at the scene, he sensed a consciousness, a tangible, inexplicable response. He mentally moved through the space as if watching events as they occurred. He was here as auditor, not participant.

It wasn't the individual elements but the gestalt. Everything was choreographed to fit one narrative: "Harold Krumm did it. Harold Krumm harmed Virginia Lawery."

Michael stood in the doorway, reliving his first impressions, filtering through what he knew and comparing it to theories that didn't involve suicide. His deep concentration was disrupted by the Margaritaville ringtone. He hesitated, thinking the tune was coming from elsewhere than his pocket.

"Michael!" It was Donahue.

"Yes?"

"Are you in the apartment?"

"Yes."

"Are you wearing the booties and nitrile gloves I gave you?"

"Yes on the booties, no on the gloves, but I haven't handled anything."

"Good. Leave the apartment."

"What's going on?"

"The DCI had a change of heart. Their crime scene people examined the car but left the apartment to our team of investigators. It seems our deputies did an exceptionally fine job. The mud and dirt they found may be a recent contribution and contains traces of oil and sphagnum moss. The oil is a specialty kind used in motorcycles. Also, the footprints and trace lifted from Harold's apartment and your home match. The wear pattern on the outside of the right foot suggests whoever it was walked with a limp, and Graves remembered that Jolly walks with a limp. He checked the interview room used when we brought in Jolly. Nobody's used or cleaned it since, and he went through it meticulously. He found trace and lifted several excellent footprints, all of which match those found in your home and Harold's apartment. The DCI wants to return to do their own workup of the crime scene. So, Counselor, leave everything as it is and please exit as you entered, ASAP."

Michael hung up and scrutinized the room one more time. Everything was in place—well almost. He closed his eyes, slowed his breathing, focused, and rehearsed the room, pointing at objects as he remembered them. Suddenly he opened his eyes. He was pointing at the homemade shelving. Sitting on the top shelf was a picture frame missing its picture. He knew from the crime scene report that the picture found leaning against the vodka bottle had been taped to the frame.

Putting on his nitrile gloves, Michael ignored what he'd been told and stepped gingerly to the shelving to study the frame. It was a digital picture frame and ugly, or rather the repair job was ugly. The glass display was cracked and the rails of the frame were held together by duct tape. The overall effect wasn't pleasing. A residual coating of powder was evidence of an investigator's search for fingerprints.

Turning it over, Michael felt something under the tape on the back of the frame that didn't conform to the smoother taped surface on the front. Aware of the need to preserve evidence, he improvised by wrapping his clean handkerchief around the frame, then exited and relocked the door.

Once inside his car, he called Donahue. "Is Terry the tech in-house?"

"I don't know. Let me check." Michael could hear the sound of Jack's hand over the receiver and a muffled call to someone. "Not right now, but he's due in shortly. Is there something I can help with?"

"I committed an indiscretion, but if what I suspect is true, Deputy Mullen may be able to prove it worthwhile."

Donahue wasn't pleased to hear what Michael had done, but since it was done, he said, "Do not take it back into the apartment. Preserve it as best you can and bring it right over."

"Will do. I'm sorry for the complication, and it may not prove to be anything, but…."

"Yeah, I know. We'll have Terry work on it. Oh, and you have a message from Barry Seward from ISU. You're to call him. He said he called your office, but the receptionist told him you were at the courthouse."

"Thanks, Jack. I'll return his call after I deliver the frame. See you in a few minutes."

47

Michael's calls and emails over the next two days connected him to all the important players, and as often happens with continued conversations, additional details emerged. Barry's call concerned a follow-up done by one of his officers.

"The two young women who helped Sally recalled that right before they found her, they heard the sound of a motorcycle, like a Harley, storming away from the far side of the library. There's a permit-only parking lot, but someone could easily park a motorcycle at night, at least for a short time, and it wouldn't be noticed. They didn't mention it before because they didn't associate the motorcycle with Sally's attack, but when my officer asked each of them to remember anything before or after they found Sally, even if it seemed irrelevant, they both said they thought it was unusual for someone to be riding a motorcycle on a cold night and that time of year. They assumed it was some student getting an early jump on spring. It's a small detail, but thought I'd pass it along."

Pam had called Sally, and Sally confirmed that she heard a

motorcycle and the sound came from the general direction her attacker had taken.

The DCI lab people were back and each discovery either confirmed what Deputies Graves and Mullen had found or added to the accumulation of evidence. They were becoming less confident in a determination of suicide.

DCI Agent William "Wild Bill" Hitchcock accompanied the mobile DCI Crime Scene Team and was working with Detective Donahue and an expanded team of investigators in addition to Jack and Michael. Agent Hitchcock shared that the DCI had been in touch with the Feds and learned the DEA was working on what they considered to be a related case in Arizona that involved Jolly Holiday. A meeting of the minds was scheduled for later in the day at the conference room of the sheriff's office.

The turning point for the DCI had been Harold's autopsy report from the state ME's office, a revelation that Dr. Phillipa Goulet desired to personally explain to Michael.

"Evidence indicates, even if preplanned, the level of intoxication was so great, that the victim was incapable of climbing the chair or inserting his head through the knotted loop in the rope unassisted. He had at least six ounces of vodka and nearly a quart of beer remaining in his stomach. His blood alcohol reading was 4.2. He was tall and skinny, and due to his body type, was dangerously close to expiring from alcohol poisoning."

"The vomit was pre-mortem. It's difficult to throw up with a rope tied tightly around your neck. The directional disposal of vomit on his shirt, the chair, and on the floor, indicates he purged while standing on the chair. Again, he would have been unable to climb onto and stand on the chair without help. There also was a gap in the vomit pattern mid-chest which suggests someone had their arm around him, likely from the back.

"I explained all this to Agent Hitchcock, and he thinks this conforms to the faint footprints found on an adjacent chair. I understand there was an attempt to wipe the footprints from the seat of the chair, but your crime scene technician was able to recover partials. They match the footprints found on the floor in the interrogation room at the sheriff's office and the footprints found in your home. The same scumbag who attacked you may have faked Krumm's suicide."

"Scumbag. Is that a clinical expression?"

"Sorry. Bit editorial, that."

"I love it when you talk dirty."

"Then you'd enjoy a few other terms I like to use. So, when's your next trip to the capital city? I have several suggestions if you're interested."

"Such as?"

"Well, dinner, of course."

"How about next Friday?"

"Really?"

"I'm working with some summer interns from the community college and, if I can arrange it, I plan to fly to Des Moines and meet with some of the people at the Law Enforcement Academy. I need to learn more about their expectations for incoming recruits. After a day of that, I'll be ready to hear some of your other terms."

"I'll make reservations. Call me the night before and let me know where you're staying and I'll pick you up. Do you have my number?"

"Yes, I have your number."

Signing off, Michael was startled to hear a voice behind him. "I bet you do."

Turning quickly to the sound of Janneke's voice, he stammered, "Hello! I didn't hear you come in."

"You were distracted. A female medical examiner. Tell me, is she an old crone lurking about her den of horrors disguised as a beauty?"

"What?"

"You know, like the wicked stepmother in Snow White."

"Dr. Goulet is very helpful."

"Oh? Just how helpful is she?"

Michael wasn't sure if Janni was serious or toying with him. "I'd arranged to meet her at the ME's office, but someone tried to crash my plane. She suggested we have dinner at the Green Oak where she explained the results of Ginny's autopsy."

Janneke gave a mock shiver. "Discordant, wouldn't you say? Talk of carving up the victim while carving the beef?"

Michael's face grew dark. "I'm not sure what you're implying, but it was business and not beef. It was duck."

"Did you say duck, or did I misunderstand your pronunciation?"

Momentarily discombobulated, Michael sat there with his mouth open not knowing whether to laugh or respond in anger. Why should he need to defend himself? He watched as a smile formed on Janni's face. He'd been had.

They both laughed, Michael in relief and Janni gleefully, as she enjoyed some of what endeared him to her. "Oh, Michael. I've said it before, you're so easy. I love you, but we're not exclusive, or at least at this point I don't think of it that way. I'll let you know if there's a change."

Michael nodded his head. "Agreed, in spite of getting skewered by your macabre sense of humor,"—Janni smiled—"I'm happy to see you."

"I'm happy to see you, too. Now, what did you want to show me?"

"What?"

"Your text said you had something to show me. I'm meeting with the county auditor next door anyway, so thought I'd stone two birds at one time."

"Oh, the picture! Detective Donahue had the department's computer whiz enhance the background of the picture of Ginny and Harold."

He pulled the picture up onto his laptop and as Janni leaned over his shoulder to better see the image, her hair brushed his cheek. Her first response was, "Huh." It wasn't a question but a statement. "May I take a closer look?"

"Here, take my chair."

Michael stood to the side and watched as Janni's face changed from curiosity to a troubled frown. "What is it?" She didn't answer. "What do you see?"

"I'm not sure."

"Tell me anyway."

"No. It's nothing. Send a copy to my phone, would you please, Michael?"

"Yes, but what is it?"

Abruptly rising, she insisted, "It may be nothing, but I'll let you know. I have to check on something first. Gotta go. Call you later." She gave him a peck on the cheek and was gone.

Michael stood staring at the open doorway. "What the hell just happened? God, she's right. Sometimes I am clueless."

48

Now war arose in heaven. Michael and his angels fighting against the dragon.

Revelation 12:7

Michael arrived for the meeting with only moments to spare. As an advocate of interagency cooperation, it was gratifying to see DCI Agent Hitchcock and Detective Donahue conducting the meeting in tandem, another example of the 9/11 effect. Donahue's exceptional memory was on display as he introduced all the players, their titles, and their roles in the investigation. It was now accepted that the two cases were one. Jack briefly covered the salient points up to the present time and then turned matters over to DCI Agent Hitchcock.

Hitchcock explained there were significant questions unanswered concerning what happened to Harold Krumm and to Virginia Lawery. The DCI had reached out to the Feds and authorities in Arizona for more information regarding Jolly and a nascent motorcycle gang he and a few known hardcore bikers had chartered while in

Arizona's prison system. Agents in Arizona were eager to cooperate with the FBI, DEA, and Iowa law enforcement. At this stage, the Dickinson County Sheriff's Department, assisted by the DCI, would continue to lead the operation.

Hitchcock distributed a binder to each of them. "This is also available digitally and includes a checklist of what is known or needs to be confirmed. We'll add to this as we go along. Let me say to begin with, we're very interested in Mr. Jolly Holiday. If you'll turn to page three, you'll see why. I'll go through it with you." Everything listed had a Jolly Holiday connection.

1. *There is trace human blood on the carpet in the "Winnie-the-Pooh" fishing shack from two donors, and they are a match for Ginny Lawery and Jolly Holiday. There is also trace on the door latch that matches Holiday. We believe he may have cut his hand when breaking into the shack.* "Although we have his blood type, we don't have Holiday's DNA on record. He was incarcerated in Arizona, and like many states, Arizona is playing catch up when it comes to the DNA of past offenders."

2. *Holiday's boot prints and trace evidence taken from Interrogation Room #1 of the sheriff's office connect him to the B&E and assault on Michael Cain and as a presence in Harold Krumm's apartment, possibly at the victim's demise.* "Thanks to modern science and skilled techs, it's possible to recover prints of shoes, boots, and so on that used to pass by undiscovered."

3. *Trace sphagnum moss found in Krumm's apartment, the home of Michael Cain, and in Interrogation Room #1 is the same as that found in bait containers distributed by Holiday.*

"The owner of the Sports Shop next to the Lodge was able to provide us with some of Holiday's used bait containers."

4. *Oil trace found in Krumm's apartment, the home of Michael Cain, and in Interrogation Room #1 matches that used in motorcycles.* "Holiday rides a Harley-Davidson motorcycle."

5. *A motorcycle was heard to be in the area shortly after the attack on Sally Grosfeldt.* "I would add that since Sally's digital devices were taken and Ginny's devices remain missing, investigators theorize that it is likely the attack on Sally and the burglary of their apartment were meant to find and eliminate any incriminating evidence that could connect someone to the death of Virginia Lawery."

6. *A motorcycle was heard to be in the area of the airport shortly before Michael Cain flew off in his Cessna.* "In case you weren't aware of it, the Cessna developed engine trouble, likely due to sabotage, and necessitated a dead stick landing. Fortunately, the Ames Municipal Airport was nearby and Mr. Cain has the skill to manage such an emergency landing."

7. *Due to an old wrestling injury to the right hip, Holiday walks with a limp similar to that described by Sally Grosfeldt and observed by Dickinson County Deputy Brian Graves.*

8. *Holiday's rap sheet includes B&E and assault. He did time in Arizona on a plea deal that omitted drug distribution.* "The drug charge was weak because the witnesses recanted their testimony."

9. *Holiday is a charter member of a mostly wannabe motorcycle gang, but a few of the members are hard-core and have long records.*

10. *Some are known to be in this area—most remain in Arizona. The DEA knows Holiday.*

11. *Sources in Arizona point to his involvement in drug trafficking. We believe his involvement extends to Iowa. We don't know how it's being done but suspect his local bait supply business is a cover.*

Hitchcock concluded the narrative. "As you can see, some of this is circumstantial, but there's a lot of it. Witness accounts and the trace evidence and boot prints suggest there's a common thread in the attacks on Sally Grosfeldt, Michael Cain, and Harold Krumm. That common thread is Jolly Holiday.

"We've asked district Judge Garner for a warrant to search Holiday's mobile home, barn, and all other buildings on the acreage, as well as his van, phone, and electronic devices. We also asked to confiscate his work boots. She's agreed to the boots but deferred on the rest. You can understand that for such a wide-ranging warrant, the judge expects more specificity. If the boots match our evidence, the judge may grant the additional warrant for what we've requested. Then we may be able to charge Holiday and any others connected in some way for these heinous crimes."

With that, Hitchcock deferred to Detective Donahue. "Holiday will be asked to come in, ostensibly to answer a few questions we still have about Harold Krumm and to help us wrap up the investigation into Krumm's assault and murder of Virginia Lawery. We want to do that today, but avoid revealing to Holiday the true scope of the investigation. Something we want all of you to keep in mind as you go about your work."

Each attendee was assigned specific tasks and the team was scheduled to reconvene early Friday with the expectation that they would then be able to execute the desired search warrant. Questions were answered and then the team, in silent resolve, decamped.

Donahue addressed Michael as he was about to leave. "Stick around, Michael." Closing the door, he said, "The DCI consented to have you assist the state and the sheriff's department in the investigation. You can't sit in on the interrogation with Mr. Holiday, but you can observe."

"All right. Thank you."

"That's not all. The Dickinson County Attorney and Sheriff Conrad want you to serve as advisor. In that capacity, you will be on hand if we arrest Holiday and search his property. Everyone understands the issues that can arise in a multi-agency, multi-jurisdictional case like this. Should the arrest and search begin to go sideways, some decisions may need to be made quickly, without bureaucratic delay—that's when you might be of help.

"Our county attorney also checked with Judge Garner and she concurs." Looking down to read from his notes, he recited, "To quote the judge: 'I agree that decisions may be facilitated better by a knowledgeable neutral party, on site, acting as advisor. Said advisor also may act, if needed, as a point person to communicate with the court.' Unquote."

"You'll be responsible for communication between our team and the judge. She'll be on hand in her chambers and is to be kept up-to-date. Judge Garner is supportive and wants this done right."

Donahue handed Michael a sheet of paper. "Here are all her contact numbers. Call the judge, confirm you've accepted the appointment, and hear what her expectations are. Congratulations! You're it!"

***

"That is one pissed off bait dealer." Michael was standing outside the interview window watching two large deputies remove a set of handcuffs and place Jolly's beefy forearms in table restraints.

"That tends to be a common state for Jolly, but probably nothing compared to what's about to happen."

"I thought you and Wild Bill said you were going to bring him in peacefully?"

"Well, you know how it is. Sometimes good intentions are mis-interpreted. A little shove becomes assault on a police officer."

"Are you going to let him cool off?"

"That's what we normally do, but not this time. We don't want to give him time to think ahead. We're going to go right at him."

An hour-and-a-half later, the bait dealer was still pissed and little had been gained. Michael understood the variety of approaches skill-fully used by the interrogators, but so did Jolly. They asked about the attack on Sally and the attack on Michael. When talking about Harold's suicide, Donahue took a different tack. "You knew how badly he felt, you liked him, you both were drinking heavily, maybe you felt sorry for him and in a weak moment, helped him end his misery."

Jolly responded, "Bullshit!"

He was questioned about deliveries the night Krumm was hanged and if anyone could vouch for him. They asked for a copy of his schedule and the locations of his vending machines. He retorted, "Get a warrant!"

They drilled him hard on his drug activities and gang affiliations in Arizona and whether he still had those connections. They asked if he had started a chapter in the Lakes area. Jolly was surly, uncoop-erative, and abusive, but in spite of his obvious anger, his responses were measured. He didn't ask for a lawyer.

They took a break, then went at it for another hour. Nothing. Finally, an exasperated Agent Hitchcock leaned right up to Jolly's face and through clenched teeth threatened, "We're going to check your barn, your van, and everything you've touched. We're going to turn you inside out. You have this one chance, and once you step out of this room, there will be no deals, no consideration for cooperation. You're screwed! You're on your own!" He slapped a piece of paper down on the table. "Oh, and by the way, here's a warrant for your boots."

Jolly went ballistic. "Screw you and screw your threats. You want my boots? Take 'em! Shove 'em up your ass. You want to check my stuff? Get a warrant. Now charge me or fuck off."

There was no arrest.

***

While they waited for expedited tests and lab results on Jolly's boots, Agent Hitchcock, Detective Donahue, and Michael dissected the interview and ran parts of the video, but the result was the same. There was no significant addition to take to the judge for the warrant. Everything rested on whether there was a match with the boots.

Sheriff Conrad joined the group while they worked in the conference room. "While you questioned Holiday, we just happened to have our K-9 unit walk by his van, but the dog didn't react. The van smells so bad, the dog probably couldn't distinguish drugs from all the crap."

Michael sat at the table's end, reviewing his personal notes. Sally's attacker walked away with a limp and smelled earthy. They had boot prints and trace that matched two crime scenes and the interview room. He had access and means, and he was capable. But what was the motive? Maybe Krumm knew something and couldn't be trusted. Could it all be that simple? Was it possible that somehow Ginny and Harold were collateral damage?

Michael looked up from his notes. "I have a suggestion."

The three men looked at him, and Jack was the first to respond. "I hope it's a good one."

"We need to approach the judge from a different direction. Judge Garner may be willing to issue a warrant if we narrow the focus and have a specific intent. I'm to keep her informed. Let me call, relate what we learned, and try a couple of 'what ifs.'"

"But we didn't learn anything."

"Actually, we did. I'll make the call."

***

Although it was still a stretch, Michael argued to Judge Garner that any evidence in the van and warehouse was elevated in importance by Holiday's known history of drug distribution. There were instances during the interrogation when questions about Krumm had overlapped with statements about drugs. Jolly's answers refuted the questions about Krumm but failed to address or deny the drug-related accusations and implications.

It turned out the boots were a match, and they held a bonus—trace vomit matching that found at Krumm's apartment. The obvious link to Harold Krumm's now questionable suicide and Michael's argument concerning a possible drug connection made for an easy decision. Judge Garner issued a warrant for Holiday's arrest and granted the warrant for the van, trailer, warehouse, and adjacent property.

Judge Garner reminded Michael, "Anything related to the death of Harold Krumm, any illegal drugs, other prohibited substances, drug paraphernalia, and anything to do with production or distribution of drugs is covered by the warrant. In my opinion, you have a compelling cause for your search. If you need to, call me, and I'll consider expanding the warrant. This isn't to be shared, but good luck. Let's get this SOB!"

Evidently Father Barney was not the only one who believed justice sometimes needed encouragement.

They assembled at 4:00 AM in the maintenance building adjacent to the Dickinson County Courthouse. With the onset of spring weather the heater was off, and the large space was as cool as the predawn air outside. The effect was negligible. The atmosphere inside crackled with tension, the anticipation was palpable, the increased flow of adrenaline pumping through their bodies barely controlled beneath a patina of discipline. They all had received the summons the evening before: Judge Garner had granted the warrant.

With so many agencies depending upon their success, the operation had evolved into a major campaign. Connie would command the assault from the communications van, a repurposed Winnebago RV. Michael was assigned to the command center with Connie. From there, they could communicate with all players, including Judge Garner.

Sheriff Conrad always insisted on extensive training for his people. He was confident in his staff but emotionally restrained by his role as sheriff. His temperament made him valuable for the role of understanding and directing the officers, yet he would rather be the first one through the door.

In addition to firearms and extra ammunition, everyone wore a bullet-resistant vest and utility belt fitted with a variety of choices to reduce force. Divided into two assault teams, Team One would spearhead the advance and approach through the roadside grove. Their target was the mobile home. Using the lane, Team Two would follow to provide backup and secure the intermediate buildings and barn. Firearms Deputy Sergeant Dexter had finished inspecting each member for weapons and ammunition. He assigned specific members on Team One the necessary equipment needed to break in or force the occupant from the trailer.

A large portable table was set up in the middle of the cavernous maintenance garage. On the table was a section from a plat map blown up to clearly show the entrance, driveway, buildings, and surrounding terrain of the objective.

At 4:30 AM Detective Donahue mustered everyone around the map, and assisted by DCI Agent Hitchcock, began the briefing. It was straightforward. Jolly had a mobile home set into a small grove on a site that used to include a house, corn crib, detached garage, utility shed, and barn. The house and corn crib were gone. The garage, utility shed, and barn remained. As far as they knew, there were no dogs or other kept animals. The deputy on overnight stake-out reported Jolly had returned late the previous evening, parked his van in the barn, and entered the mobile home where, it was thought, he remained.

Donahue pointed out the entrance lane was off Highway 9 and approximately 200 yards long.

"Team One, led by Sergeant Dexter, will approach from the highway on foot, advance through the grove, and arrive on the southern end of the mobile home. That likely is where the subject will be sleeping. When they're in place, Team Two will drive slowly into the lane and provide backup. The communications van will remain at the entrance. Mr. Cain will remain in the van as observer and representative of the court.

"Sergeant Dexter and Deputy Sheriff Thompson will approach the front door of the mobile home to serve the warrant and arrest Holiday. Team One will assist in entering and securing the mobile home. Let me stress, Jolly Holiday is capable of violence and considered extremely dangerous. When Holiday is in custody, Team Two will clear the garage and utility shed, then access the barn. After the site is secured the crime scene investigators will be allowed in to set up their equipment and begin their work. If all goes well there will be donuts for everyone. Any questions?" There were a few nervous attempts to laugh about the donuts. There were no questions.

They departed at 5:00 AM, and fifteen minutes later the convoy stopped at the bottom of a hill for a final check. They were on Highway 9, two miles from their goal. A sudden glow like the rising sun appeared in the sky but it was from the west. The van's radio crackled. "This is stakeout Charley. Be advised. The Spirit Lake Fire Department is on its way. The subject's barn just exploded into flames."

***

The fire department turned out in force but could do nothing to save the barn or the van parked inside. The mobile home was undamaged, and a small safe sat open and empty in the bedroom. If it had held evidence of Jolly's activities, it was gone.

After the convoy returned to the maintenance building where they'd gathered hours earlier, Sheriff Conrad addressed the teams. "He was thorough. The crime scene investigators will work the site, but so far there's nothing additional of interest in the mobile home. The barn and van are a total loss. We may prove arson and there may be trace for drugs, but the destruction was so complete, we're unsure what would stand up in court." Detective Donahue and DCI Agent Hitchcock were clearly disgusted and the teams frustrated. Exhaustion, exacerbated by the drain of adrenaline, was evident in them all.

Connie continued his summary. "Holiday escaped. Tracks found behind the barn indicate he pushed his motorcycle to an access path along the half-mile fence. From there, we think he remotely detonated whatever was set up in the barn. We issued APB and BOLO alerts for his motorcycle, but by now he's probably swapped out his bike with one of his buddies and is gone. Write up your reports. Team leaders will meet with me at 1:00 PM in the sheriff's office conference room to break it down."

Michael reported to Judge Garner and obtained a warrant for Jolly's bait vending machines. To be on the safe side of the law, it included any associated electronic devices. He passed the warrant on to Detective Donahue and wrote and emailed his brief report for the sheriff and the judge. Still emotionally drained by the morning's setback, he stopped at Connie's door for a final update, then thought better of it. Sheriff Conrad appeared detached, inscrutable, deeply engaged in conversation with someone from some agency, somewhere. It was an activity he would repeat until all associated participants were apprised of events. None of them would be pleased. Michael waved, unseen by his friend, and quietly left the building.

Arriving home, Michael had two messages. The first was from Janni who apologized "for falling off the face of the earth this week, but it's been crazy trying to help with the official reopening of the Lodge. Let me know if you can join me Saturday night." The second message was from Father Barney to remind him the funeral for Harold Krumm would be at 10:00 AM tomorrow.

His call to Janni rang through, but there was no answer. He left a message saying he'd try again later. His call to Father Barney was answered by the parish housekeeper. Michael asked her to thank Barney and to tell him he would be at the funeral.

He climbed the stairs, dropping his clothing as he went, and headed straight for the shower. When the hot water ran out, he toweled off and fell into bed.

50

The assaulting ring of a telephone dragged him from an uneasy slumber. The answering machine picked up, and from his haven under the covers, Michael could hear Willy's gravelly voice. He checked the clock; he couldn't believe he'd slept straight through the night until 7:00 AM. Groaning, he threw the covers back and was reminded of his lack of clothing by the air's chill. Punching play on the answering machine, he heard Willy's voice. "Mr. Cain, you owe me a favor for all my help." He added that he didn't want to talk about it over the phone. "These damn portable phones are easier to tap into than the old land phones. Come see me, today!"

Michael glared at the machine as if it was more than a messenger, then spat out in disgust, "Willy can wait!" Instead of returning the call, Michael went for a run, showered, ate a bagel and a bowl of defrosted berries from the freezer, and phoned Connie.

"No one's seen Jolly or his motorcycle. It's like the earth opened up and swallowed him. We've distributed his picture and asked all law enforcement and pretty much any public or private service that interacts with the general populace to watch for him. We also gave the news media his picture and information with a request that if anyone should see him, they are to call or text us. The tourists and summer returnees may help or hinder. More people means it's harder to pick him out but more eyes looking for him. It could work in our favor."

"Aren't you concerned that you may be overwhelmed with calls?"

"Under the circumstances, it's still the better thing to do."

"Some of the business community may not be happy about it."

"I know, but they'd be even more upset if the public hadn't been informed and someone was harmed. They'll have to suck it up and live with it, like the rest of us."

"What did the fire marshal have to say?"

"Unofficially, the cause of the fire was arson—big surprise. There were enough gasoline and other flammables that the barn and van went off like a Roman candle. We should have his report early next week. We don't anticipate Jolly returning to admire his work, but we have a volunteer reserve deputy onsite to keep away the curious. We'll reconvene the team sometime next week after we hear from the fire marshal and discuss what, if anything, we do to follow-up. I'll let you know when and where."

"Thanks."

"I don't know if Detective Donahue told you this, but we had a warrant to attach a GPS to Jolly's van a few days ago. When we released Jolly, we had a deputy follow him at some distance in an unmarked vehicle. Jolly picked up something at the barn then drove his usual delivery route. Thanks to you and Judge Garner, we opened two of his vending bait dispensers and found drugs in one and money in the other. We're in the process of setting up surveillance cameras at all the sites marked by the GPS. Other than that, it's every hand on deck for Memorial Day weekend. Last night, thank goodness, was fairly quiet, but it will pick up today. All deputies have to work the weekend, and every available volunteer reserve deputy has been assigned to direct traffic or assist with crowd control at the park, not to mention the official opening of the Lodge. There'll be a big crowd there for the fireworks."

Michael waited to hear if there was more, then said, "Man, that's a load. Impressive for the short turnaround from yesterday."

"Not much choice. I'm fortunate to have a great staff and group of dedicated volunteers."

Michael added, "And they're fortunate to have your leadership."

***

The funeral casket and flowers were tasteful. Evidently Harold's inheritance had provided for such a need. The funeral was lightly attended, even counting those whose mission was to fill some pews when it was thought the deceased would have few mourners present.

Seated near the front, huddled in their little group, were Harold's friends. His girlfriend appeared to have replenished her supply of tears and tissues and sat next to the aisle sobbing and twisting the pendant from Harold. They were clustered securely but were unsure of the ritual and responses. However, at the appropriate time, two came forward to take communion. Following their lead, the rest of the group rose as one, queued behind their communal brethren, and received the host. Whether they were Catholic or not, Father Barney treated all in attendance equally.

***

Following Harold's service, the interment, and lunch at the

parish hall, Michael decided to respond to Willy's recorded message. He carefully steered his truck around the potholes in the unimproved driveway.

Parking his truck next to the makeshift corral, Michael got out and was greeted with a whinny from the large old horse. "Isn't she beautiful?" Willy spoke from behind the screen door and stepped out to join Michael at the railing.

"I don't know much about horses, but if you say so, yes, she's beautiful."

Willy was relaxed and the stress apparent earlier by phone, noticeably absent. Having been burned once by his inopportune observation, Michael ignored the likely use of Willy's favored substance and asked how he may be of service.

"What service? Oh yeah, I forgot. I called the bastard this morning, and told him I was going to sic you onto him. You must be a mean SOB, because he got all friendly and said it was all a big misunderstanding."

"What misunderstanding?"

"It's that real estate guy, the one with the fancy new office on Highway 86. He wants to buy my place, wants to develop it, and I told him where to put his money. He's been back twice and threatened to report me to the county for animal abuse or some bullshit. But when I told him that you were my lawyer, well, like I said… Can you imagine? Threatenin' me for animal abuse? I love this old horse and Boxer!"

The water in his eyes may not have been entirely due to his love for the creatures, but Michael had no doubt of Willy's sincerity. "She really is beautiful, Willy. What's her name?"

"Bess. Dad raised and trained draft horses and was a life-long Democrat. He thought Harry Truman was one of our best presidents ever, so he named his last pair of horses Harry and Bess. Harry's gone now. So's Dad, but Bess is still with us."

At the sound of her name the horse stepped up to the fence and nudged Willy's shoulder. "Thatta girl, good Bess. Here ya go, sweetheart." Taking a carrot from his jacket pocket, Willy held it while Bess munched it down to the limp fronds.

Michael looked away as the big gruff man brushed aside tears. As he pretended to be preoccupied gazing over the fence, Michael saw what appeared to be a large horse blanket draped over the gate of the single stall in the shelter. It was distinctive, certainly a cut above what he thought a horse blanket would be made of. He pointed at it. "What's that?"

"That's Bess's special comforter. Found it in one of the construction dumpsters behind the Lodge. It was way down under scrap wood and masonry. Whoever threw it away didn't know it was just right for Bess."

At Willy's words Michael stiffened, a sudden prickle traveled down his back. "Do you suppose I could see it?"

"Sure. Come around here."

Standing before the blanket, Michael had to admire the fabric and weave. "It's beautiful."

"Yup. Jus' remember, no matter how much you like it, it belongs to Bess."

Michael ran a hand back and forth over the rich material.

"Smooth as a baby's bottom."

"Yes, it is. What's this?"

Michael's hand had brushed across something hard and sharp. Looking closer, it appeared to be a piece of jewelry. It was a single earring. Michael stared in disbelief. He knew its mate.

He took out his phone and shot several pictures of the earring. Stepping back he took more pictures of the blanket hanging over the gate. Putting away the phone, he carefully lifted up and held at arm's length the finely embroidered throw depicting a matador and a bull engaged in mortal combat. "Willy, do you remember exactly when you found the blanket?"

***

Compliments of the Memorial Day weekend, it had taken quite a while to reach Detective Donahue, but Michael had finally managed. He arrived, as requested, with his crime scene kit and camera. Donahue removed and bagged the earring. A small stain, left where the earring snagged, was field tested and proved to be human blood. Donahue tried to explain to Willy the importance of why he had to take Bess's comforter. Even with Michael's promise that he would personally be responsible to find him a replacement, it was a sad man and his horse he saw in his rearview mirror.

***

It was mid-evening by the time Michael arrived home. "Damn! I forgot to call Janni." He tried, but this time it went directly to voicemail.

He was beat. A quick wash up and he sat down at the kitchen table to gulp a Heineken and devour a meal from McDonald's. Sipping a second Heineken and munching the last of the fries, he went to his study and opened his computer. After emptying his inbox of the junk, one unopened email remained, sent earlier that day by Terry the Tech.

He was surprised to find that Deputy Mullen had some success with the abused digital frame. In an earlier email—addressed "To All Concerned"—Terry had expressed pessimism over whether anything could be done with the badly damaged device. However, the tech's persistence had paid off.

There were fingerprints on the frame, all belonging to Krumm except for one distinct thumbprint on the glass display under where the picture had been taped. The thumbprint belonged to Ginny.

Terry had checked and the frame was old and no longer manufactured. Due to its age and condition the tech postulated that Krumm likely scavenged the frame, and Ginny or someone tried to download pictures for Harold, but the frame would not display them. The lump Michael had felt under the tape was a depleted battery. For all that, with new batteries and his added expertise, Terry was able to tease some pictures and a disjointed video directly from the frame's memory onto his computer. Michael opened the attachment and scrolled first through a dozen or so pictures and then played the video. He was stunned by what he saw.

A connection clicked into place. He opened his phone to the photos taken of Bess's blanket. Switching to Google on his computer, he clicked the bookmark from his earlier research on the Lodge to compare with the photos of the blanket and found what had niggled at the back of his mind since his visit with Willy. Leaning back from the screen, he finished the Heineken and attempted to grasp the enormity of what was formulating in his mind.

Before he could react to what was becoming increasingly clear, his ringtone, suggestive of a very different mood, intervened.

51

He quickly answered. Without waiting for a greeting, a voice exclaimed, "Michael! This is Faethe Lawery. I'm sorry to bother you this late, but Hoepe and I may have done something we don't feel quite right about. You know Janneke Strauss, don't you? She used to be Janneke Sanderson before she married that nice Luke Strauss... although now that I think about it, I guess it's Sanderson, again. Such a lovely girl. Well, Janneke was on her way to tonight's big celebration at the Lodge and stopped briefly to pick up the information I promised her about the old Winchester property. You know, I do like to help women in business whenever I can. When she got here, we showed her something that was left in our mailbox today. It's something she called a flash drive. Funny looking thing, like a little pearl-white whale. It came with a gold chain. Ginny had one like it, but kept it on the end of a lanyard. I remember she used to hang it from the rearview mirror in her car...

"Where was I? Oh, yes. Janneke put the whale, or rather the flash drive, into her portable computer and there was a video and a diary that belonged to our Virginia. There also was some sort of financial spread sheet having to do with the Lodge resort and the owner, that Sandoval fellow. It upset Janneke terribly."

"She called him on her mobile phone and insisted they meet right away. Janneke told us that she was going to see Mr. Sandoval and get some answers to her questions. Hoepe and I have been worried sick. Should we have waited to have you or Sheriff Conrad look at the flash drive? We still have it here." There was a pause. Faethe asked, "Michael? Are you there?"

"I'm here. When was she to meet Sandoval?"

"9:00."

"It's 8:30 now. Do you know where?"

"Yes. I heard her say, 'in the office of his personal suite at the resort, tonight at 9:00.' After she hung up, she said she saved the flash drive to her laptop, gave us back the flash drive whale, and told us to keep it safe. She apologized for not staying longer and dashed out to her car."

"Faethe, please listen carefully, and do as I ask. I'm leaving for the resort right now. Call 911, that's the Dickinson County Sheriff's dispatcher, and tell them to send an officer, send several officers if they can, to the Lodge immediately. Janneke is in danger. Tell them it's a matter of life and death. Tell them to meet me in the lobby or if I'm not there, to go to the Sandovals' personal suite. It's very important they get there as fast as they can."

"Oh Michael, I'm so sorry. We shouldn't have shown Janneke the flash drive."

"It's okay, Faethe. Call 911. I'm only minutes away from the resort. And Faethe, tell whoever you talk to that I said they're to send someone to your home immediately. As long as you have that flash drive you and Hoepe are in danger."

There was a perceptible change in the voice, a shift from earnest apologetic concern to cold steel. "Michael! Hoepe and I can take care of ourselves. But I will call the sheriff's office right away and insist they go to the resort. You be careful."

"Don't worry, Faethe. I'm armed and determined."

Faethe heard him disconnect, and as she punched in 911, she thought, "How appropriate: Armed and determined." She added, "And dangerous."

＊＊

Michael opened his safe, checked the magazine to his 9mm Beretta Nano, stuffed the holster and gun inside his belt at the small of his back, and made a dash for the garage. Jumping into his truck, he hit the garage door opener and turned over the starter at the same time. Slamming the gearshift into reverse, he barely missed taking out the garage door. Shifting into first, he floored the gas pedal. A speed shift into second just missed blowing a transmission gear and reminded Michael that he'd not done such antics since high school. The shift into third timed with the ultimate ratio of pedal to the floor left a rubber signature and sent the old powerfully modified pick-up truck screaming forward.

Ignoring the Yield and Pedestrian Crossing signs, he slowed slightly on his approach then blew through a stop sign, and turned onto the blacktop for the Lodge. Cranking hard on the wheel, the truck fishtailed. Whipping the wheel back he regained control and rocketed for the resort entrance. With barely all four wheels on the pavement, the truck swerved around the last curve and slammed to a tires-on-fire halt just inches from the last vehicle slowly creeping toward the Lodge.

"Damn! They just had to have fireworks on the opening night."

Michael steered to the left and then right to see if there was some way of passing, but a mass of vehicles was parked on both sides of the road, and from both directions hapless drivers were attempting to maneuver into the jammed parking lot of the Lodge. The road was fast becoming the parking lot.

Michael wheeled the big truck around in a sharp U-turn. With the wheels spinning for traction, he managed to simultaneously remodel a Caution sign and the right rear panel of his truck. With another speed shift and mass to the gas, he headed to the employee parking and construction storage lot. Michael downshifted into second, slammed the brakes, and cut hard onto the narrow gravel drive. To keep out the flood of visitors, the gate was closed but irrelevant. With a grinding downshift to first, Michael floored the accelerator and, in a spray of gravel and chain links, smashed through the gate.

Like a hard set of hooks with a musky rod, he yanked control of the truck before it crashed into the wall next to the employee entrance.

***

It seemed to have taken forever, but as Michael approached the doorway, he wondered if Janni had managed to get by all the traffic. She may not even be here.

Tentatively Michael tried the door only to find it locked. Desperately trying to remember if there was another way to enter without running around the outside of the building to the lobby, he was surprised to hear a distinct clink from the door's lock. Turning the lever, the door opened with no further resistance.

The office space was as silent as a tomb. The overhead security light provided a pale patina to the scene and allowed Michael to find his way past the desks, reception counter, files, and copy machine. As he cautiously approached the door to the hallway leading to the break room, he had the odd sensation someone was near. Drawing his handgun, Michael slowly turned and did a visual sweep of the area. The fiendish red points of light from various devices did nothing to ease his sense that someone was watching.

Turning back, he peered through the narrow glass in the door. The dim night service light cast the hallway in shadows. Reaching for the door lever, he attempted to slow his breathing and clear his mind for what might come. His training and experience as a deputy had kicked in. Setting aside the various scenarios he knew were possible, he gripped and ever so slowly turned the lever. It was cool to his touch and sent a shiver through his body. Pressing forward, the door opened smoothly and yielded no sound.

Stepping into the hall, Michael was acutely aware that the restrooms on the left and the break room to the right hid potential risks. Standing in the dead air, listening to his own heart pound, Michael heard another sound, an intermittent raspy sound, like claws crabbing across the floor. It seemed to come from the nearer room on the left. Michael cautiously pressed his ear to the door but could not identify the sound or the source. With his Beretta at the ready, he quickly pushed opened the door.

Michael had to blink several times to adjust to the faint light emitted from the overhead device. "A bad bearing in the fan. No urinal—must be the women's."

Checking inside and then slipping past the break room and men's room, Michael came to the long hall and the stairs to the Sandovals' private suite. With a quick turkey neck around the corner he saw no one and quietly hurried down the corridor. Coming to the stairs, a dim glow beckoned from the landing above.

Taking one stair at a time with a stop between to listen, he arrived at the top. He now had a choice between the office suite straight ahead or the adjoining private quarters to the right. The door to the office was slightly ajar, and a soft shaft of light spilled across the carpeted floor, a path to whatever awaited him.

52

With his gun raised to firing position, Michael slowly, quietly moved toward the light. Pausing outside the door, Michael could hear voices. The first voice was Janneke's, clear and melodic. He wasn't sure, but it sounded as if she was in casual conversation. The sound of a male voice responded and was followed by a short, nasal-like laugh.

Momentarily, Michael was confused. Listening, he could gain no further purchase on the conversation. He knew there was a possibility he was mistaken but doubt in this case could be fatal. Lowering his gun to his side and holding it slightly behind him, Michael pushed open the door and stepped inside.

Anthony was seated behind his desk with a laptop open before him. Janneke was seated in one of the chairs before the desk and looked up with a start when Michael came through the door. With resignation in her voice, she said, "Oh, Michael. I am so sorry."

"Ah, yes. Mr. Cain. Come in, come in. I see you found your way. Did I tell you the security cameras are working now? I can even unlock doors from my office.

"We were just talking about you, the brilliant investigator and prosecutor, or as I said, self-absorbed judge and executioner. What is it your friends call you? The Angel of Justice? So nice of you to join us. You remember Janneke Sanderson, of course. All you Boji types know each other. Please have a seat. You need no gun. We're all friends here."

Michael took another step forward. "If you don't mind, I believe I'll keep my gun handy."

"I'm sorry you feel that way, but I must insist."

As he raised the Beretta, his head was abruptly struck from behind. All he could hear was clanging while bright colored flashes danced around inside his head.

Then Michael had the strange sensation he was carrying on a conversation with someone. He was himself but could see himself. It was an image, maybe a hallucination. But this image was talking to him. It sounded like him but wasn't. How strange! He should be terrified but instead felt calm, filled with strength. The image reassured him.

As the likeness faded, Michael heard other voices, but as he attempted to raise his head, was nearly overtaken with a wave of nausea. He was aware of someone next to him, someone tangible.

There was a soft touch and then Janni's voice. "Lie still, Michael. Don't try to get up."

Then powerful hands seized him by his shoulders, roughly dragged him across the floor, and propped him up in a sitting pose against the wall.

"He's coming around."

"Good. I'd hate to have him miss the dramatic finish to such an annoying tale. Is he bleeding?"

"Nah. Just another goose egg."

"Well done, Jolly. What's he saying? I can't make it out."

His breath like sour worms, Jolly bent close to Michael's face. "He's just mumbling."

"Empty his pockets. Get his phone and check for a backup handgun. We don't need more surprises."

"Mr. Cain! MR. CAIN!" Michael felt a kick on the sole of his shoe. "Can you hear me?"

He opened his eyes and stared blankly up at the voice. Anthony Sandoval stood over him holding the Beretta. Michael's head throbbed, but his mind began to clear. Janni was kneeling on the floor by his side. Jolly, revolver in hand, stood behind Sandoval to the side. Michael knew he needed time.

"I can hear you. The police know all about your little project."

"They do? Isn't that sweet? According to what Ms. Sanderson showed me, they don't have squat. It's all circumstantial at best, and without either of you to clarify matters, they don't have a case. Convenient of Janneke to bring her laptop."

"That's not the only copy." It was Janni's voice, clear and defiant. "There are more copies than you can find, and I emailed a copy to the police before I came here."

"Oh, nice try dear, but you're getting overly excited. According to your laptop, no emails have been sent tonight. And I see you downloaded—at 7:57 PM to be exact—the information you were so eager to use to confront me. You said it was from a flash drive. So, let me play the detective.

"When you called, you said you were at the Lawreys', had just learned of something, and needed to talk to me immediately. Considering the overwrought state you were in when you called and, in spite of the traffic, how soon you arrived, I'd say you didn't have time to copy or email anything. You don't have the flash drive on you, and we'll check your car to be sure, but most likely it's still with the Lawery sisters.

"Later tonight there will be a sad but convenient tragedy at the home of the Lawerys. It will be the end of the flash drive and any further mischief. We'll probably need to go over by boat. It should be easy to make it look accidental. There's always something about an old house that poses a risk of fire, perhaps a gas leak—then a big explosion, lots of fire. Did you really think you could bring me to my knees because of a few emails from an emotionally immature girl and a random video?"

Janneke persisted. "There's a discrepancy in your financial records. If something happens to the board's treasurer, do you really think that won't be noticed?"

"Yes, well perhaps my wife was too willing to help Ginny, but if I have to, I can explain it was simply an exercise my wife provided Ginny for practice. Or perhaps our treasurer was messing with the books. After all, we didn't have much trouble getting the law and Mr. Cain to run in circles. And neither of you will be around to dispute the matter."

Michael had to ask. "Were you the father?"

Sandoval stepped back. The surprise was evident on his face. "What?"

"Ginny was two months pregnant. Were you the father?"

For what seemed a long moment the only sounds that could be heard came through the opening in the sliding door, the distant noise of people gathering on the shore for the display of fireworks. Jolly kept his revolver trained on Michael as he glanced over at his partner. Sandoval stood there breathing deeply, his eyes misty. "I didn't know."

Michael persisted. "Then why kill Ginny? She couldn't harm you. There may have been a little scandal, but that was no reason to hurt her."

Looking downward, and as if only to himself, Anthony spoke

softly. "I suppose it's my fault as much as anyone. I shouldn't have allowed her to get so close to our enterprise. Lovely girl, tempting and gifted in so many ways. She didn't have a clue what it was all about. Still, it was too bad."

"But if she was just infatuated, why kill her?"

Regaining some composure, Anthony's answer was matter-of-fact. "We didn't. It was an accident. It got late, and she slept over. She must've had trouble sleeping and was lying on the couch here when Jolly and I met to take care of some late business. Ginny overheard us, and it put us all at risk. She still appeared enticing, standing there with the throw wrapped about her. I tried to reason with her, but when I reached out, she tripped over the throw. She fell and struck her head on the corner of the fireplace hearth." He stared, fixated on the remembered scene, then uttered sotto voce, "It was quick and painless."

"Maybe not. She was unconscious but alive when Jolly dropped her into the water."

But Sandoval was no longer listening to anyone else's voice. Tears ran down his face. He raised his eyes to meet Michael's. "Can you believe it? She said she added hotel management to her business degree and came here to tell us all about it. The poor, delusional girl. She actually thought she would be a partner in business with us. I truly believe she thought if she cared enough, the fairy tale would come true. Charming, but sad. Romantic, but naive."

"So, you plan to do to us what you did to Ginny? A good bump on the head, and anchor us to the bottom of the lake?"

The change in Sandoval was sudden and savage. "Oh, you are the clever one. No, nothing so innovative. An evening boat ride to watch the fireworks ends tragically. Two bodies recovered. A bump on the head? Good! Probably due to the accident. Cause of death, drowning. What they were doing together will be cause for speculation, and much gossip. That should keep the locals chattering for some time.

"Don't worry. Jolly is brutal but efficient. We'll need to arrange for a boat. Something without lights. Perhaps a canoe borrowed from the resort? I'll leave it to my colleague. Jolly's good at problem-solving."

"Right, like taking care of Harold? That was a little obvious."

"Yes, it was a bit clumsy, but there's no defensible conclusion other than suicide."

"He's still your biggest problem."

"Who, Jolly? That's nonsense."

"The DCI knows about Jolly."

"What do they know? He has a record. Big deal."

Desperately trying to stall for time, Michael exaggerated the truth. "No. Ginny's roommate identified Jolly as her attacker, and we have Jolly's boot prints."

"If she'd identified him he'd already be in jail. Besides, it would be the word of a confused young woman manipulated by a master investigator. And boot prints? Too facile. Easy to refute."

"He also got careless when he broke into the fishing shack and dropped Ginny through the ice."

"My, you are desperate. I don't know how you divined all this, but there is no way of proving that Ginny did a dive through the ice or that a fishing shack was even used."

Michael could sense an opening. "He left evidence. The shack Jolly used was identified and guess what? Ginny's blood was found on the floor."

"So what? Anyone could have dumped her body. It doesn't connect Jolly."

"Except Jolly cut his hand on the lock when he broke in. There's DNA which ties Jolly to the shack."

"Really, Michael. For someone of such reputed stature, I thought you could do better. Didn't you notice? Jolly wears gloves, leather biker gloves."

"Yes, with the fingertips cut away. Good for prints and blood. We got both."

Looking directly into Sandoval's eyes, Michael slowly smiled and continued. "We found the throw. Ginny's missing earring was caught in it, and both Ginny's and Jolly's blood were on it. The same throw wrapped around Ginny and pictured over your grand leather couch in your nice glossy brochure and on your website. It's only a matter of time, and we'll have DNA confirmation. Oh, and the police really are on their way. They do know Janneke and I are here."

Sandoval stood silently, glaring at Michael. "How unfortunate. It seems Jolly has not performed up to his usual standards. I believe it's time I improvised." Sandoval turned to Jolly, raised Michael's Beretta, and fired a single shot, point blank. Jolly's face briefly registered surprise before he crumpled at Sandoval's feet. Michael made a desperate lunge for Jolly's snub nose .38 as it bounced once in his direction. But as his hand closed on salvation, the Beretta was pressed to his head.

"Back off slowly, Michael. Don't complicate matters."

Janneke stood up, and in a shaky voice she begged, "No, Michael. Please do as he says."

Michael stood and backed away. Speaking in what he hoped to be a calming voice, he said, "Easy, Janneke. It's okay. It's going to be alright."

Sandoval gazed intently at Michael. "That's good, Michael. We don't want to hurt Janneke any more than we need to."

"You're not going to get away with this."

"Oh, but I will, Michael." Picking the revolver up from the floor, he set the Beretta on the desk and switched the revolver to his dominant hand. "Don't you understand? Don't you see what I see? It was

Jolly all the time. He was the one dealing drugs. Harold must've learned about it and he told Ginny. Jolly killed Ginny and Harold to protect himself. Why he took the throw, we don't know. Maybe he thought to implicate me, to force me to cooperate if there was trouble, then changed his mind. Yes, there may be some questions over the resort's finances, but that can all be managed."

"What about your wife?"

"My wife? What does she have to do with it?"

"That's my question."

"Lucia had nothing to do with our little play. She'll have doubts, but she's committed to our success and will support me. The car was a risk but I explained away the throw and Ginny's early morning departure. I'll explain away this, too. Lucia will choose our future over any spurious questions that arise."

"It's not going to work, Anthony. If you love your wife, give it up. Save her and the Lodge."

"Michael, your mindless repetition is beginning to bore me. Jolly was just a part of our business. But he had access, including to this office. He was the one who had a connection to Krumm. He knew about Ginny and Krumm. When he became concerned your investigation was getting too close to him, he sabotaged your airplane. When that didn't work, he broke into your home and attacked you. He was watching you and followed you here. You brought him here."

Sandoval began to pace but kept his eyes on his prey like the predator he was. "I was delayed in meeting Janneke and when I arrived, found this ghastly scene. Janneke Sanderson and Michael Cain, shot to death by a desperate drug dealer who was in turn shot and killed by Mr. Cain in a blazing exchange of gun fire. Exciting, don't you think? As I recall, you do have a taste for gunfights."

"The police aren't going to buy it. There will be trace evidence. Witnesses. Everything will be questioned."

"What witnesses? Do you see anyone here but us? Everyone is down by the lake ready to watch the fireworks. Questions? Certainly! Conjecture? Absolutely! But after a quick boat ride to the Lawerys' there's no solid evidence to implicate me or the Lodge. I will miss Jolly. He was resourceful and even now in death, so useful."

From the lakeside came a loud report that echoed across the water. "Ah, that's the signal the fireworks are about to start." Michael stood and staggered forward, desperate for anything he might use to distract Sandoval long enough to give Janneke a chance to escape.

"No, no, none of that. Stay put, or Janneke gets the first shot."

Frantically, Michael blurted, "There will be gunshot residue, not on me or Jolly, but on you. The police will figure it out."

Sandoval shook his head and smiled. "A good hand washing, a quick change of clothing, and I'm clean. As for you and Jolly, it was a wild shoot out. Very OK Corral. Stray bullets everywhere. What's the saying? 'From my cold dead fingers'? And with all the fireworks going off, who will notice a few extra explosions? Think of it this way, you're going out with a bang!" At that, Sandoval raised the .38, his eyes cold and expressionless.

In the slice of silence between the whoosh of the rocket and its discharge, Michael heard the hammer cock, not once but twice, two distinct clicks, metal against metal. Sandoval heard it too and spun in the direction of the sound.

At the rocket's burst a thundering boom stunned Michael's hearing. The brilliant flash seared onto Michael's retina the stark demonic vision of Sandoval suspended between heaven and hell, the space all around filled with glittering fragmented glass mixed with blood and flesh. Then—a dull thud.

Blinking his watering eyes, Michael became aware Janneke was next to him, screaming and gripping his arm as if clinging to life itself. Michael reached out and pulled her sobbing face onto his shoulder. Looking down he confirmed there was no longer a threat from Anthony Sandoval. A bloodied face was punctuated by two bulging, terror-struck eyes and a mouth agape, like a fish drowning in air. But no air would come. There was no place for air, only the garish mass of red pulp left where there had been lungs and whatever had passed for a heart.

A glow of luminescence surrounded them as Michael wrapped Janneke in his arms.

Epilogue

"I'm so glad you could come over. Michael doesn't tell me anything, and after that awful experience at the Lodge, I've been concerned about you."

"Thank you for inviting me, and don't worry about me. It was Michael who got bonked on the head, again."

"Yes, and we all know how much good that does."

"Hey, I'm right here."

"That's the point."

The kids were at the movies, thanks to Jeremy and his girlfriend. Connie and Michael retired to the deck to tend the grill. Madge and Janni remained in the kitchen, Madge finishing the salad and Janni setting the table. It was a welcome opportunity for the two women to talk privately.

"What made you suspect Anthony Sandoval?"

"It was the picture of Ginny and Harold Krumm. There were two people in the background. You could see Jolly handing a wad of money to a man who was wearing a suit. The second man's shirt sleeve was exposed and it had a French cuff. There was only one person I knew who wore French cuffs, and when Michael showed me the blown-up version, I recognized the cuff link and the wrist watch."

"Why didn't you say something?"

"I wanted to learn what they were doing before I said anything."

"Well, you found out the hard way. What's going to happen with the Lodge?"

Janneke let out a big sigh. "Everything is still on. The Lodge on Okoboji is doing well and our investors and the board of directors remain committed to the long-range plans. For now, Lucia Sandoval will continue her duties and those of her late husband. But the board already has hired a company to headhunt someone to assist with management. It's a big job with lots of potential."

"If the Lodge was doing well, why were they dealing in drugs?"

"The Lodge, so to speak, was not dealing drugs. It came down to sheer greed. Anthony and Jolly were using the Lodge as a cover for their own side business. It was a lot of easy money. Connie probably knows more of the details, but I understand that Anthony and Jolly met at a bar while Anthony was attending the University of Arizona and they shared an interest, a shortcut to wealth. Anthony also met Lucia at the U of A, and when they married, her family financed the Lodge as a combination wedding present and investment. Jolly tagged along. The bait and supply distribution operation run by Jolly along with the respectability of the Lodge was too good to pass up. For them, it was a match made in drug paradise. They could deal and launder the money through the Lodge."

"How stupid. Enough of that. Let's talk about something pleasant. How are you and Michael doing?"

***

Faethe had carried out Michael's request to call the sheriff's office and have deputies sent immediately to the Lodge, but the reply was not reassuring. The dispatch operator promised that someone would be there as soon as possible but cautioned her that all deputies and local law enforcement were tied up with other calls or responsibilities. Faethe pointed out that due to the fireworks display, someone from the Okoboji Police Department or County Sheriff's Office should be at or near the Lodge. The operator agreed and said she had already contacted the officers, but they were having trouble getting past all the traffic and large crowd. The call ended but alarmed by the delay, Faethe and Hoepe were determined to do more to help Janneke and Michael.

Within minutes of the shootings, Sheriff Conrad, Sergeant Dexter and several reserve deputies managed to break through the logjam. The dash down the hall and up the stairs to the Sandovals' suite by Sheriff Conrad and company was not subtle, but on their arrival, the grim scene brought their charge to an abrupt halt.

Michael and Janneke were transported to the Spirit Lake Hospital by two of the firefighters on hand to oversee the fireworks display. It took Deputies Graves and Mullen all night and most of the following morning to complete their crime scene work. After Dr. Matt completed his responsibilities as county medical examiner, Anthony Sandoval and Jolly Holiday were packaged appropriately—in black body bags— and transported to the state medical examiner's morgue in Ankeny. Shortly thereafter, each corpse took a turn under the knife of the state's lovely new pathologist.

Jolly Holiday's motorcycle was never found, but his saddle bags were discovered in the guest room beyond the hall to the Sandovals' private quarters. The bags held cash and keys to several safe deposit boxes in area banks where more cash and a handful of fake passports were discovered.

Also found in the saddle bags was the pièce de résistance. It was a notebook in which Jolly had kept a hand-written record of drug deals and money earned. It implicated Anthony Sandoval, dealers in the Lakes area and nearby in South Dakota and Minnesota, and a big-time source in Arizona. Together, the DCI and DEA were helping the sheriff's department tidy up the local and cross-state dealers, and authorities in Arizona were nearly giddy over the bonanza bust to Jolly's supplier.

Though she was initially a focus of intense interrogation, in the end there was nothing to incriminate Lucia Sandoval. While the drama was playing out in the Sandovals' personal suite, she was busy directing staff and welcoming guests in the ballroom. The business office was her responsibility, but there were no records under her aegis that were found to be related to drug trafficking or money laundering. Indeed, her ledger was clean, and nothing was learned to evince that she knew anything about the lawless enterprise of her husband and Jolly Holiday. She was stunned by the events, and due to concern for her well-being and safety, remained under the care of Dr. Matt and the protection of a deputy from the sheriff's department until the shock and potential danger subsided.

The ring given to Ginny by her mother was returned to the Aunties. Ginny's phone, laptop, and backpack were never recovered, and it was surmised from the flash drive she may have helped herself to Anthony's personal computer and unintentionally downloaded something no one else was supposed to see. Mysteriously, Anthony Sandoval's personal computer was also missing.

It had taken another three days in the hospital, but after that Michael was cleared for dismissal. He rescheduled his meeting at the Iowa Law Enforcement Academy, but only after calling to confirm whether Dr. Goulet was also available.

The investigations into the murders of Virginia Lawery and Harold Krumm were finished, but as Michael had conceded, violent death always left issues unresolved. Murder tainted everyone it touched and the living were left to manage in their own ways.

***

Pam Schneider was looking forward to the summer break. She was pleased by how well Michael had fit into the role as an academic and investigator. If there was an opportunity and Michael was willing, he would be an incredible addition to the staff.

Pam had found her role in the Virginia Lawery case a stimulating application of what she knew and taught. Even Michael seemed to appreciate that her patience and empathy toward others had lent balance to Michael's aggressive manner. If asked, she would be keen to assist him in future investigations. As she expressed to her husband, Darrell, "I think Michael and I make an excellent team of snoops."

***

Sally missed her close friend but completed her coursework from the previous semester and in the spring, earned her degree. Grant Laxton transferred out-of-state.

***

Harold Krumm's small group of dedicated friends gathered to bowl and have a pitcher of beer in his memory, a validation of Father Barney's words: "The true value of a person's wealth on this earth is not gold or accruements due to power, but the number of friends and loved ones that remain."

Harold had meant well, but his girlfriend knew the pendant was Ginny's and that it had to be returned. Sylvia remained unaware of the consequences brought about by her kindhearted but anonymous placement of the little whale pendant in the Lawery sisters' mailbox. She still cried, but not as much.

***

At his advanced age, Father Barney found comfort in the routine required of his office. However, still saddened by recent events, he added a daily prayer on behalf of Ginny and Harold and Harold's friends. Each time before he did so, he took a moment to reflect on the inherent goodness of Harold Krumm and the caring relationship between Harold and Ginny.

***

Willy and Boxer stood by the corral admiring the newly gifted hand-sewn quilt over Bess's back. It spread from shoulders to rump and was just the right length. "It's your color, sweetheart. You look good in quilt. Just like the race horses."

DNR Officer Piccard, accompanied by his son, had delivered the quilt. Willy offered them an excellent cup of coffee, and they enjoyed some time together talking about fishing.

***

For Lucia Sandoval, none of what had taken place diminished her dream. People were depending on her and the business would go on. They had planned well and their arrangement was successful.

Anthony was the image, but as she learned too late, the image came with heavy baggage. "Baggage," she thought. That was too considerate a description for Jolly.

The past few days had been exhausting, but she was recovering. Tomorrow she would fly to Arizona in first class, with Anthony in the cargo hold. It would be good to see family.

Lying in bed, she removed the gold cross and chain from around her neck and placed it on the night stand where she had found it the morning after Ginny went missing. She had kept it in spite of her husband's disapproval. Rolling to the other side, she rested her head where Ginny had slept. There was sleep, with tears.

***

Detective Donahue had spent the entire afternoon finishing paperwork. He shut down his computer and sat staring at the open folder on his desk. "Incredible! We don't know who shot Sandoval or why, although it probably had to do with drugs. No one saw the shooter, and the only physical evidence we have are old #5 lead pellets removed from the body." He shook his head in disbelief, then closed the autopsy report and went home to his family.

***

Faethe and Hoepe were seated at their small kitchen table. Their vintage wooden run-about bobbed at the dock. The glow of evening gilded the small waves caressing the shore.

"Did we have to, Faethe?"

"Of course we did."

"I really did like Papa's shotgun."

"I know. But it was dangerous to have around the house, and

now it's with Papa."

"With Papa—I like that. Do you think anyone knows we put it in the lake like Papa's ashes?"

"No, only you and me. Papa is happy, Hoepe. He is with Mama and the lake. And now he has his shotgun and shells. How's your shoulder?"

"There's still a big bruise, but I can lift my arm today." She paused. "Faethe?"

"Yes, Hoepe?"

"Did I do a bad thing?"

Faethe rose from her chair, stepped around the table, and wrapped Hoepe lovingly in her arms. "No, Hoepe, it was a good thing. You heard him say what he did to our Virginia. We had to, we promised God. She was your adopted daughter, and I was her godmother."

***

"I miss my Aunties."

"You're still together."

"Do they know that?"

"Yes."

"How?"

"Faith."

"I think I'm supposed to go now."

"Yes."

"Should I be afraid?"

"No."

"I think I should be afraid but I don't feel afraid. Have you been there?"

"Yes."

"What is it like?"

"It is...There are no words, time, or places like you have known, but the awareness of love and beauty is unending."

"I don't understand."

"The awareness is the gift. And you're not alone. You share the joy with those you remember here and all who are before and to come that have this gift."

"Does everyone have the gift?"

"No. Some will only know but be unaware."

"How sad...Will you go with me?"

"No."

"Why?"

"You know why."

"You're needed here."

"Yes."

"Will I see you again?"

"Yes."

"Will I remember you?"

"You will."

"I don't know your name."

"There's no need for a name."

"If you chose a name, what would it be?"

"Call me Gabriel."

Acknowledgments

Writing a novel may be a solitary task for many writers but as I wrote the *Girl in the Net*, I never felt alone or isolated. Memories of the Iowa Great Lakes and its people provided comfort and companionship. Michael Cain and the characters I created were good company and often surprised me as they evolved and contributed to their part in the story. But most important were the people who advised and supported my efforts as a writer. With deep gratitude I want to acknowledge and thank my wife Vicki, the first of all first readers and whose unwavering encouragement helped to turn a dream into reality; first editor, Dr. Zora Zimmerman who suggested the title and provided valued early advice on plot and character development; Jerry Stewart, retired ISU Chief of Police, for reviewing the manuscript and sharing his knowledge of law enforcement at the university; Sgt. Elizabeth Quinn of the Story County Sheriff's Department for background information and for suggesting how an attorney may be hired by a county on a temporary basis; Dickinson County Sheriff Greg Baloun for his time and providing facts about Dickinson County and the lakes area; Father James Secora for insight and answers into liturgical questions; and Lief Wilson, bush pilot extraordinaire of 49-Mile Air in Tok, Alaska, and Chris Schrodt, flight instructor for Central Iowa Air Service, in Ames, Iowa, for information needed to better understand aviation and confirming my method to crash an airplane! I'd also like to thank Joseph LaValley for sharing his early experiences as an author; editor, Emily Trenholm for plot and character development and for keeping me on point; and Dr. Anthony Paustian and staff at BookPress Publishing for the opportunity to publish *The Girl in the Net*.